LONE WOLFE

A LEX WOLFE NOVEL

KEVIN ROBERT ALDRICH

WARNING TO SENSITIVE READERS

This novel contains the following elements, which may be disturbing to some readers:

- Swearing
- Sexual situations and innuendo (mildly graphic)
- Depictions of and discussions about rape and attempted rape

LONE WOLFE

For Holly, Jayda, and Taegon

MANILA

1

THE HONKING WOKE HER, as usual. She could ignore the bleat of the car horns and the low blat of the rumbling trucks. But the *neep-neep* of the motorbikes drove through her sleeping brain and needled her mind awake.

Then her other senses would slowly wake.

The reek of gasoline and two-stroke engine oil through the open windows mixed with the buzz and pop-pop of the motorbikes gunning and slowing, darting like swarms of gnats through the traffic outside. During a lull, she heard mongrel dogs yapping and a rooster crowing in its raspy, strangled tongue. Pungent cigarette smoke, the kind banned decades ago in most countries, wafted into her one-room apartment, along with the occasional shout or jabber in rapid-fire Filipino.

The sounds and smells woke her, but it was her hands that opened her eyes every morning.

Fingers swollen tight in their skin. Knuckles creaking as she formed a loose fist, tearing open scrapes that had only started to heal overnight. They were a comfort, those aching bones. They let her know she was alive. They let her know she was a fighter.

They let her know she could protect herself now.

Lex Wolfe's eyes flipped up like a light switch, adding the visual to the aural and the sensual. Face-down on her pillow, belly-down on her bed, a corner of the thin sheet angled over her bare back, leaving her ass and arms and legs exposed, trying to catch a whisper of a breeze in the stifling late-September heat.

Was it September? Days and dates meant nothing to Lex anymore, and she tended to lose track.

No, it was October already. It should be chilly in October. Sweater weather. The smell of November snow should already be creeping into the air.

Instead, it was eighty degrees in the middle of the night. Ninety-five in the day. And as humid as a hot fucking shower. Lex didn't know why she stayed in this place sometimes.

Then she'd flex her knuckles again and remember.

Lex pulled in a deep breath, smelling sweat and sex and sheets that should have been washed months ago, then pressed herself up from the bed, savoring the ache of the muscles in her arms and her back. She swung her feet to the floor and stood, raised her arms over her head and arched her back. The muscles in her abdomen had been beaten so tight she barely felt them anymore, but she rolled her shoulders to feel the stretch and the ache around her shoulder blades.

Through the wide-open windows, she could see the bustle on the street two floors below as the locals went about their morning routine. Delivery trucks stopping traffic, motorbikes and side-cars weaving between through the jams, shopkeepers sitting on folding chairs outside their stalls, fanning themselves for a futile pant of cooler air, as pedestrians jumble past.

And everywhere, color. A riot of color that had taken Lex months to get used to. She was used to olive drab and dress brown. All the chili reds and robin's egg blues and pistachio greens and banana yellows in Manila gave her a headache.

They still did. Only now, she'd come to like the headache.

She didn't bother to pick up the corner of the bedsheet that had fallen on her dirty wood-slat floor. The sheet had long ago gone from white to off-white to dingy grey, absorbing the particulates that hung heavy in the smoggy air. There was no point in cleaning. Everything got dirty again. The whole world was dirty. Lex had learned long ago to focus on the battles that mattered.

She padded across the room to the bathroom, the slight breeze of her movement welcome against her naked body, cooling the pricks of sweat that seemed always to be on her skin in this place. She splashed lukewarm tap water over her face and the back of her neck, careful not to get any in her mouth. That was a lesson she'd spent her first week in the city learning, on her knees, face-down in the toilet.

She touched under her eyes. The swelling was already going down. She'd have a nice bruise on her cheekbone, but it would fade quickly. Fast healing was one gift her father had given her.

She ran wet hands through her ropey brown hair, dried them on a barely serviceable towel, but left her hair wet. She'd had long hair when she arrived here two years ago, down to her breasts. She'd cut it that same night, a pair of scissors in front of the mirror, accusing eyes watching from her reflection. Three minutes later, no more heavy head, no more sweaty neck, no more long locks for someone to wrap tight around their fist. She could stand tall and straight and look herself in the eye again.

She brushed her teeth and spat in the sink, reached for drinking water and found only an empty plastic bottle. She crumpled it in one hand and threw it skittering across the cracked bathroom tile.

"Get the fuck up," she said in Filipino to the body in the bed as she stalked back out of the bathroom.

"Mrph," replied the body.

"On your feet, soldier!"

Lex used her drill sergeant voice. The body flew to its feet.

The soldier was just a kid. Said he was twenty, so he was probably eighteen. His body proved it. Standing naked before her, instinctively at attention, she scanned his soft, tight skin.

Oh right, Lex remembered. That's why I fucked him.

His muscles had the effortless definition of youth, taut pecs giving way to abs like bookshelves, with a transversus V that led to a tangle of pubic hair and a long cock that had passed the time just fine for Lex the night before.

A moment after he jumped up, the kid came to his senses and realized where he was. He saw Lex scanning his naked body, scanned her naked body in return. He grinned a boyish grin and took a step toward her.

"Fuck off, *gago*," said Lex. His shirt was on the floor in front of her. She scooped it with one foot and kicked it at him. "Go home."

She turned toward her dresser for a t-shirt, heard him come up behind her, sweet-talking in Tagalog. She smiled grimly to herself and flexed her knuckles once more.

From behind, he put his hands on her bare shoulders,

bent and kissed the back of her neck. Lex grabbed his hand from one shoulder and spun around, twisting the kid's arm behind his back. She punched him twice in the kidneys in quick succession, then a third time for good measure. Enough so he'd feel it, but he'd probably only piss blood for a few hours.

"I said fuck off," said Lex, pushing the kid toward her door. She jerked it open, shoved him into the hallway, and slammed the door.

He banged his fist against it, complaining about being naked. In one quick motion, Lex scooped his shirt and pants off the floor, popped the door open so the kid could watch, and threw the clothes out the open window. He could pick them up from the street on his way out.

Astonishment crossed the kid's face, quickly followed by anger.

"You fucking *puta*," he said, his hands balling into fists.

The apartment was tiny, little more than a walk-in closet with a bathroom stall. In two quick strides, Lex moved from the window across the room to the door.

One shot to the gut had the kid doubled over. A jab to the throat had him wheezing for air, eyes bugged.

Lex strolled to her dresser and picked up her gun, a Sig Sauer P320 compact. She racked the slide, but held the gun loosely at her side.

"You call me a fucking whore again, asshole, and you'll be singing soprano in the church choir."

She pointed the Sig at his crotch. The kid's eyes went wide as the moon.

"Get the fuck out."

She didn't have to say it again.

2

LEX UNLOADED the gun and set it back in its holster on the dresser, smiling mirthlessly as she heard the whistles and mocking catcalls through her open window as the kid emerged naked on the street. He'd talk shit about her with his friends at the base. He wouldn't be the first. Not by a long shot.

Lex didn't give a fuck. She and the rest of humanity had decided years ago that they wouldn't be friends. And when she needed to blow off some steam in the sack? Men were easy, especially the young ones, and they couldn't resist fucking a woman who could kick their ass. Some Freudian bullshit, probably, about re-establishing male dominance. Whatever the reason, Lex would use them and lose them, just like they did to women all the time.

She debated on showering, decided to do it later. She pulled on a t-shirt, light linen pants, and flip-flops, tucked her holster inside her waistband, and headed out. She didn't bother to lock her door. There was nothing in her apartment worth stealing.

The door at the bottom of the narrow stairwell in her building opened onto a side street. Lex turned left, away from what passed for a thoroughfare, and wound her way through what was essentially a glorified alley. Clothes hung everywhere, on stands and from lines overhead. Between stretches of concrete wall, where once-colorful paint had faded into lost hope, corrugated steel walls bent and leaned, boards meant to support them broken into splinters on the ground.

Lanky dogs and feral cats shadowed her, tongues lolling and heads hung low. Lex strode through the familiar smells of cigarette smoke and sweat and piss. She'd long ago stopped thinking about what might be the source of the liquid working its way down the center of the alley toward the distant drain.

Despite the squalor, the people in the alley chattered and laughed with each other. Kids played with faded, broken toys as if they were new from the box. Potted plants were everywhere, in the alley and on the ramshackle balconies above, their broad, green leaves healthy and shining in the heat and humidity.

Lex nodded at the greetings she received as she worked her way through the alley. Everything was chipped and broken and scratched and warped and looking like the back room of the worst pawn shop in history, but the smiles of the people were bright and new. Grandparents, parents, adults, children, all living ass to tip in the poorest slum in Manila, sweating their tits off. But they were living. And they didn't take that for granted.

Lex worked through the alley, ducking clotheslines and dodging stacks of empty crates, other pedestrians, and parked scooters to a point where the alley grew so narrow the sunlight didn't reach the ground for the buildings teetering overhead. Even the wind couldn't work its way inside. Shirtless old men in plastic chairs sat in shadow, the heat hovering over them like a specter. Two motorbikes were parked along one wall in a single file. Lex had to turn sideways to edge past a man chiseling a doorjamb to fix a broken hinge.

When the alley finally widened again, Lex looked up to see a lone palm tree in the distance, arcing over the buildings, framed green against the blue sky. The only unpotted tree for three square blocks, and the marker for Lex's destination.

It wasn't much of a destination. Just a doorway with a folding table set before it, some old slat crates underneath. A triangular old woman in a faded dress and an apron leaned against the doorway behind the table, arms crossed.

"*Magandang umaga*," said Lex as she approached the old woman.

"*Magandang hapon*," the woman corrected her.

It was their ritual greeting. Lex went to bed just before dawn and rarely woke before noon, so she would say *good morning* to the woman. The old woman would correct her, saying *good afternoon* in return. When Lex had first arrived and was just learning Tagalog, it had been a helpful correction. Now, it was an inside joke.

Lex pulled a crate out from under the table, turned it over, and straddled it. She leaned her elbows against the table and watched the old woman shuffle back through the doorway to the four-burner stove in her kitchen. Her thick, bare arms were tattooed in faded patterns that looked like fish scales. She tottered more than walked, her calves swollen, her feet puffed around the straps of her sandals.

The old woman stepped up on a wooden stool and dropped a large ladle deep into a pot that was almost as large as she was. She emptied the ladle into a wide ceramic bowl, sprinkled a pinch of garnish on top from a plate beside the stove, and shuffled back with the bowl.

The smell of chicken broth, ginger, and roasted garlic was already making Lex's stomach growl. She watched the woman's slow progress toward her. Lex swore she moved slower just because she knew how hungry Lex was.

Every morning, Lex was starving. And every morning, she came to this woman's house for the same dish, *arroz caldo*. Rice and chicken gruel with ginger. The garnish was roasted garlic. Sometimes, green onions, too. On rare occasions, a hard-boiled egg, but those were precious in this part of town.

The bowl steamed in the old woman's hand. Arroz caldo was normally served in the rainy season or the cooler months, but the old woman served it year round. Lex had never seen anything else on the stove. Hell, she'd never seen anyone else seated at the table.

She'd stumbled across the old woman while exploring the neighborhood soon after she'd moved in. The old woman had eyed her suspiciously, then pushed her down onto a crate and served her the most delicious food Lex had eaten in years. Filipino comfort food, at a moment when Lex needed comfort.

Every morning since, Lex had come to this spot for arroz caldo for breakfast. Three years, not a single day missed.

"You're too skinny," the old woman said in Filipino as she set the bowl in front of Lex. "You need to eat more."

Lex shoved a greedy spoonful into her mouth. "Then I'd

look like you," she said as she chewed. "Too fat." She reached for a large plastic bottle of fish sauce on the table and squeezed some into her bowl.

"I'm old," said the woman. She patted her flanks. "This is wisdom." She pointed at Lex. "You're skinny, you're stupid."

She cackled. Lex laughed, too, and choked on the broth in her mouth. That set the old woman cackling even louder.

Lex knew the old woman's name, Cariz, and she assumed the old woman knew Lex's name, too. But they never used them. They were as anonymous in their conversation as they had been on the first day they'd met. Lex liked that. It was probably part of the reason she came back every day.

"What are you laughing at, *nanay*?"

A slender Filipino woman came from the house into the kitchen and stood beside the old woman. Her granddaughter, Aya. She lifted her chin toward the bruise under Lex's eye.

"You should see the other guy?" Aya said.

Lex grinned. She flexed her fists and felt a flush of strength at the pain in her knuckles. She shoved two more spoonfuls of food in her mouth. "You coming tonight?"

Aya nodded.

Lex held the bowl in both hands, bent her head back and tipped it high, letting the last bits of broth and rice slide down her throat. She was already sweating from the hot weather, and the hot broth had only made it worse, but she set the bowl down with a contented sigh and wiped her mouth with the back of her hand.

"Bring some of this with you," Lex said, pointing at the empty bowl.

Aya rolled her eyes and went back through the kitchen into the house, waving over her shoulder.

"Bye, old woman," said Lex as she stood and walked away.

"See you tomorrow, stupid girl," came the old woman's response.

Lex smiled to herself and kept walking.

3

LEX PROWLED between the pairs of women grappling on the floor and surveyed the gym.

Gym was far too grandiose a word for it. Even calling it a room was giving it too much credit. It was the back corner of an old export warehouse by the docks that was one strong gust from a pile of rubble. There was a single bare bulb overhead, illuminating the center of the room with a dim spotlight and casting the rest in radial shadows that deepened to half-darkness by the time they reached the walls.

On the other side of a demarcation line of deep shadow, the rest of the warehouse was brightly lit. From rumbling trucks belching exhaust smoke into the already polluted air, burly, shirtless men hauled boxes and crates and drums and stacked them toward the ceiling in neat rectangular sections, working from the front of the warehouse toward Lex's makeshift gym in the back.

The deliveries contained everything imaginable, every export that went through the North Harbor of the Port of

Manila. Bundles of rope, stacks of plywood, bags of sugar, barrels of coconut oil, and God only knew what else.

Sometimes, if the overnight activity was heavy, the last line of lamps would light, the demarcation shadow would disappear, and the stacks would pile all the way into Lex's workout space. The women would have to crowd even closer together. Always adapting to what dregs the men left for them.

Occasionally, the haul would include drums of oil or chemicals. These were illegal, but for a short time and the right price, the export official could be convinced to look away. For the greater good. To improve the economy.

Improve it for everyone but the people who lived near the docks, of course, and the women in the gym who had to breathe noxious fumes while they worked.

"Yes, Julia," said Lex as one of her students rolled her sparring partner off of her, exactly as Lex had demonstrated earlier. She prowled further between the women. "Good, Maja," she said to another student. "Almost had it. Go again. Keep working."

Tonight she had eight women, not counting herself. Four pairs. She normally had nine students, but Liza didn't come that evening. Lex wondered whether it had anything to do with her piss-face husband, but she hadn't asked when Julia had delivered the news.

Lex's self-defense classes earlier in the evening had many more attendees. Usually fifteen or twenty. Because of the size of the gym, she'd had to split them into two one-hour classes. They started earlier in the evening, around eight or nine, once the temperatures had cooled from unbearable to merely oppressive. Those classes taught the basics, including mental techniques like tactical awareness, self-defense mindset, and strategies for controlling anxiety, as well as physical techniques like how to use your voice as a deterrent and an alarm, how to stand to create the greatest positional advantage against a potential attacker, and where and when to strike your opponent to have the best possible chance of escape.

All the students were women. Only women were allowed. Men were the aggressors in nearly every case of rape, domestic violence, human and sex trafficking, and murder, all of which were prevalent in Manila, and very prevalent in slums like Tondo, where Lex and most of her students lived. Lex refused to teach men. She would not be the one to help them learn how to be more aggressive. She refused to give them even more tools for controlling women.

Instead, she was empowering women to protect themselves.

That night, she'd had the biggest turnout yet, with nearly thirty women showing up at the back of the warehouse just after dark. A dangerous time of day, but the only time most of the women could stop working and leave their homes. Lex had run three classes, back to back, ten women at a time. The women who weren't in the class would stand outside and watch through small windows clouded with decades of oil and grime. Even the women whose class had already finished would watch, practicing in the meager glow of the bulbs hung from wires strung across the narrow streets, eager to learn as much as they could.

For those who wanted to learn to do more than simply protect themselves, Lex held an advanced class. This was much more sparsely attended, and kept far more secret. The men might laugh at the notion of their women learning how to yell and run and control their anxiety, would wave them out the door after dinner and wink at their friends as they reached for more beer.

But they would not be so light-hearted about a class that taught women how to fight back. They would not wink and laugh about their women learning how to leverage their smaller size to advantage, how to lure men into bending down and then strike their necks with the edge of their hand, or how to target the soft, weak inside of the knee with the heel of their foot or the hard edge of their boot. They would not sit back and drink their beer at that notion. They were more likely to swing the empty bottle at their woman's head, then demand she get him another beer.

And so this class was smaller and later in the night. The women who attended were mostly survivors of past abuse who had somehow managed to escape their men, or whose husbands had died, gone to prison, or run off, leaving them alone and damaged in a dangerous part of town.

The lesson that night was floor work. They worked on an old mattress one of the women had found months earlier, or on a pile of old t-shirts stained with oil by a clumsy or drunk dock worker, or just on the bare concrete floor. They worked in pairs, taking turns, one student on her knees atop her partner.

Lex's instructors had called the move "countering the mount". A man's title. Lex described it simply as the way to get out from under the asshole while he fumbled to get his dick out of his pants.

Hook your right foot outside his left, and hook your right arm outside his left arm, above the elbow. Chop your upper arm down onto his forearm to bend his elbow, dropping his left side down on top of you. Then use the momentum of his fall to roll the fucker onto his back.

"No, Aya," Lex shouted. "Don't let go of that arm."

Lex stopped Aya and her partner, then switched places, getting on her back on the floor with Aya on top. She did the move, rolled up over Aya, kept Aya's arm pinned between her biceps and her chest, and kept rolling, first onto one knee, then up to her feet in a low crouch, rolling Aya onto her stomach and twisting Aya's arm behind her back as she went.

For a moment, Lex felt the usual flare of anger as she did the movement, memory impinging on reality. She'd known how to use the moves back then. She just hadn't known she would need to use them against her own side. She had been trained to follow orders, not to give herself permission.

Not anymore.

Lex took a calming breath. "You see?" she said. Aya slapped the ground, wincing, and nodded. "It hurts, right?"

"Yes," Aya croaked.

Lex released Aya's arm gently and helped her to her feet. The other women had stopped to watch. A few timid faces pressed against the windows from outside.

"Never give up an advantage," Lex said to the group, pounding one fist into her other palm to emphasize each word. Her mouth pressed into a grim line. "You won't get many." She motioned toward Aya and her partner. "Go again."

The class ran long, well after one in the morning. Lex sat on a pile of rotting rope in a dark corner of the gym, scraping the last of the cold *arroz caldo* from a ceramic bowl while the students cleaned up, chattering excitedly about what they'd learned. As usual, they'd be sore in the morning, but they'd look at their men with a colder, more calculating eye.

Aya said goodbye to two women. They always left in groups of at least two. Never alone. Three other women were chatting in the corner, waiting for Aya and eying warily the workers at the far end of the warehouse. Aya walked across the warehouse toward Lex.

"You going home?" she said.

Lex licked the spoon clean, dropped in back in the bowl, and handed it to Aya with a nod of thanks. When she didn't answer the question, Aya pursed her lips and nodded slowly.

"Just remember," said Aya. "You're no good to us dead."

She rejoined the others. Lex waved at them as they left, then leaned back against the wall. She closed her eyes and tried to calm herself, but she could feel her skin crawling, her muscles sparking with pent-up energy. The fetid reek of the moldy rope only soured her mood further. No sense resisting. She breathed it in deep through her nose and felt a dark cloud settle over her mind.

Lex heard a loud bang echo through the warehouse and looked up. A huge, muscle-bound meathead had dropped a massive crate on a pile. He stared at her down the length of the warehouse. She stared back and narrowed her eyes, waiting, until he rolled his shoulders, lifted his chin at her, and turned back to haul another crate.

Lex flexed her knuckles, felt the skin stretch and crack.

She knew this crawling, sparking feeling all too well.

She wasn't going home. Her night was just getting started.

4

Dangerous men prowled in darkness in the small hours of the night. Lex taught her students always to walk in pairs on well-lit streets. Walk in the center of the street beneath the overhead bulbs, get home before midnight, and stay home until morning.

She did not follow her own advice.

Then again, Lex was more dangerous than any man.

She slipped alone through the shadows along the narrow side streets, avoiding the thin light from the crescent moon above. As she walked, her mood grew as dark as the deepening night. A needling headache morphed into an insidious fog of pain. Her temples throbbed. Her eyes hurt when they moved. She flexed her hands into fists and kept them there, swinging them as she strode, feeling the sting on her knuckles. Her upper lip curled into a sneer with each step into the night.

The moon would see blood tonight. Some of her own, no doubt. But more from others.

She could hear the fights from a quarter mile away. The makeshift ring was a square formed by the intersection of two lanes in a shipping yard. The metal shipping containers stacked two or three high around it provided vantage points for spectators, but they also amplified the cheering and the grunting and the thud of bone striking bone. If fighting and betting were illegal, the police or the army might have broken it up. But it wasn't illegal. And most of the fighters were soldiers or cops, anyway. Exorcising demons of their own.

There was a healthy crowd that night, stacked at least five deep, with many more sitting on top of the shipping containers all around the square. Half the crowd was already drunk, the other half doing their best to catch up. Lex stood in the back for a moment. When the men in front of her turned and saw her, they parted, as did the men in front of them, allowing Lex to walk unimpeded to the ring. Like a messiah among her followers.

That made Lex's lip curl even more.

The ring was nothing more than the space formed by the line of the crowd around a bare patch of hard-packed dirt. A fight was underway between two regulars, a stocky, middle-aged sergeant from the Philippine army and a feisty, wiry kid who drove a bicycle taxi during the day. Both of their chests were heaving, blood mixing with their sweat and running down their faces, their chests, their fists. The kid's left eye was swollen shut. The sergeant was spitting blood, and he was favoring his right leg.

Lex never bet on anyone but herself, but if she were forced to choose between these two, she would put her money on the kid. The sergeant was smarter and more experienced, but the kid was younger and hungrier. And with only one opponent to worry about, the kid being blind on one side was less of an impediment than the sergeant's restricted movement.

Five minutes later, blood now gushing from his mouth and his nose and unable to support any weight on his right leg, the sergeant, down on one knee, held up both hands and yielded the bout.

Lex put her name down with the ringleader, an ancient man, wrinkled and grey, who sat on a folding chair behind a small card table in the front of the crowd, a clipboard and a cash box on the table in front of him. She gave him ten thousand Filipino pesos, equivalent to only a couple hundred bucks in US dollars, but more than most of the people in the crowd made in a year. Only the soldiers could even think of taking the bet against her, and even for them it would be a stretch. But they could pool their money. Lex had learned how lucrative the male ego could be.

There were a couple bouts set to go before her, and she still had to wait for an opponent to step up. That was getting harder and harder for Lex. Her reputation preceded her now, and the only men willing to oppose her tended to be soldiers on weekend leave from Fort Magsaysay a couple hours' drive to the north, newcomers to town, or drunken idiots goaded on by their peers. But even they were hesitant now.

The rumor had gotten out that Lex only fucked men she fought, so that provided a little extra incentive for the men. Wasn't true. Lex fucked whoever she wanted to fuck. But the rumor was good for business, and she had to pay rent on what passed for an apartment and what passed for a gym, so anything good for business was good for Lex. A minor affront to her ladylike honor was a small price to pay. She'd already paid far worse.

The two bouts passed uneventfully. Two local dipshits who had no idea what they were doing, settling some kind of grudge between them, and two soldiers, an older officer and a younger enlisted man. That one seemed to be some kind of unofficial military justice or object lesson. The enlisted man swung wildly, his punches full of rage and frustration, but lacking skill. The officer avoided most of them, except for a couple haymakers that clearly rattled his cage. But otherwise he waited for his openings and took the kid apart piece by piece, using nothing but body blows, until finally the kid fell to one knee, sweat and blood forming gritty pools on the dirt as they dripped from his face. His chest heaved with exhaustion, each breath a loud wheeze on both the in-breath and the out. He probably had at least one broken rib, maybe a bruised lung.

The officer came up to him, towered over the kid for a moment. The kid just hung his head and wheezed. The officer held out one hand, and the kid took it. Lesson learned, Lex figured. Military justice served.

Then it was Lex's turn. She stood in the center of the ring, barefoot, wearing the same linen pants and white t-shirt she'd worn when she left her apartment that morning. She regretted not putting on a sports bra. Her opponent's blood would probably ruin her t-shirt by the time she was done with him.

No one stepped forward to challenge her. There was a lot of pointing and jabbering and horse-trading in the crowd as groups of men tried to scrape together enough cash to post against her. The ringleader wouldn't post. He took a cut of every bet. He was the stock exchange, not a day trader. And Lex could reduce her stake, but she was the main event. She wasn't going to cheapen it.

Every once in a while, the crowd couldn't post enough and Lex would have to go home frustrated. That just made her all the more expensive the next time, and all the more angry.

After ten minutes, it was starting to look like one of those times. And then the tenor of the crowd shifted from angry jabbers to awed whispers.

Lex looked up and saw the crowd parting again, like it had for her. Swaggering down the center was the meathead from the warehouse. He pinned her with his stare as he approached, taking his sweet-ass time. When he finally got to the ring, the crowd closed behind him. He rolled his shoulders and pressed a fist into his palm, his knuckles cracking like pistol shots.

Lex sighed. The guy was what they used to call JAFA. Just Another Fucking Asshole.

She glanced at the ringleader, who finished counting the wads of cash that had been dropped on the table before him when the meathead showed up. The ringleader nodded at her, then at the meathead, who didn't even look. He was still trying to intimidate Lex with his scary-man stare.

Lex turned toward him, set her feet into a fighting stance but kept her arms by her side, and cocked one eyebrow at the beast.

He grinned, and came at her.

5

HONESTLY, the feisty kid from the earlier bout would have been a tougher opponent. Men always equated size with superiority. In bed, size was definitely a benefit, no matter what men with small dicks said to make themselves feel better. But in the ring, size didn't fucking matter.

Okay, sure, a bigger guy often had more strength, so if one of their clay-clod fists happened to make contact with your face, it was going to hurt. But bigger guys were usually slower, often dumber, and always cockier.

Slow, dumb, and cocky made the fights easy money for Lex.

Lex decided from the start to be surgical, to work on her precision and her patience. She took inspiration from the fights before her and targeted the man's left kidney, the bottom rib on his right side, and his right knee. Lex was tall, but the man still had at least six inches on her, so she went for the underside of the jaw only as an opportunity attack, only when it presented itself.

Which it did, more and more as the fight wore on.

It took longer to wear a big guy down, but Lex was

patient. She savored the hunt, savored the thunk of her fist against the meathead's kidneys and ribs, the vibrations through the bones of her arm all the way to her shoulder. It hurt, but in a way that let Lex know she was alive, she was fighting, she was delivering more pain than she was receiving.

She stayed out of range of the clay clods. The meathead was all size, all bluster. He had no subtlety, no technique. The only punch he knew how to throw was a roundhouse, and he telegraphed them every time, giving Lex plenty of warning to duck under his beefstick arms, blast him with three quick rib jabs and an uppercut before dancing around to his back to jab his kidney and kick the inside of his knee before dancing out of range again.

Repeat until pain, fatigue, embarrassment, and rage made the meathead twice as dangerous, but five times dumber and ten times more predictable.

He only managed to get one hit on Lex. It had been a fucking bomb, though, right in the side of the head, above her right ear. Instinctively, Lex had turned with the punch to soften the blow, but still her skull nearly spun around on her spine. She'd stumbled, but had not fallen, even though her vision was swimming. She still had enough presence of mind after the blow to duck under his next punch, duck down and toward the meathead, and get a shot to his knee, buckling it and sending him to ground, giving her time and space to back off and get her head back together.

But she would definitely be feeling that punch tomorrow.

By the end, the meathead was on the dirt, unable to stand on his right leg. His rib was broken in at least two places; Lex had felt each satisfying crack under her fists. He was breathing hard, and his skin was taking on a bluish cast. One of those rib fractures had probably punctured his lung. Lex stood over him, wary, but holding out her hand for him to resign the bout and let her help him up.

But men being men and meatheads being the worst kind of men, he slapped her hand away and struggled to his feet, putting all his weight on his good leg.

Lex took a fighting stance again, then straightened up when she saw the look in the meathead's eyes.

Funny thing about a punctured lung. You can't breathe very well when you have one. The guy was already turning blue, and when he stood up and gravity pulled the blood down from his head, he got a dazed look and wobbled back and forth. Even after accounting for his busted knee, that wasn't normal.

The meat was roasted.

Lex turned her back to the guy and walked straight to the ringmaster's table. She heard the meathead collapse like a sack of dicks behind her.

When she got to the table, the ringmaster held out her winnings, already bundled up. She didn't even break stride. The crowd parted again for her as she left the ring and headed home.

As she walked through the night, the anger she'd carried to the ring washed out with her adrenaline. By the time she turned the corner to her apartment building, she was worn down and ready for sleep.

Someone was blocking the stairway door. A shadow in the darkness.

A man, it seemed. Sitting in a chair.

Lex didn't react, didn't change her stride. She tightened her hands into fists, feeling the blood from her freshly scraped knuckles weeping over the webbing between her fingers, but she kept the rest of her body loose and ready.

She kept her head level and darted looks around the alley and up to the balconies, wishing she'd paid more attention when she'd been walking on the main street behind her.

She didn't see anyone else. No gang members, no crew. If this was one guy, he was either an innocent drunk passed out in the wrong doorway or an idiot from out of town.

"Is that what you do with yourself now?" said the shadow.

Lex recognized the voice immediately.

It was definitely an idiot from out of town.

"Fighting thugs and children for pennies?" the voice continued.

"Pesos," replied Lex, "not pennies."

The shadow grunted and stood as Lex approached. She walked past him through the doorway. He moved to follow. She turned and pushed him in the center of the chest.

"I didn't invite you in."

She couldn't make out her ex-husband's face in the darkness, but she knew he'd be smirking.

"Can I come in?" he said.

Lex pushed him again, pushed him back out the doorway.

"Fuck no," she said, and slammed the door in his face.

6

To his credit, he didn't bang on the door or demand to come in. He didn't bust it down with his shoulder or climb the outside of the building and in through Lex's windows, like other men might have done. If Lex knew him at all—and she knew him better than anyone alive—she knew that he'd wait patiently outside for her to emerge.

Above all else, Nick Hadley was patient.

Lex stripped down and lay on top of her bed, sweating in the dark. She touched her cheek gingerly. It was puffy and swollen where the meathead had clocked her, but she couldn't feel anything broken.

Just her head. The pain there pulsed with each heartbeat like the meathead was whacking the inside of her skull with a sledgehammer.

Her body tired but her mind spinning, she lay awake and watched sunlight melt the shadows from the ceiling. But it wasn't the pain or the heat that kept her awake.

Lex didn't have to wonder how Nick had found her. That was what he did. He found people. He knew things.

What kept her awake was wondering why he'd come.

She woke in full sun, sweat soaking the sheet beneath her. She must have finally dozed off. She checked the time. 8:30 AM. She hadn't been awake that early in years.

8:30 used to mean she'd slept in.

That was a long time ago.

Lex gave up on sleeping and took a lukewarm shower instead. She dressed, checked her gun and holstered it in her waistband, and went back downstairs.

Nick was still there, sitting in a chair on the opposite side of the alley.

She could see him clearly now, in the morning light. He looked exactly the same. No reason why he wouldn't. It had only been four years since Lex had seen him.

But in those four years, Lex had changed completely. It surprised her a little that he hadn't changed, too. Still the same expressionless mouth, the same Army-issue haircut, the same pale green eyes that seemed to have enough compassion to wrap the entire world in a warm hug, but could direct an airstrike to its target and watch the buildings burn on the video feed without batting an eyelash.

He wore a short-sleeved shirt and pants, trying to appear casual. But Nick had been in the Army so long that even clothes he thought were incognito still looked like Army greens, right down to the leather shoes and tucked-in shirt. Good choices for the tropics.

"You cut your hair," he said.

"Yours turned grey."

"It looks nice."

Lex snorted and walked past him down the alley.

"You still working for the cartel?" he called after her.

Lex stopped short. A woman hanging clothes on the balcony above her lifted one eyebrow, then went back to her laundry.

That fucking asshole. Is that how he was going to play it?

She turned and walked back toward him.

He smiled and said, "I was hoping we could ta—"

She grabbed him by the front of his shirt and pulled him through the doorway into her apartment building, shoved him stumbling ahead of her up the stairs and into her apartment, the door banging against the wall like a shotgun blast and swinging shut again.

"Jesus," he said. "Is this where you live?"

Lex spun him around and shoved him hard against the door, rattling the drawers in her dresser.

"We don't talk about the cartel in public here, you got that?"

"*You* don't talk about the cartel in public here," Nick said, calmly straightening his shirt. "*I* can do whatever I want. *I* am a representative of the US military."

Lex rolled her eyes. "That won't help you much when you're sinking to the bottom of Manila Bay with your arms and legs tied together and a plastic bag over your head."

Nick shrugged. "I thought the cartel didn't work that way around here anymore. Legitimate business interests and all that bullshit."

He was playing dumb.

He was good at it. Came naturally for him.

"What do you want?"

Nick shrugged. "Does a man need a reason to visit his wife?"

"I'm not your wife," Lex growled.

He was baiting her. She wouldn't give him the satisfaction. She balled her fists tight enough to make her knuckles bleed again.

"I never signed the papers," he said.

"You didn't have to, you fucking—"

Lex's hand twitched involuntarily toward her gun. She wanted to blow that smug fucking smile right off the asshole's face.

She turned away from him and took a deep breath. After two years away, she was not going to let him get to her now.

"What do you want?" she said through clenched teeth.

"We need you."

"Who needs me?"

"Your country needs you."

Lex hated that those words still triggered something in her. A lightness in her stomach, a flutter in her chest. A conditioned response from her childhood.

It made her weak.

"I'm not in the Army anymore, remember?" said Lex. "You booted me out for being a woman."

"I don't think that's what the discharge papers said."

"They never do."

"We have a situation."

"A situation?"

"We need your particular skill set."

"A fucking situation? God, when I was in the Army, did I sound like a ball-licking robot, too?"

"It's a matter of—"

"Don't say national security."

"—nat..." Nick caught himself and smiled. "Of utmost importance."

"How's Skinner?" said Lex.

Nick's smile fell.

"He the one that sent you?"

Nick turned away.

"I'm surprised you could hear the order with your head

up his ass." Lex barked a laugh. "Or was he the one up your ass?"

She balled her fists, felt the swelling and the pain.

"No," she said softly, her voice hard as a bullet, "I know where he likes to stick his dick."

Nick strolled around the room, his back toward Lex. He ran the tip of his finger along the edge of her dresser like he was doing a barracks inspection.

"You were hard to find," he said.

"Not hard enough."

"I figured you'd be high on the hog with all that cartel money."

The sledgehammer pounding in Lex's head grew to a whole fucking construction site.

"Their payroll department must have had the wrong address," she snarled.

Nick turned toward her, the smirk she knew so well on his face.

"My employer is much more reliable," he said.

"I don't work for—"

"And they pay their *contractors*"—he let a moment's pause dangle from the word—"very well."

"Why the fuck would I want to go back to that shit-house?" Lex folded her arms across her chest. "They made it very clear they didn't want me."

"That was just..." Nick shrugged, "a misunderstanding."

Bile rose in Lex's throat. This time, she didn't fight it. She pulled her gun from her holster.

"You know what goes for a fucking misunderstanding around here, Nick? In Tondo?"

She racked a round.

"Dangerous part of town," she said, pointing the gun at his chest. "Misunderstandings happen all the time."

He held up his hands. "A grave misunderstanding."

Lex lowered the gun to point at his balls.

"A hundred grand," he said hastily.

Lex clucked her tongue. "And you always said you wanted children."

Nick eyed her for a moment, then smirked and dropped his hands.

"We both know you're not going to shoot—"

Lex raised her gun and shot a round past Nick's head. She would have shot past his balls, but the walls were paper thin, and she didn't want to hit anyone on the street.

Nick hissed and grabbed his ear, pulled his hand back with blood on it.

"Huh," said Lex with a shrug. "Windy in here." She pointed the gun at his balls again. "A million."

"You know I can't authorize—"

She put a round past his other ear. She'd get an earful from the landlord, but the apartment needed more ventilation, anyway.

Nick yelled out and crouched reflexively. He always was a fucking baby in combat.

"Maybe I can get two hund—"

"A million USD," Lex said. "Wired to my account. In advance."

He stood slowly, spreading his hands out to his sides. "Lex..."

"Sometimes people even die around here," Lex said, squaring her sights on his chest again, "from grave misunderstandings."

Nick deflated, shaking his head.

"Fine," he said. "A million."

"In advance."

"Fuck—"

Lex raised an eyebrow.

Nick sighed. "In advance."

He looked pissed off now.

Exactly how Lex wanted him to look, the fucking prick.

She unloaded the gun and holstered it again.

"Okay, Nick," she said. "What's the job?"

7

Lex lay on her bed while Nick paced back and forth, explaining the job to her. He'd tried to sit on the bed beside her, but that was a hard pass. Since there was nowhere else to sit, he paced. Pacing was his natural state, anyway.

The job was par for the course in Lex's old line of work. Some new terrorist group in the Sudan had kidnapped a couple of foreigners in Khartoum. The US government was trying to figure out who the terrorists were and why they'd done it.

"Is it some kind of splinter group? From the LRA or something?" asked Lex.

"That is the leading hypothesis, but we have not received confirmation at this time."

We have not received confirmation at this time. The fucking Army was just like a goddamn corporation, with its obfuscations and double-speak. Army Intelligence was ten times worse. And just like middle management, underlings like Nick had to learn how to manage up. They used smoke and mirrors to hide their fuckups, spewed empty platitudes to make it sound like they knew what they were doing, and talked in circles to avoid any real responsibility.

They were good people with real talent, and they truly wanted to help. But the political meat grinder turned them into bland sausage.

Most of them.

"Diplomatic channels?"

"We've reached out to Kenya, Uganda, and Ethiopia, but we're getting nothing from them."

Lex frowned. "Someone bought them off?"

Nick shrugged. "Probably just don't want to stick their necks out."

"What about locals?"

Nick looked down and shuffled his feet.

"You must have someone on the ground," said Lex. They couldn't possibly be that inept.

Lex had worked with Nick in Army Intelligence until four years ago, stationed in Italy with a focus on the African theater. Nick still worked there. He'd been recruited for his analytical skills. He was one of the best at sifting through reams of seemingly disparate information and finding the slender thread that connected them all.

But analysts were a dime a dozen. Lex had been recruited for her language skills. She spoke twenty-seven languages fluently—twenty-nine, now that she'd learned Filipino and Tagalog—and could get by in another thirteen. That kind of skill was not a dime a dozen. Lex was a unicorn.

Which is why the Army had gone to the trouble of tracking her down.

"No one speaks the language as well as you, Lex."

"They speak English in the Sudan."

Nick rolled his eyes.

Lex smiled faintly. English was technically one of the two official languages of the Sudan, but Arabic was by far the more prevalent, spoken in its own Sudanese dialect. Even near the border with South Sudan, where English was the only official language, the locals rarely used it. In Dinka, the most common language in South Sudan, they called it *thok de lueth*, the *lying tongue*. Used throughout the region mainly by educated elites, government officials, and uppity assholes. In other words, corrupt politicians and the rich fucks who greased their palms.

"So what do you want from me? Translations? You got audio for me?"

Nick shook his head. "We have zero presence on the ground."

"How is that fucking possible? What about Thomas?"

"Reassigned six months ago."

"Harris, in Kampala."

"Transferred to CI."

"Jesus, Nick." Lex threw up her hands. "Bathwer in Nairobi, then. Or someone from the embassy in Addis Ababa, at least. They've got to know something."

"No, Lex, no one knows anything. The group is new. This is the first time they've done anything."

"Well, send some people in, then. Gather some Army intelligence. That's your fucking job, isn't it?"

Nick folded his hands behind him, standing at military rest, and stared at Lex.

Quietly.

Patiently.

A pit formed in Lex's stomach.

"No," she said.

Nick kept staring.

Lex sat up on the bed, not wanting to believe the

thought that was becoming painfully obvious with each passing moment.

"Fuck no," she said. She stood and strode into the bathroom, slamming the door shut.

She heard Nick's calm voice through the thin door. "You're the only one who can do this, Lex."

Lex ripped the door open. "On the fucking ground? In a war zone?" She slammed the door shut again.

"They're not technically at war."

She ripped the door open again. "It's a fucking civil war zone, Nick. Those don't just end. Not in Sudan." Slammed the door shut once more.

Nick didn't say anything. Lex knew he was standing there, waiting patiently.

"Get the fuck out, Nick," said Lex through the closed door.

"Lex..."

"Get. Out."

After a long moment, she heard the door to her apartment knock shut. Lex leaned on the sink, felt the basin bend slightly away from the wall under her weight. She stared at her pale, worn face in the mirror and sighed.

8

LEX WOUND THROUGH THE ALLEYS, lost in her thoughts, her mood fouled by her headache, her fatigue, and her fucking ex-husband. She saw the deep green palm tree against the bright blue sky, followed it to its root, to Cariz and Aya's home.

Her stomach was pinched and acidic. She didn't feel particularly hungry, but she knew she should eat. Plus, she didn't want to stay in her apartment, and she couldn't think of anywhere else to go.

When she got close, the narrow alley was crowded with men standing or leaning up against the walls, smoking and conversing. Lex pushed her way through, a stab of fear in her chest.

But when she got to the front, to the table before the doorway, she saw that her fear was unfounded. Every seat at the table was taken by men sitting shoulder to slanted shoulder, some of them eating with one hand, straddling a crate so they could find room at the table. Other men were standing behind them, holding plates and bowls and scooping food into their mouths.

The tangle of smoking, talking men Lex had pushed through wasn't a crowd. It was a line. They were all waiting for food. And the men eating around Lex weren't eating just arroz caldo. Lex saw longsilog and sisigsilog, breakfast dishes with fried rice, a fried egg, and cooked sausage or pork. She saw goto, a rice porridge like arroz caldo, but made with tripe instead of chicken. (Lex had never liked that one. She wasn't into eating cow stomach.) She even saw a few bowls of champorado, a sweet rice porridge made with cocoa powder, sugar, and condensed milk.

Lex had never seen so many people here, and she'd never seen such a variety of food coming from Cariz's kitchen. She squeezed against the corner of the table by the wall when the old woman came out with a steaming plate in each hand for two of the men.

"Where did all these people come from?" she said in Tagalog.

The old woman didn't seem surprised to see her. In fact, she seemed irritated.

"You think you're my only customer?" she said, before turning back into the kitchen.

Behind her in the kitchen, Lex saw Aya at the stove. Aya glanced over and motioned with her head for Lex to come in. Lex ducked through an alley barely wide enough for her to walk and pushed through a side door into the kitchen.

"If you're in here, you're working," said the old woman, pushing a bowl of goto and a plate of longsilog into Lex's hands and gesturing toward the crowd. Lex brought the dishes to the doorway, and two men took them from her with slight bows of thanks, leaving money on the table for Lex to collect.

Lex had no idea how long she spent carting food from the stove to the doorway to feed the seemingly endless line of men outside. Hours, it seemed. Sweat poured down her face and soaked the back of her shirt. She collected the money, but she had no idea how much the food was supposed to cost. Cariz had never asked her to pay. Lex hoped none of the men were shortchanging them.

When the last customer had paid, eaten his food, returned his bowl, and left, the silence was a balm for Lex's tired muscles and sore mind. Aya took off the apron she'd been wearing and left the kitchen. The old woman prodded Lex with her fingers like she was kneading dough, pushing her out the side door after Aya.

They went out front, cleaned up what plates, bowls, and utensils had been left lying about, then sat at the table on a pair of crates. Lex's headache, forgotten during the mad rush, came back with a vengeance, throbbing against her skull like her brain was trying to break out.

The old woman brought them each a steaming bowl, champorado for Aya and arroz caldo for Lex, set them on the table, and took the dirty dishes away.

"I didn't know you could make all that stuff," said Lex to the old woman around a mouthful of food. Feeding all those men and smelling all those delicious smells had made her ravenous. "Why didn't you ever offer me champorado?"

"You're too skinny, stupid girl," said the old woman. "You need more food. More arroz caldo is what you need. Besides," she cackled and smiled, the gap from one missing side tooth making her smile even more endearing, "you never asked."

"But that's not—"

Cariz turned back into the kitchen, still laughing.

"You can't argue with my grandmother," said Aya. "Haven't you learned that by now?"

"That's what makes it so fun." Lex grinned and ate another spoonful of food.

They ate for a while, enjoying the good food in silence after the busy, noisy morning. When Lex finished her arroz caldo, Cariz brought her a bowl of champorado. Lex gave her a broad smile and dug in. The sweet milk and cocoa and the toothy rice were heaven in Lex's mouth.

When her own bowl was empty, Aya turned toward Lex to say something, then stopped short and looked up behind Lex.

"Who's the '*kano*?" said the old woman, standing in the doorway. "He one of yours?"

Lex sighed. She knew before she turned and looked up that Nick had found her again.

"Hello," he said to Cariz and Aya with a slight bow of his head. "Lieutenant Colonel Nick Hadley, US Army."

Lieutenant Colonel? When Lex left the army, he'd been about to be promoted to major. He must have perfected his ass-kissing in the last few years.

"You don't need to introduce yourself, *Colonel,*" Lex muttered.

Nick had the decency to look ashamed for a brief moment before he smiled and held out his hand to Cariz. "It's a pleasure to meet you, ma'am."

Lex had never seen the old woman smile so wide. Hell, she'd rarely seen her smile at all. She was eating Nick up like he was her breakfast.

"I like him," she said, holding Nick's hand and running her own over Nick's skin. "Soft hands." She looked at Lex. "And he's not skinny like you."

Nick just smiled and nodded and looked increasingly discomfited. He didn't speak Tagalog or Filipino, and was probably wondering why this old Filipino lady was feeling him up and leering at Lex like she was about to serve Nick in her next dish.

"He yours?" the old woman asked again.

"Used to be," Lex replied, scooping the last of her champorado into her mouth. "Not anymore."

"Then I'll take him."

"Be my guest."

Aya stood and cleared the table, nodded politely at Nick, and took the dishes into the kitchen. The old woman motioned for Nick to sit beside Lex. Lex tried to get up, but the old woman—remarkably strong for her age—reached across the table with both hands and pushed her back down.

"Sit, sit, handsome man," she said in Tagalog, gesturing Nick toward a crate. "I'll bring you some food."

When she turned back into the kitchen, Nick leaned to Lex. "What did she say?"

"She said she doesn't like Americans," Lex replied. "Especially men."

"You're American."

"Yes, but I'm repenting. This is a very religious country. They appreciate that sort of thing."

The old woman came back with a plate of longsilog and a bowl of arroz caldo and set them before Nick. She stroked the two-day stubble on his cheeks, cooing softly before retreating back into the kitchen.

With an embarrassed glance toward Lex, Nick picked up his utensils and took a bite of arroz caldo.

He swooned at the taste.

"She seems to like American men just fine," he said around his mouthful.

"It's probably poisoned," Lex replied. "Enjoy your last meal."

"I'll die happy."

"As long as you die," Lex smiled, "I'll be happy, too."

Lex sat in silence while Nick ate, the clink of his fork on his plate and his occasional moans of pleasure the only sounds. When he had finished, Cariz brought him a bowl of champorado. Nick protested at first, claiming he was full, but Cariz just smiled and turned back into the kitchen. Naturally, Nick took a bite—to be polite, he said—and moaned again. Minutes later, he was scraping the last of the champorado from the bowl.

Aya took away Nick's empty dishes and brought them both cups of kapeng barako. The steam rising from the dark coffee brought the licorice scent of anise to Lex's nose. She breathed it in deep, then smiled into her cup as Nick sipped his drink and exclaimed. Philippine kape, or coffee, is brewed strong, and kapeng barako is a particularly strong varietal. When Cariz brewed it, it was even stronger.

Lex and Nick sipped their drinks, neither of them looking at the other. Instead, they stared straight ahead at Aya and Cariz working in the kitchen.

"I'm not going, Nick," Lex said at last.

"Lex..."

"It's too dangerous." Lex shook her head. "I'm done fucking my life up for... what? Duty? Honor?" She scoffed. "That's all bullshit. Propaganda. Doesn't exist. Not at the 207th, anyway."

She sipped her kape.

"They took hostages, Lex."

"Find someone else to free your hostages."

"Journalists. Three of them."

"Three or three hundred, I don't give a fu—"

"All women."

Lex fell silent.

"Two Brits and an American freelancer. Sar—"

"I don't want to know their names."

"Sarah Court, writer for the Guardian. 30 years old."

"I said, I don't—"

"Her photographer, Isa Margules, 31."

Lex stared straight ahead in silence.

"And Trina Huntsman."

He held a photo out in front of Lex. She didn't look at it.

"That's the American. A freelance journalist looking for a story. Twenty-eight years old."

Lex couldn't help herself. She glanced down. It was a byline photo of a pretty, young, brown-haired woman in a business suit. Her arms were folded and her look was serious, determined.

"Pretty, don't you think?" said Nick. "And talented, from what I hear. A bright future. If she can get away from the terrorists who are holding her captive."

Lex took a long, slow swallow of her kape, thinking things through. She knew what Nick was doing. After five years working side-by-side, the last three as husband and wife, she knew him as well as he knew her.

And she knew all too well what a band of terrorists in the Sudan might do with three Western women. A hard fist formed in her guts. She forced her mind to think of other things.

"Why now?" she asked. "What's so important about Trina Huntsman?"

"And the two British—"

"You don't give a shit about them. What is so important about Trina Huntsman?"

Nick's mouth pressed into that lipless line he made whenever he spouted corporate Army bullshit.

"The president is committed to freeing every American wrongly detained overseas," he said.

The president. There it was.

Nick was a shitty liar. He gave too much information when he didn't need to.

It was early October, and there was an election in the US in a month. Lex didn't follow US politics closely anymore, but it was all over the newsstand headlines, even in the Philippines. And every election was a nail-biter these days. The president would want something big he could tout on the campaign trail. An October surprise to bolster his campaign.

What better than a daring rescue, commanded by the president? America loved stories about heroes who rescued damsels in distress.

"Go away, Nick," said Lex softly as she took another sip of her kape.

"Lex..."

"I said go away."

There was no anger in her voice. Nick must have realized that. He didn't press Lex further, just nodded and stood, pulling a wad of cash from his pocket and dropping it on the table.

"I'll see you at your apartment," he said.

Whatever Nick's other qualities, good or bad, he was persistent.

"No," Lex said, stopping him as he turned away. "Come to the docks. North Harbor. Ten PM. I want you to see something."

She didn't bother to tell him how to get there. Nick would figure it out. Or Lex would find him.

She listened to Nick's footsteps fade as she drank the rest of her kapeng barako, staring into the kitchen and watching Aya and Cariz clean up. Aya came to the doorway, wiping her hands on a dishtowel. She glanced after Nick, then settled her gaze squarely on Lex.

"Why'd you tell him to come to the gym?" she asked.

"I don't want him at my apartment."

"Because it's a shithole?"

"Because it's my shithole," Lex said, "and he wasn't invited."

"Why didn't you tell him you'll do the job?"

"Because I haven't decided if I'll do it yet."

"You'll do it."

"You don't even know what it is."

"I don't need to," said Aya. "He wouldn't have come all the way to Tondo unless he knew you could do it."

"So what? I can do lots of things."

"So, if it's something you can do, you will do it."

"I don't work for the military anymore," said Lex.

Aya sighed. "You're as bad as my lola."

"Maybe that's why we get along so well."

Aya disappeared. Lex stared into her nearly empty kape, swirling the few grains of ground coffee that had slipped past the filter. Aya reappeared in the alley and sat on a crate beside Lex.

"You won't do it because it's the military," Aya said. She lay her hand lightly on Lex's forearm. "You'll do it because it's women that are in trouble."

"Lots of women are in trouble," Lex said, her voice quieter and weaker than she intended. She knocked back the last swallow of kape and set the cup down with a bang on the table.

"Yeah," Aya said, taking the empty cup and standing, "and you always help the ones you can."

Aya went back into the kitchen. She was right, of

course. Lex would do it. Aya knew it, Lex knew it. And Nick knew it. That's why he saved to the end that detail about the hostages being women. It's why he said it at all. He was trying to manipulate her.

And Lex was going to let him.

She could have told him that. She didn't need to make him come to the gym later. But he needed to see what she was leaving behind to go off on his rescue mission. She wanted him to see how many women she wasn't helping so that she could help his three hostages instead. He needed to see first-hand the impact of following orders.

And she wanted to make him sweat a little longer. He deserved it.

Lex had hoped the kape would ease her headache. Instead, it was even worse. She was starting to wonder if that meathead had given her a concussion last night.

"Aya," she called into the kitchen. "How about another cup of coffee?"

9

Nick appeared that night right on time at 10PM, Army punctuality deeply ingrained in him. Lex's first class had just ended, the women sweating and full of energy, chatting about what they'd learned as they wiped their faces with faded towels and filed into the street outside. The second class filtered past them into the gym and took their places, ready to practice for themselves what they'd just watched the other class learn.

Nick skirted the shuffling crowd and stood in the dark corner. Lex came up to him, letting Aya and Julia get the second class started.

"What's all this?" Nick said.

"My class," Lex replied.

"I never pegged you as a teacher."

"You've been wrong about a lot of things when it came to me."

Nick winced at the comment. Lex wasn't the least bit sorry.

"Self-defense," she said. "Turns out the Philippines has a problem with violence against women."

"They're not the only ones."

Obvious. The kind of thing only a privileged man would say with any kind of gravity. But it was an olive branch. A thin, brittle one, but an olive branch.

"In poor districts like this one," Lex continued, "it's a hundred times worse. These women," she gestured to her class, "serve their husbands day and night. Wash their clothes, cook their food, clean up after them, and still work day jobs for pennies to support their families. For half of them, the husbands drink that money away every night, then beat the wives before essentially raping them and passing out."

"Jesus Christ," muttered Nick.

"He doesn't seem to help much."

Nick scanned the room and the other women still waiting in the alley. Lex followed his eyes. Turnout was high that night. They would need to run a fourth class.

"And you're teaching them to stand up to their husbands?" he said.

"I'm teaching them how to defend themselves. It should help if they're out at night and someone comes at them." Lex pressed her lips together. "Getting them away from their husbands is a trickier proposition for most of them."

"Why? Are there laws against it?"

"No, though the police are men, and they do tend to take the husband's side. But it's more than that." Lex shook her head. "These women grew up watching their mothers get abused by their fathers. Most of them were abused themselves as children, emotionally, if not physically. It's what they know. It's hard to leave what you know, even when it's hurting you.

"And if they did leave, where would they go? They don't have money. They can't move to America. They can't even move to the other side of Manila. And if they stay here, the husbands and their friends will just track them down and drag them back home."

"And the police won't stop it," said Nick.

"The police won't stop it," Lex nodded.

"Don't these women have any skills? Any ways they can make money?"

Lex laughed. "Are you kidding? Some of these women are fucking brilliant." She pointed at one woman practicing defensive chops to the neck with the side of her hand. "Yasmin designed and built a pulley system for her block. Everyone hangs their laundry on the wire. With a twist of a knob, anyone can shift the laundry to keep it in the sun as it moves during the day. Frees them up to do other things. With the right opportunities, she could be an engineer."

She pointed to a face peering through the window. "Angel is a gifted artist and seamstress. They don't have much around here in the way of new clothes, but she can take a pile of old t-shirts and make a dress that you could see on a runway in Paris."

She pointed out more women. "Nadine is an amazing chef. Jackie should be a surgeon. If you're having trouble with your phone, Kim can fix it. She's amazing with computers and technology. She could have a startup in Silicon Valley, if anyone would give her the chance."

She pointed to Aya, who was demonstrating a move in front of the class. "You met Aya this morning. She can see what's troubling people and can help them through it. She should be a psychologist, but she doesn't have the money."

"Her husband spends it all?" asked Nick.

"She never married. Never wanted to. She lives with her grandmother and runs that little restaurant you ate at this morning. She just doesn't have the time or the extra money to go to school. And what's worse is that she doesn't believe she ever could."

Lex turned to Nick.

"These women are as smart, as strong and as talented as anyone you'd meet in the States. They just don't have the opportunities we do. They need someone to encourage them, to teach them, to invest in them. And they need resources to get away from the men who hold them down." She gestured to her class. "*That's* what all this is."

Nick nodded slowly. "I get it," he said. "You're doing good things here."

"And I don't want to leave them. They need my help."

Lex gulped when she said it. She'd never even thought it so plainly before, let alone said it out loud. But it was the truth.

"Those three hostages need your help, too," said Nick quietly.

Lex shook her head. When would people, especially privileged rich people, ever stop believing that they knew everything, that their priorities were the only ones that mattered?

The only way to make them understand was to speak their language.

"Ten million," Lex said.

"Ten million what?" said Nick.

Lex turned to face him, her expression stony, her eyes fixed on his.

"Ten million."

Nick looked away, back at the class. "We agreed to one."

"That was before I knew I was being sent into a fucking civil war zone in a lawless country where the so-called freedom fighters rape women before breakfast. All so your fucking president could win another election. Ten."

"He's your president, too."

"Not for a long time. Ten."

"Lex, be reasonable. That's a lot of money."

"That's a lot of opportunity for these women. You'll be helping not just three white women who shouldn't have been in the Sudan in the first place." She nodded toward the class. "You'll be helping all these women who never had a choice."

Nick breathed heavy through his nose, but Lex could see the calculations going on behind his eyes. He was thinking through the possibilities. She knew then that she had him.

"Ten million," Lex said, softer. "And I want it tax-free. None of that give with one hand, take with the other bullshit. No federal, no state, no military, no social security, none of that shit."

Nick swore under his breath, shaking his head, then let out a heavy sigh.

"If I can do this—*If* I can—I want you on a plane with me before sunup."

Lex nodded. "You get me ten mil, I'll leave with you right now."

She was enjoying the look of pained irritation on Nick's face. It was a hell of a lot better than the smirk he'd worn when she first saw him.

"Let me make some calls," Nick muttered, pulling his cell phone from his pocket. He moved past Lex, deeper into the shadows of the warehouse, toward where the workers were unloading crates in the distance.

"Nick," Lex called. When Nick turned back to her, she jerked her hand toward the alley where the last class and the next class were watching. "You'd better go that way." She grinned. "You're safer with the women."

10

IT WAS WELL after one in the morning when the fourth class finally wrapped, and nearly three by the time the advanced class was done. Lex would normally have been stricter about the time schedule, but she didn't feel the usual urgency that night. She wasn't going to see these women for a while. She was feeling sentimental.

Lex helped Aya and Julia and the others clean up after the advanced class, pushing their makeshift mats into a pile in the corner and sweeping the floor with a snaggle-toothed straw push broom. It made little difference in the moldy, dusty warehouse. Probably made things worse by kicking all the dust and mold into the air. Lex always sneezed her head off when she was the one pushing the broom. But this was her workspace, and she would do what she could to keep it clean. She didn't give a shit about her apartment, but her gym would be as clean as she could make it.

"Can I walk you home?" Lex asked Aya once the chores were done.

Aya raised one eyebrow in mild surprise, but nodded.

They said goodbye to the other women, who left in small groups, then headed down the dark, narrow streets toward Aya's house.

The streets in Tondo at that time of night were quiet, the kind of stale silence that comes between the hours that belong to the drunks and the hours that belong to the early risers, when the drunks were already passed out and the early risers were still asleep. The only things moving at that hour were Lex and Aya and the stray cats, though even the cats were sleepy, stretching long, languid legs and meowing softly in the still night air when Lex and Aya passed by.

Lex and Aya followed Lex's teaching and walked in the middle of the street, lit from overhead by bare bulbs hanging from a convoluted tangle of wires that ran like vines across and down their path. The vines ran power from sagging transformers on tilted power poles to the warrens of homes that hunched beside the cracked pavement. At intervals, the bulbs on their slim wires provided a hazy glow that mingled with the moonlight. When the wind blew, if the wires didn't snap altogether, the bulbs would sway wildly, casting the scene in an eerie, shifting, silvered yellow light.

Tonight, there was no wind. Just a humid heat that squatted over the city like a fat man's ass. And the smell was just as bad. The drunks had a tendency to piss and shit and puke in the street as they staggered toward whatever place they would collapse for the night. Lex could see one such drunk splayed beside a pile of broken shipping pallets. He was using one of them as a mattress to keep him off the pavement, away from a pool of vomit on one side and a puddle of piss on the other. As they approached, Lex could see a sheen from the overhead light reflecting off a wide, dark stain on the man's crotch and leg. As she and Aya walked past, the stench became unbearable.

Women would hose the street down in the morning and chase the drunk back to whichever unfortunate wife was responsible for him. But right then, between the heat and the humidity and the stagnant air, it smelled to Lex like she was walking through an overfull Port-a-Potty on a hot summer day.

She pushed the smell aside in her mind. They had sped up to traverse the cloud of reek, but now Aya walked quietly beside her, keeping to Lex's ambling pace, waiting for Lex to speak.

"I took the job," Lex said.

Aya didn't reply, didn't even react. Of course she didn't. She knew Lex would take the job before Lex did.

"I want you to run the gym while I'm gone."

Aya looked at Lex in alarm.

"I don't—"

"You know enough," Lex said. "More than enough. You've already been teaching the basic classes off and on."

"But the advanced class..."

"Practice what I've already taught you. And try new things. Experiment. I'll send you a copy of the Army manual, if I can find one. That will give you some ideas."

Aya walked silently beside Lex, staring at the street, her brow wrinkled in thought.

"You can do it, Aya," said Lex. "I know you can."

Aya shrugged, then nodded. "I can keep things going..." She chewed on her lower lip.

"But?"

Aya sighed. "Will you be coming back?"

Lex frowned. "Of course I will. Why would you ask that?"

A sharp, bitter laugh. Aya gestured at the street, at the buildings around them. She gestured behind her at the drunk sleeping in his own piss.

"This is hardly paradise," she said. "If I could leave, I wouldn't come back."

"I'm doing this for you," said Lex. "For us. For all of us. With the money from this job, I can get a real gym. Real mats. Equipment, even. Hell, I could buy a whole building. A whole fucking block."

"We don't need a block," said Aya. She looked at Lex. "We need a teacher."

They reached the alley where Aya's house stood and stopped in the street. Lex turned to Aya. They were between bulbs, and her face was mostly shadowed, lined on one edge with the faint glow of the bulb ahead of them. Aya's eye reflected it, like a beacon in the distance on a dark night.

"I'll come back," said Lex.

She wanted to say she promised to come back. But Lex knew where she was going. She knew the job was dangerous. She wouldn't make a promise she wasn't sure she could keep.

"If you can," said Aya, reading Lex's thoughts.

Lex pressed her lips together, looked down at her feet, and nodded.

When she looked up again, Aya was searching her face intensely. She pulled Lex into a fierce hug, then turned down the alley without another word. Lex watched until she stepped into the side alley that led to her house.

Aya never looked back.

When Lex arrived at her apartment, Nick was waiting outside.

"Do I have time to pack?"

Nick tilted his head at her. "Do you have anything to pack?"

Lex pushed past him into her building. He began to follow her inside, but she stopped him.

"Wait here," she said. "I won't be long."

Nick wasn't wrong. She didn't have much to pack. A few changes of clothes. Her gun and some spare ammo. Her toothbrush. She took a quick shower, put on a clean outfit, and brushed her teeth. Everything she needed fit into a small duffel.

Ten minutes later, she emerged onto the street again.

"Okay, Nick," she said with a weary sigh. "Let's see what kind of bullshit you're putting me through this time."

An Army jeep was already waiting around the corner.

VICENZA

11

"I'M NOT MEETING HIM."

Lex stared straight ahead as the Army jeep slowed for a speed bump. They'd just passed through Chapel Gate at Caserma Ederle, the Army base in Vicenza, Italy that, among other things, served as the headquarters of United States Army Africa. It was also the place where Lex had served her last seven years in the Army.

Tan stucco walls and a red tile roof gave the familiar gate a local Italian feel that helped to soften the visual impact of the thick iron bars and retractable auto barriers that formed the business end of the gate itself. Lex had gone through the base's three gates hundreds of times in the past. The last time was three years ago, but Private Jenkins at the guardhouse had still recognized her and welcomed her back with that bright smile of his.

Nick sighed in the back seat. "You have to meet him," he said, his voice rattling as the speed bump jostled him. "He's the colonel now."

"I don't give a fuck if he's the goddamn pope. I'm not meeting him."

"Well, he's meeting you. You don't have to participate."

After more than twenty hours in coach on an Emirates flight from Manila to Venice—including a three-hour layover in Dubai—Lex was in no mood to take orders. Especially not from her ex-husband. He'd forfeited his right to ask her to do anything three years ago, and Lex wasn't about to give it back to him.

To make things even more irritating, Lex had been forced to forfeit her gun at the airport in Manila. A minor detail she'd completely forgotten about, one that had nearly gotten her thrown into a Filipino prison. She'd gone to Manila years earlier on a private jet owned by the Envigado cartel. No prohibition on weapons there. There were so many guns on board, they could have rolled down the windows and shot down a C130.

"Then I want a gun first," she said.

When Nick said he was taking Lex to Vicenza for a job with the Army, she'd expected something a little different than a commercial flight with civilian weapons regulations. Carrying her sidearm had become as much a habit as brushing her teeth or wearing shoes. Not having the comforting weight of the Sig pressing against her hip or the feeling the butt of the pistol against the small of her back made Lex even more irritable than the jet lag.

"You know you can't carry a gun on base, Lex," Nick replied, his tone that of a weary parent with an unruly teenager.

The unruly part was fair enough. Lex had an OTH Army discharge to prove it. And she knew they wouldn't give her a weapon until she shipped out for Africa, but she was tired and irritable and she wanted Nick to suffer for it. Not super professional, but fuck these people for not hiring someone else who could do the job. Someone who was still actually in the Army.

"Okay, then I want a waiver," Lex said, "signed by someone with authority, that states in no uncertain terms that if I beat the shit out of that man again, I am not to be held responsible in any way, shape, or form."

"I don't think anyone with authority would sign a waiver like that."

"Then I'm not meeting him."

Nick sighed again. "How about we start with a shower and a nap and go from there?"

He leaned forward and clapped a hand on the shoulder of the young private who had picked them up from the airport in Venice. "Let me check us in at CPF and then you can take us to my place, son."

The private nodded sharply and kept his eyes fixed on the road ahead as he drove them slowly through the base.

"I'm staying with you?" said Lex.

"What's wrong with that?"

Lex snorted, but didn't bother replying. She didn't know if Nick had orchestrated this bullshit or if it was just typical Army penny-pinching, but she was too tired to deal with it just then. She'd find a better place to stay in town tomorrow. Maybe Simona would have a spare room for a couple of days.

When they got to CPF, the central processing facility where arriving soldiers signed in and went through inprocessing, Lex waited in the jeep while Nick went inside to make things official.

She still knew the route. It was stitched into her brain tissue with Army green thread. When Nick returned, they would turn around, go back out the Chapel Gate, turn left onto the main road, and drive to the *Villaggio della Pace*.

Literally translated, it meant the "Village of the Peace". It was a secure area a mile outside the base where the U.S. government owned a bunch of houses for married soldiers and their families. It was where Lex had lived with Nick for three years, in a tiny dump of a townhouse built in the fifties. Crumbling stucco, peeling laminate floors, and a toilet that plugged every other day. But their newlywed bliss had made it seem like paradise. For a while.

"I hope you got a more comfortable couch since I left," said Lex as Nick hopped back in and the private turned the jeep around, "because you're not sleeping in the bed with me."

She could hear the smile in Nick's voice. "There've been a few changes since you left."

Whatever the fuck that meant. Nick was being coy, but Lex didn't give enough of a shit to take his bait.

She rolled down the window of the jeep, feeling the breeze. With temperatures in the mid-seventies, the locals would have considered that particular day unseasonably warm for mid-October, but for Lex, it was a cool shower compared to Manila. When they got off the plane at the airport in Venice an hour earlier, the screens on the wall said it was four-thirty in the afternoon and seventy-four degrees. Hottest time of the day, and it was already cooler than the middle of the night in Lex's apartment in Manila. Africa would be much hotter, she knew, but for now, she could enjoy the weather.

"How long before I can ship out?" asked Lex. Despite the nice weather, she wanted to get this job started and finished as soon as possible.

"Long enough to get you kitted out," said Nick, "and get a full briefing. This is a sensitive mission, so there will be eyes on it."

"Ugh. Brass?"

Nick nodded. "Lieutenant General Torrance is scheduled to arrive on Thursday. She asked to meet you specifically."

"Thursday? What day is today?"

Lex had little reason to keep track of days and times in Manila. After the long flight and the jet lag, she had even less of an idea what day it was.

"Monday."

Lex swore under her breath. At least three days stuck in Vicenza. She would be comfortable enough, she knew. Military bases did not tend to change quickly, so she was sure she could still get around. There were plenty of locals that Lex had come to know in her seven years in Vicenza. They would still be in town, she was sure. And most of the people on base were good people, people who had been—and probably still were—Lex's friends.

Only one of them was a complete fucking asshole.

Not Nick. He was an asshole, but not a complete asshole. Nick was the pucker without the stink. Lieutenant Colonel James Skinner—now Colonel James Skinner, apparently—was the full package: shit stains, hemorrhoids, anal itching and all.

"If you make me meet him," Lex said, "you'd better not leave me alone with him. I won't be responsible for his condition when I'm through."

"Understood," said Nick. "But you won't get that in writing."

Lex leaned her head against the headrest and closed her eyes, the slow breeze through the open window cool against her face, listening to the throaty chortle of the jeep's engine as the private eased them through the base. When she felt him slow and turn right, she opened her eyes.

"Uh, it's been a while for me, Private," she said, "but I think you want to go that way." She pointed straight ahead, toward Chapel Gate.

"No, ma'am," said the private. "Lieutenant Colonel Hadley's quarters are this way, ma'am."

Lex turned in her seat to look at Nick in the back seat.

"I told you," he said, smiling like the shit-eater he was, "there've been a few changes since you left."

12

NICK'S new place was a marked improvement over the shitbox Lex had shared with him. It was brand-new, for one thing. Nick said they'd broken ground on widespread housing renovations just a few weeks after Lex had been discharged. Apparently, the entire Villaggio had been rebuilt, including a new high school, a playground, open green space, and sports and fitness areas. Plus, they'd doubled the number of available housing units, including a handful of units built just behind the base itself.

Nick's townhouse was in the latter development. Finished just six months earlier, it was two stories tall, with over fifteen hundred square feet of living space.

At least, that's what Nick told her. He was rattling off the sales pitch while giving her a tour. Nine-foot ceilings, air conditioning, plenty of windows to let in lots of light, plantation shutters if you wanted to block it out.

"I'm not going to buy it off you, if that's what you're hoping," Lex said.

Nick made a weird, strangled noise, but when Lex glanced at him, he just gave her an awkward half-smile.

There was a living room, kitchen, bedroom, and full bath on the first floor and a bedroom, half-bath, and master suite on the top floor. Nick opened the door to the bedroom on the second floor and flicked on the light switch.

"You can stay in here," he said. "You can use the shower downstairs." He jerked a thumb over his shoulder. "I'm just across the hall." He paused for a moment, then added, "You're welcome to use the shower in the master suite, if that's easier for you."

Lex stared blankly at him for a long moment. "I'll take the downstairs bedroom," she said, shouldering past him and heading back downstairs. She didn't like the idea of sleeping in the same house as Nick. She liked the idea of sleeping across the hall from him even less. And there was no way in hell she was going to share a shower with him.

"Oh, okay," said Nick, hustling down the stairs to catch up to her. "Sure. Good idea. Closer to the kitchen. It's fully stocked, by the way. Did I mention that?"

"Yep," said Lex. "You did."

She stepped into the bedroom and dropped her duffel bag on the bed. She turned to look at Nick in the doorway, hands on his hips, goggling at her.

"Um, bathroom is through there." He pointed at a doorway across the hall, one he'd already pointed out earlier in the tour. As if Lex couldn't figure it out on her own.

"I can take it from here, Nick." Lex waved him away with the backs of both hands. "Get the fuck out."

"Oh, uh, right." Nick went outside, then leaned back in through the doorway. "Shower, maybe a nap, and I'll wake you for dinner in, say..." He checked his watch.

Lex slammed the door in his face.

"Whenever you're ready," Nick's muffled voice said through the door.

Jesus fucking Christ. Living with Nick again on base in Vicenza. It was like the last four years of Lex's life had never happened.

If only that could be true.

In the silence of solitude at last, Lex could feel the weight of her own weariness. She flopped backward on the bed, fully ready to sleep for as long as her body needed. She closed her eyes and took a deep breath.

Holy shit. What her body needed was a long, hot shower. She smelled like the ass end of a pig stuffed into the ass end of a cow. There was a bathrobe in the closet, and Lex wondered idly if Nick had entertained any guests before her. She dropped her dirty clothes in a heap in the corner, headed across the hall into the bathroom, and locked the door behind her. She cranked up the shower and stood on the far side of the tub while the water slowly heated. As it got warmer, she crouched down, letting the spray hit her body, then sat, splaying her legs out ahead of her like a kid on the playground. Now that she was sitting, she felt too tired to stand up. She closed her eyes, feeling the warm water against her skin. Maybe she'd flip the stopper and take a bath instead.

She didn't know how long she was asleep, but when she woke, her hair was soaked through. Her foot was blocking the drain and the tub was half-full. The water was still hot, so either she hadn't been asleep that long or the building had a really good water heater.

She tried to drag herself to her feet, but her body felt so heavy, she slid right back down. She stretched up, grabbed the soap and shampoo that were already in the shower—Nick was the type to keep it stocked, just to be prepared—

and washed herself while she sat on the floor of the tub, the shower spray needling her head and her body.

Lex didn't really care about her living space in Manila, or anywhere else, for that matter. She wasn't really home much, after all. But she had to admit, in that moment, it was nice to have a good shower and a clean bedroom to sleep in.

And sleep she did. She wandered across the hall to her bedroom in her robe, her short hair wrapped in a towel. After locking the door, she flopped onto the bed and fell asleep instantly.

She dreamed. She was in the shower, but not the one she had just used. She was in a shower with glass doors. The water was steaming, fogging the glass. As soon as she wiped it clear, it would fog again. She looked up and saw that the glass arced up overhead and came down the other side, joining the shower basin again and forming a glass capsule. The short sides of the shower did the same, forming one curved piece of glass, like a bell jar or a snow globe. The showerhead floated like an apparition. No pipes, no controls, just steaming water spraying her from midair.

The water grew hotter. The steam billowed around her. She looked for the controls to turn the heat down, but there were none. The spray needled her skin, forming a cheese-grater pattern of tiny red circles like cigarette embers.

Water filled the shower pan. It sloshed over the arches of her feet, then rose up to her ankles. Lex swiped at the drain to unclog it, but it seemed perfectly clear. She toggled the switch to stop and unstop the drain, yet the water kept rising, now up to her calves. Her legs flushed the red of a lobster being boiled alive. She could see the skin turning red, but couldn't feel the burning. Not yet.

Cold adrenaline shot through her, her heart beating

loud in her ears. She swallowed hard and forced herself to breathe. She pushed aside the panicked thoughts in her mind and focused on what was in front of her, on what she could control.

The water was up to her knees now. She wiped at the glass, trying to see into the bathroom, but the heat steamed the wet track of her hand and obscured her view. She banged against the glass, calling for help, but the banging was muffled, her shouting voice muted, as if her ears were packed with cotton.

The water rose to her thighs, then higher. The cold adrenaline spiked again. This time, Lex didn't try to breathe. She was already breathing hard. She pounded harder on the glass. She tried to kick at it under the water, but the shower was too narrow, the water too high. She couldn't get any leverage, couldn't apply any force. She pounded with her hands, then with her fists. Her throat was raw from screaming, but still she heard only a quiet, distant cry.

When the water reached her crotch, Lex screamed. The super-heated water ran through her entire body like white phosphorous, burning her from the inside.

She pounded wildly on the glass, kicked at it, screamed over and over. Her already raw throat ripped ragged, but she couldn't hear any of it. No pounding, no shouting. All she could hear now was a faint sound, like a train whistle on a distant track, coming closer.

The water rose, up and up, up to her chest, then to her neck, then over her head. She looked at herself under the clear water. Her skin was angry and red, like an infected boil. But she could feel nothing. In the boiling water, she felt numb. She heard the sound of the train, closer, of the chugging engine and the wheels rattling on the track.

She held her breath as long as she could. She banged again and again on the glass, but her banging grew weaker. Her chest burned and tightened. She stopped, floating in the place where she would die.

A knocking on the glass, over and over, from outside. A spark of hope.

A hand wiped the glass clear. A face appeared.

His face.

Skinner's face.

Leering through the glass at her.

Lex opened her mouth, pulled in a lungful of scalding water.

This time, she could hear herself scream. It sounded like the whistle of the train engine as it ran her over.

13

When Lex woke, the room was pitch dark. Her heart was pulsing in her eardrums.

"Lex?" Nick's voice through the door.

She felt herself, felt the bed around her. Her robe had come undone, had come half-off. The bed covers were rent, her still-damp towel tangled in them. She'd been tossing in her sleep.

Nick knocked. "Lex, are you awake? Can I come in?"

"No," she called, but the word never made it past her lips.

She swallowed hard and tried again.

"No."

This time her voice was little more than a rasping whisper, her throat dry and swollen and raw, like she'd swallowed a dozen razor blades, then smoked a carton of cigarettes.

"Lex?" said Nick. "I'm coming in, Lex, okay?" She heard the rattle of the door handle.

Lex closed her eyes, pulled in a chestful of air, steeled herself for one last attempt.

"No!"

The door handle stopped rattling.

Her throat burned, but she had found her voice again, clear and strong.

"Don't come in, Nick," Lex said. "Please."

Nick was silent outside the door. "Okay," he said, his voice quiet, soothing. "Okay. I won't come in."

Lex let out a sigh of relief. Her muscles relaxed. She closed her eyes again, still sprawled on the bed. How long had she been out? She could sleep for another twenty hours. What was wrong with her? This couldn't just be jet lag. She felt like she'd been run over by a truck.

Or a train.

Her dream flashed through her mind. The shower. Drowning. Boiling alive.

The face.

She shot up from the bed, instantly on her feet, adrenaline jolting her wide awake.

A soft knocking on the door made her start and cry out.

"Sorry," said Nick. "Just me again."

Lex went to open the door, then realized she was still half-naked. She shrugged the damp robe over her shoulders and tied it tight.

"I have some clean clothes for you," said Nick through the door. "Your old clothes. I figured they might still fit."

Lex yanked the door open. Nick had been leaning his head against it. He jerked upright. In his hands were a stack of neatly folded fatigues.

"I didn't know if you brought clothes or not," he said sheepishly. "Or if you brought anything... suitable for base."

He shook his head at himself.

"You've kept my clothes all this time?"

Nick's cheeks flushed red.

"Well... I mean, they were just... they were here and I just never got around to..."

"Even when you moved to a new house?"

"I just... It was a hard time—a busy time, I mean. For me. With work. The movers just... brought everything over."

Lex frowned. Nick seemed smaller than she remembered. Despite his good looks, he'd never been particularly outgoing. He was an analyst, and they tended to be nerdier, more introverted. That's one thing she had liked about Nick. He was often awkward in social situations, but when he was in his element, at work or wrapped up in a case or a project or engaged in a topic of discussion that he was passionate about, he was confident and precise and sharp as a blade. That was the Nick that Lex had fallen in love with.

She didn't recognize the Nick she saw in front of her now.

But he did have a point. She thought about what she'd packed. A t-shirt and a pair of linen pants that were sitting in a stinky heap on the floor of the closet. Three more t-shirts and a pair of cut-off jean shorts that were great in the Manila heat, but not so great on an Army base.

"Thanks," she said as she took the stack of clothes from Nick.

He brightened immediately.

Lex looked through the clothes. Camo fatigue pants, an Army green t-shirt, a black sports bra, black panties, and a pair of tan socks. Standard issue, clean, but not brand new. It really did seem like Nick had kept her clothes.

He held out a pair of warm-weather uniform boots. They were broken in, with a small tear near the sole on one side. Three years ago, Lex had been about to trade them in for a new set, but then she'd been discharged.

"There's more upstairs, if you need it," said Nick.

She nodded and held up the stack in thanks. She started to close the door, then stopped.

"What time is it?"

"Ten thirty."

"Ten thirty at night?"

"That would be twenty-two thirty." Nick's smile was gentle. "You're back on a military base, remember? It's ten thirty in the morning."

Ten thirty the next morning? Lex had slept for nineteen hours.

"You must be hungry," Nick said.

Lex started to object, but her stomach gave a loud gurgle. Guess she was hungry after all.

Nick's gentle smile widened. "I'll make breakfast," he said, and turned away.

The clothes felt like a familiar old blanket that she'd thought she'd lost. Her parents had both been in the Army, her father a helicopter pilot and her mother a flight surgeon. Lex had spent her childhood moving from base to base in the U.S. and abroad. That was how she'd developed her skill for languages. She went to school on bases around the world. Kids wore whatever they wanted, as long as it fit the dress code, but it wasn't unusual to see fatigue t-shirts or pants worn by the kids who weren't rebelling against their parents, especially once the kids were old enough to fit into their parents' clothes. And Lex had been tall for her age, so she'd fit into her mother's clothes early. She'd been wearing fatigues in one form or another since she was an early teen.

After her discharge, she'd left everything behind. But it felt good to be wearing Army green and brown again. Annoyingly good.

The pants were a little looser than she remembered, the t-shirt a little tighter in the shoulders and arms, but they fit well enough. The boots were as comfortable as an old pair of slippers, even with the tear in the side. The only thing Nick had forgotten was the hat.

When the smell of bacon and eggs and coffee drew her and her growling stomach out to the kitchen, a camo patrol cap was sitting on the breakfast bar beside an empty plate, an empty coffee cup, and a full glass of orange juice. She slid onto the stool behind the bar and picked up the cap. Her captain's bars were stitched on the front and "Capt. Alexis Hadley" was stitched on the back. Who she used to be.

"I know it's not going to be as good as what that old lady in Manila cooked for you," said Nick over his shoulder as he stood at the stove and flipped some eggs in a pan, "but it'll get you going."

He turned from the stove and took Lex's empty plate from in front of her. "I hope you're hungry." He slid three eggs, over-easy, and five pieces of bacon onto the plate and set it before her. "I had some food I needed to use up before it went bad."

A toaster chinged in the corner. Nick scraped butter on it while Lex took a bite of bacon. She hadn't had American-style bacon in years. It was good. Fatty and rich, but good.

Nick filled her coffee cup and set a small plate of toast beside her, buttered and cut in halves. She nodded her thanks, then stabbed and pressed the eggs with her toast, forcing the bright yellow yolks to bulge and burst onto her plate. She sopped it up and savored the creamy heat of the yolk against the salty crunch of the toast. She could take the bacon or leave it, but egg yolk on toast was a taste she had missed. She could have found it in Manila, but in a poor neighborhood like Tondo, eggs weren't as common as they were in America. Or on an American military base in Vicenza, Italy.

Nick filled his own plate and took the stool beside Lex. They stuffed their faces in silence for a few minutes until Lex had sopped up all the yolk and eaten her toast and the whites of her eggs. She took just a sip of the orange juice, sweet and acidic on her tongue, and left the rest, along with most of the bacon.

She picked up her empty coffee mug and went into the kitchen to refill it. She held the pot up in offer for Nick, who nodded. Lex leaned across the bar to warm his mug, then set the pot back and leaned against the counter in the kitchen to drink her own.

"So what's the plan today?" she asked. "Just a cozy trip down Recurring Nightmare Lane, or will we actually do something useful?"

She shuddered a little as the memory of her own nightmare from the night before flashed behind her eyes, but she hid it behind her coffee mug.

"The Lieutenant General will be here earlier than planned. Instead of Thursday, she'll now be arriving on Wednesday morning."

"What day is today, again?"

"Tuesday," he smiled, sipping his coffee.

"Good," said Lex. "I've got some things to do in town."

Nick scrunched his face in thought. "We can go there, but we—"

"I said *I've* got things to do in town, not *we've* got things to do."

Nick sighed. "I need to accompany you wherever you go."

"No, you don't."

"Sorry, Lex. Colonel Skinner's orders."

Lex closed her eyes and took a calming breath at the mention of Skinner's name.

"I'm not in the Army, Vicenza is not American soil, and Italy is a free country. I can go to town alone if I want to."

Nick pressed his lips together. "You won't be able to get on or off base without me."

"On or off?" Lex set her mug down so she wouldn't be tempted to throw it across the room. She was tired, and she still needed to drink more coffee. "Why the fuck wouldn't I be able to leave base without you?"

"Colonel Skinn—"

"Skinner's fucking orders."

That goddamn asshole. She hadn't even seen the man, hadn't even been here one day and he was already making her life hell.

"And there's one other thing," said Nick. He rubbed the back of his neck. "You're not going to like it."

"I haven't liked anything you've said since I saw you again. Why stop now?"

"Skinner wants to see you in his office at noon."

"Skinner can fuck himself."

"He's really not that limber."

Lex ignored Nick's attempt at humor. Every muscle in her body tensed at the idea of seeing Skinner again, even from a distance. The thought of being in his office across the desk from him with only Nick as a witness made her want to catch the next flight back to Manila. Fuck the hostages. Fuck the ten million dollars.

"You're not going to get out of it, Lex," said Nick. "He'll just lock you down on the base, or force the MPs to haul you in."

"I'm an American citizen. He can't—"

"You're a contractor with the U.S. Army, residing on a U.S. Army base in theater."

"I'm not in his chain of command."

"Not technically, no."

Nick stared at her, leaving the rest unsaid. *You're not in his chain of command, but you're on his base, so you're under his control now.*

Lex swore under her breath. She'd walked right into the lion's den again, lured by money and her own fucking idealistic crusade.

"When do we need to leave?" she asked.

Nick checked his watch.

"Five minutes," he replied.

Lex worked her jaw. The spike of adrenaline that surged through her came from more than just annoyance. She had to admit that to herself. The slickness on her palms and the way the eggs in her belly had turned to burning coals told her that much.

"You're coming, too, right?"

"Of course."

"If you leave me alone with him, I—" Lex's voice wavered. She looked away from Nick, into her coffee cup. She swallowed hard, then lifted her chin. "If you do, I can't be held responsible—"

"The meeting is for both of us," Nick said calmly. "I won't leave you alone with him."

Lex stared at him for a long moment, then downed the rest of her coffee and collected the dishes to help clean them up.

She may have walked back into the lion's den, but this time, she knew what to expect. This time, she wasn't the prey. She was the hunter.

14

LEX AND NICK sat beside each other in the narrow waiting area outside Skinner's office. Army bases aren't luxurious places. Even the waiting area outside the office of the highest-ranking officer on base was more like the waiting room of a doctor's office or the principal's office at a large high school than it was like anything grandiose. CEOs of even small corporations had waiting rooms with far better appointments than army colonels.

The floor was covered with grey, low-pile carpet, worn thin by the tromping of decades of military boots. The chairs were simple, with unpadded wooden arms and padding on the seat and back that seemed designed more to get you to leave the chair than to settle in. They weren't uncomfortable, but they weren't what anyone would call lush, either. The walls were smooth and bare, painted a bland eggshell white. The small room was spotlessly clean, but devoid of flair, style, or imagination. The waiting area, like the base itself, was there to serve a purpose, and it did that to the letter and not a fraction of a step beyond, with no effort wasted.

Lex, on the other hand, was wasting effort all over the place. She couldn't stay still. Her knees would bounce, subtly at first, then with larger and larger amplitudes. When she pressed down on them with the heels of her hands, elbows locked to force the bouncing to stop, her jaw would clench over and over until her molars ached. When she loosened and wiggled her jaw to force that to stop, her fists would squeeze until the knuckles were white, again and again. She tried a deep breathing meditation technique one of the shrinks on base had taught her during the months of sessions she'd been required to attend. They'd never worked before. She didn't know why she thought they would work then. They didn't. But at least she tried.

The door to Skinner's office was at the far end of the long, rectangular room. The chairs Lex and Nick sat in, four chairs in a line against the wall, were at the opposite end, by the exit. Between the two was a desk, set to one side, but facing the chairs like a judge's stand faces the defendant's table. From behind that desk, the Honorable Ms. Eunice Catrell presided over the waiting room.

A matronly old woman in civilian clothes, the desk was two sizes too small for Eunice's massive frame. Tall and shockingly muscular, Eunice gave the impression of an East German Olympic gold medalist. Her hair was formed into a motionless coif that looked like the hair of a Lego figurine, every strand afraid to move for fear of death by hair spray. She wore large, round glasses, with a thin, gold chain arced behind her neck that connected one earpiece to the other. The glasses had thick frames and thick lenses that magnified her eyeballs until they each appeared like some kind of monstrous evil eye, resting their cold gaze upon those unfortunate enough to be forced to wait before them. Lex could have sworn the two eyes swiveled and darted independent of one another, casting their disdain upon every inch of the room, even the inches behind her head, missing nothing.

Eunice was typing on the loudest mechanical keyboard Lex had ever heard, clacking non-stop like she was writing a novel. The noise reverberated around the room, bouncing off the unadorned walls and rattling through Lex's skull. Lex tried to close her eyes to block out the sound, but that only made it worse. With her eyes shut, it sounded like a swarm of chittering insects or a Greek chorus of judgmental voices, muttering to each other and staring accusingly at Lex. Lex opened her eyes again. The insects and the Greek chorus disappeared, but the clacking sound remained. Her knee began to bounce again.

Eunice had no rank, but she needed none. She dominated the small waiting room the way she dominated her desk, with quiet sternness and an air of imposing authority that made Lex feel like an insignificant child. It really was like sitting outside the principal's office.

Only Lex knew the principal behind the office door was a sleazy fuckface who deserved to die for the shit he'd done. To Lex and to who knows how many other women.

Eunice had been the secretary for the previous colonel, and the one before that, and probably the one before that all the way back to fucking Adam. She could be Eve's disapproving aunt, for all Lex knew, clucking her tongue and shaking her head as she watched Eve sneak through the garden at night, up to no good with the serpent.

And it was probably just as well. Only someone like Eunice could deal with Skinner's bullshit. She was too old for him to sleaze onto, too scary for him to sass, and too mean to let any of his shit slide. She was a pro who knew her job and did it better than anyone else could.

The door to Skinner's office opened and a captain came out, carefully closing the door behind him again. He thanked Eunice, who merely nodded at the captain without missing a beat in her typing. He glanced at Lex, who didn't recognize him, and nodded at Nick before leaving, closing the door quietly behind him. Lex was quite sure that anyone who slammed the door shut—or, worse, left it open—would feel the wrath of Eunice.

With Skinner's prior visitor gone, the time had come. If Lex was going to be forced to deal with Skinner, she figured she might as well get it over with. She pulled in a deep breath, blew it out in a huff, stood, and took a step toward Skinner's office door.

The sound of Eunice's typing ceased immediately, leaving a silence that menaced the room like the spectre of death itself. Lex stopped cold, mid-stride, a chill icing her spine. It was instinctive, a defense mechanism.

Slowly, without moving her head, she turned her gaze toward the desk.

Eunice was watching her, unblinking, one eyebrow raised.

Lex was frozen like an underage freshman sneaking across her college campus at night carrying a beer keg when the spotlight of a cop car flashed on, pinning her in the center of its cone of light.

Eunice eyed Lex. Lex eyed her back, until through sheer force of will and some sort of antediluvian mind control, the power of Eunice's gaze forced Lex to shift her weight backward, unwind her single stride, and sit back down in the chair again. Only when she was fully seated, muscles unbunched, arms at her sides, did Eunice lower her eyebrow, divert her gaze back to her computer screen, and begin typing again.

A minute later, before Lex's heart rate had even slowed to normal, the typing stopped once more. Nick stood like someone had poked him in the ass with a tack. Lex looked up at him, then over at Eunice. That eyebrow was raised again, the eye beneath it staring at Lex like she was the village idiot. Lex shot to her feet beside Nick, who then strode past Eunice's desk and rested his hand on the knob to Skinner's office door.

Lex minced forward at first, then skittered past Eunice, half-expecting to be whacked across the ass or over the knuckles with a stiff wooden ruler. She made it safely to Nick's side. She took a beat to collect herself, then nodded at him. He opened the door and they stepped through.

Into the lion's den.

Predator, not prey, Lex reminded herself.

15

LEX STEPPED past Nick and into Skinner's office in three long strides. She steeled her gaze on the man behind the desk and strode with all the power and confidence she could muster. She stopped ten feet from the desk.

Skinner was sitting at his desk, head down and pen in hand, poring over a folder full of papers and ignoring her and Nick completely.

Nick closed the door and came beside her, a half-step in front, standing at attention. Lex eyed him and shook her head. Always a suck-up. But, then again, if she were still in the Army, standing before the desk of her CO, she'd be standing at attention, too.

For anyone but Skinner.

As the seconds ticked by, the confidence Lex had ridden into the room began to erode. To avoid looking directly at Skinner, she examined the desk, the floor, the room, anything that wasn't him. It hadn't changed much from when Colonel Wilson was in charge. The desk was wide and deep, but simple. A sturdy, deep brown color, it looked like the kind of desk you might buy at any inexpensive retail store. Functional, but not ceremonial. The Oval Office, this was not.

Stacks of folders, notebooks, and papers covered the desk, neatly arranged in two lines, leaving room for a telephone on one corner and a small workspace in the center. Two leather chairs stood between Lex and the desk, tall-backed and weathered. They looked far more comfortable than the chairs in the waiting room.

A gold-fringed U.S. flag hung limp on a pole behind Skinner. A computer monitor and keyboard sat on a small desk beside it, the computer itself a tall black box on the floor underneath. The monitor was showing a screensaver of the Army logo. Both the screen and the keyboard were spotlessly clean, but something about their arrangement made it seem like the computer hadn't been used in months.

"Lieutenant Colonel Nick Hadley and former Captain Alexis Hadley, reporting as ordered, sir," said Nick.

Nick used Lex's married name, the fucker. But Lex didn't bother to correct him. The fewer the words she had to say in Skinner's presence, the better.

Skinner did not respond, did not look up. Lex continued to look anywhere else.

There were two windows on the wall behind Skinner, one on either side of the computer desk, both looking over a parking lot on the base. To Lex's left, a small bookcase stood against the wall, the type with several shelves set above a pair of cabinets. The cabinets were closed, a lock on one side. The shelves were adorned with books, several framed photos, a medal in a display box, and various other knick-knacks.

The floor was covered in the same thin carpet as the waiting room, though slightly less threadbare. In the corner on the right side of the room stood a coffee table and a mini-fridge.

And the couch.

Icy sweat broke out all over Lex's body. She shuddered like a thousand cockroaches were crawling across her skin.

She turned forward again. Maybe standing at attention wasn't such a bad idea after all. She set her eyes straight ahead, staring blankly at the flag on the pole. Fuck pulling the heels together and the arms in. And she definitely wasn't going to arch her back and stick her chest out. But staring off into space and not looking at Skinner? Ten-hut, yes, sir. That was something Lex could do.

"Colonel Hadley," said Skinner without looking up from his papers, "you are dismissed."

The burning coals in Lex's belly from that morning returned.

Nick frowned. "I'm sorry, sir," he said, "I was told this meeting was for both myself and for former Captain Hadley."

"It was," said Skinner. He signed the last piece of paper with a flourish, closed the folder he'd been working on, and stared up at Nick. His eyes were steel. "And now you are dismissed, *Lieutenant* Colonel."

Lex felt her palms grow slick and thought she might actually puke those burning coals right onto the shitty thin carpet.

"Uh... with all due respect, Colonel," said Nick. Lex saw him glance at her, but she kept her gaze straight ahead. "I'm not sure that's the best idea."

Skinner pushed his fists against the top of his desk and slowly rose to standing. He stepped around the desk to stand in front of Nick.

Nick had a good five inches on Skinner, but Skinner

had the strength of arrogance and authority. Nick cowered like Skinner was ten feet tall.

"You don't think that's a good idea, Lieutenant Colonel?" said Skinner.

"With respect, sir," stammered Nick, "but, no."

Skinner stared up at Nick, eyes piercing, chest puffed. Nick stared straight ahead. Skinner let the seconds tick by. With each moment of silence, Lex felt Nick wither.

Same old Nick.

"Your opinion is duly noted, Colonel," said Skinner. His voice was smooth, deep, even friendly. But his demeanor was pure menace. "You. Are. Dismissed."

Nick's shoulders slumped. He closed his eyes for a moment, then opened them again and rose back to attention. "Yes, sir," he said. He pivoted on one heel, turning away from Lex, and strode toward the exit.

"Be sure to close that door behind you, Colonel Hadley," said Skinner. He cracked a smile. "Eunice doesn't like it to be left open."

Lex continued to stare straight ahead at the wall. Every muscle in her body was tensed. Every hair on her skin stood on edge. Every sense was extended, quivering.

She heard the clock tick the slow seconds on the wall. She tasted hot blood from biting her tongue. She smelled the stale reek of Skinner's aftershave. And she felt the snap of the latch bolt against the strike plate as Nick closed the door, like the snap of a bone breaking.

She pulled her posture up, drew in a quiet breath, pushed her emotions down.

Predator.

She let her breath ease out slowly.

Not prey.

16

STANDING JUST a few short feet away, Skinner turned toward Lex. Lex kept her eyes staring straight ahead, trying to ignore her pulse growing louder and quicker in her ears, trying to ignore the icy fist squeezing tighter and tighter around her heart. The air was close and thin, no oxygen in it. She remembered her dream, drowning, boiling, suffocating in a snow globe, Skinner's face watching through the glass.

"You seem tense, Cap—"

Skinner stopped himself. To a casual observer, Lex was sure his voice would sound kind, friendly. It had the same smooth, deep tone he'd used with Nick, but there was no menace beneath it now.

But that was to the casual observer. For Lex, the menace was all on the surface.

"No," Skinner said, "I can't call you captain anymore, can I?" Without looking, she heard him smile, heard his skin tighten, heard his white teeth expose themselves. "What would you like me to call you?"

He took a step closer, his nose just inches from Lex's

cheek. She could smell his heat, his sweat, his cum, his arm pinning her.

Her skin pocked with cold sweat.

"Ms. Hadley? Hmm?"

Lex furrowed her brow. She had to pull her shit together or things were going to get dark again.

"No," Skinner chuckled. "You're not that anymore either, are you?"

He scanned her from head to toe. He had to lean back to do it. She felt his gaze on her body like a slug leaving a trail of slime over her skin.

"You've lost so much since you left here," Skinner mused, the imitation of kindness in his voice like a slap across Lex's cheek.

He reached a hand up toward her face. She flinched, and he hesitated, then smiled wider before he smoothed a loose strand of hair against her head.

"Maybe I'll just call you Lex, okay?" he said. "We're old friends, aren't we?"

He leaned in closer, his breath hot against her cheek. His voice fell to a low growl. "Aren't we?"

At the feel of his hand on her skin, a switch clicked over inside Lex. She closed her hands into fists, not as a nervous tic this time, but in preparation. She was back in familiar territory, a man threatening her with physical violence. She trained for this. She taught this to others. She deliberately put herself in this situation four or five nights a week.

Everything else fell away. The job. The money. The military protocols and regulations. The past. All gone now. Now, all that mattered was survival.

Her eyes narrowed and her pulse steadied as she waited for an opening.

Then Skinner turned away, so quick the air of his

passing swept cool over Lex's skin. "Have a seat, Lex," he said.

He went around to the other side of his desk, bent to sit in his chair, then stood again as he saw her still upright. He gestured to the high-backed leather chairs in front of Lex. "Take your pick."

Eyebrows up, voice light, Skinner now was the picture of cordiality, all menace gone.

No, not gone. Retreated. Biding.

"Unless..." His voice and his brow dropped again. He glanced at the couch in the corner. "Unless you'd prefer to sit somewhere more comfortable."

Lex's lip curled into a snarl. She squeezed her fists so hard she heard her knuckles crack. "The chair is fine."

She stepped around the chair and sat. The leather was old, worn smooth in places, cracked and dry and rough in others. The cushion was yielding, more comfortable than it looked. As she sat, Lex slid backward into the chair. If she'd been in a different environment, she might have enjoyed it, might have relaxed. As it was, she pulled herself forward again and perched on the hard edge of the seat, her back straight, her feet flat on the floor.

"Yes," Skinner mused. He was still standing. He leaned forward, both fists on the desk, leering above her. "You've lost so much since you left." He straightened and gestured around him. "And I've gained so much." He smiled at her. "There's a lesson there, I think."

"You think so?" said Lex. She tightened her fists again. "How's your jaw?"

The smile fell from Skinner's face. His hand reflexively moved toward his chin, but he stopped it before it got there.

Lex felt a deep satisfaction at seeing that reaction.

"I broke it in two places, didn't I?" Lex screwed her face

as if trying to remember. "Or was it three?" She shrugged. "You lost a lot of pounds that year, I heard." Lex smiled mirthlessly at Skinner. "Gained some experience, though, I guess. Learned a lot about eating through a straw." She sighed. "Must have been nice around here with your mouth wired shut for six months."

A darkness flicked across Skinner's features. He blinked once, slowly, and when his eyes opened again, the darkness was gone, retreated back to wherever Skinner kept it hidden.

He went to the bookcase against the wall. "Would you like a drink?" he asked over his shoulder. He took a key from his pocket, squatted, and opened one of the cabinets. On the top shelf inside, Lex could see a small collection of liquor bottles, several glasses, and what looked like a wooden cigar box.

"Isn't it a little early for drinking?" she said.

He set two tumblers on the shelf above the cabinet and stood holding a bottle half-full of what looked like whiskey.

"This scotch is timeless," he said as he poured a finger into each glass. "It's older than both of us."

He screwed the cap back on, set the bottle on the shelf, and brought the glass over to Lex.

"So I make an exception," he said.

He held one of the tumblers out for Lex. She didn't take it. He shrugged and set it on the desk in front of her, then sat in his chair behind the desk, leaned back and took a slow, savoring sip.

"I import this Scotch straight from Scotland," he said, regarding his glass. "Special arrangement with the liquor store owner in town. Two bottles, hand-delivered every Sunday morning." He slid his tongue over his lips like a snake. Lex shivered. "You know why the best Scotch comes from Scotland?"

"Are we really going to sit here and—"

"The climate," Skinner said. "The cool climate slows the maturation of the whiskey. Takes longer to mature, so it tastes better when it finally does."

He looked at Lex. She said nothing.

"The Scots are patient," he said, staring at her, "because they know it'll taste all the sweeter when they finally get it in their mouths."

He let his eyes slide down over her body. Her skin tried to crawl out the door behind her. Lex wished she'd worn a fatigue jacket instead of just a t-shirt. She looked away, her eyes finding the open cabinet. She eyed the liquor bottles, the cigar box. Not seeing them, just trying not to see Skinner.

"Those are Cubans," Skinner said, his eyes following Lex's to the cigar box. "Not for sharing. Technically legal in Italy, but very expensive. I have them shipped from Rome. A special treat"—his eyes had slid back to Lex's body—"just for me."

Skinner got up and locked the cabinet, then turned to face Lex, leaning against the bookcase.

Lex's eyes had been fixed on the cabinet. Skinner's crotch was now in her sight line.

Skinner tilted his head. "If you're looking for something to, ah, smoke..."

Lex looked away again, back to the now empty chair behind the desk. A thin line of acid bile crept to the back of her tongue.

Skinner sat back down behind the desk. This time, Lex didn't bother to look away.

He took another swallow of his drink, draining the

glass. He puckered his cheeks and pushed out his lips as he washed the whiskey back and forth with his tongue, then finally swallowed it and set the empty glass on the desk. He nodded toward Lex's untouched tumbler.

"Try it," he said.

"Pass."

He smiled. "You might like it."

"I didn't like it last time."

"Things change."

"Doesn't seem that way to me."

His smile fell away.

"Maybe you just haven't learned your lesson yet," he said. "Maybe you haven't matured enough."

He stared at Lex for a long moment. She could feel the hatred in his stare, mixed with a want that was feral, vicious.

He reached across the desk and every one of her muscles tensed, but he was reaching for her whiskey glass. He paused, hand on the glass. He'd seen her reaction. He smiled, baring his teeth again.

Lex shivered. She couldn't help it.

He leaned back in his chair—it creaked on its springs—and held Lex's tumbler up in a beam of light slanting through the window. He stared at it, swirled it with a gentle turn of his wrist. The whiskey was dark, almost red in the sunlight. Like blood.

"I'm patient." His eyes dropped to meet hers. "Lex."

He seemed to savor the sound of her name the way he'd savored the mouthful of whiskey earlier, washing it back and forth over his tongue.

He took a small sip from her glass, swallowed it.

"All the sweeter," he said.

Lex's skin crawled for the door again, and this time she

decided to let it. She couldn't take any more. She had to be out of there, out of his office, away from him.

She stood. "Thanks for the meeting," she said. "I'll be sure not to attend the next one."

Thankfully, Skinner didn't get up. He just leaned back in his chair, swirling his whiskey in the sunlight.

"See you soon," he said, "Lex."

Lex ground her teeth as she stalked to the door, yanked it open, and strode through the waiting room past Eunice's incessant clacking. Nick was cowering in a chair by the exit. When Lex yanked it open, she looked back through the office door she'd left open. The typing had stopped. She could feel Eunice's glare. But it was Skinner who held her attention. Skinner, still leaning in the chair behind his desk, now smiling like the shitheel he was.

He held his tumbler up to her from across the two rooms. Lex exited in a hurry.

Her heart was pumping, her skin still crawling, that line of bile still staining the back of her tongue. But it felt good to be moving. Felt good to be free.

Skinner wasn't the only one who could be patient.

He was right about one thing. A lot had changed since the last time they'd met. Lex had learned some important lessons. And one of these days—sooner than later—she'd teach them to Skinner.

17

Lex had been hoping Bar Montagna might be empty at one PM on a Tuesday. She was wrong. And why would she have expected anything else from Simona Montagna, the self-proclaimed Mountain of Vicenza? *Tutti vogliono scalare la montagna, ma pochi oseranno,* she liked to proclaim. Everyone wants to climb the mountain, but few will dare. And, she would add with a wink, only the chosen will succeed.

Her bar was as lively and as colorful as Simona herself. Situated on the ground floor of the Hotel Simona, Bar Montagna had been a local favorite for generations. With the best jazz musicians in Europe playing all night, Michelin-quality food all day, and Simona all the time, the place was irresistible.

It didn't hurt that it was built inside an old palazzo on the banks of the Fiume Bacchiglione, near the Ponte degli Angeli, the Bridge of the Angels. The bar was built in what was once a court or a great hall. With the long room, stone floors and walls, and a ceiling that arched forty feet overhead, the shape of the space made for incredible acoustics, offering pristine sound quality for the acoustic jazz bands from just about any seat in the house.

And as Lex learned when she entered that day, it had become a darling of the social media set, as well. The social media influencers liked the flowers and plants that were everywhere, the colorful rugs, the eclectic furniture. Simona had designed the interior to look like her own living room. She figured she'd practically be living there every day, anyway, so she might as well enjoy it. The food and the music and the feel of the space gave it character, but it was the personality of the decor that made such beautiful images, tailor-made for social media posts.

The rarest image of all was one with Simona herself in it. She was ubiquitous in the room, but she rarely allowed herself to be photographed, especially for social media. It was all just self-centered bullshit, she said, and she would have no part in it. Lex was inclined to agree.

The narrow side street Lex was walking down was typical for Vicenza. The old buildings hunched overhead, and she had to move to the side of the alley, practically pressing herself against the wall, when a car came through. But as she neared the end of the street, she could already hear the hum of voices up ahead.

The street opened onto a wide piazza under a cloudless, blue sky. Tables under tents lined the square, and every one was full of people eating and drinking and laughing in the warm afternoon air. The piazza was ringed with small shops and eateries, but, like many palazzos in Italian cities, the entire side opposite Lex was filled by the Hotel Simona.

The building rose three stories tall, extending away from the piazza in the shape of a rectangle with a central courtyard. Not a huge structure by palatial standards, but massive by any other. Bar Montagna filled the front section of the building, an enormous three-story hall. A loggia formed by a series of archways ran the length of the facade. The center arch was wider and taller than the others, forming the entrance to the bar and the focal point for the entire piazza.

The building was hundreds of years old. Maybe even older. Simona had inherited it from her mother, who had inherited it from her mother, and on down the line into the hazy fog of history. When asked, Simona claimed her family had built the palazzo in the 1400s, but Lex knew the more likely story that someone in her lineage, some great-great-great-times-twenty-grandmother, had been the mistress of a Milanese nobleman who had died during the Great Plague of Milan in the seventeenth century. That mistress had been shrewd enough, bold enough, and brutal enough to claim—and more importantly, defend—the property as her own. It had been handed down through her lineage ever since, from mother to daughter, in an unbroken line that ended with Simona.

No woman in Simona's family had ever married, but all had borne daughters to inherit the palazzo. There were a few sons here and there along the way, too, but the inheritance was strictly matrilineal. Last Lex had heard, Simona's daughter, Azzurra, was off in Venice studying architecture and finance, or something like that, but like all Montagna women, she would eventually return.

Per family custom and inclination, Azzurra's father had never been in the picture and was not missed in the slightest by Simona or by Azzurra. When asked, Simona claimed she couldn't remember the man's name. "But I can remember a few other parts of him," she would laugh.

When the weather was good, Simona's staff would set up tables in the piazza and along the wide loggia. Lex made her way around the outside of the piazza, avoiding the crowded tables in the center, and through the main arch into Bar Montagna.

As her eyes adjusted to the dim light inside, Lex closed them and pulled in a deep breath. The smells of rich food, fine liquor, ancient stone, and fresh pipe smoke from the man seated in the loggia behind her filled her nose, and the tightness she'd been carrying in the center of her chest immediately eased. Of all the places in the world she'd been, this was the only one that always felt like home.

The acoustics of the room immediately raised the noise level, as if when Lex walked through the archway, someone had turned up the volume switch on the world. But this wasn't a muddy wash of noise. The sounds were in high-definition, as sharp and clear as if they were whispered in her ear. If she focused, Lex could almost make out individual conversations from across the room.

Almost. Bar Montagna was a free-wheeling place, where anyone could feel safe in being their true selves. But discretion and non-judgement were paramount. As far as Simona was concerned, as long as you were respecting yourself and those around you, your business was your business. What happened in Bar Montagna, stayed in Bar Montagna.

The bar itself stood directly across from Lex, on the far side of the room. Lex hadn't seen Simona since she'd left Vicenza three years ago, but before Lex had even opened her eyes again, Simona was shouting from across the room.

"Alessia!" she called.

Lex opened her eyes. Simona had stepped out from behind the bar and was on her way toward Lex. A maze of tables separated them. Some were traditional tables like you would see in any restaurant. Others were long, weathered wooden tables like you'd find in your grandmother's kitchen for a family meal. Still others were small, intimate coffee tables surrounded by high-backed chairs in a cigar-and-brandy setup. All were scattered and intermingled in a way that should have felt chaotic, but instead felt wild and energetic and freeing and improbably harmonious. Yet another reflection of the owner herself.

Lex worked toward Simona as Simona worked toward Lex. They met in the center of the room. Simona hugged Lex so hard she groaned as the breath squeezed out of her chest, then found herself laughing as Simona released her.

Simona threw one arm around Lex's shoulders. *"Ciao a tutti! Alessia è tornata!"* she said to the room. Alexis is back. The guests at the surrounding tables raised their glasses toward Lex. She heard a smattering of cheers and applause from around the room.

"You look good, Alessia," said Simona as she gave Lex a once over. She squeezed Lex's traps and one biceps. "Strong."

She nodded, impressed, then noticed the bruise under her hair above her right ear and touched it lightly. Lex tilted her head away from her touch, but only a little. The bruise had mostly stopped hurting already.

"Maybe a little worse for wear," Simona said. "Come to the bar and tell me what happened. And why you haven't said a word in three goddamn years." She poked Lex hard in the sternum. "Three!"

Lex followed Simona to the bar and took a stool at the end, near where the servers picked up orders for the tables. Without asking or waiting, Simona fixed a drink for Lex, a mix of gin, grenadine, and a fennel liqueur called finochietto. Lex had never had or even seen the drink anywhere else, but it was by far the best drink she'd ever tasted. Might have had something to do with the fact that whenever she tasted it, she was with Simona.

Simona set the drink in front of Lex, then leaned on her elbows on the bar, her face serious, eyes focused intently on Lex. "Tell me everything," she said.

Lex spent the next twenty minutes catching Simona up on everything that had transpired since she'd left Italy three years before. Simona already knew about Skinner and Nick and the shit at the base. She already knew about the discharge. Simona was the one who had helped Lex get through it all.

She'd been the only one who believed Lex's story. She'd put Lex up at the hotel that night, had talked to her until the morning birds had long stopped chirping and the sun was high. Simona knew exactly what Lex was going through. She'd helped Lex find a strength she didn't know she had.

Lex had always been strong, had always been confident. As a career woman in the Army, it was more or less a job requirement. But she'd still been subject to the same upbringing as every other American woman—most women in the world, really. Taught by society to take a backseat to men, to tend to the children and the kitchen, put up with male bullshit, and get along with everyone.

When that upbringing failed Lex, Simona taught her to stop looking to society for validation and look to herself instead. Manila had hardened the muscles on Lex's body, but Simona's counsel was what had really made her strong.

Simona listened mostly in focused silence, pausing only for the occasional clarifying question and to refill Lex's glass. She waved one of the servers behind the bar to manage the bar orders while she and Lex spoke.

"And now they've got you back here working for them

again." Simona shook her head. "You Americans and your money. You're crazy for it. It makes you do stupid things."

Lex grinned. "It brought me back to you, didn't it?"

Simona half-smiled at that. "Sometimes even stupid can be smart." She eyed Lex's fatigue t-shirt, then pressed herself up with her hands on the bar to look down at what Lex was wearing. "They even dressed you like them." She let herself back down with a huff and shook her head again, her brow furrowed in anger. "They're worse than *la mafia*. They never let you leave, even after they kick you out."

She came around the bar and waved for Lex to follow. "Come," she said. "Bring your drink."

Lex hopped off the bar stool and grabbed her glass, trailing Simona through a door on the side of the bar. "Where are we going?"

Simone called over her shoulder, "To get you some real clothes to wear, G.I. Jane."

18

Simona led Lex into the *cortile*, a central courtyard surrounded by weathered marble arcades on each of the three stories of the palazzo. The ground floor of the palazzo held the kitchen, an extensive library, and various sitting rooms and dining areas. The second floor held twenty luxurious and expensive hotel rooms, as well as quarters for the handful of live-in household staff. The entire third floor was reserved for Simona, Azzurra, and any private guests they may invite to stay. One of the spare rooms on that floor would now be Lex's for the duration of her time in Vicenza.

Grey stone tile covered the floor of the cortile, a row of greenery in pale stone pots tracing the outside of the first-floor arcade. Riotous swathes of flowers set in high flower boxes beside ironwork chairs and stone benches dotted the space, all oriented around a huge marble fountain in the center of the courtyard. The sound of the bubbling water echoed off the marble and stone before escaping into the sky above.

Simona's rooms were on the far side of the palazzo on

the third floor, overlooking the river. She led Lex through the center of the courtyard, past the fountain. As she always did when she passed through, Lex slowed to admire the gorgeous sculpture.

A nude Venus held a sword in her right hand, point-down at her side, and in her left hand a long sprig of myrtle angled downward across her thigh. This was no demure Botticellian Venus, standing coquettishly and covering herself, nor was it an armless, impotent Venus de Milo. This was a strong, proud, empowered Venus. She stood tall and straight-backed on a raised pedestal, her weight equally distributed on both feet. Her eyes were closed and her head tilted to one side and up toward the sky. In a master stroke of clever sculpting, a sun rose behind her head. It was from this sun that the water of the fountain fell. It whispered over Venus's face, then slipped around her breasts, across her waist and hips, and down her legs before chattering into the pool below her feet.

Simona claimed the fountain had been sculpted by Michelangelo himself, though Lex had always taken that claim with a large grain of salt. Regardless of its provenance, it was an incredible work of art that stole Lex's breath every time she saw it. Just like the David in Firenze, so maybe Simona's claim was true after all.

Simona's rooms were as colorful and comfortable as her bar, and her liquor cabinet was nearly as well-stocked. Lex was already feeling the two drinks Simona had made her downstairs. After they downed a bottle of wine between the two of them in Simona's bedroom, Lex was laughing with Simona like old times, times when Lex was still just an Army first lieutenant, unmarried and newly stationed in beautiful Vicenza, Italy. Times before every-thing went to shit.

That's how Lex thought of her life now. BS and AS: before shit and after shit. Or maybe Before Skinner and After Skinner. Only then it would have to be BS and ASS, really. Bullshit, and just fucking ass.

Being with Simona again was like stepping out of that timeline into a side pocket, a timeless space where Lex felt lighter, freer, and happier than she might have ever been before. It came in flashes, quick and fleeting, but it felt momentous, all the same. Even more important for its rarity.

Lex and Simona were near the bottom of their second bottle of wine by the time Azzurra got their attention. Italian techno was pumping through Simona's speakers. The clothes from her walk-in closet were strewn every-where around the bedroom: on the floor, on the bed, rumpled over chairs and dresser drawers slanted half-open.

At Simona's insistence, Lex had tried on at least two dozen outfits, not because she didn't like any of them—she didn't really care one way or the other—but just because it was fun to try them on. After the first few outfits, Simona had gotten in on the fun, too. Lex felt like she was in high school again, trying on clothes with her friends for a big party that night. Only the party wasn't out there some-where. It was right here, in Simona's room, just her and Lex.

Lex stood in just her panties. Simona never wore under-wear, so she was buck naked. They were throwing silk scarves at each other from a box they'd found at the back of the closet. The scarves were too light to really throw, so they formed a diaphanous cloud of slowly sinking color between the two women. They dropped to the floor too quickly, though, so Lex and Simona were scampering around, furiously picking the scarves up and flinging them as high in the air between them as they could, trying to get them all in the air at once, failing completely and laughing madly as they scampered and flung.

Lex noticed a flare of light or flash of movement on her left. She looked over and saw Azzurra standing in the doorway, grinning like the Cheshire cat as she filmed the scene on her phone.

Simona followed Lex's stare. "Zu-zu!" she shouted gustily. She leapt through the cloud of scarves and wrapped Azzurra in a hug, pinning Azzurra's arms and her phone between them. "Look who's back," she said, gesturing toward Lex.

"Buona sera, Zia Alessia," said Azzurra, coming over and kissing Lex on both cheeks.

Lex felt a little odd that she wasn't dressed, but Azzurra didn't seem to care. Simona sure as hell didn't, and she was completely naked.

"You look gorgeous," said Lex, stepping back to admire Azzurra. "You were beautiful last time I saw you, but now you're absolutely stunning."

Azzurra stood taller than Lex and Simona by a couple of inches, and she was wearing dark red heels that pushed her an inch or two higher. She wore a black, waist-high pencil skirt with an intricate brocaded pattern in a red to match her shoes, and a black button-down blouse with the neck open to her sternum. Her dark hair was cut short and slicked back off her face, giving her a sleek, sophisticated look. A far cry from the bouncing ball of light she'd been as a sixteen-year-old. Now, she bore the intense beauty of the sun itself. All of nineteen, she already had the presence of a woman who would run the world one day.

"Grazie mille, Zia," Azzurra said with the kind, but weary smile of a woman who is complimented often on her beauty. "And you look gorgeous as well." She scanned Lex's body, then glanced at her mother's. "I'm starting to feel overdressed."

"And under-drunk," said Simona. She grabbed the wine bottle off the dresser and held it out to Azzurra. "Have some wine, Zuzi."

"Maybe later, mamma," she said. "I'm meeting some friends downstairs soon." She looked at Lex. "I just came up to tell you that your ex-husband is in the bar asking for you."

"Tell that asshole to fuck off," said Simona. Then she frowned and turned her head to Lex. "We're telling that asshole to fuck off, right?"

Lex tilted her head from side to side, considering. She definitely did want Nick to fuck off, but she also had a job to do, and she still needed him for that.

"Tell him I'll be down in a little while," Lex said to Azzurra. "Tell him to have a drink or something."

"And charge him double," said Simona.

Azzurra nodded and turned to leave, then turned back. "Wear the black pants," she said, pointing to a heap on the floor. "Tells the men you don't give a shit about them." She turned away, then back again. "But wear heels." She smiled slyly. "Tells the men you don't give a shit about them, but you do give a shit about yourself."

Lex cringed. "I haven't worn heels since..." She frowned, then looked at Simona. "Have I ever—"

"You've never worn heels," said Simona.

"I've never worn heels," Lex said at the same time, nodding.

Azzurra's eyebrows went up in surprise. She nibbled the inside of her lip, thinking, then pointed behind Lex. "Then wear the boots."

She was pointing to a pair of black leather platform boots. They were fashionable, but still looked like they could do some serious damage. And that was coming from Lex, who spent most of her life in army footwear.

"What do the boots say?" Lex asked.

"That you'll kick their ass if they try any bullshit." Azzurra grinned.

Lex grinned back. "That's a fashion statement I can get behind," she said.

She came down to the bar an hour later wearing the black pants and boots, a fitted white t-shirt that ended an inch or two above her waist, and an ankle-length coat in red leather. The Matrix meets Milan Fashion Week. A lot more put together than Lex was used to, but it felt good.

Through the archway, she could see the lights in the piazza, casting a warm glow over the patrons filling the square as the last of the setting sun painted the sky shades of blue and the hot afternoon air cooled to warm evening comfort.

Inside, the bar was even more full than it had been at lunch, every table humming with conversation. Lex didn't know how late people stayed out in Vicenza on a Tuesday, but there was a vibe in the room that felt like they might stay all night.

A few exploratory notes from an acoustic bass thumped through the room. Lex looked at the stage and saw that the band was getting ready to start their first set. They launched into a fast jazz tune, blistering through the opening notes in unison. Lex was no jazz afficionado. She didn't listen to much music at all, really. But she could recognize good music when she heard it. And Simona— who actually was an afficionado—only invited the best musicians to her place.

"Nice of you to meet me."

Lex's eyes drifted from the stage and settled on Nick, standing beside her, a drink in one hand. Judging from the color in his cheeks and on the tip of his nose, it wasn't his first. Nick had always been a lightweight.

"I figured I made myself clear when I ditched you back at base," said Lex, keeping her eyes on the band in the distance. A drum roll crescendo launched the saxophone player into her solo, the sax wailing as it dodged through a sequence of rapid-fire intervals.

After leaving Skinner's office, it had been easy enough for Lex to lose Nick. She'd been a little nervous when she signed out at the gate, hearing in her mind Nick's warning that Skinner would issue orders not to let Lex leave. But she'd gotten through without incident. Either Skinner hadn't bothered with the order or Nick had been gaslighting her. Lex honestly didn't give a shit either way. She had no plans to spend time with either of them unless she absolutely had to.

"Thanks a lot," said Nick. "I guess that means you won't be coming home tonight?"

Lex swung her eyes to meet Nick's. "I won't be coming *home* ever again, Nick. Or do I need to define the word divorce for you... again?"

Some of the color left his cheeks, but Nick didn't say anything. At least nothing Lex could hear. She thought she heard Nick mumble something into his glass, though, as he took another sip. He was drinking something pink from a martini glass. Probably a watered-down Cosmo. Lex was surprised he hadn't asked for a twisty straw.

"I'll be here at oh-eight-thirty, then," he said, "to pick you up."

"Pick me up for what?"

"The general," Nick replied. "She'll be here at oh-nine-hundred."

Right. Lex had forgotten about the fucking brass. They would make the whole thing political, make all the ass-kissers like Nick and Skinner behave even more like jumped-up dickweeds than usual, and generally make Lex's job a whole lot harder than it needed to be.

"I don't need you to pick me up, Nick. I know where to go."

"You'll need an escort. They won't let you just walk up to a lieutenant general, you know."

"Why not? It's a fucking military base, isn't it?"

Nick didn't say anything. Lex sighed.

"I don't need an escort to get on the base. I'll meet you outside CPAC."

"The meeting's at JAG Off," Nick said.

The Judge Advocate General, or JAG, had offices on base at Caserma Ederle. JAG was the Army's corps of lawyers. Those who weren't part of that corps referred to the JAG offices as JAG Off. It was not a term of endearment.

"Why there?"

Nick shrugged. "That's where the general wants to meet. It's not for me to question her orders."

He slurped down the rest of his drink and turned behind him to set it on the bar. He had to set his hand on the bar rail to steady himself for a moment.

Total fucking lightweight.

He took a deep breath and glanced at Lex, then gathered the shreds of his dignity and stood up straight, swaying only slightly.

"Be there at oh-eight-thirty."

"I thought she wasn't coming until nine."

"Oh-eight-thirty," Nick said, then belched softly. "Out front."

He put the side of his fist against his chest and frowned, then scuttled toward the exit. He stopped once and turned back to Lex, the rising half-moon framed like a cartoon thought bubble in the doorway behind his head, and eyed her with as much gravity as he could muster with his tongue still pink from his frou-frou girly drink.

"Lex," he said, "please don't be late."

19

Lex was late.

But not by much. Nick had insisted they meet outside JAG Off at eight-thirty. Lex arrived at five minutes to nine. The lieutenant general wouldn't be there until nine, anyway. Nick was just being a priss.

Lex was late because Simona had kept her up all night. They'd spent some time behind the bar, Simona showing Lex how to make drinks. For hours, it was one drink for the customer, one drink for Simona and Lex. Then they'd found Azzurra and her friends sitting in a dim corner on a green velvet couch and three mismatched armchairs arranged around a low wooden coffee table. They had greeted Simona with boozy cheers and hugs, and had welcomed Lex like one of their own.

Unfortunately, that meant Lex had stayed up with them until the jazz band played their last set, then stayed two more hours for a late-night cutting session. Lex and Simona and Azzurra and the others, along with a smattering of remaining bar patrons, hooted and wolf-whistled along with the action on the stage. Something about the intensity of the music, the energy of the group, and the free flow of alcohol energized Lex so much that time passed in an instant and an eternity, another timeless side pocket of life. When Lex's cheek finally hit her pillow, it was four in the morning and her bedroom was spinning.

She'd woken with a start at quarter to nine. Fortunately, she was still dressed from the night before, boots, jacket, and all. The spinning of the room had slowed to a manageable rotation, more like the centerpiece vehicle on a pedestal at a car show than like the tornado she'd fallen asleep to. She brushed her teeth to get the dirty ashtray taste out of her mouth and defuse her breath, stuffed a piece of stale bread from the kitchen into her mouth, borrowed Simona's car, and headed out.

It was a ten-minute drive to Caserma Ederle. Lex made it there in three.

Nick was waiting by the curb.

"You're late," he said, checking his watch and tapping his foot as she strode down the sidewalk toward him. "And what are you wearing?"

"These are clothes, Nick," Lex said. "People wear them all the time. Turns out they make them in other colors than green. Who knew?"

Running on alcohol fumes and adrenaline, she turned past him and up the walkway to the JAG office without slowing and took the steps to the glass front doors two at a time. She burst through into a reception area that was just like every other building on that base. Just like Skinner's office.

Construction that left beautiful behind in exchange for sturdy and functional. Painted cinder block walls, thin carpet, tiled drop ceilings that were pocked and browned like the inside of a thirty-year-old smoker's lung, well on their way to emphysema but still some distance from the promised land. Round-bottomed black plastic chairs lined either side of the waiting room, oversized versions of the chairs you'd find in a preschool classroom.

Across from the doorway, a woman sat behind a glass window, her head turned toward a computer screen.

Lex walked up to the window and opened her mouth. Before she could speak, Nick shouldered her aside.

He actually shouldered her aside, the fucking prick.

"Lieutenant Colonel Nick Hadley and former Captain Alexis Hadley here to see Lieutenant General Torrance, ma'am," he said.

"Wolfe," said Lex to the woman. She glared at Nick. "Alexis Wolfe. Not Hadley."

Nick looked at Lex, sidelong, but only for a moment. He pressed his lips tight and stared at the receptionist through the glass.

The woman was in her mid-forties, with brown hair cut short and curled around her jowled face in a look that was in style ten years ago. She wore a white blouse buttoned to the collar and tight at the wrists. Black-framed reading glasses balanced on the end of her nose. She stared over them through the glass, looking back and forth from Nick to Lex with an expression on her face that showed that she knew what was going on between them and she didn't give even the tiniest of shits.

She tapped a few keys and examined her computer screen. "Please have a seat," she said in a bored voice. "We'll call you when the lieutenant general is ready for you."

Nick turned on his heel like he was on the parade ground, marched three steps to one of the plastic chairs, spun on his heel again, and sat down like his ass was looking for something it had dropped earlier.

What a dick-sniffing prick. How had Lex ever lived with him? Why had she ever married him? Had he always been like this?

Shit, had Lex been like that, too? She probably had been. She was as gung-ho as the rest of her class at West Point. When she got the word about her parents, she'd been even more so, talking the Army talk and walking the Army walk with her chin held high. Her parents had given their lives to the service, had died in theater doing their duty, like good soldiers. Lex would honor their memories by following in their footsteps.

That was during the BS times, before Lex knew any better.

She and Nick were the only ones in the waiting room. Nick took a seat in the center of one of the rows of empty chairs. Lex sat five seats down from him at the end of the row. Nick gave her a wounded stare for a few seconds. Lex stared back, arching one eyebrow. If he wanted to have a go, she was more than willing. She didn't give a shit if it was in the JAG office or in Buckingham fucking Palace. It would do her creeping hangover good to give Nick the tongue lashing he deserved.

Nick must have seen the challenge in her eyes. He backed down, of course. Nick was no hero. He was built for bureaucracy. Once upon a time he'd been full of idealism and intelligence, interested in world affairs and focused on using his brain to spread democracy and all that rah-rah bullshit. Lex had married him for it. But somewhere along the line, Nick had turned into just another ass-kissing, ladder-climbing career Army middle manager.

Nick turned his gaze to the blank wall across from them and settled in to wait, all awkward right angles as he sat on his cheap plastic chair.

Fortunately, they didn't have to wait long. After a few minutes, a young first lieutenant straight from central casting—blond crewcut, wide, beefy shoulders, and long legs—came out in Army green slacks and a collared, short-sleeve uniform shirt and tie. No fatigue pants and t-shirts here. Apparently, the lawyers liked to look the part.

The kid was probably brand new. JAG started their officers at O-2, so this one was probably fresh off the boat, straight from law school, and reduced to escorting people from the waiting room as his first JAG assignment. Oh, the glamor of the Army. Lex didn't miss it a bit.

The first lieutenant showed them to a square room with a cheap brown table in the center, surrounded by eight of the same cheap black plastic chairs as the waiting room. Nothing at all adorned the white walls. They were completely blank. Martha Stewart wept.

The room smelled stale, like a room without windows where the door is kept shut all the time. Which was probably exactly what it was. The kid offered them water or coffee. Lex and Nick both declined, and the kid left them alone to wait some more. Nick took a seat behind the table and Lex stayed on her feet, arms folded across her chest, pacing back and forth while they waited.

This was when the job really started. The lieutenant general would have the real assignment, the real details. Nick was just a gopher. A useful gopher, one who had gotten Lex's payday worked out—or better have, at least—but it was the lieutenant general who would have the real information about this job. Who, where, what, when, and most importantly for Lex, why.

The how would be up to Lex, probably. The Army liked to maintain plausible deniability for these kinds of ops, and that meant they would find an operative from the private sector, pay them an unconscionable sum, kit them out and drop them in theater, then put their hands up in the air and deny all knowledge of whatever shit that operative might get themselves into.

Unless the operative succeeded, of course. Then the Army—or, rather, the president—would take all the credit.

Lex didn't give a shit about the credit. She didn't give a shit about the Army. And she didn't give a shit about the president. She just wanted to get in, get out, and get paid.

The door swung open. The kid was back. He stepped inside and held the door while a stream of uniforms walked in. Nick shot to his feet, standing at attention.

A man and a woman in fatigues, a captain and a major, came in carrying briefcases. A tall, thin, black woman, a lieutenant colonel, in greens with the JAG insignia patched to her upper arm, came next, a brown leather bag slung over her shoulder. All three stood against the wall.

Then Skinner walked in. The hair on Lex's arms and neck stood up. She felt a cold pucker on her scalp, then felt the familiar stretch of the skin on her knuckles as her fists tightened instinctively. Skinner nodded at Nick, then at Lex, no flicker of recognition in his eyes. All business. All seriousness. He strode to the other side of the table and stood next to Nick, his back straight.

All were waiting for the person who came through the door next. The highest-ranking officer in the room, Lieutenant General Carrie Torrance, strode in. She nodded at the kid as she passed. He left the room, closing the door behind him.

Torrance was shorter than Lex by about two inches. White skin, pale brown eyes, brown hair with brown highlights cut in an A-line down below her chin. If she were wearing ankle-length crop pants with flats and a long-sleeve V-neck t-shirt, she'd look right at home on the side-line of a kids soccer game, ready with a Ziploc bag full of sliced oranges for halftime.

Instead, she was dressed in fatigue pants, jacket, and boots, three black stars stitched in a vertical line on her chest. Her eyes swept the room quickly and coolly and came to rest on Lex. She stood in front of Lex, no expression on her face. Sizing Lex up.

Lex returned the favor. She'd heard about General Torrance when she was first promoted to one star. One of the few women to reach that rank in the Army. There hadn't been many more in the five years since. Torrance had the reputation for being smart, tough, and hard-work-ing. Any woman had to be all those things in this *man's* army, but she had to be ten times more so to make it to general. Lex could see right away that Torrance was the real deal. It was there in the way she carried herself, upright, but loose. It was there in the way she took in the room, took in Lex, assessing all at once, but showing nothing about what she was thinking.

It was there in the way she made Lex feel small, even though Torrance was the one who had to look up to meet Lex's eyes. Lex was suddenly aware of her long, red leather jacket, so out of place in that room. She could feel the cool air on her bare midriff. Her cheeks warmed like a teenager caught violating high school dress code. She was acutely aware of the reek of alcohol through her pores, the gin-sweat soaked into her clothes, the stale, stank taste in her dry mouth. She felt like a fool. She felt small. She felt ashamed.

And then that feeling flipped. Nothing changed in Torrance's expression or her posture. She still hadn't said a word. But something in Torrance's eyes changed, the difference between the glint of light on a muzzle pointed at your head and the glint of light on a barrel pointed at your enemy. Lex didn't feel small or ashamed anymore. She felt seen, acknowledged. A feeling of warmth flushed over her.

No wonder Torrance had climbed the ranks. She was a fucking mind-control magician.

Nick cleared his throat. "Lieutenant Colonel Nick Hadley and former Captain Alexis Hadley reporting as ordered, ma'am," he said.

The corners of Torrance's eyes tightened just a bit, as if she wanted to laugh, but didn't. She arched one eyebrow at Lex.

Lex squared her jaw. "Alexis *Wolfe*," she said, sending an angry glance at Nick. She looked back at Torrance and added, "ma'am."

The mirth left Torrance's expression entirely. She continued to stare at Lex.

"At ease, everyone," she said.

The others in the room pulled out their plastic chairs with screeches and shuffles and sat down. Only Nick remained standing.

"Ma'am," he said, "if you'd like, I'd be happy to fill you—"

"I said at ease, Colonel," said Torrance.

She finally pulled her eyes from Lex and glanced at Nick, who sat down with a jerk, as if with her glance Torrance had shoved him into his seat.

Torrance looked back to Lex, raised her eyebrows, and held out one hand toward the table. "Please sit down, Ms. Wolfe," she said. "We have a lot to talk about."

20

THE KID WHEELED in a cart with two steaming silver jugs of coffee and several cups, along with some water and a tray of pastries. If his mother could see him now.

At the very least, three years of law school had taught the kid how to pick good breakfast foods. His tray was laden with biscotti, bomboloni, cornetti al pistacchio, and Lex's favorite, maritozzi di Roma. She smelled the sweetness of the fresh creme filling before she took a bite. The rich flavors of honey, orange, and vanilla lit up her tongue, tempered perfectly by the faint, round taste of the olive oil enriching the dough. Amazing breakfast pastries were one of the benefits of being stationed in Italy. If they had been having this meeting in America, the kid would have wheeled in a tray of glazed Krispy Kremes and a pile of sad, flat danishes from Costco.

As they sipped their coffee and ate their pastries, Torrance confirmed that three hostages had been taken in Khartoum, two British nationals and an American. All women. One of her aides, the major, slid a stack of folders across the table to Torrance, who distributed them to Lex,

Nick, Skinner, and the JAG colonel. The colonel had been introduced as Lieutenant Colonel Grace Harrow.

Torrance gave each of them a packet of three folders. Lex flipped the top folder open to find a dossier with a photo of a woman clipped to it, the same photo Nick had shown Lex in Manila. Trina Huntsman, the American journalist. Young, pretty, determined-looking. A wholesome, hard-working American woman in need of rescue. Probably a Democrat, otherwise the current president would have let her rot in Africa.

Lex opened the other folders and saw the two Brits. Also young, also pretty, also determined-looking. Lex supposed you had to be determined to go to Khartoum as a Western woman in search of a news story about the civil war in Sudan. And only someone that young would be foolish enough to go alone and get themselves captured. And the pretty part, well, that's just the hand you're dealt. Helpful at times on the home front, not so much when you're bound and gagged in a cave in the Sudanese countryside.

Torrance had opened Trina Huntsman's folder, too, and the others followed suit. Torrance launched into Huntsman's background.

"I'm gonna stop you right there," said Lex.

A stunned silence hung in the air for a moment. Clearly, Torrance didn't get interrupted very often. Across the table, Lex saw Nick's body become so rigid she thought if he tipped over, he might shatter into a million tiny pieces on the floor.

The general fixed her cool eyes on Lex. Lex stared straight back. Deep down, a part of her was shivering. She'd just interrupted a general in the U.S. Army. What the fuck was she thinking? Was she suicidal? But she pushed that part of her down even deeper. She wasn't in the Army anymore. She was a person talking to another person about a job. And Lex wanted to get the important stuff out of the way first.

"With all due respect, General, first things first." She pointed at Nick. "My friendly neighborhood recruitment officer has made some pretty big claims to me about this job. I want to make sure you're on board with them before we go any further."

Torrance lifted her chin at Lex. "Your fee, you mean?"

"My fee, I mean."

Torrance smiled faintly and nodded. "I won't lie to you, Ms. Wolfe. Ten million dollars raised a few eyebrows in Washington."

"How high did it raise them?"

Torrance's smile became sardonic, and more genuine. "High, but not hairline high. Between Big Pharma, Big Oil, and Blackwater, the government gets some pretty big invoices." Torrance shrugged. "I suppose it helps when you can print your own money."

"I should have charged you double," said Lex.

"You charged us plenty," Torrance said, "and we'll pay it." Her eyes bored into Lex's skull. "When the job is done."

Lex had demanded the payment in advance, and Nick had agreed, albeit under duress. Lex knew she was making a deal with the devil. Religion had nothing to do with it. If you were small and they were big, it was a deal with the devil. She knew she should push for some payment in advance. She was off the record, and if the U.S. government decided to stiff her on payment—or silence her altogether —that would be off the record, too.

But the U.S. had a reputation to uphold, and they would need shady contractors in the future. The last thing they wanted was a rep for not paying. Lex figured the odds were good she'd get her money, and the look in Torrance's eye didn't make it seem like she was open for negotiation.

"Thank you, General," she said. "I apologize for inter-rupting, but assurances are only as good as their source." She cast a disdainful glance at Nick, then looked back to Torrance.

"I understand, Ms. Wolfe." Again, Torrance smiled only at the corners of her eyes. Almost like a secret handshake.

"If we're going to work together, you might as well call me Lex."

That faint smile again. "Ms. Wolfe will do."

They pored over the dossiers. The British government was aiding the mission through back-channels and helping out with Lex's fee. Neither government wanted to be on the hook for sending military operatives into a sovereign nation without their permission, and getting permission from the Sudanese government to enter a region decimated by decades of famine and civil war and currently claimed in part by at least five different factions was a non-starter.

For their part, the Sudanese government was already officially under sanction by both the U.S. and the U.K., and neither country was going to ease those sanctions. Without that, Sudan couldn't give a fuck about three foreign women who had stepped in dog shit. As far as the government was concerned, the women should have watched where they were walking. They should have stayed home with the chil-dren where they belonged.

The plan was just as Lex suspected. She would outfit herself from the armory on base, taking whatever matériel she felt necessary, but she would have no ground support. This was going to be a solo job. She could take what she could manage herself, and nothing more. Her mission was to obtain and verify the location and status of the hostages. Extraction was a bonus—for which Lex successfully negotiated an extra two and a half million dollars a head—but the mission objective was intelligence gathering.

"The USS Truxtun is currently patrolling the Red Sea off the coast of Port Sudan," Torrance continued, "and will be for the duration of this mission. The Navy has agreed to let us use it as a staging area for your insertion in-country."

"General," said Skinner, raising his hand. Torrance nodded for him to speak. "With all due respect, maybe it would be worthwhile for Lieutenant Colonel Hadley to accompany Cap—" He winced. "To accompany Ms. Wolfe at least as far as Khartoum. Ms. Wolfe can relay periodic updates via satellite link, and Colonel Hadley could serve as a local point of contact in case things go sideways. And in the meantime, if they don't, he can provide us with on-the-ground intel and liaise with local government, as needed. If necessary, he can retreat to the Truxtun and work from there once Ms. Wolfe is safely inserted in Khartoum."

Nick's face was white as a sheet. He hated boats, and Lex was sure he would be dreading the prospect of days at sea on a destroyer. She figured Skinner hadn't consulted with him before offering his services in a war zone.

And Skinner certainly hadn't consulted with her. Nick would be as useful in Khartoum as a thick, down parka. Maybe less. At least Lex could use the parka as a pillow.

"The Truxtun can serve as a point of contact," Torrance said to Skinner, then gave Lex a hard stare, "but only for exfil. There is to be no communication from within the borders of the Sudan, understood?"

Lex nodded, then glanced at Nick. She could see the color return to his face as he tried to hide his relief.

"But, General—" said Skinner.

"I will not have U.S. military personnel on the ground in the Sudan," said Torrance, skewering Skinner with her glare. "We cannot risk the perception of interference in a Sudanese civil war. The Truxton will be the POC."

"What about the embassy in Khartoum?" asked Lex. "Why wouldn't they be my point of contact?"

Torrance glanced at Lex. "We closed the embassy two months ago," she said, then looked back at Skinner. "It's the Truxtun or nothing," she said. Skinner's brow furrowed, but he nodded.

Torrance let that decision settle for a beat, silently emphasizing who held the power in the room, then turned back to Lex. "We'll get you to the Truxtun on military transport," she said. "C-130 to Jeddah, then an MH-60R Seahawk to the Truxtun. From there, we've arranged a ride to Port Sudan on a civilian fishing vessel. After that, once you're in country, you'll be on your own."

There was no smile around her eyes as she said it.

It was roughly four hundred miles across the Nubian Desert from Port Sudan to Khartoum. Last Lex had heard, there was a paved road between the two, but who knew what condition it was in after years of civil war. Lex would be finding out soon enough.

She'd have to ask around in Khartoum, try to dig up an old friend, see if he was still alive and still friendly, and hope for some intel she could use to find out where these women had been taken. The cave in the countryside came back to mind. It wasn't a joke. If she were a kidnapper, she wouldn't stay in the city. She'd head for the wilderness. There was plenty of it in the Sudan.

"I can handle it," Lex said, even though she had no idea how. "I'll need clothes. And money for bribes and incidentals. Sudanese pounds and US dollars."

Torrance nodded.

Lex flipped through the folders. "Do we have any idea who took these women, or where they're being held?"

"Not much, unfortunately," said Torrance with an angry glance at Skinner.

"Intel is sparse in the region," Skinner said. "Especially since we lost our language expert."

Lex didn't bother looking up at the barb. She'd be happy to use her language skills to tell Skinner how to fuck himself in every language spoken on the African continent.

"We think they're being held along the border with South Sudan," Skinner continued, "but we don't have a more precise location than that. And no one has claimed responsibility for the abductions yet."

"It's not much to go on," said Torrance, "and it's a dangerous mission, which is why we agreed to your exorbitant fee. If you want to back out, now's your last chance."

Lex flipped through the folders, examining the dossiers. All white women. All single, though one of them had a boyfriend. Cute. A sous chef in Shoreditch. All had living parents and siblings. Families who would mourn for them.

"How long have they been missing?" Lex murmured.

"Seven days," said Torrance softly.

Families were already worrying, then, wondering why their texts and calls weren't being returned. If they knew where their daughters had been going, they were even more worried. Out-of-their-minds worried.

And what about the women themselves? Lex pulled all three photos out of the paper clips, lined them up next to each other. None of the women were smiling in their photos. All had the hard, serious look of journalists who knew what humans did to each other and were determined to report it to the rest of the world. But how would they react when humans were doing those things to them? Would they still be hard, serious women? Would they still have the same determination when it was the will to live, not the will to advance in their career?

Truth be told, after seven days, with no ransom notes or contact from the kidnappers, the odds were slim that the women were even still alive. This mission was probably a lost cause already.

But even without the women in tow, Lex would still get ten million dollars. And if there was still even a glimmer of a chance of finding them alive...

"I'm not backing out," Lex said.

How could she?

She looked Torrance square in the eyes.

"I'm not backing out."

Torrance stared back for a long moment, eyes hard and clear. She knew what those women were up against. And she knew what Lex was signing up for.

Torrance nodded.

"Then let's get to work," she said.

21

THEY SPENT the next two hours discussing strategy and logistics and timing, discussing entry points and exit plans. Torrance made it very clear that there would be no rescue operation on this mission. If Lex got captured, she would become one more American hostage on the list. Period.

Lex didn't have much experience with field work. Not the kind she would need for this kind of job, at least. Her role in Military Intelligence had mainly been interpreting audio files and intercepts, decoding transmissions from hostile foreign actors and the occasional foreign diplomat. She'd been to Khartoum twice before on intelligence-gathering missions, and she'd even been to some parts of town where nasty things happened. But you could say that about Chicago or L.A. as easily as you could say it about Lagos or Kinshasa. There are places in every city that are empty and innocuous in the light of morning, but which turn deadly when darkness falls and the demons wake. And even in the morning light, Lex had always had a team with her, people whose job it was to keep her safe. Now, she would be the only one she could rely on.

Turns out it had been like that all along, anyway.

She studied the folders Torrance had given her, scanning them not to memorize the facts they contained—she would do that later, when she was alone and things were quiet—but to look for omissions, information that she might need that wasn't in the file. She found nothing. Torrance knew her shit, and the files were remarkably detailed. All that bullshit about privacy in the EU and back at home apparently didn't apply to the U.S. Army. They could find out what you had for breakfast, if they wanted to, and how long it took you to shit it out, too.

Lex knew that they would hang her out to dry on this mission, if it came to that, but Torrance seemed to be taking it seriously. Her demeanor, her professionalism, her attention to detail, and her clear concern for Lex all told her that much. Torrance would give Lex what she needed for the job, within reason and within the confines of the mission parameters. But even with all that concern and all that aid, Lex knew that once she stepped foot on Sudanese soil, she would be alone.

She'd been alone before. She'd been alone for the last three years. You could argue that she'd been alone for at least a year before that, after the shit went down with Skinner. You could even argue she'd been alone since her parents died ten years before that, a month before she graduated from West Point.

Maybe she'd been alone her whole life, without realizing it.

She could handle it.

The more she said it to herself, the more she believed it. Sort of.

"Is there anything else you need from us, Ms. Wolfe?" said Torrance.

"Just a ride to the armory," Lex said.

Torrance eyed her in silence for several seconds. "Very well," she said at last. She stood up. There was a loud shuffle and screech of chairs as everyone else, including Lex, stood up after her.

"Ms. Wolfe," said Torrance, "you'll leave tonight at 2300 hours."

In twenty-four hours or so, Lex would be alone. A white Western woman alone in Khartoum. What was it she'd been thinking earlier about the hostages? She was making the same mistake they had, being stupid and arrogant. She would just have to be smarter than they were. If she could.

"Thank you, everyone, for your assistance," said Torrance. "You're dismissed." She touched Lex on the arm. "Ms. Wolfe, please stay behind for a moment. You, too, Colonel Harrow." The older black woman, the lawyer, nodded.

Lex saw Skinner's eyes narrow at Torrance, then flick toward Lex before he and the others filed out. Nick tried to mouth something to Lex as he went, but she frowned and shook her head at him. When he tried to mouth something again, she gave him the finger and looked away. She had no idea what he was saying, and she had no inclination to figure it out. If he had something to tell her, he could say it out loud like a real man.

Torrance saw her interaction with Nick. "I'll be sure not to get on your bad side," she said, smiling with the corners of her eyes again.

"It's the only side I have left," Lex replied.

Colonel Harrow closed the door as the last of the others exited the room. The stale smell of the air came back, this time layered with the sour reek of man sweat. There are times when Lex loved that smell, like during good sex, when her hands were spread over a sweaty, muscular back. Now, it just smelled rank.

The three of them sat down at the table again. No one said anything for a few moments, leaving Lex to wonder what the hell she was there for. She'd already gotten her orders and worked out the mission plan. What else was there to discuss?

The cart with the coffee and pastries was still against the wall. Lex was eyeing a leftover maritozzo when Torrance finally spoke.

"It's not Army protocol to hire people with other-than-honorable discharges," Torrance said.

Fucking hell. A lecture to make sure she would be a good little girl while she infiltrated a Sudanese terrorist group all on her own and rescued three hostages so the president could win re-election. For that, Lex would defi-nitely need a pastry. And more coffee.

Lex went to the cart and poured herself a cup. "I imagine it cuts down on your contractor candidate pool if you only hire Eagle Scouts."

Torrance did not seem amused. She shook her head when Lex held up the coffee jug in offer, as did Colonel Harrow. They waited while Lex loaded a napkin with the maritozzo, sat back down, and took a large bite, licking powdered sugar off her thumb while she chewed.

"Colonel Hadley recommended you for this mission," Torrance said. "Colonel Skinner passed it on to me, but only with..." Torrance smirked. "The deepest of reserva-tions, I think, were the words he used." Her eyes were steel. "Or so he claimed."

Lex took another bite. "Last time I saw him," she said around a mouthful of bun and sweet cream, "some of those deep reservations were still healing."

All humor fell from Torrance's expression. "Assault on a superior officer will never be condoned or tolerated in the United States Armed Forces, Ms. Wolfe. You do understand that?"

Lex sneered. "What about assault on an inferior officer?"

Torrance's stony expression didn't change, but she had one hand resting on the table. It curled into a fist. "That is equally unacceptable."

"And yet, in my case," said Lex, popping the last bite of the maritozzo in her mouth, "it was accepted." She wiped her hands on the napkin. "More than accepted. They rewarded it. They promoted the fucking asshole. *You* promoted him." She balled her napkin and threw it on the table.

Torrance drew in a deep breath and looked like she was about to say something. But she gave a heavy sigh instead and nodded to Colonel Harrow.

Harrow leaned forward in her chair. "Three years ago, your allegations against then-Lieutenant Colonel Skinner were dismissed by Colonel Matthew Wilson due to lack of evidence."

"I guess I should have scraped some of his cum off my thighs before I stumbled home and showered for two hours trying to get his stink out of my skin." Lex twisted her mouth in a rueful grimace. "But then they would have dismissed the evidence as circumstantial."

She took a sip of coffee. Even though Italy was known for strong, flavorful coffee, Lex drank it black. She was used to the high-test barako Cariz brewed back in Manila. But the shit in her cup wasn't Italian or Filipino. It was one-hundred percent U.S. Army joe, bitter and weak.

"Sexual assault cases have been notoriously difficult to

prove," Harrow said. She looked pointedly at Lex and added, "In the past."

Harrow reached into her brown leather bag, pulled out a thick file folder, and set it on the table.

Lex frowned. This didn't sound like a good little girl lecture anymore. What the hell were these two getting at?

"Do you know what this is, Ms. Wolfe?" asked Colonel Harrow. She set one spread hand slowly, almost reverently, atop the folder. "These papers contain evidence obtained from six female officers detailing abuses that occurred over the last ten years of Colonel Skinner's service."

The coffee had been as weak as dishwater when Lex swallowed it, but now it felt like battery acid burning in her stomach. That cocksucker had been doing this for that long? To that many women?

"Why haven't you done anything about it?" she asked, her voice low and hard.

"We are doing something about it," replied Harrow. "We're gathering evidence. Testimonies from victims and witnesses. Careful, meticulous evidence to establish a pattern of behavior from a variety of unrelated, uncon-nected sources with no particular axe to grind or power to obtain. No hint of ulterior motive that Skinner could use to dismiss the claims."

"He's the fucking rapist and we're the ones who have to be careful? We're the ones who have to be meticulous?"

Harrow's lips pressed into a tight, thin line. "This is the system we're working in."

The system created by men, run by men, abused by men, and adjudicated by men. Lex lifted her chin, ready to unleash her thoughts, but she held her tongue. It would do no good to unload on Torrance or Harrow. They weren't the problem.

"Why are you telling me this?"

"We want to invite you to join the case," said Harrow. "Add your testimony to the evidence."

"You want to *invite* me?" Like they were asking her to join a fucking sorority.

"We're asking you to help," said Torrance. "We're trying to track down every woman Skinner has abused." Her eyes flashed cold steel. "So we can take him down for good."

"You're the general. Why don't you just demote him? Discharge him. Or put him in fucking Leavenworth."

"Everyone has the right to due process," said Harrow.

Lex snorted. Due process. Rule of law. That was the kind of bullshit she used to believe. Until it happened to her and she found out the rule of law came down to the opinions of men and the rhetoric they could manufacture to justify them. Due process was a convenient lie that did nothing but protect the status quo. Created by men, run by men, abused by men, and adjudicated by men.

Lex stared at the blank wall and shook her head. Then Torrance's last comment echoed in her head. *Every woman Skinner has abused.*

"How many women are there?" she asked.

"Six women," said Harrow, patting the folder like some kind of talisman.

"No," said Lex. "That's how many gave their testimony." She looked hard at Torrance. "How many have there been, in total?"

Torrance, to her credit, did not flinch from Lex's stare. Her mouth pulled down into a harsh frown. "We don't know," she said. "We can't be sure. We've found six so far. You're seven. We have a line on four more."

"Eleven women?" Lex's mouth fell open.

Torrance nodded slowly. "There may be others." Finally,

she looked away from Lex's stare, dropped her eyes to the floor. "There are likely to be others."

"Just in the last ten years?"

"We're doing everything we can to document Colonel Skinner's pattern of abuse," said Harrow. "His timelines, his tactics, his..." She swallowed hard, then regained a look of quiet fortitude. "His tastes."

Tastes. Like food. Like a predator.

I am not prey.

"We need your help, Ms. Wolfe," said Torrance. She leaned forward, reached her hand across the table. "Lex," she said, "we need your help."

Eleven women in ten years. Maybe more. And he'd been promoted how many times in those years? Promoted into positions where he would have more power, more trust, more opportunity.

Lex stood up, her chair screeching across the floor.

"You don't need my help," she said. Her eyes jumped from Torrance to Harrow and back. "You need to grow up."

She stomped toward the door. Torrance and Harrow both stood.

"Ms. Wolfe," called Torrance.

Lex stopped with her hand on the door handle, twisting it open, but holding the door shut. She looked over her shoulder at Torrance.

"I'm here to do a job, General," she said. "Leave me alone and let me do it." A lump formed in her throat. She swallowed hard. "That's what the Army does best, anyway," she muttered.

Torrance opened her mouth, but did not reply. Lex yanked the door open and left her standing there like a fish on the dock, gasping for water.

KHARTOUM

22

THE BREEZE somehow made the air feel hotter as Lex walked through the streets of Khartoum under the burning afternoon sun. The breeze brought not just heat, but the smell of gunsmoke and faint garlic. Dark smoke like storm clouds billowed and bent overhead like a ribbon in the wind. To the north, Lex could hear bursts of automatic gunfire, pockets of popping sounds in the distance as the Rapid Support Forces and the Sudanese Armed Forces battled for control of Omdurman Bridge, a critical crossing point over the White Nile.

The popping was punctuated by the occasional bass boom. From this distance, it reminded Lex of the jazz band back in Bar Montagna. The jazz band had used an upright bass for its thumping bass sound. The RSF and the SAF were using bombs laced with white phosphorus. Hence the faint garlic smell in the air. Funny how death can evoke something as life-affirming as good Italian food.

Funny, from a distance. Up close, there's nothing to laugh about.

Lex had been in Khartoum for nine days already,

141

staying in one of the few hotels still open in the city. Nine days with no leads. Which meant the hostages had been missing for sixteen days. At this point, Lex expected to be identifying corpses. But as long as she found those corpses, she'd get her ten million dollars.

Khartoum sits at the point where the White Nile from the south joins the Blue Nile from the southeast to merge into the Nile River and meander its way north through the desert to Aswan, where the dam stops the water, collects it, before dispensing it judiciously to bring verdant life to the river valley in Egypt. On a map, the Egyptian Nile is a blue line bordered in green, surrounded by endless beige, culminating in the alluvial fan of the Nile River delta between Cairo and Alexandria. Zoomed out, the delta looks like a human brain, and the river valley below like the spinal column, ending in the sacrum at Anwar in the south.

Which made the tendril of river wandering through the desert below the dam seem like one long varicose vein, Khartoum a festering ulcer, inflamed by two factions vying for power.

The ulcer wept around the Nile junction, *al-Muqran,* which cut Khartoum into pieces. Khartoum North stood to the northeast, Omdurman to the west, and Khartoum proper to the southeast, in the land between the rivers. They fought at *al-Muqran,* fought for the bridges, for control of North Khartoum and Omdurman. One month the RSF would have it, the next month, the SAF. The RSF had owned the balance since the fighting began, but the SAF in their recent offensive had seized three bridges, including the Omdurman Bridge, allowing them to bring much needed supplies and food to their dwindling forces on the west side of the river. Until, that is, the RSF regrouped its armies and reclaimed control the next month.

Lex couldn't care less who controlled what. Wars were about politics, and politics were about ego. Lex didn't give a shit whether Abdel Fattah al-Burhan and his SAF regained control of the Sudan or Hemedti and the RSF managed to steal it from him. Al-Burhan took power in a coup d'état, and now Hemedti was trying to do the same. Turnabout is fair play for everyone who wasn't in the path of a flying bullet. But anyone who believed the war was about anything but those two men vying for power was a fool. It was not about religion. It was not about righteousness. And it was certainly not about freedom. People were dying for those men and their egos.

Lex would not be one of those people. She just wanted to stay low and get her job done. The fighting was at the junction north of Khartoum, so Lex stayed central and to the south. Not far enough from the fighting to walk in peace, but far enough to avoid stray bullets.

The city itself was empty. Every unoccupied home that hadn't been destroyed by bombs had been looted, windows smashed, doors hanging broken on their hinges. Anything of value—monetary or nutritional—had been stripped from the houses.

It was a far cry from the Khartoum Lex remembered from her previous visits, a far cry from the thronged *souks* with their jewelry merchants and chai stalls and food sellers and clothing stands, all filled with friendly faces and laughter. The civil war had robbed the people of their joy, had forced them to abandon their peaceful everyday lives in search of a place where they could simply feel safe.

And yet, not every home was abandoned. The city was empty, but not deserted. Lex estimated that one in every five homes still had inhabitants, even if only to act as a deterrent for the looters.

A searing moan lifted Lex's gaze to the sky. A fighter jet passed overhead, low above the buildings. Lex looked up just as a missile dropped from under one wing, fell wobbling for a moment, then streaked ahead in a flash of flame and a tail of dark smoke. A moment later, she heard the bass boom of impact, close enough and powerful enough to rattle what glass was left in the windows around her.

Lex's headscarf had slipped when she looked up. She pulled it back over her head, using it to shade her face from the sun and from the eyes of suspicious onlookers. Most people kept their heads down. It was the ones who didn't that worried Lex.

She wanted to attract enough attention to get the information she needed from the people who had it, but she didn't necessarily want to advertise her presence to everyone else. The same people that had abducted the three journalists would likely be just as interested in abducting Lex, and if she could avoid it, she didn't want to have to kill them in the streets. For a woman, self-defense wasn't a compelling argument in a Sudanese court of law, if such courts still existed.

In an attempt to blend in, Lex wore a traditional Sudanese thobe, a light wrap that covered her head, arms, and body. General Torrance had outfitted her with two of them, one in pale yellow chiffon and the other in a light pink cotton. Lex wore the pink one that day. Not her preferred color scheme, but it helped her to blend in, as much as a woman with short, brown hair and beacon-white skin could blend in anywhere in the Sudan. Despite three years in the Manila sun, her skin was still as white as bone.

Underneath, Lex wore a tunic dress with long sleeves to cover her arms. Like the thobe, the tunic dress was traditional garb for women in Khartoum, fitting in with the predominantly patriarchal Muslim culture. But while the long sleeves helped hide Lex's whiteness, they made her sweat like a rhinoceros. Her armpits chafed against the fabric of the dress and against the side of her chest. She wore a thin crop camisole under her dress. Sweat soaked it along the underside of her breasts. She had no idea how local women could wear these outfits, especially in the hot season when temperatures were pushing 110 degrees.

They probably just suffered and dealt with it, like women everywhere in the entire fucking world. Though it wasn't as strict as some Arab Muslim nations, in Khartoum, women were still expected to cover their heads and their bodies, mainly—incredibly—to protect them from the male gaze. Like everything else, the rule was based completely on what helped the men, not on what helped the women who were the ones forced to wear extra layers of clothing in hundred-degree heat, the women who were the ones who would suffer yet again for the weakness of men.

As much as she could, Lex stayed in the shade of what shop awnings still provided it, though most had fallen or been torn down. The shade helped her avoid the heat of the sun, but it also helped her avoid being seen. The street was empty, but who knew what eyes were peering through the windows?

In nine days, she'd found few people, fewer who were willing to speak with her, fewer still who would do anything but shudder and walk quickly away when they heard her questions. Even in an active war zone, people didn't like to talk about abductions. Lex hadn't yet been able to figure out yet whether they feared the subject itself or feared reprisals from the abductors.

For herself, Lex wasn't worried about reprisals. She knew she could protect herself from a lone attacker, or even a small gang. And if a larger gang came along, she was armed well enough to make an escape. The handgun pressed against the small of her sweaty back was just part of her arsenal. Hidden behind an armoire in the hotel, she had a duffel bag filled with two M16A4 rifles, two Sig P320 full-size handguns, a dozen magazines, hundreds of rounds of ammo, thousands of dollars in USD and Sudanese Pounds, three M8 white smoke grenades, and even a few M67 frag grenades just for good measure. Plus a smart-phone with a satellite hookup, currently turned off, to be used only if and when Lex had exfilled the hostages. Gifts from General Torrance.

And, by special request, a Sig P320 compact, Lex's favorite handgun for concealed carry. She'd cut a slit in the back of her tunic dress, wore the holster on a belly band so she could access it quickly. But as she walked in this heat, it rubbed the skin of her back raw. Sweat pooled beneath the grip and ran down the swale of her back, down her ass crack, and onto her thighs, making them chafe when she walked. The tunic dress restricted Lex's movement. She was used to walking fast, with long, purposeful strides. The dress forced her to take three steps when she would normally have taken two. And it squeezed her legs closer together, making her thighs rub. After hours of walking in the heat, the spot where her thighs touched felt like fire.

The long sleeves, the thobe, the restrictive skirt, the oppressive heat, and the rivers of sweat on her back, her sides, her ass, her legs. Lex honestly could not imagine why the local women put up with this bullshit. They should all be hanging out cool and comfortable in bikinis and making the men wear fur-lined straightjackets to keep their hands to themselves, and Saran wrap around their thighs to keep their dicks in their pants. Fuck the male gaze.

Of course, she knew why the local women put up with it. No matter where you are in the world, the patriarchy is deep, wide, and pervasive, ingrained in both men and women since birth. For most women, fighting against it was as hopeless as fighting the need to breathe air or eat food, and nearly as unthinkable. In Khartoum, any individual would be punished or killed for disobedience, and the odds of enough women rising up at once were slim to none, especially in a place where the men played war games to stroke themselves.

Lex had spent the first few days in Khartoum looking for cafes and restaurants, waiting and attempting to strike up casual conversations with the patrons. Difficult to do in a culture where women are not expected to be so forward with strangers, especially with strange men. When that didn't work, she asked questions of the desk clerk at her hotel and the few other guests staying there. Those who were willing to treat with her had little useful information to give.

In the last two days, Lex had become more desperate. If she didn't find something, some piece of information she could use, she'd have to slink back to Nick in Vicenza with her tail between her legs and ask for his help. She'd rather die alone in Khartoum than give him that satisfaction.

She'd taken to wandering the streets all day, looking for anyone who would talk to her. She prowled neighborhoods further and further from the center of the city.

Yesterday, she'd come upon a small group of women sitting in a circle beneath the weak shade of a threadbare moringa tree. They were a colorful group, dressed in thobes of green and yellow and blue and pink. Between the distant sounds of warfare, the buzz of insects and the chirp of birds mingled with the chatter of the women. In another time, it would have been a languid, pastoral scene.

That illusion broke as soon as they saw Lex approach. Their chatter ceased. Even the insects and the birds seemed to fall silent. Their faces turned to her, all of them, hard and impassive and unwelcoming.

Lex smiled and spoke to them in the local language, a dialect of Sudanese Arabic. Lex was fluent, her accent flawless, but the women stared at her as if they had no idea what she was saying.

Finally, a tall woman who couldn't have been more than twenty-five years old pulled Lex away from the group. Lex heard the chatter resume once the woman had pulled her some distance away.

"Thank you for speaking with me," said Lex.

The woman surveyed Lex, from her hair to her face to her thobe to the flat-heeled, closed-toe markub shoes Lex wore on her feet. They were typically worn by more prosperous women, which risked attracting more attention, but Lex needed to cover more skin than the more commonly worn sandals would allow.

The woman just raised one eyebrow when she saw them, then looked up at Lex's face again. Her eyes were hard, her expression stony.

"You should not be here," she said.

"I'm looking for three women—

"Please leave now."

"—white women, journalists—"

"Your presence endangers us all."

"—who would have been here two or three weeks ago."

The woman took a long breath. "We cannot help you find these friends of yours," she said quietly.

"Cannot," said Lex, "or will not?"

The woman's eyes revealed a level of suffering that made it obvious that Lex's problems were inconsequential to her, that they should be inconsequential even to Lex.

"What does it matter?" the woman said. "There is no help for you here." She turned back toward her group, then paused. Over her shoulder, she said, "I am sorry," before walking back to rejoin the others.

For Lex, it was the same response she'd gotten from everyone. Sorry, we can't or won't help you, delivered with varying degrees of sympathy.

As she shuffled away from that group of women, continuing through the empty neighborhood, she had stopped not once, but three times, listening, looking, thinking she was being followed. The third time, when she stopped and whirled in place, she thought she saw someone duck out of view behind a corner. But when she finally got there at the slow pace forced on her by her restrictive dress, there was no one to be seen.

Now, as the oppressive morning heat turned to a baking afternoon swelter, she walked through yet another neighborhood near the south of the city, and had the same feeling of being watched, of being followed. Only this time, when she whirled around, her sweat-slick handgun drawn and ready to fire, there was a man standing behind her.

When he saw her gun, he put his hands up.

He was smiling.

23

THE MAN WAS TALL, over six feet, lean and muscular without being lanky. His head was shaved to a smooth polish, glinting the sunlight in the same way as his dark eyes.

Lex pointed the gun at the man's heart. His broad smile never faltered, impossibly large, white teeth bright against his deep bronze skin. The smile and his easy, relaxed demeanor were disarming.

That set Lex on edge. She scanned the shadows and the windows and the rooftops of the buildings along the street behind him.

"Are you the one who's been following me?" she said.

The man's smile grew even wider.

"You knew I've been following you?" His voice was deep and smooth as a river, but carried a childlike playfulness as he clicked his tongue and shook his head. "I thought I was being so careful."

"What do you want?"

"When did you know?" he said, that smile still on his face. "Was it yesterday, after those women you met?"

Lex cocked her handgun.

"It was, wasn't it?"

He didn't react to the gun, didn't seem to even notice it. He clicked his tongue again, dropped his head, and laughed softly. The music of it made Lex want to laugh with him.

"I knew I was getting too close to you." He looked up, catching Lex's eye and sending a sharp flutter through her chest. "I couldn't help myself. I just wanted a better look."

"At what?" said Lex.

"At your face." The man's smile changed, grew more thoughtful as he tilted his head, regarding Lex. "It is a lovely face, you know."

And now he was hitting on her? Lex ignored the flutters that went through her chest again. He was obviously trying to distract her, maybe to allow the other members of his gang to close in from behind. She would not be sucked in by a charming smile and a perfect jawline. Lex glanced over her shoulders, scanning the road and the buildings behind her.

"There is no one else," the man said. "You don't need to worry. I'm alone."

"Then I'll ask you again," said Lex, gun still pointed at the man's heart, "what do you want?"

"To help." The man shrugged. "I just want to help."

Lex managed to keep herself from scoffing out loud, but barely.

"How can you help me?"

"You've been asking questions around town, looking for three women. White women," he smiled again, "like you."

"And you know something about these women? Are you the one who took them?"

He looked sheepishly at Lex. "My arms are getting tired. May I put them down?"

There was something odd about this guy. He was obviously perfectly comfortable having a gun pointed at him, but maybe that wasn't so odd in Khartoum these days. He could be ex-military, either SAF or RSF or one of the other factions. The Sudan People's Liberation Movement-North was allied with the RSF now. So was the Sudan Liberation Movement down in Darfur. He could be a deserter, or an emissary.

His skin was darker than most of the residents of Khartoum, but not as dark as you would find in southern Darfur or South Sudan. That fact didn't tell Lex much. There was a lot of movement within and between nations in Africa, even more so in Sudan and the neighboring countries since the fighting began. This man could be from anywhere, but he didn't look like he was from Sudan.

His accent was flawless to Lex's ear. She was no expert, but she was very good, and Sudanese Arabic was a very specific dialect.

"Where are you from?" she asked in English, testing a hunch.

"We are all from the same place, are we not?" He replied without hesitation in perfect English with a slight British accent. They could have been standing in the halls of Oxford discussing Yeats' use of imagery.

He lowered his hands slowly, eyebrows raised in question as he did so. His smile grew wider when Lex nodded, and his eyes caught the sunlight once again.

He clasped his hands in front of him, keeping them in Lex's full view. "And we all go to the same place, as well," he said, then raised one finger. "But are those places the same, I wonder?" He grinned that charming, disarming grin again.

Great. Lex's stalker was a fucking philosopher.

"What do you know about the women that were abducted?" Lex said, switching back to Arabic.

The man's smile fell. His face darkened and furrowed in worry. "I know where they were taken," he said.

"Where?" said Lex. "Tell me."

"I can't—"

"Tell me," Lex said again, pushing the gun closer to the man's chest for emphasis.

He raised his hands once again. Once again, that charming smile spread across his face without a trace of concern for the gun aimed at his heart.

"I can't tell you where," he said.

"Why not? You working for them? The kidnappers?"

"No," he said, shaking his head and smiling softly. "I can't tell you because it's too difficult to tell. Sudan is not like New York City. There are no street signs or addresses on a square grid. Not in the countryside. In some places here, navigation is by sight and by memory."

Lex paused to consider that. If what the man was saying was true, the hostages weren't in the city. They were somewhere rural, or perhaps hidden somewhere in the wilderness. That meant they could be anywhere. Without a guide, Lex would never find them.

She flipped the safety on the gun and returned it to the holster at her back.

"You'll take me to them?" she asked.

"I will."

Lex regarded him for a moment. "Why?"

The man pressed his lips together and looked off toward the horizon. "I don't care about this war," he said. "President Al-Burhan, Hemedti, some other man down the line... They will all rule in the same way." He looked to Lex, eyes blazing with a heat that hadn't been in them before. "Unjustly."

He looked down at the ground and shoved his hands in his pockets. Lex slid her hand to her back, gripping her pistol, thumb on the safety. But the man just kicked at a pebble in the road and looked up at the horizon again.

"I suppose I want to do what's right," he said. "Bring some justice to this place, for once."

Lex watched him carefully for a moment longer. When he glanced back at her, his eyes were serious and determined, but not dangerous. Not to her. She eased her hand off the pistol grip.

"How long will it take to get to this place," she asked, "where the women are being held?"

"It is a long journey," the man replied. "We can take a car some of the way, though that adds more danger. But we will have to hike at the end. And there will be some climbing."

Climbing. That meant the mountains. The hostages could be over the border in the Ethiopian Highlands, where the mountains ranged as much as fifteen thousand feet high. But the U.S. government was working closely with Addis Ababa, and she was sure the Ethiopian borders would be well guarded, even in that difficult terrain. It was unlikely the hostages would have been taken there.

The only other location where there was anything you could call mountains was much more likely. It was in Western Sudan, in Darfur, near the border with Chad. War-torn, chaotic, only nominally under RSF rule, and even that was disputed with at least two other factions that were only loosely allied with Hemedti's forces. It would be a perfect place to hide a few hostages. That's where Lex would take them.

Problem was, that region was more than eight hundred

miles away. Under normal conditions, it would take days to drive there, given the erratic road conditions in the Sudan. During a civil war, it would take even longer. And they'd be traveling through the front lines, then through the churned up, empty, lawless lands that armies always left in their wake while they continued to advance, then finally into the mountains, where no army would bother to patrol, leaving the rugged, barren land to cartels, convicts, and kidnappers.

Didn't matter. It had to be done. It wouldn't be easy, but Lex had dealt with difficult conditions before. And she'd dealt with cartels before, too. She could do it again. She would do it again.

"We'd better get moving," Lex said. She put her hands on her hips, waiting, then shrugged at the man. "Well? Lead the way."

He smiled that same bright, disarming smile, with the same perfect teeth and that same goddamn perfect jawline.

This time, after he'd turned and begun to lead her toward a side street, Lex couldn't help but smile, too.

24

THEY RODE in the man's car, a boxy Hyundai in robin's egg blue. Old, but surprisingly well-maintained, both inside and out. The exterior had no rust, no holes, and was even mostly clean, difficult to pull off when the air was constantly swirling with dirt and tiny particles of debris thrown up by the bombs and the bullets.

The interior was spotless. Lex had expected ripped vinyl, crushed beer cans, and molding food wrappers. Instead, she got pale beige fabric seats that looked like new and carpeting that seemed like it had just been vacuumed.

The engine had started immediately and ran quietly and without incident. The car was perfectly fine.

It was Lex that had the problem. She was in the passenger seat, and she was getting pissed off.

"We can take the Rabak road along the White Nile to Kosti," she said, gesturing left out the windshield with the blade of her hand, "then go west from there. We're going west, aren't we?"

The man smiled as he drove the car through the deserted streets of Khartoum at well under the posted speed limit. That was another reason Lex was getting pissed off. The streets were empty, yet the man still drove like a nearsighted nonagenarian out for a Sunday drive.

"That's correct," he smiled. "We are going west."

"Then we'll need to be on the El Ingaz road. We can catch it in Kosti."

"You are very clever," he said with a tone of pleasant surprise.

Lex's tone was far less pleasant. "Yeah, and you're going the wrong way." She pointed out the windshield. "Turn left."

"Very clever, indeed," the man said as he drove past the left turn. "You are fluent in Sudanese Arabic. You know our customs. You know how to use weapons." He jerked a thumb toward the trunk, where Lex had stashed the duffel with all of her guns. A backpack with her clothes was in the back seat beside a shoulder bag the man had brought. "And you know your way around Khartoum. Have you been here before?"

"Sure, my family spent every summer here when I was a kid," Lex said drily. "We'd come over from Kansas to get ice cream and watch the public floggings."

The man held up one finger. Seemed to be his favorite gesture.

"Now you see, *that* is the more typical assumption I would expect from an American," he said with a faint smile. "Americans seem to think all Africans are stupid or corrupt—"

"There is a hell of a lot of corruption here, you gotta admit."

"—and all Muslim nations are brutal theocracies meting out harsh justice like in biblical times. This is simply not the case."

"Spoken like a man in a patriarchy." Lex pointed to the next left. "Turn here."

"But you," the man said, again ignoring the left turn, "you are different from the others. You are more educated, more... what's the word?" He thought for a moment. "Savvy," he said, in English. "You are a savvy woman."

"And you are a typical man," said Lex, also in English, "refusing to follow fucking directions."

The man switched back to Arabic. "Please. There is no need for profanity."

"There won't be if you just turn. Left. Here."

Lex reached over to push the steering wheel. The man resisted her, then set one hand on her outstretched arm, gently, but firmly. Lex felt the intense warmth of his hand, even through the thin cotton of the thobe and the thicker sleeve of the dress, like he held a tiny sun in his palm. In this heat. She wondered if his whole body was as hot.

The man looked over at her. Their eyes locked for a long moment. Lex stopped pushing, but kept her grip on the steering wheel a moment longer. Then she let go. She watched the corners of the man's mouth bend slightly up, watched his full lips purse forward just a touch.

He released her arm.

"Under normal circumstances," the man said, both hands on the steering wheel again, "you're absolutely right. The road to Kosti is paved and in acceptable condition. It would take us to El Ingaz in approximately four hours."

"Exactly," said Lex. She pointed out the windshield. "Turn left up here."

The man smiled again as that left turn, too, slipped past.

"These are not normal circumstances, I'm afraid," he

said. "You are clever. You know our land and our customs, but you don't know the shape of our war."

General Torrance had briefed Lex on the positions of the various forces, the different factions at play, the shifting lines and alliances. But that had been before the SAF offensive in Omdurman. And African civil wars—hell, African peacetime, in some countries—were notoriously fluid. Torrance's intel was probably outdated the moment she received it.

"The Rabak road," the man said, "will take us from RSF territory into SAF territory just south of Al Qutaynan."

His voice was calm and patient. They were driving toward the bombs and the bullets in an unarmored civilian vehicle, a Hyundai Atos, for fuck's sake. Yet the man was as relaxed as if they were driving to the beach for a picnic on a Saturday. Who the hell was this guy? And what was his experience with war and weapons that would make him so sanguine? Even Lex was on edge.

"If we made it through that crossing," he continued, "then into Kosti and onto El Ingaz, we would need to cross the front line once again, this time from SAF territory into RSF territory, at Um Ruwaba. You see? That route would have us cross the front lines not once, but twice."

Lex sat back in her chair. The man nodded, seeing Lex's reaction.

"Now you understand, yes?"

Lex sighed and looked straight out the windshield. She nodded.

"Alternatively, we can take the Ishreen Road from Um Bada," the man continued. "It is slower, admittedly, and not as well maintained. And it will no doubt have many abandoned or destroyed vehicles that we will have to negotiate.

But it will not cross the front lines even once. It is securely in RSF territory—"

Lex scoffed. "For now."

The man nodded. "For now. And it will take us to El-Obeid by tomorrow."

Lex nodded, then stopped nodding and frowned. They were headed northwest.

"Okay, fine. But why are you going this way?" she said. "The bridge over Jabal Awliya Dam was destroyed. We should still be heading south, to the crossing at Al Gitaina."

The man smiled that wide, charming smile again. "The bridge over the dam has been repaired," he said. He shrugged. "And I have a friend."

"Are you fu—" Lex spluttered herself to a stop before the swear word could come out. "Are you kidding me?" she said with a laugh. In English, she said, "You're telling me you know a guy?"

"I know a guy?" the man repeated in English. He looked at her, confusion on his face. Then the confusion cleared and his face brightened like the sun had just emerged from the clouds. The man laughed, a deep sound that rolled around the inside of the car like thunder. "Yes," he said, still using English. "Ha! Yes." He slapped the steering wheel and grinned at Lex. "I know a guy."

When they rolled up to the security checkpoint in front of the bridge, the man asked for the guy. While they waited, Lex scanned a dozen soldiers in desert camo and helmets, a hodge-podge of Russian AKs, Tigr DMRs, and Saiga-MK rifles carried loosely at their sides or resting muzzle-up against their shoulders. They eyed the Hyundai with the typical mix of boredom and wariness seen in all soldiers on routine patrol.

The guy himself turned out to be a squat, round man

with a neck like a battering ram and a personality to match. Lex couldn't see the insignia on his uniform, but judging from the deference the other soldiers showed, the guy was a commander of some kind.

He conversed with the man through the open car window in Neanderthal grunts and gestures. That kind of men sound the same in Arabic as they do in English, sublingual and menacing, with a lust for violence thinly veiled behind reptilian eyes. When those eyes glided over Lex, she looked away and stared straight out the windshield.

They rolled forward toward the bridge, the guy walking beside the car, still grunting with the man through the car window. They halted just before the turn onto the bridge to allow a tank to finish crossing.

To call the bridge repaired was like calling a cow in a field a medium-rare steak. The bridge itself was narrow, allowing only enough space for a car to pass in one direction at a time, and ran six feet or so above the waterline. The section closest to Lex's side had been damaged and cleared away, leaving a gap of maybe forty yards.

The repairs consisted of a single M3 amphibious bridging rig in the center of the damaged section, with the gaps on either side filled with a handful of amphibious troop transports with their sides cut off lashed together like makeshift rafts. A few more M3s and it would have been solid as a rock, but the monstrosity outside Lex's windshield looked sketchy as hell. Lex wouldn't have walked over it, let alone driven. She would have forced the man to head south to the bridge at Al Gitaina if she wasn't watching a tank cross to their side of the dam right in front of her while the man grunted with his sour-faced friend.

The tank was halfway across, currently on top of the M3 and holding fine. As it moved over the M3's ramps onto the transport raft, the raft canted steeply, dipping below the water line. Water sloshed over the lip and halfway up the tank's treads. But the raft held. Whether it floated or rested on the bottom of the spillway, Lex didn't know, but as the tank rolled forward, the raft leveled off, then repeated the horror on the other side as the tank crossed to the next raft.

In this foolhardy and ludicrous way, the tank made the crossing. After that, Lex couldn't complain. If a tank could do it, the much lighter Hyundai would make it, too. Probably.

Once the tank had crossed and cleared out, headed north toward the battle zone, the guy slapped the roof of the car twice and walked beside the car as the man maneuvered it to the crossing and inched onto the first raft. Lex held her breath as the man eased the front tires forward. The nose of the car dipped down sharply, forming a shallow V with the raft. Lex glanced out the window at the White Nile waters swirling past. The man revved the engine, pulling forward until the full weight of the car shifted onto the raft and balanced there. They dropped a stomach-wrenching few inches, bobbing in the river flow. It was only a single tense moment, but it felt like a year to Lex, imagining herself sinking to the bottom of the river, trapped in a fucking Hyundai. She cranked the window down furiously, preparing an escape route.

But the raft held, and no water came over the edge.

Fifteen teeth-chattering minutes later, they were safely on the other side of the dam, winding through the troops and the tanks and the artillery without even a casual glance from the soldiers around them. Eventually, they found themselves in the war-crumbled neighborhoods of Um Durman and Um Bada on the western side of the Nile. Roads that would normally be clogged with traffic were barren. Not long after, they left the damaged and desolate city behind and drove southwest on the slightly less damaged, but equally desolate Ishreen Road, headed for El-Obeid.

With the windows down and the warm wind blowing through the car, if it weren't for the occasional smoking ruin of a bombed-out vehicle, Lex could have been driving through the countryside on a warm summer day in rural Pennsylvania or Oklahoma or anywhere else in small-town America. She closed her eyes and lifted her face to the falling sun, its warmth a comfort on her skin.

It was then, when the risk of drowning was past, when the threat of detainment and questioning was gone, when the shell-torn buildings and shuttered windows had shifted into wide vistas of untended fields and sparse, scattered stands of trees, that Lex fully realized her situation.

She was alone in a car with a stranger, in a war zone miles from any city. She didn't know where they were going or how they would get there. She didn't have any food or water or supplies, other than the small cache of weapons in the duffel bag behind her. She had only a smartphone to use to call for help, if she needed it, with no way to know if the phone would even work, no way to tell a rescuer where she was, if it did, and no way to keep herself alive while she waited for that rescue to arrive.

And, oh, wait. It never would arrive. The sat phone was for intel transfer, not for exfil. What had Torrance said back in Vicenza? *Once you're in country, you'll be on your own.*

Lex was definitely on her own now.

She looked over at the man behind the wheel of the car. He glanced at her and smiled, then turned back to focus on his driving.

Lex looked out her window again. They passed squat

homes with no children playing in the hardpan yards, empty livestock pens with their gates open and knocking in the breeze, tractors idle and rusting in fields already overgrown with weeds. This was not small-town America. This was civil war in the Sudan, and Lex was not welcome here.

She pulled in a deep breath and let it out slowly. This might not have been her smartest plan ever, but it was the plan she was following. She had a job to do, and she was moving forward for the first time since she'd arrived.

For good or for ill, this was the plan. And Lex would see it through, one way or another.

25

"We are going to be traveling together for some time," said the man.

That was an understatement. They'd already been in the car for hours, driving through the empty landscape like moving through a memory. They'd stopped to siphon gas from an abandoned petrol filling station, a small, low building with a covered area out front, where the electricity had failed and the two lone pumps had stopped working. They were lucky there was still any gas in the storage tanks. Lex figured the RSF would have taken it all when they rolled through with their tanks and artillery.

The man produced some jerky from his shoulder bag and shared it with Lex. She didn't ask what kind of meat it was. She was hungry enough not to care. The jerky was tough and salty and delicious. They ripped chunks with their teeth and sat in the front seats of the car in the shade with the doors open and their legs hanging out, gnawing silently as the gas tank filled.

"We may as well get to know each other, at least a little," the man continued. "Don't you agree?"

"What if I don't?"

Lex wasn't about to tell the man the truth about herself, and she didn't feel like making up a cover story just for her travel guide. Cover stories were lies, and lies were traps laid for the future, traps that you would eventually step into and trigger. That was a good way to lose a limb. Or a life. Lex didn't have time for lies.

The man laughed softly. In the car earlier, his laugh had sounded like thunder. This time, his soft chuckle was like thunder far in the distance, after the storm had passed.

"Can we at least share our names with each other?" the man asked. "I would like to be able to refer to you as something other than *short-haired white girl.*"

"You've never called me that."

"That is how I refer to you in my thoughts."

Lex shrugged. "It's accurate."

"But not very kind. I would prefer a proper name." He shifted in the seat so that he faced her. "I'll go first." He touched his hand to his chest and bowed his head slightly. "My name is Babatunde Eze, but please call me Baba."

He held out his hand to Lex. A Sudanese man would not normally shake hands with a woman who was not in his family. He offered it as a Western gesture that was undoubtedly meant to set Lex at ease. She wondered if he would have bothered to set her at ease if Lex were a Sudanese woman. She wondered if he would have bothered even to learn her name.

"*As-salamu alaykum,*" Baba said as Lex shook his hand. It was the traditional greeting in Arabic, meaning *peace be unto you.*

"Unlikely," replied Lex.

Baba clucked his tongue. "It is a greeting of hope for the future, not a comment on the present."

Lex grumbled, then grudgingly muttered the traditional response, *"Wa alaykumu s-salām." And peace be unto you.*

His hand as she shook it sent the same wave of heat into Lex's body as before, when he had held her arm in the car. The man must have a core temperature of a hundred degrees. Touching him was like touching a furnace.

"Eze," said Lex. "That's an Igbo name. *Ị bụ onye Naijiria?"*

Baba laughed distant thunder again and smiled, bright and instantly charming. Lex would need to be careful with that smile. It was a currency some men would use to get anything they wanted.

"*Abụ m onye Naijiria*, yes. My family is from Nigeria. You speak Igbo?" he said. He shook his head admiringly. "So clever. So intelligent." He winked at her. "For an American."

"What are you doing in the Sudan?" said Lex. "You're a long way from home."

"Are you from the Sudan?" The man made a show of inspecting her quizzically from head to toe. Lex felt that heat inside her again. Even the man's gaze burned like the hot sun. "You do not seem Sudanese to me. You seem to be even further from your home."

He grinned.

"Touché," said Lex. "But you know why I'm here."

Baba's smile faded. His expression grew serious. He nodded slowly. "We will find your friends."

"They're not my friends." Lex ripped another bite from her jerky. "I've never even met them."

"And yet you endanger yourself to find them?"

"I have my reasons."

Baba regarded her. "If they are not your friends, then what are they to you? Compatriots? Colleagues?"

"A paycheck."

Baba's eyebrows shot up. "You are a mercenary, then? I

would not have guessed so. Although," he nodded his head toward the trunk of the car, "that would explain the arsenal you carry."

Mercenary. That's not a word Lex would have chosen. She didn't like the way it felt on her tongue. It felt cold, and tasted sour.

"Just because I'm getting paid doesn't make me a mercenary," she said sharply. Then, quieter, "Money isn't my only motive."

"Are you a soldier? Do you do this for your country? From a sense of duty?"

Lex scoffed. "Duty is just a fancy word for following someone else's orders." She shook her head and stared into the distance, away from the man and his knowing eyes. "I'm not a soldier anymore."

"I see." Baba nodded sagely. "You are a crusader, then."

Crusader. Lex didn't like that word, either. Had an air of desperation to it. Crusaders tended to wind up as martyrs, and Lex had no intention of martyring herself for anyone or anything. Not anymore. She was more useful alive than dead, especially to herself. But crusader was better than mercenary, and a hell of a lot better than soldier.

"Let's just say these women and I are..."

She scanned the empty landscape. The bones of a burnt-out Sarsar-2 troop transport hulked slant in a ditch up the road, its 12.7mm machine gun flopped to the side like a lifeless limb. The door of the house across the street banged against its jamb, again and again in the warm breeze, as if crying out for its owners to come and secure it. A scattering of bullet casings on the road glinted in the angled sunlight, spread across the cracked pavement like the smile of the devil.

"Let's just say we're fellow combatants."

"A rescue, then," Baba said, nodding. "For love. And honor."

For love and honor. A little cheesy, maybe. Lex didn't know those women, let alone love them. But she did feel a kinship with them already. Women, taken and held against their will. Part of a larger system that didn't give a shit about them. Yeah, Lex could understand that. And understanding someone always sparked a kind of empathetic love.

"Their families deserve closure," Lex said. "They deserve to know what happened to their loved ones, so they can put them to rest."

Baba frowned. "The women are not dead," he said.

"What?" Lex's heart started racing.

"When last I saw them," Baba nodded, "they were still alive."

"When was that?"

"A few days ago."

"How many days ago?"

Baba thought for a moment. "Three days."

"Then step on it, Baba," said Lex, turning to face squarely out the windshield. "Looks like this could be a rescue after all."

And an extra seven and a half million dollars in Lex's bank account.

"See?" said Baba. "Love and honor. In my mind, I will now refer to you as the honorable short-haired white girl." He grinned again. "Unless, of course, you honor me with your name."

This time, Lex let Baba's smile pay the bill for what he wanted.

"Alexis Wolfe," Lex said with a smile of her own. Keep the change. "You can call me Lex."

"Wolfe?" Baba leaned back and nodded slowly. "Lex Wolfe." He said the name like he was tasting it, rolling it around his mouth and savoring it, studying its flavors. "Do you know that the wolf is a powerful creature in Arabic culture?"

Lex nodded. She was aware of the folklore. Just about every culture had their stories of the wolf. Some feared them, some revered them.

"In Arabic culture," Baba said, "the wolf is wise and loyal, but also fearless, merciless, and cunning."

He leaned forward and shook Lex's hand once more. She was ready this time for the wave of heat that his touch sent through her. He held her hand softly and nodded as he peered into her eyes.

"Love and honor," he said. "Yes. The wolf is a being to be respected. As, I would say, are you."

"It's just a name," Lex said, trying to ignore the flush of... of what? Pride? Flattery? Was she really such an easy mark for a handsome face and some kind words? She shook it off. "The same name my father used all his life."

Baba stopped nodding, but held Lex's hand still for a moment longer. "Perhaps."

He dropped her hand and spun out the door, pulling the siphon tube from the gas tank. Lex hadn't noticed the sound of the gas overflowing and plopping wetly against the hardpack dirt of the filling station. It was like Baba had put her into a trance. A stupid smitten schoolgirl trance. Maybe it was the heat or the wide, empty landscape or the silence that made it seem like she and Baba were the only two people left in the world.

Whatever it was, it was bullshit, and Lex was smelling it

because she had her head up her own ass. Time to pull it out into the real world again before she did something stupid.

Baba bent to pick up a small rock from the ground, then disappeared inside the small, low building. This was no convenience store like gas stations in America, but there was a counter, a cash register, and a series of shelves and racks on one side and a single repair bay on the other. Lex watched Baba put a few dollars on the counter and weigh them down with the rock. He went through a doorway into the repair bay and came out the open bay door with a rag in his hand, wiping spilled gasoline from his skin.

"Do you need anything from inside?" he asked. "Something else to eat, perhaps?"

"You going to leave money for that, too?"

"Of course," said Baba, a confused look on his face. "I am no thief."

"No one is going to get that money," said Lex, shaking her head. "Some actual thief will just come along and take it. And even if the owner did come, they wouldn't know what it was for."

"God will know." Baba nodded, his face earnest and serious. "That is all that matters."

He went into the repair bay to return the rag, probably folding it neatly and straightening the place up a bit before he came back and got in the car. Without another word, they bumped from the dirt of the gas station up onto the paved road and drove off, continuing their journey.

Lex figured they were still at least three or four hours from El Obeid. The sun was setting quickly and darkness would be upon them soon, with no street lights, no rest stops on the side of the road, no hotels to sleep in between here and the city. And at night, the danger of stopping would be much greater.

Lex considered Baba as she watched him drive. She didn't know if the danger was greater in the car or out in the world, but the more she got to know Baba, the more she was inclined to trust him.

And that was the most dangerous thing of all.

26

Lex's estimate on the length of the drive turned out to be optimistic. The little blue Hyundai pulled into the heart of El Obeid five and a half hours later. The sun had set three hours before. The night was pitch black and starlit, pierced only by the occasional light from one building or another, accompanied by the loud, chugging rhythm of generators and the sharp smell of diesel fuel.

Lex had kept her head down at the RSF checkpoint on the way into town. Spotlights high on the roofs of two buildings turned the checkpoint into an oasis of light. Lex kept still in the passenger seat, her head down, while Baba spoke to a guard on the driver's side of the car.

A second soldier strolled up outside her window on the passenger side. Lex felt his stare through the glass and was grateful she'd thought to roll the window up as they approached the checkpoint, even though the night air was still warm.

She could see the soldier's AK in her peripheral vision, but he held it casually, loosely, at a downward angle across his body. No alarm in his posture. Yet.

He bent down to examine Lex more closely. She could feel him peering through the thin gauze of the cowl of her thobe, trying to see her face. Lex ducked her chin closer to her chest. She hoped the soldier would read it as a gesture of modesty, but the real purpose of the gesture was to droop the cowl more fully over the side of her head, and to allow her hair to fall forward along her cheek. The last thing she wanted was for the soldier to see her white skin.

The soldier knocked on Lex's window. When Lex didn't look over, he pulled a flashlight from his belt and clicked it on. Lex tensed. This was going to be a problem.

Lex didn't know what she should do. Should she warn Baba, who was still engaged in conversation with the other guard? Should she roll down her window and speak to the soldier herself, try to sweet-talk him as Baba would? Or should she follow her own instincts and strike first, use the element of surprise to jab the soldier hard in the Adam's apple or shoot him with his own weapon, then hope Baba had enough presence of mind to step on the gas and speed away before the guns began to fire on them?

The question became moot. Just as the soldier began to swing the light up to shine it through Lex's window, the guard on Baba's side slapped the roof of the car twice. Baba rolled the car slowly forward.

Lex watched in the side-view mirror as the soldier on her side watched them drive off. He pointed the flashlight after the car for a thoughtful moment, then switched it off and strolled back to his duty post.

Lex eased her tense muscles and let out the breath she'd been holding. Baba had talked them through smoothly, with his characteristic ease and charm. Lex was beginning to wonder why he was given such free passage by these RSF soldiers. What he'd said to this guard and to the guard at the bridge in Khartoum had been innocent enough. Passing through to join his family, he said both times. No, not here. They live in the West, near Nyala.

That was roughly where Lex figured they were headed. The lies had come easily from Baba's lips, so easily he might have been telling the truth, more or less. All the best lies have a grain of truth in them. after all. But why were the soldiers so inclined to believe him?

They passed down the main street toward the center of town, back under the blanket of near-total darkness. There were only two other cars on the road, one well ahead and one far behind them. As they approached the town center, the lights grew brighter and more numerous. The brightest lights were centered on the mosque straight ahead, its two minarets lit like the edges of twin daggers aimed into the inky sky.

The car ahead of them went straight. Baba turned left at the mosque.

A sports stadium rose ahead of them, wreathed in light, where a local soccer team had played before the war. Judging from the soldiers streaming in and out of the stadium, laughing and smoking, rifles slung over their shoulders or across their backs, it now served as a staging area for the local RSF forces.

Again, Lex lowered her head, tensing as Baba eased past the stadium.

None of the soldiers seemed to notice them. They were not followed.

Baba released a light sigh once the stadium was behind them. Lex hadn't noticed that he was tense, too.

He turned right and took them through dark residential streets, driving slowly and swerving around piles of rubble as they appeared in the short, narrow beam of his headlights, until finally he pulled down a narrow alley beside a nondescript, two-story concrete building halfway to the edge of town. He squeezed the Hyundai through the alley into a small parking area in the back of the building and swung into a parking spot, the front of the car aimed toward the building. He switched off the engine, but kept the headlights on.

"What is this place?" said Lex.

She peered out the window. Aside from the car's headlights, she could see no light anywhere in the building or the area around it. When Baba switched the headlights off, then on again, then off again, they were thrown into complete darkness.

Baba ignored her question. They waited in darkness and in silence.

A door opened, a small rectangle of yellow light on the near side of a hallway that ran through the building to the other side. Lex could just make out Baba's smile in the faint light.

"A safe place," he said as he released his seat belt.

He got out of the car. His door thunked shut, leaving Lex inside. Without Baba, the car suddenly felt very quiet, very empty. Baba came around the front of the car and pulled Lex's door open. He held his hand out for her.

Once again, she was putting way too much trust in him, this man she'd only met a few hours before. But she took his hand, anyway, his palm soft and warm against her fingers, and let him help her from the car.

She followed him toward the building. No one stood in the doorway. No silhouette disrupted the yellow rectangle in the darkness. The door had been opened and left open.

As they approached, Baba turned back toward Lex, his face hidden in shadow.

"You don't have to wear that here," he said. Lex assumed he was referring to her thobe, or perhaps just to the head covering. "Here, you can relax. Maybe even have fun." Even in the shadows, she could see him smile. "Can a wolf have fun?"

Lex didn't bother to respond. Baba chuckled and turned away again.

Lex let Baba enter the doorway first, hanging back for a beat. If someone was going to get shot, Baba could take the bullet. When no bullet came, Lex followed.

She stepped through the doorway into a narrow, concrete vestibule roughly six feet long. Baba stood in the center of the room. A large man stood behind a half-door on the opposite side. His face was hard, and his massive bulk nearly filled the opening above the half-door.

He held a pistol aimed at Baba.

Lex immediately tensed and reached to her back for her own gun, but the man was already relaxing his aim. His hard expression broke into a smile and a rough laugh rang through the air. He stepped through the half-door and wrapped Baba in a warm embrace. Lex kept a wary eye on the pistol, still in the man's hand as he hugged Baba, but the man slipped it into a shoulder holster as soon as they broke their embrace.

"Okot," Baba said, swinging his arm toward Lex, "meet Lex Wolfe. Lex Wolfe, Okot Eltayeb." To Okot, Baba said, "Lex is a friend."

"A friend of Baba is a friend of mine," said Okot. He did not offer to shake Lex's hand, but he bowed his head slightly. Lex nodded back.

Okot stepped past her—Lex pressed herself against the wall to afford the man room to pass—and shut the door to the outside. A dragging sound drew Lex's eye to the floor, where a tightly rolled towel had been duct-taped to the bottom of the door. The tape slid over the concrete with a sound like the hiss of a rattlesnake, but once the door was shut and locked, Lex knew no light would be visible and no sound audible from the outside.

Okot threw his arm around Baba's shoulder with a wide smile and turned him toward a set of stairs on the other side of the open half-door.

"Come, my friend," he said. "The party is just getting started. And now that you're here, we can truly begin."

Okot was tall and wide, with the kind of bulk that suggests power, not paunch. He barely fit down the stair-well, width-wise, and he had to duck to avoid hitting his head on the sloped concrete ceiling above the stairs. Wearing a black button-down shirt tucked neatly into a pair of dark jeans, with a brown leather belt and boots, Okot would have looked as at home in a trendy club in New York as he did here amid the dark, quiet rubble of El Obeid.

They descended, turning once, then again. They walked through a door at the bottom of the stairs and along a short, narrow hallway, then down another twisting staircase to yet another hallway, this one dark and much longer, lit only by the glow of a small flashlight Okot switched on. The light bobbed with his stride, and Lex worked to control the fear bobbing with it in her throat.

As they approached a door at the end of that second hall, Lex could hear a faint thump. As they got closer, a muffled ringing joined the thump. Okot opened the door.

Lex could have been in that trendy New York club. The thump was the thump of a bass drum, the ringing the sound of guitar and keyboard and steel drums. The room she stepped into had all the same vibes as an exclusive underground New York speakeasy. Crowded with people, warm with their heat, rich with the scent of their sweat. A band played from a stage at the far end of the long, low room. Music echoed off the concrete walls, floor, and ceiling.

A mass of people on a sunken dance floor in the center of the room bounced and swayed in time with the polyrhythmic beat, with the pulse of bass guitar, with the staccato speech of a woman's voice rapping. The room must once have been some kind of maintenance bay or delivery room, with a sunken area in the center originally intended for trucks to enter or for mechanics to work.

The lights on the stage shifted from red to orange to blue and back again. The wooden stage had been built across the sunken area, built up to the level of the rest of the room. The wall behind the stage was solid concrete now, but in the occasional flare of the shifting lights, Lex could see cords hanging from the ceiling which once had probably opened a rolling bay door of some kind.

Toward the back of the room, lamps along the walls added a dim yellow glow to the mix. A thick cloud of smoke hung from the ceiling. It smelled of pot and harsh tobacco. Lex felt lightheaded just walking through it. She'd heard that alcohol and marijuana were consumed in private in the Sudan, even during the years of strict Sharia law, but as an outsider, she had never expected to witness it herself.

Okot led them through the crowd toward the side wall on the far side of the room, where various tables and couches and high-backed chairs had been set up. If Lex didn't know better, she could almost have been back in Vicenza at Simona's bar. The seating style was not much different.

Through the smell of the pot, Lex picked up other smells. Her stomach identified them before her brain did.

She felt it growl. She spotted a long table against the wall with all sorts of food on it, like a pot luck dinner at a church. Lex could see plates stacked high with falafel, baskets of kisra bread, steaming pots of soup, and a plate stacked with skewers of meat. Aside from a few bites of jerky, Lex hadn't eaten since breakfast, and she was hungry.

Okot followed her eyes and laughed. "Sit, please," he said, gesturing to a couch against the wall, ringed with other chairs. "I will bring you both some food and something to drink."

Baba and Lex flopped down onto a small couch. Lex squirmed and eventually found a comfortable position in her restrictive dress. She glanced at Baba, who was surveying the crowd, his leg already bouncing in time with the music. Lex looked around the room, as well. People smoking and drinking, talking and laughing, dancing and grinding and flirting and having all the fun the night can offer. It was not what she had expected to see in the middle of the night in the middle of a civil war.

And no one was wearing a thobe or a traditional tunic dress. Everyone was dressed like she would see in Italy or America or Milan. Jean, t-shirts, tank tops, skirts, light dresses. Comfortable, individual, even sexy. Lex pulled off her thobe and balled it on the couch beside her. She wished she could take off her tunic dress, too, but all she had on underneath was her camisole and her underwear. As casual as the scene seemed to be, it wasn't casual enough for that.

"What is this place?" she said, almost to herself.

The music wasn't too loud for conversation, but Baba leaned toward her, anyway. His warm breath tickled her ear and sent shivers through Lex's body.

"This, my clever white wolf," he said, "is the real Sudan."

27

LEX LIVED up to her name when Okot brought the food back. He handed Lex and Baba each a plate piled high with homemade food, and Lex wolfed hers down. The falafel was crisp on the outside, soft and flavorful on the inside, and not at all dry like most of the falafel she'd eaten. The skewers were chicken, something Baba called agashe. Baba started to say something else, but Lex had already stripped an entire skewer of chicken from the stick into her mouth, chewing with her cheeks bulged like a squirrel. He laughed when the spice hit her tongue and Lex's eyes bulged like her cheeks and began to water. She swallowed the chicken as fast as she could, then chased it down with whatever was in the cup Okot had handed her. It looked like rusty water. Baba called it sharbot.

Lex had been to the Sudan twice before, had studied the language and culture. She'd heard of agashe and sharbot, but had never seen them, had never tasted them. These were foods made by families in homes, not typically served in restaurants or hotels. Not in this form, unadorned, honest, heartfelt.

They tasted incredible. The spice of the agashe had taken Lex by surprise, but she was prepared for her second bite. The heat of the hot pepper blended perfectly with the crushed peanuts and the other spices that coated the meat, grilled to a delicate char. And the sharbot, a wine made from fermented dates, with cardamom, cinnamon, ginger, and raisins, was complex and delicious. And strong. Lex didn't know if it was the wine or her mostly empty stomach, but she was feeling the sharbot halfway through her first cup.

Her comfort food tour of the Sudan didn't stop there. She tasted mullah ahmar, a delicious red soup with wheat balls like dumplings, and ful medames, a flavorful fava bean stew with a few pieces of thin kisra bread to dip into it. There was even a piece of homemade baklava for dessert.

By the time she'd finished it all, Lex was little more than a lump on the couch, sated and happy and floating on a cloud of sharbot. That's when Okot brought to the table a clay pot called a jebena. It was a round jug small enough to fit in Lex's hand, with a long spout and a small handle extending from the top and a smaller spout extending from one side. Okot set it on the table in a wicker holder shaped like an egg cup. He poured Lex and Baba each a tiny cup of bunna, Sudanese coffee that rivaled Cariz's kapeng barako back in Manila for its strength. And the flavor was unlike any coffee Lex had ever tasted. The coffee beans were ground with clove and cinnamon, Baba explained. The result was a tiny cup of coffee that dazzled Lex's taste buds and cut through the sharbot haze.

While Lex and Baba ate, Baba's friends had slowly come to sit in the chairs around them, each one giving Baba a warm hug when they arrived, each one giving Lex a friendly nod and a bright smile. Baba's friends were as good-looking as he was, and as stylish as Okot. They ranged from tall to short, thin to fat, dark-skinned to light-skinned—what the locals would call "red"; none were nearly as pasty-white as Lex. What they all had in common, though, were sharp minds, sharper tongues, and wicked senses of humor.

As she ate, Lex listened to Baba and his friends talk about the roads, the town, the war. They spoke of Al-Burhan and Hemedti with equal derision. They spoke of the inconvenience of not being able to travel freely. They spoke of the indignance of not having any control over their own lives in their own country. In tones of quiet anger, they spoke of the indecency of the soldiers and what they did to the women and, in some cases, even the children in the towns they conquered and re-conquered and conquered again as the battle lines continually shifted.

Baba's friends were artists, musicians, journalists. They were architects and engineers and photographers. One had taught computer science at SUTES, the Sudan University of Technology, Engineering, and Sciences in Khartoum before an errant shell had destroyed one of the dorms and the university had shut down. She had studied herself at MIT and worked for a time in Silicon Valley before returning to her home country to teach the next generation of students. Now, many in that next generation were gone, having either fled the country, gone missing, or died.

Once Lex and Baba had finished their coffee, joints were passed as they talked. Baba didn't partake, just passed the joint along when it came to him. In fact, Lex hadn't seen him drinking sharbot, either. Just water. Didn't matter to Lex. She'd definitely enjoyed the sharbot, and she happily took healthy tokes from the joint, too, when it was her turn.

The conversation ranged from serious to sublime to

side-splittingly funny. The humor was often dark, usually witty, and occasionally crude, but always hilarious. And Lex saw a side of Baba she hadn't seen before. Not that she expected to know him at all after only one day traveling together, but she now knew that the man she had seen that day—unflappable, content, polite—was only one part of him. The Baba speaking with his friends was passionate and political. He was eloquent and inspiring. He saw the world tilted just a few degrees off-axis from everyone else, enough to expose the cracks and inconsistencies. And he was smart enough to turn those cracks and inconsistencies into subtle comments and asides that left everyone falling from their chairs, clutching their stomachs from the ache of laughter or, in Lex's case, from fear of throwing up her excessive dinner because she was laughing so hard.

The hours passed in a moment. Baba's friends asked Lex about herself, honestly curious about her and her thoughts and impressions of their homeland. She answered as honestly as she could, which wasn't always as honestly as she would have liked. They sympathized with Lex's concern for the three journalists who had been abducted, with what Baba told them was Lex's crusade. They admired Lex for her determination and her courage in attempting to bring the women home.

But even through the sincerity of their empathy and the haze of the enormous joints they passed and the sharbot that, thanks to Okot's attentiveness, never seemed to drain from her cup, slowly eroding the caffeine jolt of the bunna, Lex did not forget her real purpose there. Hers was a mission, not a crusade. She had a job to do, and she had to be careful not to forget that. If she relaxed too much, spoke too loosely in front of the wrong people, she could wind up kidnapped like the others. Or she could wind up dead.

But she didn't think this was the kind of crowd that would cause those kinds of problems. Every one of them had already expressed sentiments that would see them killed by the RSF or the SAF or both. These were dissidents, not informants. Even being there at an underground party, drinking alcohol and smoking pot, might be enough to get them imprisoned.

Eventually, Baba's friends peeled off in singles and in pairs and made their way to the dance floor. From where she sat on the couch against the wall, Lex had a good view across the room. The heads of the dancers were just below her eyeline. She lounged on the couch, watching the heads bob, the hips sway and grind, the hands of the dancers move over each other, from shoulders to backs and beyond.

From where she and Baba sat on the couch, Lex could see the band clearly. A man playing drums, a woman playing bass guitar, a man playing a kind of large lute with a muted, almost sitar-like sound. A female singer stood in front, her ample figure clearly outlined by her dress, her tight-curled, shoulder-length, copper-dyed hair framing her face. The metallic blue of her eye shadow and the gold of her septum piercing shone in the light when she closed her eyes and tilted her head back, as if in those moments the gods themselves looked down to admire her beauty.

In the shadows at the back of the stage, a man hunched over a laptop on a stand. Lex didn't know if he was making music or recording it or both, but the band was good. In one song, the singer alternated between complex rap rhythms with angry lyrics about bombs and soldiers and lives torn apart and a sultry, seductive alto voice repeating a chorus that spoke of rising above, rising to the heavens, rising to meet a future where all would be at peace. It was a striking contrast, and a haunting one.

It all rode on top of a driving bass and pulsing drums that ducked and beat and built like an EDM tune. The band played all night, song after song, never repeating, each song building on the intensity of the last, the pulse and the rhythm working the crowd into a late-night frenzy. Lex didn't know if it was a touring band, a band someone in the region would recognize, or just a well-hidden local talent, but the music would cause the same frenzy in LA as it did in El Obeid. The band was that good.

Before long, both of Baba's legs were bouncing in time to the music and his hands were drumming on his knees, and even Lex's head was bobbing to the beat. One of Baba's friends, Aamira, the computer scientist, came up from the dance floor. She was a sultry, hourglass-shaped beauty with full, inviting lips and dark brown eyes that seemed to take in more than they saw. She took both of Baba's hands and pulled him off the couch. Baba stood, tucked his shirt into his pants, and held his hand out to Lex.

"Oh, no," Lex said, shaking her head. "I'm not a dancer."

That was an understatement. Watching Lex dance was like watching a car drive off a thousand-foot cliff. You didn't want to stay for the horrific and inevitable explosion at the end, but you couldn't tear your eyes away.

"Everyone is a dancer," said Baba. "It is a part of being human." He held his hand out still. "Come. Please."

When Lex hesitated still, he tilted his head, a gleam in his eyes.

"Wolves are not known for being afraid," he said, teasing, not unkind. "Is that what I see here?"

"No," said Lex, "but wolves are known to bite off a head or two when they're backed into a corner."

Baba raised his eyebrows, then chuckled, soft thunder rolling through Lex's chest, and left with Aamira.

As soon as he was gone, Lex felt Baba's absence. She watched him work onto the crowded dance floor with Aamira. Her arms went into the air. He shadowed the sway of her hips. They lost themselves in the music, eyes closed.

Lex looked across the dance floor at the faces smiling, at the bodies bouncing.

At the hips grinding.

She found Baba again. The crush of the crowd had pressed Aamira close to him, pressed her breasts against his chest. Aamira's upraised arms were draped loosely around Baba's neck. Baba's hands rested on her shapely waist. Their hips swayed together, pressed together, ground against each other. Lex watched the swaying, the press, the grind of Aamira's hips slowly migrate Baba's hands toward her ass.

Lex felt a gnawing low down in her core.

Fuck it.

She stood from the couch, threw back the rest of the sharbot in her cup, and headed for the dance floor.

28

THROUGH THE CLOUD OF SMOKE, redolent of the smells of
marijuana and tobacco, Lex descended to the dance floor.
She descended from one cloud into another, the second
one invisible but no less present, rich with the hot and
heady scent of sweat and sexuality.

Aamira and Baba both clapped and shouted with
delight when Lex came up to them on the dance floor. They
parted to allow her into their circle, and Lex didn't see even
a hint of irritation or jealousy in Aamira's eyes. From what
she had watched from the couch, they had looked like they
were getting more than just friendly, but maybe she'd
misread the situation. Lex was no dancer, and she rarely
went to places where people danced. Drinking, yes. Dancing, no. Maybe this was what real dancing looked like,
seductive and sexy.

Lex knew sex. Lex liked sex. A lot. But seduction? Not
her thing. And looking sexy? She didn't have a clue. When
she wanted to fuck someone, she just looked at them in a
certain way and they came along willingly. She had never

consciously tried to look sexy before, not since high school, before her body filled out.

Maybe that's why dancing felt so strange to her. Baba may have said dancing was a natural part of being human, but it sure as hell didn't feel that way to Lex. As she stood in the crowd on the dance floor, she felt like everyone was watching her, watching the girl with the glaring white skin and zero rhythm try to dance in a sea of dancers, an alien among natural humans.

"Relax," said Baba, surveying the awkward, tentative, jerking motions that constituted Lex's attempt at dancing. "Just move."

When Lex scowled at him, he laughed.

"Close your eyes," he said.

Lex glanced at Aamira, but she had already turned to dance with another group. With a frustrated sigh, Lex did as Baba asked.

Baba touched both of Lex's temples gently with his fingertips. She started as a jolt went through her, like his fingers carried an electric spark.

"Do you hear the music?" he asked.

His voice was loud enough for Lex to hear him over the band, but somehow it felt soft in her ears, soft and low.

She kept her eyes closed, let out another deep sigh, and nodded.

"Do you hear the bass?" Baba said. "The beat of the drum?"

He pressed his fingers lightly against her temples, in time with the beat.

Lex nodded. She focused on the pulse of the rhythm, the pulse of Baba's touch.

"Let your heart find the rhythm, match it," Baba said. "Then, feel it." He moved his hands to her shoulders, his touch hot against her skin, even through her tunic dress. "Feel it here."

He moved Lex's shoulders, gently swaying them with the music.

"Feel it here."

He moved to the side and put one hand on Lex's back, between her shoulder blades, the other on the top of her chest, just below her throat. His touch felt like a furnace blast through her chest. Her heartbeat stuttered and quickened. Lex wondered if Baba could feel it.

He squeezed her gently between his hands and moved her chest back and forth. Her shoulders and her arms swayed with it. Lex felt her body loosen.

"Feel it here."

Baba slid his hands to Lex's lower back and her belly, squatted so his head was even with her breasts, and rocked her waist in small arcs, loosening her body even more. She felt her spine pop, felt some muscles loosen, even as other muscles, lower down, tightened at the slow tease of Baba's touch. The tip of Baba's spread pinky pressed just above Lex's pubis. That low gnawing she'd felt earlier became a wanting growl.

"Feel it here," Baba said, standing before her and moving his hands to Lex's hips, rocking them gently back and forth and up and down in small ellipses, adding their motion to the movement of her shoulders and her chest and her abdomen.

Lex dropped her head down, let all her muscles relax, let the beat of the music move through her. It felt good, like long-pent tension was finally finding release, moving out of her muscles and bringing new blood and fresh oxygen to old wounds. How long had she been so tense? It was nearly two weeks since she'd left Manila. She'd been tense ever since then.

Hell, she'd been tense for years before that.

"Good," said Baba. Though only his hands were touching her, Lex could feel Baba's body moving with hers. "Very good."

Very good was right. Lex didn't know if it was the pot or the sharbot or the pheromones in the air or just being in a new place with new people far from her home and her past, but she felt like light was filling her, from her feet to her hips to her gut to her heart. She flopped her head back and opened her eyes. A light in the ceiling directly above shined bright and hot against her face, but that light and that heat could as easily have come from her, coursing up through her body and into the air, instead of the other way around.

"Yes, wolf," said Baba with a laugh. "Now you have it. You see? Now you are a dancer."

The wolf was loose and in the wild. Lex laughed with Baba, then howled up at the ceiling. That made Baba laugh even louder, the sound deep and melodic. Others around them turned their heads, and they laughed, too. Some of them howled along with her.

Lex dropped her head again, her short hair falling in a tousle over her eyes. She looked through it at Baba and smiled. He looked radiant, joyful.

And so fucking hot.

Was he always so fucking hot?

So. Fucking... Hot.

So hot. Jesus, Lex was so fucking hot. She pulled at the neck of her dress. God, she could barely breathe. Her collar felt like a noose. Sweat poured down Lex's face, down her arms and her chest beneath her dress. She felt like she was swimming in it, like she would drown if she didn't do something.

She tugged and pulled at the long sleeves of her dress, freeing her arms, then stretched the collar until the stitches creaked and popped. It didn't tear, but it stretched enough for Lex to get her arms through. She shucked the dress to her waist, tied the sleeves in front of her like a belt and shimmied it down to just above her hips, exposing as much of her stomach as she thought she could get away with. She slid her belly band down with it, not caring if the grip of her pistol was exposed. Surely she wasn't the only one in the room with a firearm.

Relief was immediate. Even though the sweaty, tightly packed crowd was hot, the air was still blissfully cool against her sweat-slick skin, against her arms and her bare belly. Lex was suddenly thankful that she'd worn the crop camisole instead of something longer. Her legs were still restricted, sweat still running down her thighs, but at least her torso was free.

She tilted her head back, closed her eyes, and raised her arms high above her head, reaching for the heat and the light above her, raising her arms as much for the feel of her own skin in the open air again as for the cooling relief it brought. Her skin felt alive for the first time in over a week. Every breath of air, every movement of muscle, every bit of heat from the lights or the bodies around her felt vivid and bright, like she was feeling—feeling anything at all—for the first time in her life.

Okay, this had to be the pot talking. And the sharbot. Mixing alcohol and pot had always been a risky proposition for Lex.

But in that moment, she didn't care. It all felt too good. The sway of her shoulders, the slow twist of her midriff, the rolling of her hips, all sent sparks of sensation shooting through her body. Now she understood. This was why people danced. This was the feeling they were all after, this feeling of joy, this feeling of sensuality in the movement of their own bodies. The music added to it, the bass and the beat pulsing and throbbing through the air, through her body, aligning her movements and her sensations. Dancing was just like sex, only even more. More sensation, more rhythm.

More, and not nearly enough.

She opened her eyes, dropped her head, and looked at Baba. Sweet, helpful, sneaky-sexy Baba.

He smiled back at her, moving his body with the music, moving with her, moving his hips in a way that made Lex want to wrap her legs tight around his back and ride him into the sunset.

She was going to fuck that man. Tonight.

She locked him with her gaze, moved close to him, slid her hands over his rough-shaved head, down the sides of his face, and wrapped them around his neck. She pulled him closer. He smelled of spice and smoke, a heady scent that made Lex want to bury her face in the side of his neck.

So she did.

Baba did not resist.

Their hips swayed with each other. Lex slid her hands from his neck to his shoulder blades, felt the muscles bunch and release beneath his shirt as he danced.

She slid her hands further, felt the long, hard muscles in Baba's lower back working. Lex leaned her head back, pressing her hip against his, and saw Baba's eyes darken, saw something come into them, some thought.

The same thought Lex was having, she hoped.

Baba's eyes trailed across her face, trailed down over

her body, down to her bare stomach. She felt the heat of his stare as it moved, felt it like the trace of his fingertips, traces she would feel later, soon, hot across her skin.

Pinning him with her eyes, with that look, Lex slid her hands to Baba's ass, full and muscular, took a handful and jerked him hard against her hips. He grunted. She gasped as he slipped his body to one side, slipped himself across her, and let his thigh push against her crotch. She ground herself against it, dropped her head back and felt a pressure build in her core, felt it press through her body, her skin, felt it in the pulsing beat of the music, in the light above. Was it coming to her or from her, or both?

It didn't matter. One way or another, it was coming.

Lex moaned in frustration. She cursed her fucking dress for not letting Baba's leg push all the way under her. She would rip it. She didn't have another one, but she didn't care. She would tear the fucking dress in half with her bare hands, tear it off so she could feel it all, feel him against her.

Baba took his leg away.

Lex throbbed. It felt like a hole had opened in her, like she'd been gutshot with a cartoon cannon, a clean, round hole all the way through her, the cold air whistling through.

Baba stood in front of her, holding her at arm's length, unmoving. His face was kind, but his eyes were intense and searching, staring into hers, roving over her face. She wanted them to rove over her body, wanted his hands to quickly follow. She pushed closer to him.

But Baba stepped back, keeping her at arm's length, eyes still searching hers.

And then he took her hand and turned, leading her off the dance floor.

A flush of heat raced through Lex and pooled low in her body, anticipating.

She followed Baba eagerly. He grabbed her thobe from the couch and led her through the crowd and out the way Okot had brought them in. Through the door, up the long hallway. The sound of the band muffled when the door swung shut behind them, then silenced once they had gone a short way down the hall.

They walked in near total darkness. Unlike Okot, Baba had not brought a flashlight. After a moment, Lex's eyes adjusted. The blackness shifted to a dark grey, but Baba's stride never faltered, his grip on her hand never loosened.

They stopped halfway down the hall and Baba pushed open a door that Lex hadn't noticed on the way in. A bare lightbulb hanging on the other side threw a sharp yellow spear of light into the hall.

Now Lex could see why she hadn't noticed the door. It was cut right into the concrete, like a secret door in a haunted house. Lex had no idea how Baba had found it so easily. There was no door handle, and when he pulled Lex through and shut the door behind them, there didn't seem to be any lines or markings along the concrete on the inside.

The air was cool there, and quiet. The weak bulb lit another narrow hall, lit only a patch before darkness returned, and then light spilling from the top of a staircase in the distance, leading up.

Lex swayed as she looked, put one hand on the cool, rough concrete wall to steady herself. Something about the hallway, about the sudden shift from darkness to light, made her feel dizzy and disoriented.

Or maybe it was the pot and the sharbot, extracting the cruel cost of their dark magic.

Baba took Lex's hand again, led her up the stairs and down yet another hallway. Though it was concrete like all the others, this hallway was wider and more traditional. Doors opened at regular intervals on both sides. Numbers hung on them.

Hotel rooms.

Baba stopped at one and held the door open while he pulled Lex inside. He flicked a switch to reveal a tiny room with barely enough space for a double bed and a side table. A door led to a bathroom the size of a narrow walk-in closet, with a toilet, a sink, and a basin set in the floor beneath an open showerhead. Simple. Unadorned. Effective.

They could use the shower later. Lex turned to Baba and backed toward the bed. She took off her belly band, dropped it on the floor with a thunk, and wriggled her dress down over her hips.

"You showed me how to dance, Baba," she said. "Now let me show you what I can do."

She stumbled when her dress got down to her knees, then bumped into the bed backwards and fell into it on her back. She shut her eyes and laughed. The bed was old. The springs creaked and groaned beneath her. But the bedcover was soft and warm and comforting. And Lex didn't give a shit how much noise they made. The more, the better.

She opened her eyes. The tiny room was spinning.

Baba appeared at the side of the bed. There were three of him. The three Babas leaned over her. Hands under her arms. The Babas slid Lex further up the bed.

"This is not America, little wolf."

He pulled her dress the rest of the way off. Lex's bare legs felt cold.

"It may have seemed that way, with the music and the drink and the dancing," said Baba.

He pulled the bedcover down underneath Lex's body. She pedaled her feet to help him. Her dry skin scratched against the soft bedcover.

"But this is still the Sudan." He lay the cover atop her gently, tucked it up under Lex's chin. "And I am still a gentleman."

Lex tried to kick the covers off again, tried to say she wished he weren't such a gentleman, that she was no lady. But her legs shuffled feebly under the sheets, and she didn't know if the words made it past her lips or just curled on her tongue and went to sleep.

Which suddenly seemed like a lovely plan.

"Good night, little wolf," said Baba.

Lex heard his footsteps as he walked toward the door. The lights went out, and she slept.

29

IN THE NARROW BATHROOM, the shower was running. Steam everywhere, clouding Lex's view. The water boiling hot, filling the room. The toilet bowl was submerged. The water up to her thighs, burning her skin bright red. The super-heated water rose to her crotch, then seared through her, white hot.

Her name, shouted, the man's voice dampened by the wooden bathroom door.

She waded toward it, each slow step igniting a fresh flare of heat against her skin. The water was already up to her chest. She slapped the door with her hand, then pounded it with her fist.

The voice called for her through the door again and again.

She shouted in response, screamed for help, but the water was up to her chin, then to her mouth. With each scream, she choked on the water, gagged on it. It scalded her tongue, scorched her throat. She spit it out and screamed again, choked again, gagged again.

She shut her mouth and held her breath and pounded,

but now the water was over her head. Her pounding fist moved through it in slow-motion, like a hand around her wrist was holding her arm, holding her back, holding her down. Her head felt swollen, the skin on her face stretched in the boiling water, as if it might split open like a soft-boiled egg and blood and brain would mist the water around her and a loose eyeball would float away and watch her struggle from afar.

Still she pounded.

The voice shouted again, muffled by the door, muffled by the water, reduced to incoherent bass tones, like grunts or moans.

Lex looked down, saw the brass door handle through the cloudy blue water, twisted it.

The door opened, but the flood did not lower. It quivered in the open doorway like gelatin.

Through it, outside it, Lex saw his face.

Skinner.

Predator.

He leered.

Lex screamed.

The sound was muffled. Water filled her lungs. Choked her. Gagged her.

Silenced her.

With a smug smile, Skinner reached a languorous hand toward her body.

Lex sat up straight in bed.

Her head pounded so fiercely she felt like she could actually hear the hammer strokes of her heart.

Then she realized it wasn't just her heart. Someone was pounding on the door of her hotel room, shouting her name.

Lex stood, wobbly at first, the concrete floor cold

against the soles of her bare feet. Each step toward the door felt like nails being punched into her skull.

More pounding. More shouting.

"Okay," said Lex. It came out in a raspy whisper. Her tongue was swollen and dry, her lips glued together. Her mouth tasted like a pig's ass. The inside, not the outside.

One hand on the bed for balance, she shuffled past her dress, her gun, and her shoes in a heap on the floor. She looked down to see she was wearing just her crop cami and panties. Not naked. She couldn't remember why not. Couldn't remember anything past Baba taking off her dress, and then a hazy image of his face hovering over hers.

More pounding. Her head and the door. More shouting.

She forced the wind from her lungs to make an actual sound this time. "I'm coming," she shouted back, then immediately staggered from the noise, put one hand to the wall to steady herself, the other to her temple to keep her brains from oozing out her ear.

Sharbot and pot. Never again.

Pounding. Shouting.

The room had been small the night before, hadn't it? Now it was ten miles long.

She finally reached the door.

"Fucking Christ." She jerked the door open. The handle slipped from her grip. The door banged against the wall. Lex winced at the sound. "What?"

Baba pushed her back into the room, closed the door behind himself, checked to make sure it was locked.

"Get dressed," he said. "Now."

"Fuck you," said Lex, "and good fucking morning to you, too." She leaned against the wall, closed her eyes and massaged her temples. "If it even is morning. What time is it?"

"It's time to go."

Baba darted past her into the bedroom, grabbed her dress from the floor by the bed, gathered its length into his hands and held it up in front of Lex, holding the dress open for her to step under and into it. When she didn't move, he shook it insistently, then looked hard at her.

Lex glared back at him. She might have the mother, grandmother, and fucking Eve herself of all hangovers, but she'd be fucked if she was going to let some asshole force her to get dressed like a little girl who doesn't want to go to bed being forced to put on her nightgown.

Baba's look was fierce, darting back and forth between Lex's eyes.

"You need to get dressed, Lex. Immediately. Please, there is no time to waste."

"What's the fucking rush?"

Baba pulled open the door, just a crack. Just enough for Lex to register through the haze of her hangover the sounds of people running, shouting, scrambling in the hallway outside. In the distance, she heard gunfire.

In the distance, but not far in the distance.

Baba slammed the door shut again.

Lex needed no more explanation. She could get the details later. She took the dress from Baba and pulled it over her head, then stepped toward the bed to grab her gun from the floor. The dress shortened her stride, nearly made her fall flat on her face. Lex pulled the dress back over her head, ripped a seam up one side with a single strong yank, then pulled it back on. Finally, she could walk like a normal human being again.

She bunched the dress up under her armpits, held it against her chest with her chin while she strapped her gun around her waist. She should have put her gun on before she put the dress back on. Stupid fucking clothes.

Finally situated, she slid her feet into her shoes and looked up to find Baba holding her thobe out to her.

"Fuck off."

He shook his head, his lips pressed into a tight line. "With where we are and what's going on outside, it will call more attention if you don't wear it."

Lex snatched the thobe from his hand and strode toward the door as she struggled to wrap the huge piece of fabric over her head and around her body. Stupid, stupid fucking misogynistic religious fashion bullshit.

Baba darted past her—moving easily, of course, in his fucking pants and short-sleeved shirt. He cracked open the door and peered out, then opened it wide, stepped through, and waved Lex forward.

Lex strode out the door as she finished a half-ass job with her thobe. At least she got her head covered.

Then she looked up and didn't care about the damn thobe anymore.

They were in the center of the main hallway through the building, on the ground floor. The sun was rising, the hallway still cast mostly in shadow. To her right was the parking lot, hazed in the blue darkness of dawn.

To her left, through the square entrance at the end of the hall, the rising sun lit the street in sharp, angular light. Men, women, and children, couples, families, were running, stumbling, racing away from the city center. Some had suitcases or bags or arms loaded with valuables. Others ran with just the clothes on their backs and the hands of their children in their grip. Their shadows stretched long ahead of them, tugging them forward, urging them to run faster.

Gunfire sounded in the distance, a rapid rat-tat. But there was no answer, just the one report. It wasn't a gunfight.

And if the soldiers weren't shooting at someone who could shoot back, what were they shooting at?

Lex heard a deep, rasping rumble. A troop transport truck, a camo-painted pickup with a large-caliber machine gun mounted in the bed and a dozen soldiers piled around it, sped down the center of the street, no concern for the people around it.

It was quickly followed by the source of the rumble, a large truck that looked like a shipping container on wheels. Had to be Soviet. No one designed ugly better than the Soviets.

Painted light tan, stained with flares of carbon and pocked with bullet holes, the truck lumbered past. Lex watched a soldier drag a beautiful young woman by the back of her neck. She clawed at his hands and wrists. He threw her in the back of the truck before clambering in after her.

Instinctively, Lex started down the hall after them.

Baba grabbed her arm.

"Are you fucking—"

"Lex, no," Baba said. "We have to get to the car."

"No, we have to—" She pointed toward the street. "Did you see what—"

"The car, Lex," Baba said quietly, patiently, pointedly.

Lex looked past him down the other end of the hallway, through which she could see the parking lot, could see others fleeing in their cars. She recognized Okot, directing a few others before jumping into an old Mercedes with Aamira behind the wheel and driving off. Behind the

Mercedes, Baba's blue Hyundai waited innocently for them.

Lex's guns and money were still in her bag in the trunk. If she was going to do anything at all, she needed that bag.

She cast one look back over her shoulder at the street, then nodded and ran with Baba to the car.

30

BABA LED them through narrow dirt streets and hard-packed alleys, back roads to the back roads, leading them away from the city, away from the main road, away from the fleeing citizens.

"What help can we provide?" said Baba when Lex protested. He shook his head. "We must avoid the soldiers or we will be no help to anyone. These roads are too small for their trucks and their artillery."

"But this way takes us north," said Lex. "I thought we needed to go west."

At an intersection of two alleys, Baba stopped for a man, a woman, and two children in a tiny, rusted hatchback. The man raised his hand in thanks as Baba let them pass. Baba returned the gesture. The faces of both men were solemn, furrowed in determination, but Lex could see fear behind the other man's eyes.

Panic was plain on the face of the woman in the passenger seat and the older child, a girl of perhaps thirteen, behind her in the back seat. A small boy was asleep next to her, his face squashed against the windowpane, oblivious to all but the early hour and his interrupted slumber. Lex could see his teeth and his gums where his lip had been pulled back by the slide of his head against the window, a lifeless half-rictus behind the glass.

When they had passed through the intersection, Baba gunned the car forward.

"We can go north through Mazrub to Sodiri," he said, "and from there, we go west to Al Fashir."

"Sounds like the long way around."

"It will avoid the soldiers," Baba said, his words sharp. After a moment, he sighed and said, more quietly, "It should avoid the soldiers."

"Well?" asked Lex. "Will it or should it?"

"I don't have a map of current military movements in my mind, little wolf."

Baba hunched forward over the steering wheel, nosing the car out of every intersection, peering ahead and down the cross streets before driving forward.

"How much time will it add?"

Baba sighed. "If we see no soldiers, maybe three days."

"Three days!"

"If we see no soldiers," Baba nodded. "And if the roads are clear."

Three fucking days? Lex crossed her arms and huffed in the passenger seat. It was already going to take a week to get to wherever these hostages were supposedly being held. Now it would be three more days. She was never going to be done with this fucking job. And if the hostages really had been alive four days earlier, each extra day made it more likely they would be beaten or dead. Or worse.

Baba's last sentence finally penetrated the cloud of annoyance and registered in Lex's brain. "Why wouldn't the roads be clear?" she said. "There's no fighting north of here, is there?" She scoffed. "There's nothing to fight over. It's all just desert."

"The people who live there might disagree," Baba muttered.

Lex opened her mouth to retort, then closed it again. "Fine," she said, "but why wouldn't the roads be clear?"

Baba sighed, a heavy, frustrated sigh. "Rain."

"It's a desert."

"You are smarter than that," said Baba. "Deserts have rain." He inched into an intersection, then gunned the engine across. "A few years ago, Sodiri flooded during the rainy season. Hundreds killed, thousands of homes destroyed. And many of the roads washed away, as some do every year."

"When's the rainy season?"

Baba frowned and shook his head in irritation. Lex felt her cheeks burn. She had come into a foreign country in the middle of a civil war without even the most basic information, like an understanding of their seasonal weather patterns. She was being a stupid Westerner, but at least she knew it.

"It just ended," Baba said, "perhaps a week ago. That's why the fighting has resumed."

But the RSF trucks and the soldiers in El Obeid had been moving west. If the fighting was back on, they should have been moving east toward Khartoum and Port Sudan, the industrial and commercial centers of the country, where the political and economic power resided.

They were retreating.

"Is that why the soldiers were moving? Was there an attack?"

Baba came to an intersection with a larger dirt road. He looked for a long time to his left, rolled down the window, listening, then finally eased onto the road, turning right. He left the window rolled down.

"They say one of the generals in the East, in El Gezira, changed sides," he said

"From who to who?"

"From RSF to SAF."

"Why would he do that?"

"Why else?" said Baba. "Money."

"And that caused all of this fighting?"

"It's a boon for the SAF to gain his support. RSF supply lines that were once secure are now cut off. Troops that were once allies are now enemies. And then there is the political support, and the boost to morale for the SAF soldiers."

"Yeah," said Lex, "but who's to say he won't switch sides again if he gets a bigger paycheck?"

"He almost certainly will," said Baba. "This is the business of war."

His expression grew hard, harder than Lex had yet seen. For the first time, she saw on Baba the face of a fighter.

"But you ask the wrong question, little wolf. The question isn't whether or not this general will switch sides again." He looked at Lex. "The question is, who is signing the paychecks?"

Within thirty minutes, they had cleared El Obeid. After that, they drove for hours in silence through sun-blistered hills and sand. The occasional farmstead they passed was always empty, as they had been when they'd left Khartoum the day before. It was like driving through a hot, reddish-brown Mars-scape.

The sun glared through Lex's window. She rolled it down soon after they left the city, feeling the cool morning breeze against her cheek as it blew in her window and out Baba's.

But by mid-morning, the cool air had become a furnace. The hard-packed dirt road grew narrower as the land around them grew flatter and more sparse, from two wide lanes to two smaller lanes, then down to one lane.

They pulled over at one point to allow someone to pass in an old truck heading south. Baba flagged the driver down and spoke briefly with him. Lex watched in her side-view mirror as the driver carefully turned his truck around and followed them north again.

By the time they passed through Mazrub, the sun was high overhead. Baba stopped to negotiate the purchase of two small cans of gasoline from a farmer outside of town. Lex paid what seemed a pittance from her cache of Sudanese pounds, but the farmer looked like he'd scored the deal of a lifetime.

Two hours later, at Sodiri, Baba turned west. He poured both cans of gas into his tank and tried to negotiate with a man driving by in a rattling old truck to sell him a refill. Even with an offer four times higher than what they'd paid in Mazrub, the man would only part with one can's worth of fuel.

"The soldiers have taken most of the fuel for their trucks and their vehicles," Baba explained once they were on the road again. "These small towns get very little of what's left over. They need the fuel more than they need the money."

The single-lane dirt road became rougher. Lex's teeth chattered over the washboard surface. Even crawling along at less than forty kilometers per hour, Baba's tires occasionally slipped and skidded on the rock-strewn dirt.

Soon, the road became rutted with deep twin tracks set wider than Baba's wheelbase. He was constantly weaving the little Hyundai back and forth, bouncing through the ruts and trying as best he could to keep his tires on flat ground.

The oranges and reds had left the sky when they approached Umm Badr, leaving only blues behind to wither into night. Baba pulled off the road into a flat clearing, hiked back to a house they'd just passed, and returned with a small pot filled with mullah stew and a stack of folded kisra bread wrapped in a towel. They used the bread to eat the stew, wiped the stew off the sides of the pot with it, then scarfed down what bread remained. It was the first thing either of them had eaten all day.

Baba returned the pot to the house and came back to the car with two small plastic bottles filled with water.

"The sweet old nini there insisted we take this water with us," Baba said as he opened the glove box and stuffed the water bottles inside. "Boiled lake water. Should be safe to drink." He shut the glove box with a click. "She wanted to give us a place to sleep, but I told her we had to move on."

"Do we?"

"No, not tonight," he said. "But a white woman traveling here will attract attention."

"We'll be gone before anyone could do anything to us."

"Yes," said Baba, "but the nini won't."

Lex got out of the car and stood to stretch her legs, turning in a slow circle as she did. They were on a small rise above the town. Below, Umm Badr was pitch dark. The locals used gas generators for electricity, but none seemed to be running.

The only light came from the moon. It silvered the water in the lake in the distance on the far side of town. Lex could just make out the dark form of the river dam. The lake was high. It must have been filled by the rains.

Lex followed the silver light up into the sky. The moon was a crescent just shy of half-full. Lex didn't remember if it was waxing or waning. Waning, she thought. It had been full last week, hadn't it, when she'd been in Khartoum?

She couldn't remember, and she didn't care. It didn't matter. That was one good thing about being on a job. Nothing mattered but what was in front of you. Nothing mattered but the job, getting it done and getting paid. What mattered was the moon above her head, not the one in her memories.

And the moon above her was stunning, bright white in a dappled darkness. With no ambient light anywhere around her, the stars covered the sky like snowflakes in a blizzard suspended in time. Lex shivered at the thought, even though the air was still warm, its heat not yet stolen by the desert night.

"Are you cold?" asked Baba, suddenly beside her.

"No," said Lex.

"We can sit on the hood of the car," he said. "The engine will still be warm."

"I said I'm not cold."

"Well, maybe I am." Baba's smile gleamed in the moon-light. "Besides, it's a nice place to sit and watch the sky."

And it was. They sat side-by-side, their backs and heads resting against the windshield, looking up at the stars. The hood had cooled to near body temperature, neither warm nor cool to the touch, but as comforting as the embrace of a friend.

They lay in silence, letting the stars and the silence and

the darkness dissolve them. For a moment, Lex felt like she was floating in space, surrounded by starlight.

"I often come out at night." Rather than ruining Lex's trance and pulling her back down to earth, Baba's voice wrapped around her like the tail of a shooting star. "When it's quiet and peaceful like this."

"Is it dark like this where you live? At night?"

"Yes," Baba said, "though I'm often traveling and cannot enjoy it. This is a special treat."

Being driven days off course by a fleeing army during a civil war didn't seem like much of a treat to Lex, but she admired Baba's ability to find something positive to focus on. That was not a skill Lex possessed.

Yet, even she had to admit that the experience was special. The wide sky filled with stars, the utter darkness all around them, the peaceful, soundless night, and the air still warm from the day. She'd never experienced anything like it before. She supposed she would quickly take it for granted if she saw it every night, but in that moment, it was new enough, unique enough, to pull her away from her thoughts, her concerns. To pull her away from herself.

The war probably had something to do with that. Such craven narcissism, such senseless violence, such ephemeral human gain juxtaposed against such vast, sublime, and eternal beauty. Lex was no poet, about as far from it as you could get, but she was struck in that moment with the poetic dissonance of her day. It ended under a soft blanket of natural beauty, but it had begun with the harsh cut of man-made suffering.

She thought about the woman thrown into the back of the truck, followed eagerly by the soldier that had dragged her by the back of her neck. Lex knew what he was doing to her in there, probably egged on and even joined by his comrades in the truck with him. She could feel the woman's fear, feel her desperation, feel her powerless shock. She could smell the man, could taste his sweat like gritty motor oil on her tongue. Would the woman try to scream? Would anyone hear? If they did, would they care? Would they stop to help, or would they run by to save themselves? Would any of it even matter, the screaming, the stopping, the running by?

"Something is wrong."

Baba said it quietly, kindly.

"What?" replied Lex, pulling herself from her thoughts. "What's wrong?"

"You tell me."

His face was a shadow, the moon behind him. Lex looked up at the stars again, at the infinite nothing above her. She shook her head, ready to dismiss him, to say nothing was wrong. But the words caught, choked by a swelling in her throat, a hot stain of sudden tears against the top of her cheeks.

"What isn't wrong?" she said, her voice strangled.

Baba took her hand in his. She thought about pulling away, but his touch was so soft, so warm, so soothing. So unthreatening. It was a touch of empathy, the touch of a friend.

Not a predator.

Lex swallowed hard. "The woman," she said, her voice low and quiet. "In town. Did you see her? The one the soldier dragged into the truck?"

"No," said Baba, "but I have seen it before."

Lex nodded, her lips pressed tight together.

"Have you ever done it?"

Baba didn't protest. He didn't take offense or object to the question. He simply paused, then said, "No."

Lex believed him. She shouldn't have, but she did. Men were liars, cowards, and selfish pricks, and Baba was a man. She shouldn't let herself be lured into thinking he was any different from all the others.

But Lex knew he was. Baba was different. She didn't know exactly how or exactly why, but she knew in her gut that he wasn't like most men.

He wasn't like Nick.

He wasn't like Skinner.

"But you," Baba said, "have had it done to you."

It wasn't a question. It didn't need to be. One way that Baba was different? He paid attention. He observed, and he understood what he saw.

Lex took her hand back from his, worked it in her other hand against her stomach. She stared up into the star-littered abyss, opening her eyes wide to dry the tears that were trying to come. She would shed no more tears for what had happened to her. She'd shed too many fucking tears already.

"My husband didn't believe me," she said, her voice a husked whisper.

Baba was silent.

"He kept asking me if I was sure."

Lex laughed, a single, bitter bark. Acid bile burned and soured the back of her tongue.

"As if I wouldn't know if I'd been—"

She bit back the word, swallowed the bile, let out a long breath.

"'Are you sure he didn't misunderstand?' he said to me. 'Are you sure you didn't lead him on somehow?' Lead him on. As if it was my fucking fault."

She shook her head, feeling again the incredulous anger she'd felt so many times. Every day since that night.

"My husband cared more about his career than his wife," she said. "He was too afraid to come forward and accuse his boss. Too afraid he might lose his promotion. Too afraid he might become a pariah, get kicked out of the boys' club. It's not that he didn't believe me, he said. He just needed proof. Solid, incontrovertible proof." Lex balled her hands into fists. "I was his wife. I gave him my word. What more fucking proof did he need?"

Baba lay silently beside her.

"Can you even understand how it feels? Can any man understand how it feels to have no control, no say, no way to resist what is being done to you? To your body? To your—"

Her chest hitched. She squeezed her fists hard, hard enough to fight back her emotions, to fight down her weakness. No more fucking tears. Not for that asshole.

Lex's blood pulsed in her ears, her head throbbing with each beat of her heart. She stared up into the night again, stared up at the cold, white moon. Instead of a beauty that dissolved her, she saw only an impassive observer, watching the cruelty of humanity and doing nothing to stop it.

Quietly, after a long while, Baba said, "I do have some experience with this."

Lex frowned up at the sky, but said nothing.

"Not exactly, of course," Baba continued, "but I do know what it feels to be powerless."

Lex released a long sigh through her nose. Baba was a good man. She was sure he was only trying to be sympathetic. But Lex knew he was about to give her another typical male false equivalency. Some story about how he'd been passed over for a job or someone had told him he couldn't have what he wanted. Some experience that was nothing like what Lex and a million other women had experienced, what millions of women experienced every day, what that woman in the truck was trying to deal with that very moment, trying to put the shattered pieces of her mind, her heart, her body, her life back together. Trying and probably failing.

But Lex stayed silent. She stayed where she was, prepared to endure, lying there looking up at the asshole moon doing nothing.

"When I was a boy," Baba said, "in Nigeria, my family went to visit my uncle in Maiduguri for the holidays. My uncle and his wife and daughter were in the church choir, and they asked my parents and me to sing with them at midnight mass on Christmas Eve, so we were in the church late that evening. I was only nine years old at the time. I remember being very tired, but excited to be up so late, and excited by the joy I felt in the people around me in the choir. Christmas was always my favorite time of year, back then."

Lex could hear the smile in his voice. Her frown eased.

"We heard the doors bang open in the back of the church. It was a windy night. I thought maybe someone had not shut them all the way and the wind had blown them open. Instead, a group of men in black face masks came in, holding machine guns. They fired from the back of the church into the choir up on the altar. No warning. No statement. They just started shooting at us."

Baba delivered this information with a flat, detached voice, as if he were reading an uneventful weather forecast. Lex kept quiet, kept still, kept looking up at the night sky, every one of her muscles tense.

"Some of the choir escaped through the side doors, went to find help. Many others were wounded. I still have a scar on my arm from where a bullet grazed me."

He paused for a long moment, then continued.

"Six people were killed, including the pastor and my uncle. And both of my parents."

Jesus. Lex knew what it was like to lose both parents at once. It was fucking awful. But hers were killed in a helicopter crash in war time, shot down by the Taliban in the mountains in Afghanistan. Her parents knew the risks, and so did Lex. Didn't make it any less painful, but at least it wasn't completely random. They were doing their duty. Baba's parents were just celebrating Christmas in a fucking church.

"And while people were lying there weeping, bleeding, dying, the men in the masks came up onto the altar and stepped through the bodies. One man who was already injured tried to stand up to fight them. They shot him dead."

Lex braced herself. "Did they rape the women?"

"Mercifully, no," said Baba. "Not to my knowledge, at least."

Lex relaxed, letting out the breath she'd been holding.

"But they took the young boys," Baba said. "They took the three of us that were still alive and relatively unharmed. They took us into the wilderness, to their camp, and raised us to be like them. If we tried to escape, they would beat us and withhold our food and water, or make us sleep outside in the cold and the rain.

"Once we had been trained to use weapons, if we refused to fight or to kill for them, they would do the same. This continued until we grew older and either learned our lessons," Baba sighed, "or died in the process."

Lex reeled. For a moment, she didn't know if she was lying down looking up at the sky or falling into it. She opened her mouth, but had no idea what to say.

"So, you see, while it isn't at all the same as what you have endured," Baba continued in that same flat, dispassionate voice, "I do know what it feels like to be powerless."

He said nothing more after that. Lex tried in silence to piece together what she'd heard, tried to fathom what it must have been like for Baba. It took her a long time, and still she couldn't come close.

"How did you ever recover from that?" she finally managed to whisper. She wasn't sure if she was saying it to Baba or just to herself.

Either way, Baba heard her. "I finally noticed my own power," he said. "Unwittingly, through their training, my captors were pushing it upon me, forcing me to take it. In their name, of course."

He rubbed one arm absent-mindedly, folded his arms across his chest.

"I played my part. I did as I was told. I acted like a loyal soldier, and I was commended. Rewarded. I rose in the ranks. But most importantly, I stayed alive."

Lex felt a pit open in her stomach. She knew of only one Nigerian organization that would do such a thing. Boko Haram, the group that had kidnapped hundreds of schoolgirls a decade ago. He said he rose in the ranks. Could Baba have been a part of that?

"Are you still a member of this group?" she asked, steeling herself for the answer.

"No," he said, and Lex's stomach eased, but only a little. "I finally took the power I had all along and used it to free myself."

"How did you do that?"

"One by one," he said, "I killed the men who killed my parents. And then I left."

"And you came here? To the Sudan?"

"I found a place where I thought I might be able to do some good." For the first time since he'd started telling his story, Lex heard emotion creep into Baba's voice. "It's what my parents would have wanted me to do."

They lay in silence for a long time after that, staring up at the sky. After a while, Lex reached over, took Baba's hand in her own, and held it.

31

Lex slept rough that night. She and Baba fell asleep beside each other in the moonlight on the hood of the car. When the temperature dropped too low, they moved inside the car and slept on the front seats, reclined. Comfortable enough when you're in the dead of sleep, staggering and cold and looking for anywhere to lay your head, but Lex was aching and still tired when the sun glared through the windshield and made more sleep impossible.

She opened her eyes to see Baba across from her, turned on his side, his shoulder jammed into the shallow slant of the seat back and his torso contorted at an unsupported angle that made Lex's back twinge. His eyes were squeezed shut, still fighting the sun.

She watched him sleep. How could anyone have gone through what he did and still function in normal society? He should be a total sociopath by now, not a pleasant, well-mannered man who dances in underground speakeasies and debates science and politics with his friends.

Baba took the power he had all along. That's what he'd said the night before, that the training Boko Haram had forced on him actually helped him to recognize his own power. And then he finally decided to use it for himself.

That's how he did it. That's how he survived without losing his humanity.

Is that what Lex had done? Is that why she'd learned to fight, why she put herself in the ring with men who had ten inches and a hundred-fifty pounds on her? So she could use her power?

Or was she still trying to find it?

"Good morning," said Baba, fluttering his eyes open and squinting in the sunlight. "Did you sleep as badly as I did?"

"Worse."

"That cannot be possible." Baba groaned as he sat up. "These cars were not designed for sleeping."

They both got out of the car and stretched. Lex's vertebrae popped like firecrackers as she twisted her torso first one way, then the other. That relieved the pain in her lower back, but her upper back felt like someone had wedged a cattle prod between her shoulder blades and left it on fry. She pulled her arms forward, bent over, twisted around, trying in vain to get the ache to stop. Nothing helped.

Baba came over and massaged her back for her, quickly finding the points of tension. His hands were large and his fingers strong. Lex moaned, half in pain, half in relief. She felt the heat of Baba's touch through her dress and her camisole. It helped to loosen her bunched and blocked muscles.

She wondered again what those hands and that heat might feel like elsewhere on her body.

It turned out that the small town Lex had seen from the bluff the night before was just one part of Umm Badr. The lake was dammed on this end, the north end. But there was another, larger development on the west side of the lake.

Where the north side was small and compact, with the homes set close to each other, the west side sprawled down the length of the reservoir. There were at least three times as many homes as there were to the north, and even a hospital. It was far from a bustling metropolis, but it was much more than the tiny outpost Lex had envisioned the prior night.

Baba stopped to refill his gas tank and secure four more cans of fuel from three different places. They found a vendor selling fenugreek porridge and ate their fill. Lex would have liked something more substantial than the sweet custardy dish, something with meat or beans, some kind of protein to sustain them, but the fenugreek was the only food they saw.

And so they drove, the greenish-brown lake waters on their left slowly fading to brown mud, then to light brown dirt and sand. They drove for hours, the air so hot and the land so yellow that Lex thought for sure they were driving across the surface of the sun itself. The light brown dirt and sand persisted for the duration of their trip, as far as Lex could see. They were driving through an ocean of dirt and sand, with nothing but the stifling, breezeless air and the jouncing knock of the car's shock absorbers against the rutted roadway to accompany them.

With the roads as rough as they were, progress was much slower than the previous day. Baba was forced to drive slowly, weaving back and forth, often driving on the side of the road with one tire elevated on a ridge or a dune to avoid the ruts.

But at least the car was running well. Lex could see shimmers of heat radiating from the hood, but the engine never stuttered, never faltered, never whined. As long as they could keep gas in the tank, the little robin's egg blue Hyundai seemed like it could run forever.

Which was more than Lex could say for herself. The tension of the morning and the persistent gnaw of her thoughts had kept her mind off of her hunger the day before. That, plus the massive meal and the even more massive hangover the party had given her.

But today, the fenugreek porridge did not last. Within a couple of hours, her stomach was growling and groaning like there was a gremlin under the passenger seat. Lex did her best to ignore it, but there wasn't much around to occupy her mind.

Other than Baba.

"Was it Boko Haram?" she asked, breaking the long, monotonous silence as much for the distraction as for the information.

Baba looked at her, startled from his own thoughts, then looked back at the road.

"Yes," he said.

"And the schoolgirls?" What was the name of the town they'd been stolen from? "From Shibuk?"

Baba pressed his lips together.

"Chibok," he said. "They were from Chibok.

He said nothing more. They jounced along in silence.

"Were you involved in that?" asked Lex.

Baba sighed.

"I was a young boy," he said. "I was only thirteen when the girls were abducted."

"So you were involved."

"I did as I was told."

Lex tried to imagine what it must have been like for Baba. Witnessing the murder of his father and his uncle, being stolen from his wounded mother, then forced to live a life of brutality, violence, and religious extremism that ran counter to everything he'd been raised to believe was right. They must have brainwashed him, Clockwork Orange-style.

Again, she could not believe he was sitting beside her now, re-integrated into a normal life. It defied belief. When he first approached her in Khartoum—only two days ago, though it felt like forever—she had gone along with him out of necessity and desperation. Over that first day in the car and at the party, against her better instincts, she had grown to like him. But now, after learning what he'd endured, what he'd overcome in his life, now she admired him.

The wind had picked up outside. Both front windows were down to try to cut the heat in the car, but Baba rolled his window up to keep the sand from blowing in. He rolled the back window behind Lex open to compensate.

Lex let her mind drift like the sweeping sands as they drove through the featureless landscape. The sun rose high overhead. Even with two windows down, the car felt like an oven. She was still dressed in her thobe and her long-sleeved tunic dress. She'd worn it two days ago. She'd worn it again yesterday, then she'd slept in it. Now, she was sweating in it. She felt like she'd been sweating for two weeks straight. She needed a shower and a change of clothes. She was choking on her own reek.

Enough was enough. They were out here in the middle of nowhere. They hadn't seen another human being since Umm Badr hours ago. There was very little risk of Lex being caught improperly dressed, so why should she endure it any longer?

She squirmed in the passenger seat, pulled off her thobe and pulled her dress over her head, balled them both, threw them in the back seat, and sat in her crop cami and her panties, holding her gun in her lap, finally getting some relief. She could feel the hot wind on her bare arms and thighs. It was hot, but it was wind. Dry wind, at that, sipping the sweat from her skin. Lex closed her eyes, flopped her head against the headrest, and sighed with relief.

Baba, when he saw what she was doing, had protested as she undressed. He appealed first to her respect for local custom, then to her need to stay hidden, and finally to her sense of basic propriety. His pleas didn't fall on deaf ears. Lex just didn't give a shit.

Once she'd finished undressing and he saw that she was perfectly content to sit in her underwear for the duration of the trip, Baba pulled over so Lex could get a pair of jeans and sneakers—aside from a grey t-shirt, the only familiar clothes she'd brought—from her bag in the trunk.

Jeans were not the coolest thing she could have worn, but they were comfortable. They were a little looser around the waist than usual, almost loose enough to fall off on their own. She must have lost weight in Khartoum. But with the denim worn soft and broken-in to fit her shape and her movements, she felt like herself for the first time since she'd arrived in country. That was worth a little extra heat. And it was nowhere near the sweatbox her dress and thobe had been.

Besides, if she got too hot in the jeans, she could easily strip them off again for a little while. Baba had endured a lot worse, and Lex got a kick out of watching him struggle to avoid looking at her half-naked body.

Truth be told, she wished he'd struggle a little less. Lex hadn't had sex in weeks, and she was getting even crankier than usual. Whoever said women had no sex drive was clearly a man who sucked in bed. Lex liked sex, she wanted sex, she needed sex, and she wasn't about to apologize to anyone for it. And with every passing day, Baba looked better and better.

Her stomach growled. Lex didn't know which need was more pressing, her hunger for food or her hunger for sex. She looked at Baba and imagined him as a side of beef, figuratively and literally. She could fuck him, then roast him and eat him for dinner. She laughed and shook her head as she turned her face toward the window, toward the hot breeze. The heat and the hunger and the horniness were clearly making her crazy.

They spent another night under the stars, this time literally in the middle of nowhere, parked behind a tall sand dune beside the road, their car mostly hidden from any traffic that might drive by in the night. As if that was likely. Still, better safe than sorry.

When they'd taken their places on the hood of the car, Baba brought a parcel wrapped in a towel from under the front seat. Inside was a stack of kisra bread and four round falafel cakes.

"A little extra from the nini back in Umm Badr," he said with a grin.

"You were holding out on me," said Lex as she took her portion of the food and tore into it. She didn't like that Baba had kept the food secret. There were several times during the day when a nibble of kisra or a bite of falafel would have been a lifesaver. But Lex had survived, and rationing the food was probably a smart thing to do.

Both the bread and the falafel were a day old, and they tasted like it, dry and a little stale. But Lex's stomach didn't care, and her taste buds could go fuck themselves. Food was food, and Lex was ravenous.

They sipped the water from the glove box while they ate, helping to soften the bread and falafel and wash them down more easily. After they were finished, they lay looking up at the stars as they had the night before. With a full belly and comfortable clothes, for the first time in God knew how long Lex felt content, peaceful. Almost happy, even. She could see how someone could get used to the space out here, the quiet, the stars. A simpler life. A human life.

Except for the inhuman atrocities being committed just a few dozen miles away. Lex couldn't hear them or see them, but she knew they were happening. And who could enjoy a quiet life knowing others were being raped and murdered nearby?

Bile crept up the back of her throat. She choked it back down and sat up straighter, leaning forward off the windshield.

"How did you take your power?" she asked Baba over her shoulder.

"What do you mean?"

"You said you took your power and freed yourself. From Boko Haram."

"Yes."

"How did you do it?"

"It was during a night raid on a small village near Kiyawa. We were looking for supplies, money, valuables we could sell. The village was better defended than we expected, and a firefight broke out. During the commotion, I snuck away through the forests, hoping the others would assume I was—"

"No, not how did you get away. How did you take your power in the first place? How did you even know you had it?"

Baba didn't say anything for a moment, but Lex could see his face, staring up at the night. The furrows in his forehead formed stark lines in the moonlight.

"Is there ever a time," he said, "when we don't know the power we have, really? You know it right now, don't you? Can't you feel it inside you?" He chuckled softly. "You are a wolf. Of course you can."

Lex wasn't as confident about what she felt as Baba seemed to be. She could kick anyone's ass, sure, but the power Baba was talking about seemed deeper, stronger.

Fortunately, Baba didn't wait for a confirmation from Lex.

"We hide our power from ourselves," he said. "We let others pressure us to do things we don't want to do, things we may even believe are wrong. This helps us to make friends and work within our society, but it requires us to ignore our power. Every decision that runs counter to our power trains us to ignore it."

"Well, you can't just go around doing what you want all the time."

"Why not?"

"Then you'd be a selfish asshole, stomping on everyone else just to get your way. If the whole world worked like that, it would be even more miserable than it already is."

"That's how the world works now," said Baba. "It's just that most people give their power away. They let those who don't, those who are bold enough to use their own power... how did you say it? Stomp all over them?"

"So everyone should just be an asshole?"

"You don't think our power can be used to help others? That people would honestly choose to use it that way?"

Lex had never really thought of that before. If everyone did use their power, would the world really be a selfish, dog-eat-dog place? Or would there be more people willing to help others than there were people who would step on their neighbor's head just to reach their own front door? She'd always assumed the latter, but what if she was wrong?

"It doesn't matter," Baba said. "We're trained early on that to use our power is to be selfish, as you said. We're taught that honoring ourselves is wrong. And yet, that means that to dishonor ourselves is right. How could that possibly be true? It makes no sense.

"But we don't think like that. We don't ask those questions. We go along with the world, dishonoring ourselves, hiding our power, ignoring it, giving it away so that we can get along with others. So we can have our jobs and our friends and our possessions. So we can feel like we belong.

"If we used our power, we would risk all of those things. Or so we believe. So we fear. And that is a cost greater than most people wish to pay."

"So you gave up all of your friends and your possessions to take your power back?"

"I had no possessions," said Baba softly. "And the only people I cared about had already been taken from me."

"So you had nothing to lose."

Baba looked up at the moon, then slid his gaze to Lex. "The power never goes away," he said. "It's always there, waiting for the moment when we're brave enough or desperate enough to finally use it."

"Which was it for you, bravery or desperation?"

"One often leads to the other."

Lex didn't feel desperate. She'd escaped. She'd leveled up. If anyone tried now what Skinner had done, Lex would hand them their teeth in a Ziploc baggie. Skinner found that out when he tried to come after her a second time. Lex had learned how to defend herself.

She thought back to the meeting in Skinner's office in Vicenza a few weeks ago. Alone with him again for the first time in years, with his greedy eyes on her body, she'd felt like she was right back in his office that night. Handing her a drink, inviting her to sit, then pushing her against the couch, pinning her down, her long hair in his fist, his fist on her back, the leather cushion cold and close and suffocating over her nose and mouth.

"I didn't even try to fight," she murmured.

"Most people don't," Baba replied. "They've been taught to be afraid."

Lex frowned. "I'm not afraid of a fight."

She looked hard at Baba, challenge in her voice.

Baba met her gaze and held it, unsmiling. The moonlight shimmered in his eyes, but his face was hard and deadly serious.

"No," he said. "I wouldn't think so."

Lex watched him for a long moment. Why did she even care whether this man believed her or not?

She lay flat against the windshield again.

"Not now, anyway," said Baba. "But were you afraid then? And have you forgiven yourself for it?"

Lex didn't respond. She folded her arms over her chest.

They said nothing more, just looked silently up at the stars.

Long after Lex heard Baba's breathing slow and settle, she lay awake in the encroaching cold, glaring at the cruel moon.

32

LEX WAS EVEN MORE sore and tired when she woke than she had been the morning before. The sun was already up, the air inside the car still, stale, and already baking hot.

Outside Lex's window, the landscape seemed flat and dull and washed out in the harsh glare. Or maybe her eyes had been burned to senselessness by staring at the dirt and sand for too long. The sun was already well over the horizon. How late had she slept?

Baba was already awake, standing atop the sand dune beside the car. They didn't say a word to each other. Lex got out and stretched, then they both got back in the car and went on their way.

Lex was still stewing over what Baba had said the night before. It's true that she was raised in a society that taught people to tamp down their power, to subjugate themselves. Hell, that was practically the definition of the U.S. Armed Forces.

But in the Army, it was always a voluntary subjugation. Soldiers learned to follow orders because that's what kept everyone alive during battle. Hesitating to debate the merits of an order would earn you a bullet in the brain or a mortar fragment in the gut.

The little Hyundai jounced over the ruts in the road like it had done all day the day before. Baba weaved the car, trying and failing to find a smooth path.

But if an order came down that was clearly wrong, clearly unethical or immoral, soldiers had the right to refuse to follow it. The military never took that power away. Soldiers chose to give their power to their commanding officers, to loan it to them. For the greater good. Always to serve a greater good.

But how many times did a case come up when a soldier would refuse to follow an order? Not very often. And where was the line? Sure, killing an innocent person, a fellow soldier or an innocent bystander, these seemed like clear red lines. But those red lines had been crossed before, in Iraq or Afghanistan or any other war fought by any army in history. The U.S. military was the finest in the world, but it had even happened there. How much more did it happen in other militaries?

The bottoms of the ruts in the road changed from light brown to dark. Soon after, the whole rut was dark, then the entire road. Baba slowed even more, weaved onto the side of the road to drive around the deepest chasms.

Lex could not deny that she had learned, from her parents, from society, from the military, to tamp down her own desires, her own power, and to do what she was told. To follow orders.

And she'd learned that lesson very well, always trusting her superior officers to be honorable men and women, honorable soldiers seeking that greater good.

Until the day her trust was shattered.

The car's jouncing softened, leaving tire tracks dented

into the peaks of the ruts they weaved around. The dark dirt in the valleys shone in the sunlight. Small puddles began to appear in the deepest grooves.

Baba slowed even more, driving no more than twenty miles an hour. The dark dirt became mud, the tires picking up wet clods. When the clods rolled underneath, Lex could feel the car lurch up, then down again, like a person walking with only one shoe. When the clods came loose, they banged against the fender liner with a thunk and a rocky clatter.

Baba slowed the car to a stop, then shifted into park. "The roads are getting worse," he said.

"I can see that."

"We may need to turn back."

"Turn back?" Lex didn't recall seeing any turnoffs since they'd left Umm Badr. Hell, she hadn't seen any since Sodiri. "How far back?"

Baba didn't respond, just muttered to himself.

"How far back, Baba?"

"To Sodiri," he said.

"And then to El Obeid?" said Lex. "No. Fuck that. We've already wasted two days on this detour. We're not turning back now."

"If the roads are impassable, we'll have no choice."

"The roads aren't impassable yet, Baba." Lex huffed in frustration. At ten million for this job, Lex was starting to feel underpaid. "Are there any turnoffs up ahead?"

Baba weaved around another muddy rut, his front tire slipping briefly before it caught dry dirt and the car lurched to the side.

"There should be a turnoff up ahead that connects to the El Ingaz road between Umm Kaddadah and Kureit," he said.

"Fine, we'll take that."

"But I don't know how far it is, or whether we can make it there. And even if we do, there's no guarantee the turnoff is even passable. It could be washed out, too."

Lex had had enough. Enough of this fucking car, enough of this road, enough of Baba and this job and this whole fucking country. At this point, she was tempted to fire up the satellite phone, call for a pickup, and just get the hell out of there and abort the whole mission.

Then she remembered there would be no pickup. The sat phone would register her location. If it was within the borders of the Sudan, the call would go unanswered. Pickup denied.

"I am not going backward," said Lex. Baba wanted to lecture her about using her power? She was using it now. "The roads are still passable. Until they aren't, until there's no way we can go forward or around, we are not going back. Got it?"

Baba stared hard at her, his lips pressed tight together, then looked down the road ahead for a long moment.

"Fine," he said, shifting the car into gear. "As you wish."

As I fucking wish. Lex liked the sound of that.

Two hours later, Lex wished she could go back in time and choose differently.

They'd driven carefully over ruts that were getting muddier but were still passable, making slow but steady forward progress. Lex was feeling good about their chances of making it to the turnoff.

And then they'd topped a small rise and found themselves sliding down a steep hill into a massive wadi, a huge gash of mud and debris that sliced across the landscape. It must have been flooded not that long ago, the waters reaching all the way to the top of the rise before receding, leaving the roadway slick as glass.

Baba tried to stop, tried to steer, tried to maneuver them onto drier ground, but the Hyundai slid inexorably to the bottom of the wadi, jamming nose-first into the two feet of soft mud that filled the ravine. The right headlight was buried. Baba gunned the engine forward, then in reverse. Both resulted in the same spinning screech of the tires in the mud, with no movement whatsoever.

The car listed to the right. Lex couldn't open her door more than a crack. She had to climb out the window.

They tried throwing sand under the tires, but they were already dug in too deep. They tried finding sticks or logs to jam under the wheels for traction, but found nothing but dirt and desiccated scrub in the barren landscape. A mountain rose above them in the distance, looming and leering and laughing at their plight. There would probably be sticks up there, Lex thought.

"Jabal Teljo," said Baba bitterly. "Six thousand feet. Probably where all the flooding came from."

For another hour, they revved and rocked and pulled and pushed, Lex stripped off her jeans and shoes—this time, Baba didn't bother to protest—and stood up to her knees in the mud in front of the car, sweat streaming down her body under the hot sun, trying to push it free while Baba worked the wheel and the gas. Then they switched places and tried again. The only thing they succeeded in doing was making themselves tired, hot, muddy, and angry.

"Now what?" said Lex.

"You're the one making all the decisions," said Baba. "You tell me."

It was the first time Lex had seen Baba be anything but polite and patient. She liked it. He was acting like a fucking baby, but it made him more human.

"Don't be a dick," said Lex. "We made a decision—"

"You made a decision."

"Fine, *I* made a decision, and *you* decided to go along with it. And it didn't work out. That's done."

Baba shook his head and kicked a rock into the wadi.

Lex softened her tone. She was just as pissed as Baba, but the last thing she needed was for them to be pissed at each other. They were alone in the desert a long way from help. And Lex was not about to lie to herself. Out there, she needed Baba more than Baba needed her.

"You know this place better than I do," said Lex.

"That didn't seem to matter earlier."

Lex bit back a blistering retort just before it left her lips. It took every bit of self-control she had, but she did it. She said nothing.

Baba looked at her and sighed heavily.

"Forgive me," he said. "I'm just—" He shook his head again, then pulled in a deep breath and stepped back from the car, slipping once on the slick mud, and stepped higher up the rise. His whole body seemed to change, to straighten and grow taller.

He surveyed the landscape. The sun was high in the sky now. It was just after noon. Aside from Jabal Teljo hulking in front of them, the land was the same endless expanse of light brown dirt and sand they'd been traversing for days.

"There," Baba said, pointing.

Lex looked where he was looking, squinting in the sun. A thin tendril of smoke rose in the distance, so faint that Lex had looked right at it earlier and hadn't even seen it.

"Where there's smoke, there's fire," said Baba.

"And where there's fire, there are people," Lex replied. "How far do you think it is?"

Baba considered the distance. "I think we can make it by nightfall, if we get moving."

Baba had only a small bag with a change of clothes. Lex grabbed her own small pack of clothes and her duffel bag of weapons from the trunk of the car, stuffed the pack inside the duffel and slung the handles over her arms to form a makeshift backpack. A heavy, dangerous backpack, but it would be easier to haul the gear with her back than with her hands.

They slogged through the mud to the other side of the wadi, Baba rolling his pant legs over his knees and carrying his shoes. Thankfully, there was still a rivulet of water working along the side of the wadi, enough for them to clean themselves up once they'd crossed to the other side.

Clean, dressed, and loaded, they set off at a rapid pace toward the smoke on the horizon.

33

On the other side of the wadi, the muddy road inclined and slowly became dry and hard again. They made excellent time, trading the heavy bag of weapons back and forth as they walked, and reached the source of the smoke before the sun touched the horizon.

The sun had slipped partially behind the mountain, casting the land to their right in a long finger of shadow. The smoke came from that side, a few hundred yards off the road. They stepped into the half-night, dark enough that it took Lex's eyes a few seconds to adjust.

When they did, the source of the smoke became obvious. It was not the friendly group of travelers Lex was hoping for, eager to feed her and Baba, welcome them around their campfire, and give them a ride to El Fasher in the morning.

Instead, the smoke came from a downed cargo plane, a Russian-made Ilyushin-76 with tail markings from the United Arab Emirates. The pilot had clearly tried to make an emergency landing. A wide skid line carved deep through the sand and dirt for several hundred yards behind the wreckage. The plane was mostly intact, but the landing hadn't been as smooth as the pilot had hoped. The fuselage had split just behind the wing, cracked open like a matryoshka doll. The tail section lay a dozen yards behind the nose section, its round opening gaping, shadowed, ragged with debris, like the maw of one of those giant, carnivorous sand worms in the science fiction novels.

Lex and Baba stopped far back from the wreckage and dropped their bags to the ground.

"Supply drop?" asked Lex.

"Could be," nodded Baba. "There's still an SAF enclave holding out in El Fasher."

"What else could it be?"

"Troops." Baba shrugged. "Bombs."

"If there were bombs," Lex mused, "they would have blown up by now. If there were troops, we would see them." She shook her head. "Whatever is in there is detonated or dead." She turned to Baba. "Except for one thing."

"What?"

"Shelter," said Lex, starting toward the plane. "Come on. It's getting dark. Let's check this thing out."

They approached carefully, slowly. Even if there were no troops walking around, they could still be inside, injured and pissed off and ready to shoot a curious intruder. Lex unholstered her pistol.

They scanned the tail section first, quickly, and found nothing but shattered wooden crates and debris from the airplane. In the nose section, they found three SAF soldiers in uniform and two pilots in civilian clothing. All were very clearly dead.

Lex found two shoulder bags behind the pilots' seats. She holstered her weapon and sifted through them while

Baba went back to the tail section to check through the debris for anything useful.

Along with some porn magazines, a half-empty bottle of Jack Daniels, and a whole mess of what looked like Turkish power bars, Lex found two passports, both Russian.

"Supply run," said Baba, returning to the cockpit. "Weapons, ammunition, and food."

"You recognize either of these guys?" said Lex, handing the passports to Baba.

He looked at them both, tilted one toward the fading light coming through the cockpit window.

"I've heard of this one. Yuri Antonov. Runs weapons all over Africa. Used to work for Devin Minsk."

"The arms dealer? I thought he died."

"Murdered, I heard," Baba nodded. "Occupational hazard, I suppose. Once he was gone, his jackals went rogue, trying to conquer his empire, or whatever scraps they could tear from it."

"And the U.A.E. is footing the bill?" When Baba looked confused, Lex said, "The tail markings are U.A.E."

Baba shrugged. "Just someone else signing the paychecks."

The sun was dropping. The air in the sunlight beyond the mountain's shadow tinted orange, then red, then blue as they searched. The broken fuselages opened to the east, away from the setting sun, and it was getting dark inside. Baba found a battery-powered lantern and turned it on. The strong white light gave everything a sterile, black-and-white appearance, almost like they were walking through a Japanese manga. The open-eyed corpses leered up at them like ghouls. Lex rolled one of the ghouls onto its side and found a flashlight on its utility belt.

They moved to the tail section and began searching through the crates and the debris. Lex was mainly looking for the food Baba had mentioned. Now that the excitement of finding and searching the plane had passed, her stomach was growling and noisy. There had been nothing for breakfast, and now her belly was clenched tight as a fist.

"Over here," said Baba, pointing toward the back of the fuselage.

Half of the crates were shattered, their contents strewn across the floor. The others were tumbled all over. Some of them were stamped as ammo, others as weaponry, mostly AKs, a few RPG-7s, and even a box labeled "Kornet", though why the SAF would need anti-tank missiles when the RSF didn't use tanks was beyond Lex. *I guess more firepower is better firepower.*

Further back was a tumble of crates stamped with a blue logo showing what looked like two olive branches curved around a bundle of corn and grains. Lex tilted her head to read the upside-down words beneath the logo.

"World Food Programme?" she said, incredulous. "Tell me this plane is on a humanitarian mission and these supplies are headed for the refugee camps."

Baba looked at her, deadpan. "Assault rifles don't have much nutritional value."

"Tell me the SAF isn't stealing food from the fucking U.N."

Baba shrugged and resumed his searching. "SAF, RSF, they all do it." When he looked up again and saw that Lex's jaw had dropped, he shook his head. "It's war, little wolf." His voice softened. "After everything you've seen, are you really that surprised?"

She shouldn't have been. Rape, murder, looting, indiscriminate killing of innocent civilians. All of these things were happening every day in this war. But somehow this was a new low in Lex's mind. This food was supposed to go to the refugee camps where all the civilians who had been displaced by the war were gathered to find food and shelter. From the briefing Lex had seen, most of them were starving, literally wasting away because the food convoys couldn't get to them. She thought it was because of the fighting. She had no idea it was because the fucking armies were stealing the food for themselves.

And now she was about to do the same. Life was an ironic fucking bitch.

Most of the foodstuffs were grains and powders intended to be cooked or added to other food, but there was a spray of foil packets amid the shatters of wood on the floor. "High energy biscuits," they said on the wrapper, in five different languages. When Lex ripped one open, the biscuits looked like fat, rectangular Ritz crackers.

She stuffed one into her mouth. They were no Pop-Tarts, but they didn't taste half bad. Even had a little bit of sweetness to counteract the taste of all the vitamins and nutrients they'd no doubt jammed in there. She shoved a packet in her back pocket and tossed another to Baba.

She pried opened a crate and found boxes of white bars. The bars looked like soap, but they smelled vaguely edible, so Lex took a bite. Pasty, tasteless, and very dry. Lex was about to spit it out and throw the rest on the floor when she thought of the refugees who were literally dying for want of the food she was holding. Starving children in Africa.

She ate the rest of the bar.

When she finished, her mouth was as dry as the sand outside the plane.

"You seen any water bottles?" she asked Baba. That

morning, they'd finished the last of the water the nini had given them outside Umm Badr.

"Not yet," he said.

Lex waded through the debris to dig through the still-intact crates in the back of the plane. The light from Baba's lantern faded. She looked over her shoulder and saw Baba wandering through the fuselage toward the opening, staring up at the ceiling and the walls.

"If you're bored," Lex said, "you can help me look for water."

"Why did this plane crash?" Baba said, musing as he examined the ceiling.

Lex pawed through more crates. "That bottle of Jack in the cockpit might have had something to do with it."

"I'm going to take a look outside."

The light swung as he headed out, casting menacing shadows over the walls and the busted crates. The shadows looked like Count Dracula in the old movies, rising up in his cape, ready to pounce on the poor, unsuspecting woman asleep on the couch.

Ghouls and vampires. Lex shook her head. She was losing her mind.

She clicked on her flashlight and resumed her search.

Baba had a nagging feeling in the back of his mind.

It wasn't irritation. He'd gotten past his anger from that morning. Anger was uncharacteristic for him. It served little purpose, and he'd long ago learned to control it. But Lex Wolfe had a gift for getting through his defenses. What was that phrase Americans liked to use? Getting under his skin. Yes, the little wolf had a gift for using her sharp teeth to get under his skin.

He knew he was pushing his luck escorting her across the Sudan. If she wasn't U.S. military, she was clearly backed by them. It wasn't easy to gain access to the Sudan these days. Not for a white American woman. And despite her attempts to blend in, Lex stuck out like a sore thumb to anyone who was paying attention. Fortunately for her, in wartime, it was often better not to pay attention.

Lex insisted she wasn't a mercenary, and Baba believed her. No mercenary who was that well-armed and that well-funded would waste their time rescuing a couple of journalists. There was much easier money to be made in Africa these days.

No, she was certainly military. Or ex-military, if she was to be believed. U.S. military, of course. Given her impressive language skills, she had to be military intelligence. The only others with those skills would be CIA or a cryptologic linguist. A career spy would blend in better than Lex did, and a linguist wouldn't dare to leave her desk.

An ex-U.S. military intelligence officer in Khartoum looking for the three abducted journalists. Yes, Baba was a fool to agree to take her. But he'd been a fool many times before, and he was still alive. There was something about Lex Wolfe. His instincts told him to take her, and he'd learned long ago to listen to his instincts.

His instincts were the reason he was walking around the outside of a downed cargo plane in the encroaching dark and cold. He had a suspicion, a dangerous suspicion, and he wanted to prove it right before he subjected Lex and himself to a cold night in the open desert.

Because if he was right, they could not stay anywhere near the cargo plane that night.

He circled the tail section, moving close to hold up his lantern. He could see no bullet holes, no carbon scoring on the fuselage. The tail fins were intact. That was a good sign. Maybe his instincts were overcautious this time. Maybe this time, his instincts were wrong.

He walked to the nose section. Miraculously, the massive wings were still attached to the fuselage, reaching twenty meters to either side, listing slightly onto the engines. The pilots were skilled. They'd nearly pulled off a solid landing. That last drop to the ground must have done them in.

Or maybe it was something else.

Baba walked wide, out around the starboard wing and back, holding his lantern high, looking for damage and finding none. The tight ball in the center of his chest eased slightly.

The lantern light grew softer, more yellow. The batteries were dying.

But as he walked back down the nose side of the wing, he still had enough light to notice the large hole in the underside of the fuselage, to notice that the front half of the starboard engine was missing, the remainder shredded, hanging on by a quirk of fate.

The ball in his chest snapped tight again like the bolt of a rifle.

It was as Baba feared.

This plane hadn't crashed. It had been shot down.

And if a cargo plane had been shot down, the ones who shot it down would not be far behind.

The light from Baba's lantern weakened, flickered, and went dark.

They needed to get out of there. Fast.

As Baba groped in the dark for the edge of the wing to

guide his way back, his eyes still light-blind, spears of white bounced around him, illuminating the wing and the destroyed engine for a moment before swinging past. He heard the deep roar of a truck engine and the crunch of tires on dirt, then the whine of brakes and the skid of wheels as the truck came to a stop on the other side of the fuselage.

Too late.

34

Baba came around the nose of the plane and walked directly into the beam of the truck's headlights, his hands held high. He squinted into the light, heard from the darkness behind it one heavy door swing open on croaking hinges, then slam shut again.

Maybe they would be lucky and there would be only one soldier.

A second door opened and banged shut.

No luck tonight.

The driver stood in the shadows beside the tall hood of the truck. "Identify yourself," he said.

He stood to the side of the headlights, probably intending to keep Baba blinded. But enough light spilled over for Baba to see that, though the soldier was holding his rifle, he still had it pointed down to one side. The soldier did not see Baba as a threat. Yet.

Baba put a nervous stammer into his voice. "I'm just a traveler," he said, "headed for El Fasher. I needed somewhere to sleep tonight. I had hoped..." He gestured to the downed plane behind him and smiled weakly.

The soldier stepped closer. The muzzle of his rifle raised slightly. He smelled the lie.

Baba could feel the second soldier to his left, somewhere further back in the darkness. Baba knew that soldier's rifle would be pointed straight at Baba's heart.

"If you're a traveler," the first soldier said, "then where is your vehicle?"

Baba shrugged sheepishly. "Stuck in a wadi, a four-hour walk back toward Umm Badr." He pointed in the direction of the Hyundai.

That much was not a lie at all. The soldier relaxed slightly. He looked across the headlight beams to his comrade and nodded. Baba heard the second soldier start toward the fuselage. Clearly, of the two soldiers, the one in front of Baba was the commander.

"I'm alone," said Baba over his shoulder, much louder than necessary. He knew it was a foolish risk, knew it would raise the soldiers' suspicion. But Lex was back there, unaware of their visitors, and he hoped she would hear the warning.

The second soldier didn't stop. He headed toward the nose section of the downed plane, his crunch of his boots against the dirt fading.

The commander gestured for Baba to approach, surveying Baba carefully as he complied. Close enough now that the glare of the headlights was no longer in his eyes, as the commander frisked Baba for weapons, Baba took in as much information as he could.

The truck was large, but not military. It was a typical civilian supply truck, the kind used to haul equipment and large loads. It had a snub-nosed front, a box cab with wide fenders that doubled as steps, and a long bed with metal-slat sides. Baba could see no mounted weapons, no armor. It was a big truck, that was all.

That told him something. It told him that even if one soldier was the commander of the other, both soldiers were low-level grunts that didn't rate armored transport to protect them against the risk of attack. It told him they were ordered to find whatever useful material survived the crash, load it up, and bring it back. It told him that their superior officers didn't think twice about forcing these two men to potentially unload an entire cargo plane at night by themselves.

It told him these soldiers were unimportant.

And that meant, if worse came to worst, they would not be missed.

But Baba would prefer to avoid that scenario, if possible. Low-level grunts or not, someone would come looking for these men if they didn't return, even if only to find out what happened to the cargo they were supposed to deliver.

Finding no weapons on Baba's person, the commander slung his rifle down and told Baba he could lower his hands. At this point, for Baba, it was a matter of ingratiation, negotiation, and luck. He'd been in this situation many, many times before during this war, and he knew he could find an amenable resolution. All he needed was for the soldiers to let him go on his way, and he could disappear into the night while they searched the downed plane for bounty.

It would be simple.

If it weren't for Lex.

Baba and the commander spoke back and forth for a few minutes. Soon enough, Baba had the man laughing. The commander even offered Baba a cigarette. Baba didn't smoke, but when you're stranded in the middle of the

Sudan and a man with a gun offers you a cigarette, you take it and smoke it with a smile.

"I left my bag inside," said Baba, gesturing toward the tail section of the wreckage. "Do you mind if I gather it before you start your search?" He broadened his smile. "I promise I won't take anything."

It was a feeble tactic, but Baba didn't have much time, and he couldn't think of anything better. He hoped he'd built enough goodwill with the commander to get away with it.

The commander returned Baba's smile, pulled his cigarette from his lips in a cloud of smoke and spit a loose piece of tobacco onto the ground.

"My comrade will fetch your bag for you," he said. With the hand that wasn't holding his cigarette, he patted his rifle almost absent-mindedly, but Baba got the message. Goodwill or not, if he took one step toward that plane, Baba was a dead man.

Baba saw the other soldier come out of the nose section with the pilots' bags that he and Lex had searched earlier. The commander met him on the opposite side of the truck to confer. They kept Baba under close watch and spoke too quietly for Baba to overhear.

The commander returned to Baba's side as the other soldier stowed the bags in the cab of the truck, flicked on the flashlight at the end of his rifle barrel, and walked toward the tail section of the plane.

Toward Lex.

Baba paused a beat, letting the soldier get further away, then turned and shouted across the night air. "Excuse me! If you happen to see a brown shoulder bag inside, it belongs to me. If you could bring it back, I'd appreciate it."

It was a ridiculous thing to say in that situation, but if

the soldiers picked up on that, they didn't react. People probably said a lot of ridiculous things when rifles were trained on them.

"Your belongings will be fine," said the commander. "My comrade will take very good care of them." He said it with a smile that was so clearly fake that Baba began to fear that he might not be able to talk his way out of this situation after all.

His fears grew when the commander's eyes glided idly past Baba and that fake smile fell like a hammer blow. His rifle came up, pointed at Baba. Baba immediately stepped back and raised his hands, then followed the commander's eyes.

Behind Baba, twenty meters away, half-lit by the truck's headlights, was a duffel bag.

A suspicious-looking duffel bag.

It sat in the middle of the dirt. It didn't have the soft, round curves of an innocent duffel bag stuffed with clothing. The outline of this duffel was sharp, pointed.

Threatening.

Suspicious.

It looked that way, of course, because it was suspicious. That particular duffel, Lex's duffel, was filled with weapons provided by the U.S. military.

"Is that your bag, too?" asked the commander.

Baba didn't respond.

The commander made a twirling motion with one finger. Baba turned to face the bag. The commander jabbed the muzzle of his rifle into Baba's back and pushed him forward.

~

The inside of the cargo plane was a mess. It might have been tidy when it took off, with crates stacked in rows from floor to ceiling. But nothing had been strapped down very well, and once that plane hit the ground, everything flew everywhere. Half the crates were totally smashed. Others had been knocked over, but were still intact, lying around like a giant's toy blocks. In the back of the plane, some of the crates still stood in head-high stacks.

And Lex was trying to sort through it all.

If it weren't for the fact that she and Baba were completely out of potable water, she would have thrown in the towel already. It had been a crazy day, and she was dog-tired. They could have just cleared a space to sleep for the night amid the debris and headed out in the morning with a few packets of biscuits and the pilots' bottle of Jack Daniels in their bags.

But after a long afternoon of walking, Lex was parched. And that nutritional bar she ate had eased her stomach, but made her thirst ten times worse. She needed a drink, and whiskey was not going to cut it. If they were going to be walking all day tomorrow, too, they would definitely need water.

Which was why she was shoving crates around and wading thigh-deep in spilled ammo, dehydrated foodstuffs, and broken wood slats in the back of the airplane.

There were two hatches on either side of the back of the plane, each with a single porthole window, the only windows in the entire fuselage. Through one of them, Lex saw Baba wandering with his lantern outside the plane, holding it up like a cop from Old London, studying the fuselage intently. Lex had no idea what he was looking for, but she wished he'd stop fucking around and get his ass back in here to help her. He would be thirsty tomorrow, too.

She could use his help. Aside from all the debris, the crates that weren't busted up were very heavy. There was no way Lex could have lifted one on her own. Whoever loaded the plane must have used a forklift. Lex had to rock and lever and grunt and sweat just to tip a crate off a stack.

At one point, just as she finally managed to work a crate off a head-high stack, she thought she heard Baba yelling outside. Once the smash and splinter of the crate had faded, she listened for a moment, hoping he was on his way to help, but she heard nothing more. Lazy fuck. She went back to her rummaging.

Lex had worked her way down to the bottom crate in one of the last remaining stacks at the very back of the plane. The side of the crate came up to her waist, and Lex was bent over the edge, her head so deep inside that her feet were kicking in the air. Her head was thick and pulsing with all the blood rushing into it.

She held her flashlight in her mouth, pawing with both hands through little individual-sized bags of a nutritional supplement the label called Plumpy'Sup—the manufacturer really needed to fire their marketing department—when she finally heard Baba come back inside behind her, clomping through the fuselage. Wood shards and ammo rattled against the steel of the fuselage as he kicked the debris out of his way.

"About fucking time you came back," Lex said from inside the crate. Her voice was muffled by the flashlight. She pulled it out of her mouth. "Get over here and help me out of this goddamn crate."

As she heard Baba come closer, Lex dug deeper in the box, hoping there might be a layer of water bottles at the bottom. It was an irrational hope, but she'd been looking through all this crap for a long time, and irrational hope was the only kind of hope she had left.

She brushed back one last layer of Plumpy'Sup... and found it. The holy fucking grail. Four long, round metal cylinders that she hadn't seen in any of the other crates. She grabbed one with both hands and shifted it back and forth. The whole crate wiggled with her. Inside the metal cylinder, she heard a liquid splashing back and forth. It had to be water. It had better be water. Thank fucking God.

"I found water," she called, stretching further into the crate to get a better grip on the metal container. "Pull me up."

Baba pushed her legs down so that she was jackknifed over the edge of the crate. Her feet weren't touching the ground and her butt was in the air, right on the edge of the crate. Baba pressed himself against her, pulled her hips tight against his.

Lex could feel Baba grow hard against her ass. She felt a heat in her core as her body responded to his. Kind of a weird place for it, but Baba was smoking hot, and it had been a long time. A woman had needs, after all.

"I thought you said you were a gentleman, Baba," Lex said, smiling. "Aren't you at least going to buy me dinner first?"

She craned her neck to look behind her.

Her smile froze.

Her heart froze.

Her entire body froze.

The soldier pressing against her was definitely not Baba.

"No," the soldier said, his smile slow and predatory. "I'm not."

He had Lex pinned. She tried to wedge herself up and out of the crate, but she couldn't reach the bottom to push herself up, couldn't even lever her torso upright from that position. She reached for the side of the crate and the man smashed his fist down on her fingers. She tried to lift her head and he punched it from behind. She slumped forward, seeing stars, her head pounding.

The soldier pulled the gun holster off the back of her waistband, stepped back, and jerked her jeans to her ankles with one quick pull.

Lex felt cold air on the backs of her thighs before the soldier again pinned her legs with his own. She wriggled her hips, trying to slip free, but the man leaned in harder.

Lex's face was buried in the bags of food, the plastic cold and close and suffocating over her nose and mouth. She smelled plastic. She smelled leather.

The man leaned back, his knees digging into her thighs, heard the tinkle of metal as he fumbled with his gun belt, a thunk as it fell to the ground.

"You're a filthy whore," he sneered.

He reached down and grabbed a handful of Lex's hair, too short for a solid grip, but still long enough to bend her head back. The muscles in her neck felt like they would tear loose. She could barely breathe.

He pulled her up until his cheek was against hers.

"A Western whore," he said, his breath hot in her ear. "Even better."

He leered over her shoulder, down her body. Lex punched him in the face, flung her head backward to head-butt him. He put her in a choke hold that pinned one arm straight up in the air, tucked her other arm under his and ran his hand down her the skin of her long neck, along her collarbone, over one breast, and down her bare stomach.

Lex shivered at his touch. Her body went numb.

She knew how this would go. She'd lived through this once before.

He sucker-punched her in the temple and shoved her down hard, back into the crate. Blackness shrouded the edges of her vision and lights burst in her vision.

Lex felt him fumbling behind her, heard his zipper pull down

She'd lived through this before, but that was a different place and a different man. This was a war zone, and this man was a soldier. To him, Lex was a piece of meat. She would not survive this time.

And this time, she didn't want to.

She grabbed for the side of the crate, twisted her right hand back, searching for the top edge, searching for leverage to pull herself up. The soldier seized her wrist, bent her arm and pinned it in the center of her back. White-hot pain bloomed in her shoulder.

She screamed. Her head was inside the crate, but she screamed anyway. She screamed from the pain, screamed with rage, screamed for help, not knowing if Baba was still alive, if he would hear, or if he would respond if he did. With her free hand, she grabbed fistfuls of Plumpy'Sup and flung the bags behind her, hoping she was aiming at the soldier's face. She heard soft smacks, plastic against skin. He laughed, a low, cruel sound, and twisted her arm further up her back. Pain seared her shoulder. She screamed again and he laughed again and pressed himself harder against her from behind.

Lex scrabbled her hand in the crate, looking for anything more substantial than a plastic bag. Her hand closed around the cold metal of her flashlight. She threw it, heard a satisfying thunk and a grunt of pain and surprise from behind her.

The soldier growled, shoved her arm higher up her back. Lex shrieked as her shoulder popped from its socket.

The man's hands were massive. He held the wrist of Lex's dislocated arm in one hand and still could grab enough of her shirt to yank her backward. He put his face next to her ear from behind.

"You filthy fucking whore."

Lex swung her fist at his face again, punching him in the ear, in the eye. He grunted with the impact, but his grip did not weaken. She punched again. He grabbed her other wrist.

"I'm going to fuck you," he said.

Lex forced herself to focus, focus through the haze of pain, through the rising panic. She forced herself to look around her. For weapons. For advantage. For something that would give her power.

"I'm going to fuck you right now—"

She shifted one foot. It knocked against the soldier's belt.

"—then I'll make your boyfriend out there watch as my commander fucks you, too—"

Metal water bottles in the crate.

"—then make you watch as we kill your boyfriend slowly—"

Her gun in its holster balanced on the corner of the crate.

"—then we'll both fuck you again and leave you to die in the desert with the jackals."

He shoved Lex forward hard, letting go of her wrists, bending her over into the crate again.

As she fell forward, she flung out her hand and swept

her gun into the crate. It disappeared among the bags of Plumpy'Sup.

He grabbed a fistful of her hair, bent her head back again, held her down inside the crate, pinned her from behind with his hip while he fumbled with one hand to work his pants down.

Her head bent backward, all Lex could see was a stack of crates in front of her. With her free hand, she rummaged blindly through the bags, searching for her gun.

He tugged at her underwear, growling like a feral animal, trying to rip them off. She could feel him stabbing against her through the fabric.

She swept her hand back and forth, flailing for the gun, her throat burning, gasping for air.

He tugged twice on her underwear, then a third time.

The first time Lex had ever been thankful for military-issue panties.

Underneath the plastic bags, her hands found hard metal just as her underwear finally tore loose.

She felt the head of his cock against her thighs as he tried to align himself. She wriggled her hips, kept a moving target while she tried to wedge her gun out of its holster with one hand.

He let go of her neck, shoved her down hard into the crate, grabbed her hips with both hands to stop her wriggling.

Her right arm was useless, her shoulder dislocated.

But her right hand still worked.

She held the holster with her right hand, pulled the gun free with her left, flicked off the safety.

He tugged her backward, bent his knees to thrust up into her.

She pushed up with her feet, lifted her ass high, dove her head down into the crate.

She couldn't see, totally blind amid the plastic.

She was upside down, shooting with her off hand.

She might miss. She might shoot herself.

She didn't care. She'd shoot through her own leg if she had to.

She'd rather die than let that fucking pig inside her.

Upside-down, left-handed, blind, and out of time, she aimed her gun at the wall of the crate, screamed with all the rage and fear and pain inside her, and fired.

35

When Baba heard the gunshot, instinct came first, but cold reason came close behind.

Cold reason told him that if the soldier had shot Lex, Baba would be next.

Cold reason told him that if Lex had shot the soldier, the commander would kill them both.

Unless Baba killed him first.

Instinct didn't bother to tell him anything. It acted. Immediately.

Baba heard the gunshot just as the commander slung his rifle to his back—rifle stock by his left ear, barrel by his right hip—and bent down to look inside the duffel bag Baba had unzipped for him.

Startled by the shot, the commander jerked his head toward the fuselage.

In that same moment, Baba stepped behind the commander, grabbed the rifle at the stock and the barrel, and pulled backward with all his weight.

The force yanked the commander to his feet. The nylon rifle strap slid up his chest, snagged under the jut of his chin. The commander's right arm stuck straight up in the air, caught tight inside the circle of the strap.

Baba turned the rifle in his hands, twisting the strap, tightening it around the commander's neck.

The commander flailed at Baba with his free hand, clawed at the back of his neck with his stuck arm, then jerked the arm down, once, then twice, trying to free it.

Baba let up on the pressure, loosened the strap just a little, just enough for the commander to yank his arm free. Then he jerked it back again, the noose now even tighter around the commander's neck.

The commander gurgled and spat foam. He scrabbled at his neck. He swung his arms wildly behind him, trying to reach Baba.

Baba turned the rifle again, then once more, taking up all the slack, then grunted as he turned it one more time. The nylon creaked as it pulled taut. Baba wondered idly if he could snap the commander's neck with a few more twists of the rifle.

An inhuman shrieking came from inside the fuselage.

Or maybe it was inside Baba's head.

Baba kicked the back of the commander's knee, dropping him to the ground, then pushed him face-down on his stomach. Baba planted one foot in the center of the commander's back, hooked his elbows under stock and barrel and leaned back against the push of his foot, his knee locked straight, letting leverage and body weight snuff out the man's life.

Another gunshot from inside the fuselage.

The commander clawed and scratched and squirmed and writhed. Baba ignored it all, eyes closed, breathing long and slow, holding fast and waiting, waiting.

The clawing and squirming grew slower, half-hearted, feeble, then stopped altogether.

The commander's body twitched and shivered beneath Baba's foot.

Still Baba held on. Still he leaned back, long after all reason told him the commander was gone. It never hurt to be sure. It could mean the difference between life and death.

Finally, Baba eased forward, loosened the tension, ready to tighten it at any sign of movement.

There was none.

He tucked the rifle stock under his arm, cautiously bent down and pressed two fingers against the commander's neck, feeling for a pulse.

None.

The commander was dead.

From inside the fuselage, Baba heard the sound of splintering wood and banging metal and suddenly wished the rifle wasn't twisted quite so tightly around the commander's neck.

Someone was coming out.

Inside the crate, the sound of the gunshot was deafening.

Lex was still screaming as pain seared through her thigh like the slice of a hot blade.

Still screaming—her throat felt like gargling razor blades in salt water—but the sound was distant, muffled.

The soldier let go of her hips. Lex tumbled forward into the crate. Her back banged against the water cylinders and her legs landed in a heap on top of her, her knees banging her face.

She stopped screaming.

She knew she'd stopped screaming because the pain in her throat went from salt water and razor blades to merely swallowing a hot fireplace poker.

Through the dull whine in her ringing ears, she could still hear screaming, distant and muffled.

Lex scrambled upright, ignoring the pain that flared again in her dislocated shoulder. She held the pistol in front of her in her left hand and slowly stood, peering over the side of the crate.

She could still hear the screaming because it wasn't her making the sound.

It was the soldier.

Bare-assed, pants around his ankles, he was hunched a few feet back from the crate, screaming like a hyena and staring down at the bloody, spurting stump of his cock and the empty space where his balls used to be.

He looked up at Lex, screaming, eyes wide and incredulous, then back down at the hole between his legs. He From his inner thigh, he pulled a bloody splinter the width and length of his ring finger, held it in front of his face and goggled at it like he'd found a severed toe in his soup. He screamed again.

Lex aimed the gun at the soldier's head.

"Hey, asshole," she shouted over the din of the screaming. "You still want to fuck?"

The soldier looked up again and seemed to register Lex for the first time, seemed to comprehend what had just transpired. What Lex had done to him. The incredulity on his face washed away in an instant, replaced with a rictus of pure hatred.

He lunged toward her.

She shot him in the face. A red spray of blood and bone

and brain splatted against the crates and the food and the curved metal of the fuselage behind him.

With a dull thump, his faceless, dickless body whunked to the floor in front of the crate like a tall tree felled in a wood.

Lex stared down at the corpse. "Fuck that," she said quietly, then hissed as the pain in her thigh seared again. She looked between her legs at an angry red streak torn across her left inner thigh, angling back and up toward her ass.

A bullet graze.

Blood was dripping past her knee. Lex tried to step out of the crate, but couldn't lift her leg. A cold chill washed through her for a brief moment. She thought she was wounded, that maybe she'd shot her own leg off after all, nicked a nerve and paralyzed herself or something.

Then she realized her jeans were still around her ankles. She pulled them off over her sneakers and held them in her hand while she hoisted herself gingerly over the side of the crate.

She stepped up to the soldier, rolled him to the side with one foot, and found her torn underwear beneath his body. She wrapped her wounded thigh with the fabric to staunch the bleeding, then tested her weight on that leg. Painful, but manageable.

Like her shoulder. It wasn't the first time she'd dislocated it. It wasn't even the second time. Didn't make it any less painful, but she could handle it. Using her mouth and her free hand, she fashioned a quick shoulder sling with her jeans and picked her way through the debris toward the front of the wrecked fuselage.

At her fourth step, her skin suddenly itched all over and her knees turned to jelly. She steadied herself against an overturned crate. The itching crawled up her throat, closed it tight. Panic and itchy heat flushed through her from her toes to her scalp. Her breath wheezed as her chest hitched, struggling for air.

Fear shot cold up her spine. She spun behind her, gun aimed and ready.

All she saw was the soldier's mangled body lying amid the bloody crates and debris. Still dead.

Lex had never killed before.

She'd beaten men senseless, countless times.

But she'd never killed.

No.

She hadn't killed that man.

She'd saved herself.

She closed her eyes and pulled in a long, slow breath.

She shivered all over as if she were freezing cold, even as sweat welled from every pore on her body.

She pulled in another long, slow breath.

She had killed that man. She wouldn't lie about it, especially not to herself.

But she had killed him to save herself.

He had chosen to come after her, and she had done what she needed to do to survive.

Lex opened her eyes and pushed to her feet, willing strength back into her legs, willing power back into her step. Fuck the pain. She'd felt pain before and survived.

She strode forward, kicked away a pile of debris. It banged against the metal fuselage, the wood splintering with a satisfying crack.

She'd done more than survive.

She'd fucking saved herself.

36

LEX STRODE out of the fuselage into the night. She was naked from the waist down, wearing only her crop cami and her sneakers. The desert air was cold. Goosebumps prickled over her ass and her bare legs.

Truck headlights speared toward her from directly ahead. To her right, Baba squatted beside her duffel bag, bent over a body. He held a rifle in his hands.

Lex angled toward him, her gun held out.

Baba dropped the rifle and stood, staring blank-faced at Lex. He scanned her body.

"Eyes on mine," said Lex, aiming the gun at Baba's head.

Baba's eyes snapped up, as did his hands, raised beside his shoulders.

As Lex got closer, she saw that the body at Baba's feet was that of another soldier, like the one cooling inside the plane.

Lex shot the soldier on the ground.

Baba didn't even jump.

"He was already dead," he said.

Lex retrained her pistol on Baba's head.

"Now he's deader," she replied.

"It doesn't..." Baba started, then clapped his mouth shut when he saw the look on Lex's face.

Smart man.

Lex kept her gun on Baba as she approached, only lowering it once she stood over the dead soldier and had kicked his corpse twice to make sure he really was dead.

She didn't know why she did it. She didn't think Baba would come after her. He didn't seem the type. Plus, he'd had plenty of chances over the past few days. And even if he was that type, he was certainly too smart to try anything while Lex was holding a gun on him.

But why take the chance?

She flicked on the safety and dropped the gun in the duffel. "You can put your hands down," she said as she hoisted the bag over her good shoulder and stalked toward the truck.

Baba fell in beside her.

"I'm driving," said Lex.

She felt Baba looking her over, but she let it slide. It was more of an assessing gaze than a leer.

When they got to the truck, Baba helpfully pulled open the driver's side door for her, then stood on the other side of the door to give Lex some privacy.

She heaved the duffel into the driver's seat, rummaged through her pack for a new pair of underwear, and wedged the panties on one-handed.

She eased her arm out of the sling she'd made with her jeans, grabbed her right wrist with her left hand, and pulled her arm forward and straight in front of her, trying to pop her shoulder back into the socket. She hissed as the ligaments stretched. The ball of her arm bone ground against the outside of her shoulder socket, a bone-on-bone scrape that sent shivers through Lex's body. She squeezed her eyes shut and bit down hard on her lip, then pulled her arm even further forward, wiggling it side to side, trying to find the socket. But it wouldn't budge.

Lex sighed and pulled the strap off one of her rifles, slipped it over her arm as a sling, and untied the jeans from around her neck.

"You can look now," she said once her jeans had been pulled all the way up.

Baba came around the door as Lex struggled to fasten the top button of her jeans with one hand. Baba came forward slowly, carefully, eyebrows up in question, hands raised in offer.

Lex hesitated for a brief moment, then nodded.

Baba's hands were warm against her ice-cold belly. Lex shivered all over at his touch, this time from the pleasure of that warmth, not from pain.

He seemed to notice. Lex saw his brow furrow, but he didn't look up, didn't say anything. He moved slowly, kindly, buttoned her jeans, then surveyed her shoulder.

"Dislocated," he said.

"It's fine." Lex put one foot on the fender to climb into the cab.

"I can help you put it back in."

Lex paused, eyed Baba. She could manage with one arm if she had to. The pain was bad, but bearable.

But it was her right arm, her dominant arm, that was dislocated. Until she got the bone back in the socket, that arm would be useless. Once it popped back in, she would still have to baby the arm until it healed, but the pain would be a lot less and the arm would be usable.

"Lex," said Baba softly, "please. Allow me to help you."

Lex nodded.

Baba led her to the back of the truck. He climbed into the bed, helped Lex do the same. A pile of burlap sacks was heaped in the corner. Baba lay them out near the edge of the truck bed, forming a mattress. He helped Lex lay flat on her back, then scrambled off the truck.

"Just relax," he said.

He ran his hands over the length of Lex's arm. The warm shiver coursed through her body again.

Baba's hands were rough, but his touch was gentle. He palpated the dislocation carefully, then nodded to himself and slipped the rifle strap off of Lex's shoulder and eased her arm out until it rested straight by her side on the edge of the truck bed.

"You've done this before, yes?"

Lex nodded.

"Good," said Baba. "Then you know what to expect."

Both of his hands held Lex's right wrist. He slid his left hand up her arm to her shoulder, rested it on top of the bulge where the bone distended her skin.

"Breathe in," said Baba.

Lex pulled in a breath.

"Now breathe out, slowly."

As she did, Baba pulled her arm slowly outward, pumping it up and down gently, holding his left hand on her shoulder. She could feel his fingers working, probing. She glanced at him. His eyes were screwed shut in concentration. Dr. Baba, now accepting new patients.

Lex hissed as a spear of pain ran through her arm. Immediately, Baba eased her arm back a touch, probed with his fingertips on her shoulder as he pumped her wrist up and down. He changed the angle of his motion, then brought her arm outward again. The pain eased.

"Breathe in again," Baba droned, his voice low and soft as a hypnotist, "and slowly out."

Lex could feel her muscles relax, could feel her body rearranging, reassembling itself as Baba worked her arm outward, worked her wrist up and down.

When her arm was at a ninety-degree angle, pointing straight out from her body, Baba shifted. He stepped inside her arm, slid his left hand from her shoulder to her wrist— the sensation of his warm touch along her cold skin sending shivers through Lex's body again—then brought his right hand to her shoulder. Again, his fingers probed her shoulder, feeling the bone, feeling the socket, his eyes screwed shut as he visualized what was happening inside Lex's body.

"Once again," he intoned, "breathe in."

As Lex pulled in a breath, Baba rolled her wrist slowly, first forward, then backward.

"And out."

As she hissed a breath through her lips, Baba pushed her arm higher. He paused and adjusted his right hand. Instead of just palpating her shoulder joint, this time he wrapped his hand around it, his thumb pressed into her armpit.

"One more deep breath, Lex," he said.

Lex pulled in a long, slow breath.

"Now blow it out, hard."

When she did, Baba raised her arm with his left hand while pulling back on her shoulder with his right. Lex screamed as her shoulder popped back into place with an audible clunk.

Immediately, the pain dissipated. Her shoulder was sore, but the sharp pain she had felt with every subtle movement was gone.

Baba kept his right hand on her shoulder, rolled and bent and twisted her arm gently, testing, then brought her arm slowly back to Lex's side and re-affixed the rifle strap.

"You'll need to keep the sling on for a little while to give your arm a chance to heal. There will be inflammation, and any time you dislocate a joint, there is an increased risk of future dislocations."

Lex sat up on the truck bed and worked her shoulder in a circle. Baba stepped close and palpated the joint again.

"Good as new," Lex said. "How did you learn how to do that?"

Baba shrugged. "I picked some things up along the way."

"Well," said Lex. She put one hand on Baba's cheek, pulled him close, and kissed him on the lips. As she'd hoped, they were as soft and warm as his touch. "Thanks."

A slow smile crept over his face. Lex smiled back.

In her mind, she heard a gunshot, saw a flash of the soldier's face leering down at her, of Skinner's face.

She shoved Baba hard enough for him to stagger back a step, then jumped down from the truck.

Baba frowned.

"I'm still driving," said Lex, and stalked around to the front of the truck.

37

THE TRUCK HAD A MANUAL TRANSMISSION. Lex tried to work the gears with her bad arm, but the truck was old and the gears were rough and gritty with sand. Every shove of the gear shift sent a needle of pain through her arm, so she finally agreed to let Baba help. She still refused to let him drive, but she allowed him to work the stick, calling out "Shift" every time she pressed the clutch.

Once they found their rhythm, the drive was uneventful. The roads were bumpy, but dry, and the truck had no trouble getting through. Each squeaking jounce made Lex's shoulder ache, but she relished the pain. It let her know she was still alive. It let her know she was a fighter. A survivor.

Not just a survivor.

She had saved herself.

She was a savior.

They drove through the night in silence, aside from the occasional "Shift". The road was deserted, the desert around them empty. Lex had been tired earlier, but she was wide awake now, despite the soporific lull of the engine and the soft yellow glow of the headlights carving a wan circle of light in the darkness all around them.

"Shift," Lex called.

The whining engine eased as Lex stepped on the clutch and let up on the gas, then revved again as she reversed those steps in their usual rhythm, whining louder than before when she let up on the clutch in the same gear she'd been in before.

"I said shift."

Lex glanced over and saw Baba sleeping, his head slumped against his shoulder, his hand still on the gearshift. With his face relaxed, he looked peaceful, younger than he looked when he was awake.

Lex slowed the truck to lower the RPMs. They didn't need to shift. They could take it slow.

She thought back to the kiss. She'd kissed Baba on instinct. Maybe it was just a thank you. Maybe it was a response to the pain in her shoulder suddenly disappearing. Maybe—okay, probably—it was a response to his touch, to his warm, rough hands on her skin. His gentle touch that made her feel better. Made her want to feel even better than that.

A woman has needs.

Lex shivered, remembering being face-down in that crate, looking back over her shoulder, expecting to see Baba and seeing—

A cold chill ran through her. Her skin prickled.

She didn't even want to think about it. Could barely think about anything else. All her energy was spent trying to keep her mind away from that memory.

It had been months after Skinner before she could touch herself without the memory taking over her mind. Two years before she slept with a man again. The fear, the nights waking in a cold sweat, Nick shaking her awake because she'd been screaming, switching on the light and looking at her like she was a mental patient. Like she was broken.

Like she was an inconvenience.

Not long after that, after she'd kicked Nick out, the screams woke only her, alone in the darkness. She'd started sleeping with the lights on, just so she wouldn't have to fumble for them when she woke, to dispel the last wisps of her nightmare.

She despised those years. She'd moved halfway around the globe to get away from the sound of those screams. Every time she fought, she heard those screams in the crowd. Every time she beat the shit out of some meathead, some arrogant asshole, some douchebag who thought a woman would be easy prey, she heard those screams.

But when she fought, the screams didn't come from her. They came from the meathead, from the asshole, from the douchebag.

And over time, the screams in the night had faded for her. It was like she had pushed them outside herself, inflicted them on others. The first night she brought a man into her bed again, it had been just like the fistfight they'd had an hour earlier. Their sex had been a battle for dominance, to see who would gain control over the other.

Just like the fistfight, Lex won. But in the morning, they both went home happy.

Was that fear going to come back again now? Would those screams begin again?

No. Fuck that. Lex wouldn't let that happen.

But would she have a choice?

Lex woke Baba as the horizon in the side view mirrors was beginning to pale. They'd rejoined the main El Ingaz road a couple of hours earlier, but aside from that junction there had been essentially only one road the entire way from the wreckage, with empty landscape all around. But as they approached El Fasher, signs of life were appearing. In the greying darkness and the edge-glow of her head-lights, Lex could see empty houses and farmsteads and abandoned vehicles. And turnoffs, roads that Lex didn't know whether or not she should take.

Baba woke with a hissing intake of breath, like a knife cutting paper, eyes wide, head turning quickly from side to side, before his shoulders relaxed and he remembered where they were, remembered they were safe.

Lex had saved them both.

When Lex again refused to let him drive, Baba sat up in the passenger seat and gave directions. They were close to El Fasher, he said, and they would need to be careful to avoid running into any soldiers. Their truck was of civilian make and markings, but some soldier might still recognize it. They probably wouldn't yet be wondering why it hadn't returned, but there was no point in taking unnecessary risks.

And, he said, Lex would need to let him drive at some point. They would have to go through El Fasher eventually, and a Western woman driving a truck—especially one with bare arms, wearing only a crop camisole for a top—would definitely attract undue attention.

Lex sighed. Back to the fucking patriarchy.

She pulled over. Her arm was aching like a mother-fucker, and if she was being honest, she was glad for the break. But she would never admit that to Baba. Hell, she was barely willing to admit it to herself.

While Baba found a few cans of gasoline in the bed if the truck and refilled their tank, Lex managed with difficulty to slip her thobe over her clothes. Thankfully, Baba said there was no need for Lex to change into the tunic dress, or even to change out of her sneakers. In the Darfur region, especially with all the refugees coming in, it was not unheard of for women to wear Western-style clothing under a headscarf or a thobe. But she would still do well to keep her pale skin hidden as much as possible.

"Too bad the back of the truck isn't covered, huh?" said Lex drily. "You could just put me in a crate and hide me back there." She grinned.

"Yes," said Baba, his face grave. "That would have been better."

Lex's grin dropped like a stone. She'd meant it as a joke, but Baba had taken that suggestion far too seriously for her liking.

Fucking patriarchy.

Baba jammed the truck into gear with a scrape and a clunk of the gears and pulled them back onto the road, guiding them toward the city.

El Fasher is the capital of North Darfur state and the largest city in Western Sudan, situated at the feet of the Marrah mountains, the tallest mountains in Sudan. Compared to Umm Badr and the other places they'd been in the last few days, El Fasher was a thriving metropolis. But it was half the size of El Obeid and a third the size of Khartoum. By Western standards, in the best of times, El Fasher was tiny, about the size of Toledo, Ohio.

From her briefings, Lex knew that these were not the best of times. Like the volcanic mountains towering above, El Fasher was a seething cauldron of death and destruction. Years of war, siege, starvation, and mercenary opportunism had decimated El Fasher and its population. It was now a husk of what it once was, and still the fighting continued.

Hundreds of thousands of internally displaced persons lived in several refugee camps around the city, with the largest, Zamzam camp, located about nine miles south of El Fasher. Four hundred thousand refugees lived there, suffering from overcrowding, malnutrition, diarrhea, cholera. All because of the arrogance and ego of the men who led the militias fighting this war, made worse by the cynicism and heartlessness of the men who capitalized on it.

Baba turned onto a side road that was barely more than a cow path and wound them through the desert, occasionally bouncing across what looked to Lex like nothing more than a sand-swept field, rutted and rocky.

From a distance, they passed two northern refugee camps—Al Salam and Abu Shouk, Baba told her. Lex could see what looked like a vast scatter of makeshift tents among the sand and the scrub trees, A-frame tents made from bedsheets and twine. constructions that wouldn't withstand a light breeze, let alone the soaking rains Baba had described.

She saw a line of white along the ground, but couldn't make out what it was. Too low to be boxes, too irregular in shape to be bags of rice. As the road took them closer, she saw men behind the line of white, men visible only from their waists up. They were digging. The line of white wasn't supplies or food. They were corpses, wrapped in white sheets. And the men behind them were digging a mass grave.

Lex swallowed hard, looked up past the men, fighting her emotions. In the distance behind them, she saw a tilting, ramshackle structure with a corrugated tin roof and no walls, one of many such structures dotting the camp. They were aid stations and food stations, used to distribute medicine, supplies, and sustenance when they were available.

Each of these camps was home to tens of thousands of refugees, all Sudanese, most from nearby in the Darfur region. They had all been forced from the homes with little more than they could carry. They needed food and medicine. But this particular structure, like the others in the camp, was empty. Baba had told Lex there had been little food or aid for weeks, if not months.

Lex clenched her teeth, her jaw muscles flexing. She knew why those aid shipments hadn't arrived. She cursed herself, wishing she and Baba had taken the time to load the supplies from the downed cargo plane into the back of the truck so they could have delivered them to the refugee camps.

But that was not her mission, and she'd had other things on her mind when they left the airplane wreckage.

They finally saw the outskirts of El Fasher on the horizon ahead, low buildings made from brick or mud or clay, arrayed around dirt paths that served as streets. They were lucky to have the truck. Lex had no idea how they would have navigated the sandy, uneven terrain in Baba's little blue Hyundai.

"The SAF still hold the airport and the western gate."

"The Tawila route," said Lex.

Baba nodded.

"All the other routes in and out of the city are controlled by the RSF."

"But Tawila is where we need to go," she said. "I thought you wanted to avoid the SAF."

"I want to avoid crossing battle lines," said Baba. "I have no affiliation with any of these militias." He stopped at an intersection and studied the crossroad for a moment before pulling forward. "And we're not heading toward Tawila."

"I thought we were heading west."

"We did head west," he said. "Now we need to head south, through Nyala."

"Nyala?" said Lex. "But you turned us west."

"We can't go around to the east," said Baba, shaking his head. "Not in this truck. There's too much risk that the RSF soldiers would recognize it."

"So we're doing exactly what you said we shouldn't do," said Lex. "We're crossing battle lines."

"Not exactly," Baba sighed.

A feeling of dread settled over Lex at the tone in Baba's voice.

"What are you getting us into now, Baba?"

Baba looked at Lex, his eyes frank, his expression stony.

"You'd better get your money out," he said. "We're going to need it."

BABA HADN'T BEEN KIDDING about the money.

They'd managed to skirt far enough west of El Fasher on back roads and cattle paths to avoid the main RSF forces and the SAF enclave. But that brought them square into the territory of the Sudanese Liberation Movement.

Specifically, the faction of the SLM led by a man named Abdul Wahid al-Nur. According to Baba, he'd been born in West Darfur, accumulated a following, and formed the SLM when he refused to sign the Darfur Peace Agreement in 2006. He and his followers had worked as a rebel group in the region ever since, and they controlled the road from El Fasher to Tawila.

Al-Nur wanted to turn the Sudan into a Western-style country, with a liberal and democratic government which maintained the separation of church and state. Seemed well enough, until Baba explained that al-Nur had been trained in Khartoum as a lawyer.

That explained why Lex had so little cash left once they'd finally made it through all the SLM blockades along their route.

After skirting the northern refugee camps, they'd bounced and jounced through abandoned streets and neighborhoods on the outskirts of western El Fasher until they found a solid dirt road that took them toward the mountains, then picked their way south and west until they went down into a steep wash and up the other side onto the Tawila road.

From El Geneina on the western border with Chad, the Tawila road ran roughly east through a mountain pass toward El Fasher, then dipped southeast to a point roughly ten miles south of the city—just south of the Zamzam refugee camp—where it joined the main road that ran north-south from El Fasher to Nyala.

They'd successfully skirted El Fasher. The only things keeping them from reaching the main road to Nyala were the SLM checkpoints.

Or, as they should have been called, card-cash-or-check-points.

Every so often along the Tawila road, a line of traffic would force Baba to stop the truck. They would inch forward car length by car length until they reached a blockade that was little more than two stacks of tires with a piece of splintered wood across the top. The tires and the wood weren't much of a deterrent for a driver to stop their vehicle. But the SLM fighters and their AK-47s were enough for people to think twice about blowing through the feeble barrier.

At each stop, SLM soldiers searched the truck, starting in the back. Lex tried as best she could to keep her face hidden when the soldiers stepped up on the fenders to have a look inside the cab, but there was nowhere for her to hide, and these soldiers were not as bored and inattentive as the soldiers in El Obeid had been. Inevitably, just as

Baba was negotiating a price that fell into the category of mere highway robbery, a soldier would notice Lex and her white skin. The toll would then double or even triple, pushing the cost to levels only a terrorist group run by a formally trained lawyer would have the balls to demand.

Even in Sudanese Arabic, it was clear to Lex that the extra toll was essentially a pay-us-not-to-rape-your-white-woman tax. Every time Baba counted out the bills, every time Lex's money went to fund the assholes who perpetrated this heinous system, she dug her nails into her palms and squeezed her fists hard enough to stretch tight the skin over her knuckles. Instead of taking the money from her duffel, she wanted nothing more than to take the guns out instead and mow down every one of those assholes. Then, when her ammo ran out, she'd kill them with her bare hands.

But she couldn't kill them all. And so she couldn't kill any of them. Not like that.

Even when your own life depends on it, how do you fight a system that dominates the entire world?

After the fifth checkpoint, Lex started keeping count. By the time they passed back into RSF territory—a transition that was not guarded, all the RSF soldiers being occupied with the siege further north in El Fasher—they had endured thirteen SLM checkpoints over the course of only ten miles. And Lex had spent nearly two hundred thousand Sudanese pounds to keep herself from being violated.

It worked out to about three hundred fifty U.S. dollars, a small price to pay to avoid being gang-raped at gunpoint. But the fact that she'd had to pay it at all gnawed at a place deep within Lex's soul.

And to add insult to deep injury, even though it was Lex's money, it was Baba who did the paying. Lex had to sit there in the passenger seat, staring down at her shoes, while the menfolk haggled over the price of her virtue.

Fucking patriarchy.

Once they were clear of Lawyerland and securely on the road toward Nyala, Baba had the good sense to keep his mouth shut. If he'd tried to explain it away, to call it the cost of doing business, or even to apologize, Lex would have unleashed all of her anger on him, undeserved though it may be.

Fortunately, Baba had plenty to keep his attention occupied. Though it was only a hundred twenty miles to Nyala, the rocky, rutted road slashed with wadis filled with half-dry mud made passage incredibly difficult. Under those conditions, Baba figured it could take them as long as two days to get to Nyala.

They had no choice but to grind on.

Along both sides of the road, lines of displaced persons trudged through the sand and the dirt and the mud, their possessions balanced on their heads and their children held tight in their hands. They were walking in the opposite direction from where Lex and Baba were driving, heading north toward El Fasher, toward the already overcrowded Zamzam camp.

"There are half a million refugees in the camps around Nyala," Baba explained. "Though the fighting there has lessened, the food shortages and the overcrowding are even worse than in El Fasher." He glanced out the open window, looking down from the truck's cab at the faces of the refugees they passed. "These people are willing to walk for days, sleeping rough, risking theft, rape, and death from gangs and bandits in hopes of finding what they need in El Fasher."

"But Zamzam is just as bad. Don't they know that?"

Baba shook his head. "They may have heard," he said, "but to these people, those are just rumors. How can a rumor stand in the face of hope?"

"Fuck hope," muttered Lex. "They should use common sense."

"Look at them," said Baba.

Lex looked out her window. Most of the people stared down at the ground. Those who looked up at her had eyes hollowed by hunger and deadened by fear. They didn't smile, didn't wave, didn't ask for assistance. They just watched her pass with those flat eyes, then trudged on.

"For these people," Baba said, "hope is all they have left." His lips pressed into a thin line. "And nothing makes sense anymore."

They pulled off the road for the night, sleeping in two-hour shifts with pistols in their hands. When it was her turn to rest, even as tired as she was, the ache in her arm made her sleep as broken and disjointed as her shoulder. Even with the windows shut tight, Lex could hear the refugees still walking outside, using the moonlight to guide them, risking death on the road to escape death in Nyala.

But all that lay ahead was the same death in El Fasher. The men that were fighting to rule these people were the same men causing their needless suffering.

Lex tried to push the thought from her head. It hurt too much to think of it, hurt too much to feel so powerless to help.

How do you fight a system that dominates your entire world?

But why would that system change if no one fought against it?

Exhausted, they reached Nyala late the next day, stopping only to refuel, then continuing southwest until late in the night. The lines of itinerant refugees disappeared. The road followed a natural draw between the hills and mountains that rose on either side and ahead of them. In this direction, Lex figured they would eventually reach the border with the Central African Republic.

Baba stopped for the evening in a small village in an empty dirt lot in front of a homestead. He secured some water and a small portion of food, which Lex scarfed greedily. The last of the high-energy biscuits she'd taken from the plane wreckage had run out before they reached Nyala. With the memory of the refugees still vivid in her mind, she felt guilty eating real food. But her body didn't care about starving strangers. It needed sustenance.

They spent the night in the truck again, but Baba said there was no need for weapons this time. Even though they slept sitting up in the cab, the ache in Lex's arm had subsided enough for her to get a reasonable night's sleep. She woke with her arm still sore, but better than it had been.

Baba had parked facing west, so the sunlight wouldn't wake them quite so early in the morning. When Lex did wake, Baba was outside the truck talking with a local man. Baba shook his head and gestured passionately. The local man was calm, holding a single index finger upright, wagging it back and forth like a stubborn schoolmarm.

After a minute or two of discussion, Baba shook the man's hand and stalked back toward the truck.

"Where to now?" said Lex.

She'd given up guessing where Baba was taking her. The usual faint niggling in the back of her brain warned her against blindly following strange men, but she and Baba had been through enough by this point that Lex felt he had earned some measure of trust. Plus, if she'd had few other options before, she had practically none now.

"Due south," said Baba.

He opened the door and stepped up on the fender on the driver's side of the cab, but he didn't climb in. Instead, he reached across the seat for his bag and packed his water and the clothes he'd used as a pillow inside. He zipped the bag, grabbed the keys from the truck's ignition, and climbed down off the fender.

"Get your stuff," he said, then slammed the door shut.

Lex's mouth fell open. Get her stuff? What the fuck was Baba up to now? Those niggling doubts in the back of her brain became a little bit louder.

Incredulous, she watched through the windshield as Baba walked around the front of the truck and pulled open the door on her side.

"Get my stuff?" she said, glaring down from the cab. "Why?"

"This is the end of the road," said Baba.

A possibility occurred to her, changed her whole attitude.

"Is this where the hostages are?" she asked.

Excitement zinged through Lex's body. Finally they were getting somewhere. She threw her things into her duffel, not even bothering to zip it shut, and climbed out of the cab.

Baba slammed the door behind her.

"No," he said. Lex's mistrusting mood slammed back down like the door had slammed shut. "We're headed due south, and in that direction, this is literally the end of the road."

Baba walked away and handed the truck keys to the

local man, who pointed toward a low building nearby. Baba nodded and headed in that direction.

Lex shifted her duffel up onto her shoulder and hurried to catch up. The local man smiled and chuckled to himself as she passed. When Lex scowled at him, the man's chuckle became a high-pitched laugh.

The building was low, but it was large, made from a patchwork of corrugated steel squares, its roof on a shallow slant. It had a wide barn-like front door that slid open from side to side on a rusting metal track.

"So how the fuck are we going to get there without a road?" Lex said as Baba reached the building and Lex caught up. "Are we walking the rest of the way?"

Walking took time, and every passing hour made it less likely the hostages were still alive.

"I told you from the very beginning," said Baba, "we will have to hike and even climb, at some point." He grabbed the handle of the sliding door. "But not yet."

Baba leaned back, pulling on the handle with his body weight to get the rusty wheels moving on the track. With a screech, the door rattled open.

The smell of the place reached Lex before her eyes could make out any detail amid the darkness inside. It reeked of livestock and musty straw.

When her eyes finally did adjust, Lex saw three empty livestock stalls, two bales of stacked hay, and an old tractor in front of a door on the far side of the building, identical to the door Baba had just opened. In front of them, canting so dangerously on loose kickstands against the packed dirt floor that they seemed to defy the pull of gravity, were two of the rustiest, most beaten-down dirt bikes Lex had ever seen. The bikes belonged in a junkyard. Or a museum.

"You know how to ride a motorcycle?" asked Baba.

"Yes, I do," said Lex, dropping her duffel to the ground with a heavy thunk. "Are you planning to sell these pieces of shit to buy one?"

Baba grinned and loaded his bag onto the back of one of the bikes.

"I just sold the truck to buy these," he said.

Lex's jaw dropped. "You sold a working truck to buy two bikes that probably haven't run since before either of us were born?" She scoffed. "Remind me not to use you as a financial advisor."

"They work," said Baba, smiling.

"Oh yeah? How do you know?"

"The man outside said they did."

"And you believed him? Again, remind me not to use you as a financial advisor."

Baba hefted Lex's duffel onto a rusted metal rack on the back of the other bike, securing it with twine that he found wrapped around the rack. He tied the bag tight, tugged on the twine to make sure it was secure, then looked up at Lex.

His smile was gone. His face was serious and earnest.

"The men in power, the men who are running this war and profiting from it, they cannot be trusted. But these people," he pointed out the open door in the direction of the local man, "the Sudanese people. These are good people. Honest people. Hard-working people. They love their children. They respect their elders. They enjoy haggling,"—Baba grinned—"but they will not cheat you. And they do not lie."

Lex had been cheated plenty of times in markets in Khartoum, even before the war. Locals saw a foreigner and immediately tripled their prices. But she didn't blame them for that. And she didn't mention it to Baba.

"Okay," she said, gesturing toward the bikes. "Let's see if you're right."

Baba straddled the bike with his pack loaded on the back and twisted the key in the ignition. He flicked on the battery, squeezed the clutch, and pumped the gear shifter down to first gear. With a glance up at Lex and a grin on his face, he stood on the foot peg and stomped down on the kickstarter.

The engine coughed and wheezed like an elderly smoker in his death bed.

Baba's grin faded, but only a little.

Lex had to admire his faith.

He cranked down on the kickstarter again, then a third time.

Same emphysemic wheeze.

Baba's grin flipped to a scowl as he double-checked the ignition, the battery, the clutch, the gears. With a dubious frown, he reached down to the engine on his left side and pulled out the choke.

This time, when he hit the kickstarter, the engine roared to life like a possessed lawn mower. A cloud of blue smoke blasted from the tailpipe, and the building immediately filled with the stink of gasoline and burnt motor oil.

The engine roared for a moment, coughed once, then knocked, sputtered, and died.

"See?" said Baba from amid the blue cloud. "Told you it would work."

"Yeah," said Lex. "You're a real man of the people."

But she couldn't help but smile at the look of triumph on Baba's face. She stood next to her own bike, sighed, and set about figuring out how to make the damn thing run long enough to get her out of the local man's front yard.

39

ONCE THEY FILLED the gas tanks and changed the oil, the dirt bikes actually ran surprisingly well. They were old and heavy and had obviously endured a lot of use and abuse, but the engines must have been recently rebuilt or, at least, very well serviced over the years. They ran steady. The Sudanese people know how to care for things, Baba boasted, and they're not concerned with external appearances. Unlike Americans, who throw everything away at the slightest blemish, in the Sudan, people understand the value of their possessions and work hard to maintain them.

Lex couldn't argue with that. Despite their rusty appearance, the bikes hauled the two of them and their gear over rugged singletrack dirt lines that would have busted the shocks on a lesser bike, even a brand-new one. They just don't make em like they used to.

Baba had originally offered to have Lex ride behind him, to let her shoulder continue to heal. But Lex told him to fuck off. Her arm still hurt, and the vibration of the bike engine and the judder of the shocks every time she went over a bump or a rock made it hurt even worse, but she was

290

well enough to ride. And she wasn't about to give any man the satisfaction of Lex depending on him for anything. She was already dependent on Baba for too much as it was. She put her sling across her torse like a bandolier, gripped the throttle with gritted teeth, and ignored the pain.

Once they were out of sight of the village and well into the wilderness, Lex took off her thobe and stuffed it back in her pack. Though the morning air still had a chill that she felt on her exposed skin, she immediately felt more like herself again and less like someone squeezing themselves into a narrow box. Like a coffin. That's what the patriarchy felt like. It felt like squeezing yourself into a coffin two sizes too small.

Lex was done feeling small.

The singletrack wound between sand and scrub on one side and a wadi caked with mud from the recent runoff on the other. The mud in the wadi was lifting and cracking as it dried, revealing lines of darker mud underneath. The cracks formed a mosaic of odd-shaped mud tiles, like the skin of an elephant, viewed from up close.

The bikes carried them over sand and dirt and rock, through the harshening light of the sun and the increasing heat of the dry air. Even as the terrain angled upward toward the mountains and the brown landscape gave way to patches of green grass, then to shrubs and small trees, even as the trails sloped up bare rock and slipped down through trickling ravines, the bikes chugged tirelessly.

The local man—for an additional fee—had sold them full tanks of gas plus two additional cans to strap to the back of each bike. He had also given them each a sack of food, free of charge.

"He is a good Muslim man," said Baba. They had drained their first cans of gas into their empty tanks and now reclined in the shade of a squat acacia tree, munching on disks of falafel from their sacks. "It is a pious deed to feed a hungry traveler, earning blessings from Allah."

"So he fed us to help himself," said Lex with a smirk.

Baba sniffed a laugh and smiled. "I suppose even the most virtuous act is not entirely selfless."

Lex pulled off her gun and holster, eased her arm into its sling, and lay down, staring up at the sunlight filtering green through the slender-fingered acacia leaves. The ground was hard against her back, but it was warm, and with food in her belly she felt like she could easily fall asleep right there. She reached up lazily with her good arm and with one finger batted gently at a cluster of red-and-black berries hanging from the branch over her head.

Baba lay beside her. Even with the heat of the ground against her back, Lex could feel the new heat of Baba's body next to hers. The man was a walking sun.

"Rosary peas," he said, looking up at the cluster of berries. "My father called them crab eyes." He laughed and wiggled his index fingers up beside his temples, like the eye stalks of a crab.

Lex smiled. She shifted slightly against the dirt to work a small pebble into a more comfortable spot against her back. Her shoulder pressed against Baba's. She left it there. He didn't move away.

"Why do they call them rosary peas?" she asked.

"People will dry the seeds and string them together to make rosaries for Catholics."

Lex wasn't religious, but she recalled seeing old women in Vicenza clutching strings of beads hung with a large cross, walking the streets and muttering prayers under their breath.

"The berries are beautiful," she said.

"Yes," said Baba. "Beautiful, but deadly. If you ate that cluster, you'd be dead within hours."

"So much for dessert," said Lex. Baba chuckled. "If it's so poisonous, why do they make jewelry from it?"

"A rosary is not jewelry," he said with a chastising tone. "It is an item of religious devotion."

"It's still poisonous."

Baba shrugged. "Devotion has never been without its dangers. Besides, you would need to ingest the seeds to be affected. You'd have to grind your rosary and sprinkle it in someone's tea."

"That's all it takes?"

"If you have enough seeds," said Baba. "Or, you can break open the outer shell, soak the insides in water and grind it into a paste. From there, you can shape the paste into a cone shape or a needle and dry it in the sun to harden. If you then stick your enemy with it, breaking it off under their skin, the hardened paste will dissolve into their blood and kill them very quickly."

"Can't they just pull the needle out?"

"It takes very little poison to kill. Only micrograms."

Lex frowned. "How do you know all this?" she asked, then grinned. "Personal experience?"

Baba smiled back, but it was half-hearted.

"Any local in this region would know these things. It's a weed, common throughout Africa and many other places in the world. Parts of the plant, prepared properly, actually have medicinal properties. Useful for pain relief, treating cuts and infection. It even has some nutritional value."

"Just don't eat the berries."

"Right," Baba nodded.

They lay in silence for a moment. The sunlight filtering through, lighting the leaves bright green. The vivid red and black of the berries. The warmth of the rough earth beneath their backs. The smell of the heat and the mud and the gas and oil of the bikes. It all mixed into a heady, fecund concoction in Lex's mind, almost like being drunk or high, but clearer, sharper.

Her hands had been folded across her chest. She dropped them to her sides, letting the length of her arm rest beside the length of Baba's arm. She felt his heat. She felt the electricity between them. She felt the hairs on her arm rise, and though she didn't look, she could swear she felt the hairs on his arm rise to meet them.

"It's not uncommon as a method of assassination," Baba said casually.

It took Lex a moment to pull her mind back to follow what he was saying.

"The body absorbs the poison and dissolves the delivery mechanism, leaving no traces behind," he said. "There are even stories of an Indian caste long ago that would poison sacred bulls this way, later claiming natural death so they could take the hides and use them for their own purposes."

Lex had a mind to use Baba for her own purposes.

"And the Russians seem to favor this technique, as well," Baba continued, "for political assassinations on foreign soil."

That shook loose a thought. A Russian operative assassinated near London not that long ago.

"I thought they liked to use radiation for that kind of thing," Lex said.

"Techniques evolve."

Baba reached up, severing the connection between their bare arms, and batted absent-mindedly at the cluster of berries above them.

Lex felt the loss of Baba's touch like the sharp chill of an opened door on a wintery night. She reeled her thoughts back. She'd thrown herself at Baba once before and been rejected. Granted, Lex had been pretty wasted at the time, but it still nicked her pride. She focused on the conversation.

"Have you ever killed someone like that?" she asked. "With the rosary berries?"

Baba frowned up at the underside of the leaves.

"No," he said quietly. "But it doesn't hurt to know how it works."

Lex glanced at Baba's wrist as it turned gracefully in the air above her. He must have been Catholic once, back in Nigeria. Or his uncle had been, at least, if they celebrated Christmas in a church. He'd said he killed the men who had killed his parents. Maybe he'd used a rosary to do it.

What did they call that kind of shit? Poetic justice. Baba had just said he'd never killed anyone that way, but it would have been better if he had. Poetic justice for those assholes. Give them what they fucking deserve.

Baba sat up, scooped a handful of sand, and dusted his hands with it.

"We'd better get moving before we both fall asleep."

"Would that be so bad?" asked Lex. She reached her arms over her head along the ground, groaning as she stretched her legs and her arms. She arched her back, feeling every painful knot in her muscles, twisted and bunched from too many nights sleeping in a truck cab.

She slitted her eyes mid-stretch, caught Baba scanning her body. She felt a low flush of heat and held the stretch a little longer than she had intended, curling her body toward him to afford a better view.

Her thoughts spooled out again in a rush. There were

other things they could do under that acacia tree than sleep.

Baba tore his eyes from her body, looked into the distance, and shook his head slightly. He threw down the sand in his hands in what Lex interpreted as a gesture of frustration—though that could have been wishful thinking—and stood.

"Come," he said, holding his hand out to help her up. "This is not a place we would want to be caught sleeping."

When he pulled her up, Lex stood close to him, practically embracing. She lay her hand on his chest, stared into his deep, dark brown eyes, then slid them down to the arc of his lips, full and deep apple-red. She licked her own lips involuntarily. In that moment, she wanted to bite that fucking apple, more than she'd ever wanted anything.

She could feel his heat under her hand, could feel his heartbeat thump and quicken. Or maybe it was her own.

"We still have a long way to go," said Baba, his voice a dry rasp. With effort, he swallowed, then cleared his throat and stepped away. "We should get moving."

He dropped her hand and got on his bike. When Lex straddled her own, she was acutely aware of the feeling of the seat between her legs. The bike was not what she wanted to be riding in that moment.

Baba kicked his bike's engine to a roar and eased down the trail. Lex started her own engine, felt the bike vibrating through her thighs and her arms.

Yeah, she thought as she eased the bike back onto the trail, they should definitely get fucking moving.

40

THEY SPENT that night sleeping on hard dirt under the stars. The terrain had begun to slope up toward the mountains and Baba found a rocky outcropping, two tall boulders that leaned beside each other and provided some shelter from the night breeze, from the nocturnal animals, and from whatever else might be out in the night. Baba wouldn't specify, but Lex could imagine some possibilities easy enough.

Using a rock and a fallen tree limb, they dug a pit in the soft dirt and built their fire within it. The pit kept the fire from the wind and kept it hidden as much as possible. Between the pit and the rocky outcropping, they should have enough camouflage to pass the night, but they each kept a gun close at hand, just in case.

Baba pulled his only blanket from his pack and gave it to Lex. She offered to share it with him, but he politely refused, choosing instead to sleep on the opposite side of the fire.

It was the politeness of the refusal that chafed Lex more than anything. If Baba had been irritable, she'd know he was as horny as she was. If he'd been cold toward her, that would also be a sign. She had seen his frustration that afternoon. She knew it was there.

But instead of showing it, he was polite, as usual. As kind and considerate as always.

What a fucking asshole.

Lex lay under the blanket, her back against the dirt, her hands on her bare stomach. She considered getting herself off. God knew she could use the release, and if she made a show of it, moaning and squirming around so Baba knew exactly what he was doing, maybe he'd give in and let her fuck him.

But, horny or not, Lex still had her pride. She'd never thrown herself at any man, and she wasn't about to start now. She turned on her side, stared through the flames at Baba's profile as he lay, unmoving, staring up at the stars. Lex fell asleep to the smell of the dirt, the glow of the fire, the faint crack and shush of animals shifting in the distant wilderness, and the yearning ache in her core.

Thunder cracked the night. The dark sky split open.

Lex's blanket was gone. Thick drops of rain like a thousand tiny fists battered her face and body.

The fire was out, the pit already a pool of rainwater. Baba was nowhere to be found.

The wind rose from a moan to a howl, from a howl to a shriek. It whirled in a wild tumult, driving the rain left, then right, then straight down, pounding against Lex from all sides.

She stood, walked around the boulders that formed the rocky outcropping.

In a flash of lightning, she saw the wadi in the valley below. The afterimage hung ghostly in her vision as thunder boomed overhead.

The wadi was overrunning its banks.

Another lightning flash.

The entire valley was filling with water, the flood racing up the slope toward her with astonishing speed.

How could that be? How could the water be rising that quickly?

Lex didn't have time to figure it out. She could already feel the water swirling around her bare feet, the dirt softening beneath them, her feet sinking in the new-formed mud.

She scrambled up the rain-slicked boulders. The rock cut her skin, a dozen scrapes and nicks on her hands and feet. She felt one sharp angle of rock pierce her sole, felt a spear of pain and a hot gush of blood. She slipped, fell to one knee, felt hot blood again beneath her jeans.

She climbed on, to the apex, stood atop the boulders in the lashing rain.

A line of lightning like the slash of a knife overhead, a thunderclap all around her, deafening, like her head was within the storm clouds, like her ears had been boxed by a vengeful God.

In the flash of light, she saw the floodwater all around her, lapping at her feet, drowning the boulder she'd just climbed.

And across the water, in the distance, a dark silhouette.

A man, walking toward her.

In the darkness, the water rose.

To her ankles.

To her knees.

She expected it to be cold. It had been cold before.

But now it was scalding hot.

The rain turned to flame, staining the sky angry red around her, each battering fist hissing and welting and burning her skin.

The scalding water rose to her thighs.

Another deafening thunderclap. Another lightning strike.

The man stood before her, no longer in silhouette, his face illuminated by the lightning, by the flame.

Smiling. Leering.

Skinner.

The water rose to her crotch, burned white-hot through her.

Skinner reached one hand toward her, a casual gesture of unchallenged ownership.

Lex screamed.

Skinner's smile became a grin. He reached out with the other hand, both hands reaching out to grab her, to take her.

Lex screamed again. Her hand scrabbled at her back, found the grip of her gun, cold steel against the scalding heat of the rising flood.

She pulled it around, aimed it at Skinner's face.

Another slash of lightning, another boom of thunder.

Skinner hesitated in his reach.

On his face, confusion.

It morphed into a rictus of pure hate.

As another shock of lightning rent the sky and yet another bellow of thunder shook the earth, Lex pulled the trigger.

～

Lex woke to the smell of dirt and the feeling of being smothered.

A hand over her mouth. A weight over her body, pinning her down.

Instinct took over.

Hook your right foot outside his left. Hook your right arm outside his left arm, above the elbow. Chop your upper arm down onto his forearm to bend his elbow, dropping his left side down on top of you. Use the momentum of his fall to roll the fucker onto his back, pin his arm and keep rolling, first to one knee, then to a low crouch, rolling the fucker onto his stomach and twisting his arm behind him as you went.

Just like she'd taught her classes in Manila.

She didn't teach them to grind one knee into the fucker's spine, to draw their weapons and jam them against the back of the fucker's head.

Maybe in the masterclass.

The fire was low, but still glowing. Once Lex had regained control, it gave her just enough light to see who, exactly, she was controlling.

Baba.

One hand held his arm twisted behind him, one knee dug into his spine.

Why the fuck was Baba trying to smother her in the night?

"Stop," Baba hissed, his cheek pressed against the dirt, his free hand flopping up and down like a wrestler tapping out. "You were shouting."

Shouting? Lex hadn't been shouting. Had she?

She eased Baba's arm down to his side, let him roll over under her, but stayed straddling him. She lowered her gun from his head, but still aimed it at his chest.

"I was shouting?" said Lex.

Baba shushed her, his eyes wide with angry pleading.

"You were dreaming," he whispered. "A nightmare. Let me up."

"Why were you on top of me?" Lex said. She lowered her voice, but kept her gun trained on him. "Your hand was over my mouth."

"Let me up," Baba hissed.

Lex slowly came more fully awake, her mind catching up to her body. She realized the position they were in.

Baba tried to sit up. Lex pushed him back with a hand on his chest.

His hips wriggled beneath her. She felt that ache in her core again.

This time, she ignored it.

"Why was your ha—"

She stopped mid-sentence when she heard a voice, faint and distant, but clear on the dry night air. Lex looked at the sky, was surprised to see stars.

A clear night. No rain.

She'd been dreaming.

Baba's words sank in.

She'd been shouting.

Shouting, dreaming, when there were voices nearby.

Lex rose to a crouch and crab-walked to the edge of the boulder, squatted down and peered around it. She heard Baba get up and sweep dirt into the fire pit. What faint red glow there had been went black. Baba came up behind her, crouched above her. He lay his hand on her back, hot against the cool night air. Its heat seeped into Lex's skin through the thin cotton of her camisole.

She could see nothing across the valley that she knew lay before her. Only darkness. What sliver of moon had been in the sky the last few nights was gone, leaving only the pale light of the stars.

She waited, listening, her senses growing sharper with each passing moment. She heard the squeak of a desert mouse ten feet from the boulder. She saw the shine of the stars in its dark eyes.

But she heard nothing from further away. No more voices. No hint of movement.

Her mind flashed to the valley, flooded. To a man in silhouette, a face twisted with rage.

To the sound of a gunshot.

She gripped her pistol tighter, finding comfort in the press of the firm metal against the bones of her hand.

She and Baba waited for what must have been thirty minutes, crouched together against the rock. His hand never left her back. His warmth countered the coolness of the rock against her cheek, the air against her skin.

At last, he stood and took his hand away, leaving a fading afterimage in its place.

"Go back to sleep," he said quietly. "I'll take the first watch."

He walked off to fetch his gun, then stopped, turned back.

"Try not to have any more nightmares," he said.

41

THEY RODE the dirt bikes up the mountain until mid-morning, when the trail became too steep, too rocky to ride safely. They left them in a shallow indentation in the rock, hidden by a stand of trees. Lex could have sworn she saw an old oil stain on the ground when she leaned her bike against the rock, but Baba was already starting up the trail, shrugging his pack onto his shoulders. Lex untied her gear and followed.

The terrain was steep, but manageable. There were a few places where Lex had to take her arm out of its sling and scramble on all fours to traverse a slide or to climb up a steep rise. After the exertions the previous night and the bike ride that morning, her injured shoulder was scream-ing, but she chewed the inside of her cheeks bloody and said nothing. She'd endured a hell of a lot worse. She wasn't about to complain about an aching shoulder.

They were both sweating and breathing hard by the time Baba stopped them for a bite to eat. They sat on a ledge overlooking the valley while they ate. Green trees and yellow grasses spread below her. To her right, the landscape grew denser, greener. They weren't in the desert anymore. They'd left that behind in El Fasher and Nyala. But Lex hadn't seen this much green since she left Italy.

Where were they? They'd passed through Nyala, heading southwest toward the border with the Central African Republic. Then they'd turned due south.

Kafia Kingi.

They had to be in Kafia Kingi, a disputed territory between Sudan and South Sudan. Which meant the green to Lex's right was Radom National Park. It dominated most of that area.

And so did smugglers and bandits. Disputed territory from the last civil war, bordering on the edge of the current civil war, made a perfect hiding spot for criminals. Kafia Kingi was notorious as a staging ground for smugglers of Congolese ivory, preparing to ship their wares north.

Was that what they'd heard the night before? Smugglers?

Ivory smugglers were ruthless. She and Baba were lucky not to have been discovered, or else they might not be breathing today.

"We are close now," said Baba when they'd both finished eating the last of their food. They shrugged on their packs. "We'll arrive before nightfall."

He scanned the valley and examined the area around them, listening closely for a moment. Lex hadn't heard or seen anything, but if the smugglers had been poking around last night, it made sense to keep an eye out for them now. Apparently seeing and hearing nothing out of the ordinary, Baba turned to move on. Lex stopped him with a hand on one arm.

"What happens when we do get there?" Baba turned back to her, his brows raised in question. "Won't the kidnappers have lookouts? Won't they kill us if they see us coming?"

Baba nodded slowly. "We will have to be careful. We can't know what will happen." A mischievous light came into his eyes. "But that's what keeps life interesting, isn't it, little wolf?"

~

A few hours later, the trail flattened at a plateau along the side of the mountain, sloping gently upward to the mouth of a wide cave. As they climbed toward the cave mouth, two guards emerged from the darkness within and took positions on either side of the opening. They carried rifles in their hands, ready, but the muzzles were pointed at the ground.

For now. The looks on their faces told Lex that could change in an instant.

Lex heard a noise, glanced around, and started when she saw two more armed guards who had materialized on the path behind them. She and Baba must have walked right by them without even noticing.

These guards were skilled.

This must be the place.

As they topped the rise, another man stepped from the cave mouth. He was dressed like an off-duty U.S. Army soldier, with dark green fatigue pants, heavy black boots, and a dark green t-shirt. An off-duty soldier, or a mercenary thug. He carried no rifle, but had a pistol holstered at his hip. His chest bulged under his shirt, his tattooed arms massive under his short sleeves as he folded them across his chest. Though the cave mouth opened ten feet on either side of him, his bulk in the center seemed enough to prevent anyone or anything from passing.

Baba and Lex stopped in front of the man. He eyed Baba up and down.

"You must be lost," he said, his voice deep enough to shake the ground. He swung his eyes toward Lex. "You're a long way from the shopping mall."

The four other guards chuckled. Lex clenched her fists and stepped forward to show that fucker just how funny he was. Baba gave her a sharp look of warning, and, reluctantly, she backed down.

"We've been for a long time," Baba said. "We're tired and hungry."

"And badly in need of a shower," said the man. He sniffed and made a face, waving one hand in front of his nose.

The guards chuckled.

"Yes, actually," said Baba. "We are."

The man grinned. It quickly faded to a threatening hiss. "This isn't a resort," he said, "and it isn't an aid station."

"You have something that doesn't belong to you," said Lex. "You have *someone* that doesn't belong here."

"Ah," said the man, nodding slowly. He looked at the guards. "A rescue party." He scanned Lex from head to toe, clucked his tongue and tilted his head back and forth. "Not much of a party. Unless you're the stripper?"

More laughter from the guards. Lex stepped forward. She'd taken down meatheads like this one before. She'd be happy to do it again.

Baba put his arm out to stop her. Lex shoved it aside and growled in frustration.

The man laughed, loud and deep. The guards whistled and laughed with him.

"You have a live one here, Baba," the man said. "How have you survived this long with her at your side?"

Baba sighed. "It hasn't been easy," he said.

The man laughed again and clapped his arm around Baba's shoulders. "I'm glad you made it back safely," he said. "Reports have been concerning since the rains stopped. Come inside and take some rest."

Lex's mouth dropped open. "You know these assholes?"

"Come inside, Lex," said Baba. "There will be time for introductions later."

"Fuck the introductions," said Lex. "I want some explanations."

"There will be time for those, as well."

The guards from behind walked past Lex, joined the two front guards, and went inside the cave. The large man turned Baba away and led him inside. Baba cast a look back at Lex over his shoulder.

"Come, little wolf," he said. "This is the place you've been looking for."

They disappeared into the darkness of the cave mouth. Lex stood outside, alone, her hands on her hips.

Un-fucking-believable. She racked her brains, back to the day she'd met Baba. He said he knew where the hostages were. He said he didn't work for the kidnappers.

He didn't say anything about being friends with them.

What the fuck else wasn't he telling her?

She pulled in a long breath and blew it out, turned her back to the cave, looking off the edge of the mountain trail over the green treetops of Radom park.

What option did she have at this point? She still hadn't seen the hostages. She had no guarantee they were even inside, or that they were still alive. She could demand to see them, but what would she do if they refused? Leave? With no food, no shelter, no transportation except a dirt bike with a quarter-tank of gas, and no idea where she was, in a region with little government and plenty of dangerous people?

No, Lex had chosen this path back in Khartoum, and she had to stay on it. The only way out is through.

She turned back to the cave, stared into the gaping darkness in front of her.

The only way out is through, but the question was, through what?

42

ONCE LEX ENTERED the cave and her eyes adjusted to the darkness, she found a surprisingly clean and efficient operation in place. The mouth of the cave was kept dark —intentionally, it seemed—but it curved sharply to one side and opened into a bright, spacious vestibule lit with solar-powered lanterns set into niches in the rock walls. Three corridors branched off from the vestibule, and people milled around and through the space from one corridor to another. Most of them were men—some in fatigues, some in civilian clothes—but there were some women, too, and even two children that darted past, playing chase.

The walls were natural rock, rough and cool under Lex's hand, with no signs of any adulteration. Was this entire space natural? It seemed too perfect, too well-suited to human habitation to be true, but Lex couldn't fathom the resources it would have required to build such a setup, or even to shape it from an existing cave system.

"Lex," called Baba from halfway down the left-most corridor, "this way."

The guards had gone. Only Baba and the burly man from the cave mouth walked with Lex.

"Alexis Wolfe," said Baba, "this is Ezenwa Ebike."

"I apologize for the fun at your expense, Ms. Wolfe," said Ezenwa, his voice now as deep and rich and sweet as honey. "Though your teeth do seem as sharp as your name would suggest." He laughed, a booming laugh that echoed off the rock walls and brought involuntary smiles to the face of the people walking by. "Welcome to our humble dwelling. We are happy to have you here."

Lex wanted to be pissed off at the man, but it was difficult, even for her. His energy was big and loud and infectious as hell. She managed to grumble something back at him, but he just laughed again. This time, Lex couldn't keep from smiling herself. But only for a second before she regained her scowl.

"What is this place?" she asked.

"This is *udo n'etiti ara*," said Ezenwa, "our home."

Udo n'etiti ara. Peace among the madness.

"Our home, and our base of operations," Baba added.

Fucking hell. First he's friends with the kidnappers. Now Baba was talking like he *did* work for them. Had he lied to her in Khartoum? If so, why?

They walked by an opening in the corridor that revealed a large space filled with tables where people were sitting and eating. Men, women, children of all ages. It looked like a restaurant in a small town on a Saturday afternoon. The smell of roasted meat and hot bread made Lex's stomach growl.

"This is where our families live and grow," said Ezenwa, "free from fear and oppression and prejudice."

"It's a commune."

"Yes," Ezenwa nodded, "of a kind."

"How long has it been here?"

"Not long," said Baba. "A few years."

They turned left into a smaller corridor lined with doors fitted into the rock.

"And how long have you been kidnapping innocent people?" said Lex, venom in her voice. She waved at a small group passing them in the corridor. "Are any of these people hostages?"

They stopped. Ezenwa opened a door.

"You can stay in this room," said Baba. "It has a private shower and toilet. There is a change of clothes in the armoire that should fit you well enough."

"We have no hostages here," said Ezenwa. "Only family and honored guests."

He spoke with a sincerity and a quiet dignity Lex found hard to discredit. It was the same dignity, she realized, that Baba carried. No histrionics, no games. Just honesty.

Honesty always made Lex suspicious.

"I can come back in, say, one hour to bring you to the cafeteria," said Baba. "Unless you would prefer to rest first?" He glanced at Lex's shoulder, then back to her eyes. "We have a very skilled doctor here that can take a look at your injury. Perhaps it would be best to see to that before anything else."

"I would prefer to see the hostages I came for."

She leaned on the word *hostages* and stared at Ezenwa. He just laughed, like she was only teasing him.

"You will have time for that when you're cleaned, fed, and rested," said Baba.

"I want to see them now."

"I would prefer that you have a more open mind when you meet them."

"My mind doesn't open. It's a steel fucking trap, rusted shut."

Ezenwa laughed again.

"Sharp teeth and a sharp tongue," he said. "I hope to never see your claws, Alexis Wolfe."

"It's Lex," she said, "and you won't if you bring me to the hostages."

"We have no hostages here," said Ezenwa, "only honored—"

"Just show me the fucking women," said Lex.

Baba put his hands on her shoulders and stared into her eyes. She felt his heat pour into her, as always. She felt herself melting in the gaze of his dark eyes.

"Soon, Lex," he said. "You've trusted me this far. Please, just be patient for a little while longer."

Fucking men. When would she ever be free of them? When would she ever be able to do what she wanted to do without having to wait for permission from a fucking man?

Fuck them. Unless they planned to lock her in, they couldn't stop her from looking around. She'd find those hostages with or without them.

"Fine," she said. "One hour."

She'd wait until they left, then sneak out of her room and make her own tour of the facilities.

"And then dinner," Baba said. "A hot meal, freshly cooked, I promise." He smiled. "No more cold, day-old falafel eaten on the hard ground."

Lex's stomach growled. Maybe she could have a meal first. That couldn't hurt, right? The hostages wouldn't be going anywhere.

"There is a fresh towel folded on the shelf beside the shower," said Ezenwa. "Be careful not to turn the heat up too much. The water can get very hot."

A hot shower, too. It felt like Lex hadn't had a hot shower in forever.

Okay, a shower and a meal. Then she'd find the hostages.

Baba and Ezenwa left. She shut the door behind them and sighed.

The only thing she hated worse than being forced to do what men told her?

Finding out that they were right.

Lex could have stayed in that shower forever.

Ezenwa wasn't wrong. The water was scalding hot. Lex dialed it down just enough to sting her skin, but not enough to burn. She examined the wound on her thigh. It was already mostly healed, reduced from a seeping slice to a pale red line. Probably wouldn't even leave a scar.

The hot stream sluiced over her shoulders and down her body, rinsing away days of dirt and grime. The small bathroom filled with so much steam she could barely see the door handle.

She shuddered for a moment, remembering her dream from El Obeid. That triggered a memory of her dream at the rocky outcropping, which triggered a whole string of other memories. Unpleasant ones.

She sat down in the shower basin, letting the water beat against her head and run over her skin, letting the heat ease sore muscles and untie her knotted mind. She would not let Skinner control her, in body or in mind. She would not let that asswad at the wrecked plane inside her head. She had survived Skinner, and she had saved herself at the plane. She was a survivor and a savior, and she would never let those men or those memories dominate her life again.

She stayed in the shower for a long time, at least twenty minutes, then dried and dressed in the clothes from the armoire Baba had mentioned, loose muslin pants and a gauze tunic. A little big, but light and comfortable.

She sat on the bed for just a moment to put on the strap sandals that came with the outfit. When Baba knocked on the door half an hour later, Lex's eyes popped open. She sat up on the bed, feeling like a new woman, staring around the room for a moment while her mind came back online.

The room wasn't large and had no windows, but it didn't feel the least bit confining. Furniture was sparse, just the armoire, a bedside table with a lamp, and a double bed that was surprisingly comfortable. Or Lex had been so tired that it hadn't mattered.

But after her quick power nap, she was raring to go. She combed down her hair with her fingers as she approached the door. Didn't need Baba to know she'd fallen asleep.

Just as she opened the door, her stomach made a gurgling growl that practically echoed through the hallway, it was so loud. If Ezenwa had been there, he probably would have given one of his big, booming laughs again, but it was only Baba outside the door. He just smiled, that twinkle in his eyes that Lex had come to know.

"Your dinner is waiting for you," he said. He held out one arm. "This way."

Lex ate like she would never see food again. Spicy roast chicken and stew with kisra bread and salatat banjar, a bright red salad made from beets. Remembering the party in El Obeid, she demurred on the offer of sharbot, eliciting a quiet chuckle from Baba beside her, but drank cup after cup of what they called karkadey, a cool, sweet, dark-red tea made from dried hibiscus flowers.

When she thought she could eat no more, they brought out a plate of kaak, sesame seed biscuits covered in icing sugar. They tasted so good after her meal that, despite already being full to bursting, Lex ate almost the entire plate herself.

It wasn't until Lex was sipping a cup of bunna that she remembered the hostages she'd come to see. The strong coffee again reminded her of Cariz in Manila, which made her think of Aya, wondering how the self-defense classes were getting along without her. That brought her mind back, shadowed with guilt, to the women she had come to rescue, the three journalists that had been abducted from Khartoum more than a month ago.

Abducted by Baba, it seemed.

"Sarah Court," said Lex as she set down her empty coffee cup.

Baba had been smiling. His smile faded.

To his credit, he didn't ask who Sarah Court was. He didn't feign ignorance. He just nodded slowly.

"Let me bring you to see Dr. Dembélé," he said. "He can make sure your shoulder is healing properly."

"30 years old," Lex continued. "Writes for the Guardian."

Baba sat back in his chair, folded his arms over his chest.

"Isa Margules, her photographer. Thirty-one years old. Both British nationals."

Baba stared at his empty plate.

"Isa has a boyfriend, a chef in Shoreditch. Did you know that?"

Baba sighed. "Lex—"

"And Trina Huntsman," Lex continued. "Twenty-eight

years old. Freelance journalist. A good one, from what I understand. Could even be a great one. Bright future ahead of her. That is, if you—"

"Would you like to meet them?"

Lex was caught off-guard.

Baba pushed back his chair and stood.

"Right now?" said Lex.

"You've settled in, had a shower, a meal, a change of clothes. Even," he grinned, "a quick nap." Lex felt her cheeks redden. "You're ready to meet our other honored guests."

Honored guests, my ass. If Baba considered being chained to a wall and fed table scraps in a dank, dark dungeon an honor, then his worldview was even more fucked up than hers.

But she didn't have time to say that to him. Baba was already walking toward the corridor. Lex hustled after.

She had figured she'd be in and out of Sudan within a week. Ten days, tops. Now, after twenty-one days in the Sudan, she was finally getting to the end of this fucking job.

43

BABA LED Lex back up the corridor into the vestibule near the entrance, then down another corridor. The grade here was steeper, leading deeper into the mountain. Baba turned right, then left, then right again, working through a maze of hallways.

Down to the dark, dank dungeons, no doubt. Lex braced herself to find three bedraggled women. Probably starving, emaciated after a month with nothing but moldy bread and rancid water to eat and drink. They'd be dirty and smelly. No hot showers for the hostages. Maybe a bucket of cold water thrown on them once a week.

There might not even be three of them left. Maybe two, or only one. Maybe just a dungeon full of corpses. How would Baba know? He'd been traveling. And the other guards probably just tossed food in the cell and didn't even bother to check if anyone was alive to eat it.

If those women were dead, if they had been harmed, if Lex saw any signs of rape or sexual assault of any kind, there would be fucking hell to pay like Baba and his band of merry men had never seen. Lex had been schlepping a

318

heavy bag of weapons all over the Sudan for the last three weeks. She'd be happy for an excuse to finally use them.

They turned one last corner and stopped before a windowless doorway. Baba looked at Lex.

"Are you ready?"

Lex dug her nails into her palms, took a deep breath, and steeled herself for what she was about to see.

"Open it," she said.

"Open it?" Baba replied. "Without even knocking? That would be rude." He rapped quietly on the door.

Lex frowned. She heard footsteps approach from inside.

Trina Huntsman opened the door, locked eyes with Lex. Lex recognized her from her picture. Same pretty face. Same serious, determined look. She looked perfectly healthy. Clean, well-fed and well-rested. She looked just like her photo. Better, even.

Trina's eyes slid from Lex to Baba. Her serious, determined look softened to a bright smile.

"You're back!" she said, wrapping Baba in a warm hug. Lex felt a twinge of territorial jealousy as Baba returned the embrace.

Trina kept one arm around Baba's shoulders, but broke the hug and turned back toward the room.

"Hey, you guys! Baba's back!"

Sarah Court and Isa Margules rushed out of the room, exclaiming and giving Baba hugs of their own, like an old friend had returned from a long trip.

They all looked just like their pictures. They all looked perfectly healthy. Completely untouched, untortured, unabused.

If Baba was keeping them hostage, he was doing a shit job of it.

"Ladies, this is Alexis Wolfe," Baba said. The corner of

his mouth twisted in a wry smile. "She's been sent by the U.S. military to rescue you all and take you home."

The two Brits chuckled. Trina skewered Lex with what Lex figured was probably her signature journalist stare, a well-tuned blend of arrogance, intelligence, and mockery meant to cow even the toughest interview subject.

Wasn't about to work on Lex.

"Our savior," Trina said. Lex felt her cheeks burn in spite of herself. "Here to rescue us from the greatest story of our careers? Don't you have an innocent country to invade or something?"

Well, at least Lex had gotten something right. Trina Huntsman was definitely a Democrat.

"The U.S. government and the British government"— she stared at Court and Margules—"sent me here because you three disappeared off the face of the earth in a country embroiled in civil war. They're worried about you."

Trina scoffed.

Lex glared at her. "Your families and loved ones are worried about you. You could have sent a fucking text, at least. You know, call your mother?"

Trina looked suitably chastened, and annoyed by that fact. But she didn't shy away from Lex's glare. The woman had some nuts. Lex had to give her that much, even if she was an ungrateful asshole.

"We haven't been able to send word to anyone," said Sarah in a soft, lilting accent that sounded more Scottish than English.

"This is a very remote area," said Baba. "Communication is challenging."

"Not a lot of cell towers in Kafia Kingi," said Trina. "You'll have to send our apologies to our respective govern-ments. Maybe if they took some of that tax money they're giving to the billionaires and used it to help less-developed nations build out their infrastructure, we wouldn't have this problem."

"I'll be sure to give that note to the president," said Lex drily. "Fortunately, I do have a way to communicate. But we'll need to get off of Sudanese soil first. We'll head to the CAR in the morning. The border shouldn't be far from here."

She looked questioningly at Baba.

"Just a few hours' walk," he said.

Lex nodded. "We'll leave at oh eight hundred." She glared at the women. "Don't sleep in."

Finally, Lex could get the fuck out of there and get paid.

"We're not going anywhere," said Trina. She shifted in the doorway to a stance like a nightclub bouncer, arms folded, feet wide. "Not until we've finished getting what we need for our stories."

Lex matched her stare and her stance. She wasn't about to let some prissy journalist tell her how to run her operation.

"Your stories are not what's important here," Lex said. "Getting you all home safe is what's important. That's what I was hired to do, and that's what's going to happen. At oh eight hundred tomorrow."

"Oh, we'll be up," said Trina, "but we're not going anywhere." She gestured at herself and the two other women. "*We* have a job to do, too, and we're staying until it's done."

That ungrateful fucking bitch. "Do you know what kind of shit I went through to get here?" Lex said. "To rescue your sorry asses?"

"Probably the same kind of shit we went through to get here," Trina replied. "And we didn't ask you to come. We don't need rescuing. So you can just run back to your generals like a good little soldier and tell them you did your job, get yourself a nice pat on the head and maybe a new rocket launcher to play with. Tell the mommies we're fine and let the adults stay here and do some important work." She turned to Baba. "Baba, can we debrief tomorrow morning? I want you to verify what I've got and fill in any missing details."

Baba nodded. "Of course, Trina," he said with an apologetic glance at Lex.

"Great," Trina replied. "How about we meet at, say"—she was still speaking to Baba, but she stared at Lex —"eight AM?"

Her stare was anything but apologetic.

Lex spun on her heel and stalked away. Fuck these fucking idiots. They don't want to leave? Fine. Lex would leave without them.

She turned left, right, right, not thinking about where she was going. It had been such a maze getting in there, anyway, and Lex had never had a great sense of direction.

"Lex!" she heard Baba call from behind her.

She turned left.

"Lex!" he called again.

She turned right at a wall sconce on a rock outcropping that looked vaguely familiar.

"Alexis!" shouted Baba in a voice Lex had never heard him use before. Imperious, forceful, cold. It sounded like the voice of a man who would gouge your eyes out for crossing him, then wash up and sit down to finish watching his six-year-old daughter's dance recital.

She stopped in the hallway. Baba approached her, not running, but walking in long, rapid strides. His face was dark, irritation flashing in his eyes. Lex prepared for another fight, but when Baba caught up to her, searched her eyes with his own, that irritation softened.

"You're going the wrong way," he said quietly.

All the defensiveness in Lex drained away, revealing frustration, fear, hurt, and, most of all, fatigue. Even with the nap she'd taken earlier, Lex had never felt so tired in her life.

Baba must have noticed. He put his arm around her, steered her in the direction she'd been headed.

"I thought you said I was going the wrong way," she said.

"Change of plans," Baba replied. "I'm taking you to see Dr. Dembélé."

He led her through the maze to another room. It looked just like her room, with a simple bed and nightstand, an armoire in the corner, bathroom to one side. The only difference was that this room had a wooden desk and chair beneath a window that looked out into the night.

There was no doctor in the room.

"A pit stop first," said Baba, walking to the armoire and pulling a bottle and two glasses from inside. "The medical facilities are just down the hall. You seem like you could use something to help you relax first."

He filled each glass with two fingers of a clear liquid and handed one to Lex. He clinked her glass with his and took a long sip.

Lex sniffed her glass. Definitely alcohol. Baba had drunk from the same bottle, so Lex figured it was safe, unless Baba had been working on his immunity to iocaine powder.

She took a sip. Strong, but smooth.

"Tequila?" she said.

"Araqi," Baba replied. "A local drink. It's like... what do Americans call it? That liquor you make in your bathtubs."

"Moonshine?"

Baba snapped his fingers. "Yes, moonshine. This is araqi." He held up his glass in salute. "Sudanese moonshine."

He grinned and took another swallow.

Lex smiled and took another sip herself. "I didn't think you drank alcohol, Baba."

"Only among friends," he said, "and only in a safe location. We are safe here."

He refilled his glass, topped off Lex, then put the bottle back in the armoire. He gestured for her to sit on the bed, then turned around the chair by the desk and sat facing her, ten feet from the bed.

"I brought you here under false pretenses, Lex," said Baba.

"I can see that," Lex said, holding up her glass.

"Not about the doctor," he said. "About other things. Small lies, but lies, nonetheless. It is not right to lie. I am sorry."

"Jesus, Baba," said Lex. "Don't get all sanctimonious about it. I've lied to you, too. We're even."

Baba frowned. "When did you lie to me?"

Lex shrugged. "I don't know. I don't remember. Maybe I didn't. But I probably did at some point, so don't worry about it."

Baba looked confused, but shook it off. "I brought you here the same way I brought the women. I found them in Khartoum, looking for a story. I told them I could show them the Sudan, give them stories no one else would have. Just like I told you I could help you find your hostages, even though I knew they were not hostages at all."

"Those aren't lies, Baba," said Lex. "You did bring me to the hostages. It doesn't matter whether they were here of their own free will or not. I needed to find them, you said you could help me, and you did."

"I lied about my association with the kidnappers, as you called us."

"Yeah, you did. But who gives a shit? I don't. Not anymore."

"I'm sorry."

"For fuck's sake, Baba, stop apologizing. No one cares about some little white lies."

"I care, Lex."

"Fine. I forgive you."

Baba nodded, but sat brooding in silence on the chair, staring down at the stone floor.

Lex took another sip. She was already feeling the effects of the alcohol, a warm, soft feeling all through her body, like she was floating in a white cloud. It was good stuff. Did the trick.

"Hey," said Lex. Baba looked up. "Drink your drink. It'll help you relax."

Baba smiled wanly and took another sip. Lex threw back the rest of her glass, then stood. She wobbled slightly, but regained her balance. She sauntered to Baba's chair, leaned over to set her glass on the desk, leaning close to him as she did, closer than she needed to. She could feel the heat from his body. She could smell him, a subtle, sweet scent, like rosewood or something.

"You know," she said quietly, her voice low, "there is something else that would help me relax."

She took his glass from his hand and set it on the desk, then straddled him in the chair. She eased her arm from the rifle-strap sling, let it drop to the floor.

"Lex," said Baba in a parental tone.

She ran her fingers over his shaved head, grown stubbly

in their travels. It felt like sandpaper, tickled her fingers and palms, sending electricity through her body.

"Lex," Baba said again in that same discouraging tone.

"Shh, shh," Lex said. She brought her hands to the softer stubble on his cheeks, put one finger under his chin and tilted his face up toward her, stared into his dark eyes, slid her gaze to those apple-red lips and finally, finally tasted them, felt them full and soft against hers, timid at first, then eager.

Baba slid his hands around her back, pulled her toward him. Lex moaned at his touch, cursed her gauze tunic for being so long, so modest. She wanted to feel his skin against hers, his heat against hers. She ground her hips down against his lap, felt him swell beneath her, gasped at the sensation, her wetness releasing in a gush.

Baba wrapped his arms tight around her, held her hard against him, stood from his chair. The heat deep in Lex's core surged, like a volcano ready to erupt. She wrapped her arms around his neck, wrapped her legs around his waist, kissed him harder, deeper, plunged her seeking tongue deep into his mouth.

He reached behind himself, untangled her legs, lowered her slowly to the ground. They broke their kiss, stood forehead to forehead, both of them panting.

"Alexis," he whispered.

Her name never sounded so good.

Slowly, Baba squatted down in front of her. Lex dropped her head back, felt her heat surge in anticipation.

Baba stood again.

He had the rifle strap in his hands.

Lex stood agape, confused, as he slipped it over her head, gently set her arm into it.

"We should take you to see the doctor," said Baba quietly. "You need to make sure your arm is okay."

He put one arm around her shoulder and led her to the door, pushed her softly into the hallway, and led her down the hall.

Lex swallowed hard, her mouth dry. She couldn't believe what had just happened. Her body was in shock. It was still tingling, the volcanic heat still roiling within her, but the air of the corridor was like cold rain on her caldera.

Her shock turned to anger. She shook Baba's arm off of her shoulder.

"If you're trying to get me to relax," she growled, "you fucking suck at it." She stomped ahead of him, even though she had no idea where she was going. "We'll see what your doctor says about that."

44

Lex lay in her bed, staring up at the ceiling in the dark. She'd tossed and turned for hours before throwing off the covers and just lying there, her mind swirling with thoughts.

And frustrations.

The doctor's office had been surprisingly well equipped. They had even had a portable X-ray machine that sent the image straight to a computer in the office, instantly. Lex wondered again how the hell the cave complex had been built, let alone equipped.

The doctor confirmed that her shoulder had reset properly and was healing nicely. He gave her a real arm sling and told her things she already knew—rest, take ibuprofen for pain, try not to use the shoulder, and so on. Baba seemed relieved, but Lex had grown even more frustrated and angry with each passing minute.

And that frustration had not subsided since Baba led her to her room and said goodnight, backing away before Lex could do anything to stop him.

Her insides ached, a tight pain in her abdomen. She

had fucking blue balls. The female equivalent, anyway. She'd never had that problem before, but she'd heard about it, and she was pissed as fuck that she had it now.

She supposed she could find someone else there to sleep with, but she wanted Baba, goddamn it. And she knew that he wanted her, too. That much was obvious when she'd been straddling his lap. But he was too fucking sanctimonious to do anything about it. Or something like that. Lex didn't know what the fuck his problem was, but she knew what her own problem was. Her problem was Baba, and if she had to sit around waiting for Trina Huntsman and the others to do whatever the fuck they were doing, Lex was going to find a way to solve her problem.

She was up early the next morning, dressed in her freshly laundered jeans and t-shirt, and about to leave the room to wander the facility when she heard a knock on the door. She yanked it open, ready to chew Baba a new asshole, but it was Ezenwa standing in the corridor, not Baba. His bulk filled the doorway. When he saw the look on Lex's face, his laugh boomed down the hall. Lex shoved past him and stalked down the hall toward the cafeteria. She knew the way that far, at least.

They collected their food and ate in silence, Lex gnawing on some kind of bread dipped in a bowl of vegetables, crumbled cheese, yogurt, and a hummus-like paste. Ezenwa called the dish shahan ful. It was delicious, but Lex didn't care. Her blue balls were still gnawing away at her insides like she was gnawing at her bread, and it was doing nothing to help her mood.

Ezenwa sat across from her, his amusement clearly visible on his face, his periodic chuckling reverberating like thunder through the cafeteria.

"Where's Baba?" said Lex.

"Baba is occupied this morning," Ezenwa replied. "He asked me to show you around."

That's right. Baba had to meet with Trina Huntsman this morning. Lex remembered the warm hug Trina had given him the night before. Maybe Baba was already fucking Trina. Maybe that's why he wasn't responding to Lex.

"So you're my babysitter," she said to Ezenwa. "Lucky you."

"Not a babysitter," he replied. "Your companion for the day." He grinned. "And I do feel lucky. It's an honor to show you our home."

Lex eyed Ezenwa. He was wearing fatigue pants and a dark green t-shirt again, just like he had been when he met them at the entrance to the cave. His t-shirt sleeves looked like they were about to split open. His biceps were the diameter of Lex's thighs. The man was a tank.

Three chattering children ran through the maze of tables in the cafeteria and crashed into Ezenwa from all sides. He gave a mock groan, then scooped all three kids in his massive arms and gave them a bear hug that left them giggling and groaning and gasping for air.

A tall, beautiful woman who looked to be in her late thirties came up behind Ezenwa and put her hand on his back. With long slender limbs, chiseled features, and a shaved head, she bore an otherworldly grace and elegance that awed Lex. When she smiled at Lex, her smile radiated a joy and peace and welcome that elevated her beauty. Somehow, just seeing the woman and her smile actually eased Lex's frustration a little bit, took her mind off things for a moment.

"Alexis Wolfe, meet my wife, Nailah, and our children, Makena, Ola, and Xolani."

He patted the heads of the children in turn as he said their names. They were all girls, beautiful, ranging in age from maybe seven years old up to twelve or so. Their smiles were as bright and healing as their mother's, their laughter as infectious as their father's.

"Welcome, Alexis," said Nailah. "It is a pleasure to meet you."

"Nice to meet you, too. You can call me Lex."

"You're another white girl," said the littlest one, Xolani, in a sweet, innocent voice.

"Have you seen a lot of white girls?"

Xolani thought for a moment, her face screwed in concentration. "No," she said at last, "just you and the other ones. The new paper people."

"*News*paper," Nailah corrected her.

Xolani frowned. "That's what I said."

Ezenwa gave her a kiss on the head and another squeeze that set her giggling again.

"Lex and I have work to do, children," he said, "and you all have school. Get some breakfast and get moving, now." He kissed each of them and they ran off toward the food.

"Don't let him bore you today, Lex," said Nailah, standing behind Ezenwa with her hands on his broad shoulders. "If he gets lost in one of his stories, just tell him to be quiet."

Ezenwa's face took on a look of mock offense. "Don't you bias her against me, woman," said Ezenwa. "She may like my stories."

"She'd be the first," said Nailah, laughing.

Ezenwa roared in feigned anger and pulled Nailah's arms forward, pulling her smiling face close to his. Lex watched them kiss, a brief kiss, but a deep one, a loving one.

The gnawing feeling in her insides came back.

After they left the cafeteria, as they were walking down the hallway with Ezenwa nodding and smiling and greeting seemingly everyone they passed as if they were his oldest and dearest friends, Lex asked, "What the hell is this place? It's like a village in the middle of nowhere. Why are you all here?"

"We are all running from something," explained Ezenwa. "For some, it's war or smugglers or terrorists. For others, starvation and famine. Corruption, oppression, prejudice. A few are running from the police. And there are some here who are running from nothing worse than a life of boredom and routine."

"What are you running from?"

"Boko Haram," said Ezenwa, his usually smiling face grim.

Lex's eyebrows raised. "We're you taken, too? Is that how you met Baba?"

"Taken?" Ezenwa frowned. "Taken by whom?"

"Boko Haram."

"I was never taken by Boko Haram, thank goodness. We lived in Damboa, suffering through Boko Haram's attacks for years. Makena and Ola were very young when they took the schoolgirls in Chibok. That was the last straw. My wife and I swore we would never let harm come to them, so we fled our home and wound up here."

"Oh," said Lex. "Then how did you meet Baba? You two seem to have known each other for a long time." Though, to be fair, Ezenwa seemed that way with everyone they passed.

"Our families know each other in Nigeria. We went to

school together, though Baba was much younger than me. We were friends when we were boys."

"I'm sorry," said Lex, her tone sympathetic. "You must have been devastated when he was taken."

Ezenwa stopped in the hallway, frowning. "What is this taken? Who was taken? No one was taken. Why do you keep saying taken?"

Lex stopped, too. "Baba was taken." All sympathy was gone from her voice now. Ezenwa was starting to piss her off. "By Boko Haram."

"Baba?"

"Yes, in Maiduguri. At the church."

"Baba was never taken. And Baba," he laughed, "would never go to a church."

"He was just a little kid. His uncle was in the choir. He went there for Christmas."

"Lightning would burn the church to cinders if Baba stepped inside."

Lex was definitely getting pissed off now. "Baba went to Maiduguri for Christmas. He went into the church for choir practice on Christmas Eve, before midnight mass. Boko Haram came in and shot everyone, killed Baba's uncle and his parents—"

"His parents are in Nigeria."

"—then abducted Baba and forced him to join Boko Haram."

Ezenwa paused. "That's what Baba told you?"

"Yes," said Lex, "that's what Baba to—"

She went silent.

Ezenwa kept his mouth shut.

Was all that shit a lie? All that shit about Boko Haram and being forced to fight as a child and finding his power and escaping, fleeing to the Sudan to do some good, like his parents would have wanted. Was that all bullshit?

Ezenwa's shoulders began to shake. Lex looked over at him and he burst into laughter, loud and deep and reverberating through the long stone hallway. Lex punched him in his massive biceps. It made a dull thud, like punching a side of beef. She punched him in the side of his stomach. Same feeling. Ezenwa just laughed even harder. He was hard as a fucking rock. He had to lean one hand against the wall to steady himself as he bent over in laughter.

"Your face," he said when he could catch his breath again. "Your face was so..." he waved his fingers in front of him, then curled them into claws and made an angry face before bursting into laughter again.

Lex punched him again, twice in the arm, twice in the ribs, then stalked away.

Ezenwa caught up to her a minute later.

"Are you done?" Lex said.

"I can't promise anything," said Ezenwa. "But I think I'm done for now."

"You better be done for good." Lex stomped down the hall, then stopped short. Ezenwa stopped with her. "Why the fuck would he lie to me?" she said. "What good would that do?"

"I don't know," Ezenwa said, brow furrowed, "but he usually has his reasons. You should ask him."

"Fuck that." Lex stomped off again. "Next time I see that asshole, I'm gonna punch him in the face."

"Then I should definitely warn him first." Ezenwa winced as he rubbed his arm where Lex had punched him. "You may be gullible"—Lex glared at him—"but you know how to throw a punch, woman."

45

THE TOUR of the facility turned out to be fascinating. Lex was still seething from the knowledge that Baba had lied to her, but if the tour wasn't enough to distract her completely, it was enough to push her anger to the back of her mind.

The complex had been there for hundreds of years, Ezenwa explained, told of in legends of nomads and raiders and political refugees. Most people thought the location was just that, mere legend. But Baba had found it somehow. They'd made improvements over time, like rigging hydro power to an underground river that ran beneath the caves and provided both fresh water and a natural sewer system. They'd brought in computers, medical equipment, and other tools, and had built modern amenities, but the basic structure was completely natural. A gift from God, Ezenwa said.

The facilities were impressive, but so was the organization. Ezenwa said there were over three hundred people living there, including two hundred fifty men and women and fifty or sixty children, with more being born at a steady rate. He and Nailah had been living there for ten years. Led by Baba, they were among the first to settle there, and so had risen to levels of leadership within the group. There were cleaning crews, cooking crews, medical staff, even a financial organization, half bank, half government, to manage money for both the individual families and the entire compound. Nailah led that function.

And, of course, there was a significant security apparatus. Forty men, more than a platoon, with Ezenwa as their leader. The biggest danger, he told her, was from the bandits and ivory smugglers in the area. They would happily slaughter the entire group to seize the caves for themselves, but they'd never been able to find an entrance.

"Didn't seem that hard to find," said Lex. "The cave mouth is not exactly hidden."

"That's because Baba knows where to go. The trail that leads to that entrance is not easily accessible, not something a random traveler would stumble upon."

It was true. Lex and Baba had climbed some grades steep enough to deter an uninformed hiker, and they'd scrambled over some dicey slides to get to the trail that led to the cave mouth. She wondered if Baba and team had caused the slides in the first place, to discourage those random travelers.

"There are other entrances, of course," Ezenwa continued, "but they are all very well hidden."

That was why Baba had been so secretive, so careful, when they were traveling to the cave. Lex had thought he was just looking out for threats, but he was also making sure no one was following them, tracking their path to determine the location of the caves.

Ezenwa showed Lex the armory, well-stocked with crates of rifles, rocket launchers, grenades, and box after box of ammunition. Lex shuddered involuntarily at the sight of the wooden crates, remembering the crashed airplane fuselage. She pushed the feeling away, stuffed it down deep, and focused on what was in front of her.

It was clear that Baba's group had indiscriminately raided both the RSF and the SAF to build their weapons cache. Lex saw crates that bore the markings of both groups. There were even a few crates with markings from Russian and U.S. militaries. If anyone did find the caves, they'd be in for one hell of a fight before they could take it for themselves.

They walked for hours through the maze of corridors. Lex barely noticed the time flying by. It wasn't until they walked under a natural skylight and she glimpsed the sky above turning dark that she realized they'd been touring all day. They hadn't even eaten lunch.

Ezenwa ended the tour with the medical facilities Lex had visited the previous evening. Baba met them in the hallway afterward, Trina and the other two journalists in tow.

"I hope you enjoyed your tour," said Baba. "Hopefully, Ezenwa didn't bore you too much with his stories."

"My stories are not boring," growled Ezenwa in mock affront. "And, anyway, I didn't tell any."

"You spared her?" Baba seemed surprised. "Lucky you, little wolf." He grinned at Lex.

Lex glared back and said nothing, just folded her arms over her chest and did her best to burn Baba's eyes to ash with her stare.

Baba's grin faded. He looked at Lex for a long moment, his face inscrutable. What the fuck was that man thinking? And why the fuck had he lied to her? There was absolutely no reason for it. Lex was offended by the lie, but she was even more offended that Baba had gone out of his way to deliver it with such conviction. Did he get off on messing with people like that?

Watching the interaction from behind Baba, Trina laughed once, out loud. Lex shifted her glare. She wanted nothing more than to wipe that smirk off Trina's pretty little face. There were a few things back in the armory that Lex would be happy to test on Trina Huntsman right then.

"Well, you must be as hungry as we are," said Baba. "Why don't we go to the cafeteria for some dinner?"

Ezenwa led the way down the hall. Baba fell into step beside Lex. He held her elbow and leaned in toward her.

"Lex," he said quietly, "you seem upset. What is the matter? Did something happen during the tour?"

"All this time," Lex replied, shaking her head, "I've been wondering how you could have turned out so well, so... normal."

"What do you mean?"

"After everything you went through, with your parents—"

"I see." Baba released her elbow.

"—the church, fucking *Boko Haram?*" Lex's voiced raised, echoing in the corridor.

Walking behind them, Lex felt Trina Huntsman lean closer. Lex spun to face her.

"How's that story coming, Trina? Huh?" She poked Trina in the chest with one finger. "You writing for the fucking Enquirer now?"

Undeterred, Trina grinned. "I think I just found a new angle. I'm thinking Guardian? New York Times? Hell, if it works out, this might get me a Pulitzer."

The whole group had stopped in the hallway. Lex cocked her fist, ready to give Trina an award she would never forget.

Ezenwa calmly hooked one meaty arm under Lex's raised elbow, wrapped the other around her waist, and held her in place. Not so tight that she felt squeezed, but tight enough that she couldn't move. She wriggled in his grasp and went absolutely nowhere. The man was as hard as the rock walls all around them.

"Why don't you all go on ahead," said Baba, quietly. "Lex and I have some... issues... to discuss. We'll catch up."

Trina smirked again. Lex flinched, throwing her fist toward Trina's face, hoping to catch Ezenwa off-guard. No dice. He lifted Lex up like she weighed nothing and turned her to face the wall until Trina and the others had passed.

Once they were well down the hallway, Ezenwa released Lex and turned her around to face him. He put his meaty hands on her shoulders and looked her deep in her eyes. It was almost like he was apologizing without apology. A "no hard feelings?" kind of look.

Lex avoided his eyes, but Ezenwa was insistent, moving his head to put it in front of her gaze every time Lex looked away, until she finally broke out in a smile. She punched Ezenwa once in the chest, playfully, then a second time. Ezenwa shocked Lex by pulling her into a bear hug for a moment, a surprisingly tender embrace for such a muscular man. Then he jogged after the others toward the cafeteria and left Lex alone in the hallway with Baba.

She and Baba looked at each other for a long moment. The smile she'd given Ezenwa fell away, defiance coming back into Lex's stare. Baba glanced around the hallway, where a smattering of people were walking by.

"Why don't we talk somewhere more private?" he said.

He led Lex down the hall to his bedroom and again poured each of them a drink of Araqi from the armoire in the corner. He held one glass out for Lex. She turned her back on it. Baba set the glass on the edge of his desk and sat on the bed with his drink while Lex paced back and forth in front of him, her anger rising with each pass.

"Ezenwa told you," said Baba.

"What did Ezenwa tell me, Baba? Huh? What do you think Ezenwa told me?"

"He told you I was never in Boko Haram."

"Yeah, he did. He told me you were never in fucking Boko Haram."

"He told you my parents are alive and well—"

"He told me your parents are alive and well."

"—that my father is working as a dentist in Lagos, as he has been his whole life—"

"That you father..."

"—and that my mother is still teaching schoolchildren there."

"Your mo—" Lex stopped pacing, shaking her head in confusion. "No, he didn't tell me that shit."

"He didn't?"

"Why would he tell me that?"

"Then Ezenwa showed remarkable restraint today."

"A dentist? Your father is a dentist?"

"The man can't hold a secret any longer than he can hold a boiling potato."

Lex shook her head, trying to reconcile all of this new information. She'd just traversed a war zone with a man she thought had been abducted by a terrorist group. Now he was talking about dentistry?

"Where do your parents think you are now?"

Stupid question. Why the fuck did she ask that?

A smile touched the corners of Baba's lips. "Is that what you want to ask me? Are you angry because you think my parents are worried for me?"

Lex jabbed her finger at him, ignoring the burn on her cheeks, ignoring the way that slight smile made her want to bite the corners of Baba's lips. "How about you answer my fucking questions instead of feeding me a bunch of bullshit?"

"I have never fed you bullshit, Lex."

"Oh, sorry, my mistake," Lex replied. "I only know forty languages. Maybe I'm using the wrong term. What do they call it here when everything someone tells you is a complete fucking lie?"

Baba sighed. Lex resumed pacing.

"Everything I've told you is true," he said.

"Not fucking Boko Haram."

"Except for that."

"Kind of an important thing to lie about, don't you think?"

Baba shook his head. "I would say I'm sorry—"

"You better say you're fucking sorry."

"—but I'm not sorry."

Lex jerked to a halt.

"What the fuck did you just say?"

"You needed to hear that story, Lex. In that moment, you needed to hear it."

"The fuck are you talking about?"

"You were feeling powerless and alone. You needed to feel like someone understood you."

"So you lied to me?"

"I understood you," Baba said. "I knew how you felt."

"You understood me, so you lied to me. Fucking asshole."

Lex started pacing again.

"If I had simply told you I understood, you wouldn't have believed me."

"You lied to me so I would believe you?" Lex threw her arms in the air. "You're even more fucked up than I am."

"I told you a story that helped you at the very moment you needed that help."

"You told me a lie."

"I told you a story. There's a difference."

"Fuck you. You told me it happened to you."

"That's how all the best stories are told."

"What else have you told me that was 'a story I needed to hear'?"

"Nothing. Just that."

"No other lies?"

"Aside from the lie about my relationship with the people in this facility, no."

Lex cursed herself for trusting Baba. She'd known all along that she was being stupid, that trusting a total stranger was a dumbass thing to do, especially as a white Western woman trusting a man in war-torn Sudan.

And yet, as she paced back and forth, she felt her anger weakening. She felt her instincts telling her yet again that Baba was trustworthy.

How could he be trustworthy when he'd just admitted to lying to her? Even the way he admitted it was bullshit. A story she needed to hear? He lied because she wouldn't have believed the truth? What the fuck kind of doublespeak mantalk was that? *Oh, no, honey, I was only fucking that other woman because I was missing you so badly.* Was Lex really going to fall for that shit?

And yet, she could feel herself slipping. With every line she paced back and forth in front of Baba's bed, her anger lessened, her trust returned.

"Why did you even tell me that story, then?" she asked. "What help did you think I needed in that moment?"

"You needed to know that your power is still there, waiting for you to use it."

"I already use it. I can kick anyone's ass. Anyone in this whole place. Even Ezenwa."

She wasn't entirely sure about Ezenwa, but she'd taken down beefy guys before. She might not beat Ezenwa, but she'd definitely make him think twice about fighting her again.

"That is not the kind of power I'm talking about."

"Then what the fuck are you talking about?"

"I'm talking about your inner strength. Your faith in yourself. Fists are one thing, but your real power is inside you."

"Oh, okay. Thanks, Oprah," Lex scoffed.

"It's the power you seized in the airplane wreckage."

Lex stopped mid-pace.

"What the fuck do you know about that?"

"Nothing," said Baba, "except what know about those soldiers, and what they tend to do when they find a beautiful woman all alone." He paused. "And what I saw in your eyes when you came out of the wreckage."

Lex squeezed her hands into fists, digging her fingernails into her palms, feeling the skin stretch over her creaking knuckles. She could hear the gunshot and the soldier's screams. The acrid smell of gunpowder, the iron reek of blood. Her thigh stung fire along her still-healing wound.

She turned toward Baba. "What did you see?"

"The power you said you lacked before. I wanted you to know that you aren't the only one."

"The only one of what?"

"Who lacked power when they needed it most."

"You've felt that way, too?"

"I have," Baba nodded, "but my experience was nowhere near as serious as yours. Meaningful to me, but the circumstances were trivial in comparison."

"So you made up a story?"

Baba nodded. "One that I hoped would resonate with what you had been through. Same understanding. Same learnings that I gained. Just a different set of circumstances."

Still total bullshit. But at least Lex could understand now what Baba had been thinking. In a way, it was kind of thoughtful.

Total bullshit, but thoughtful bullshit.

"You wanted me to know that I could still seize my power."

"And you did."

"And you haven't lied about anything else? Just those two things?"

"Just those two things."

"Lies can be in the things you say," Lex stepped toward the bed, toward where Baba was sitting, "but they can also be in the things you don't say."

"I... suppose that's true."

Lex stepped closer, just a foot away from Baba.

"What haven't you told me, Baba?"

"I don't..." Baba gulped. He squirmed where he was sitting on the bed. "What do you mean?"

"I mean," said Lex, pressing her legs against the foot of the bed, on either side of Baba's knees, "what haven't you been telling me?"

Baba leaned back, away from Lex.

"Nothing," he said nervously.

Lex leaned over him, put her arms on either side of his chest on the bed.

"Don't lie to me, Baba," she said, lifting one knee onto the bed, her gaze drifting from Baba's dark brown eyes to his full, red lips.

"I'm not lying," Baba said, his voice dropping to a whisper. "I wouldn't."

He scrambled backward. Lex climbed after him, on all fours above him, straddling him with her knees.

"No?"

Baba gulped. "Never."

Lex slid one hand down his chest, feeling the heat of his body, his muscles rippling under his t-shirt as he shifted underneath her, pulling himself still further up the bed. His hips bucked up against hers as he moved, sparking an inferno within Lex.

Lex shifted with him. She slid her hands to his waist, unbuckled his belt.

"Don't," Baba said. "What are you doing?"

Lex leaned close, slid her hand down Baba's pants, felt the length of his desire.

No matter what the lips say, the body never lies.

"What am I doing?" Lex whispered. "I'm seizing my power."

Baba's lips were hard when Lex first kissed him. Then they softened, opened to her probing tongue. Baba shuddered, moaned. His hands—so firm, so hot against her back—pulled her down to him.

46

LEX DIDN'T KNOW if there were other bedrooms near Baba's room. If there were, they would have gotten a show.

Lex did not hold back her screams. They drowned out the screams in her head. Her orgasms dissolved all thought, all memory in a white heat, again and again and again until she and Baba lay sweaty and panting on the bed.

Then they went for another round.

Lex had no idea how long they spent pleasuring each other. After the depravity they'd witnessed, the pain and suffering they'd passed through, Lex wanted to spend as much time as she could inside that blissful cocoon.

And Baba obliged.

When they were finally spent, Baba's sodden sheets tossed and twisted around their naked limbs, they lay on their backs beside each other, their ragged breathing slowly calming, staring up at the rock ceiling.

Lex's stomach growled, a sound as loud and long as a creaking door opening in a haunted house in a movie.

One hunger sated, another brought to the fore. Lex hadn't eaten since breakfast.

Baba burst into laughter at the sound.

"The wolf is hungry," he said. "And here I am in bed with her. It's not safe to lie in bed with a hungry wolf."

Lex rolled on her side, ran her hand over the ridges of Baba's muscles, lay her hand on his stomach and felt the rise and fall of his breath, felt the sticky heat of his skin. She leaned in, pressed her nose against his chest, breathed in the musk of sex and sweat. She felt yet another stirring deep in her core. She slid her hand lower.

"This wolf," she said, looking up at him as her head followed her hand down his torso, "is going to eat you up."

She felt him stiffen in her grip, bent down to take him in her mouth. Baba moaned again and arched his back, arched his hips toward her.

A banging on the door.

They ignored it.

A pounding on the door, hard and insistent.

"Yes?" called Baba, his voice hoarse. "Who is it?"

The door handle rattled. Luckily, they'd thought to lock it at some point during the evening.

"Baba." It was Ezenwa's voice. Gone was the playful lilt that it usually carried. Ezenwa sounded serious. Stressed. "Baba, open the door."

Lex stopped what she was doing. She and Baba shared a glance. A chill fell over both of them.

They stood from the bed. Baba pulled on his pants as Lex tugged on her t-shirt, then located her jeans on the floor. Baba glanced back to make sure she was decent before opening the door.

Ezenwa barged in. He looked at Lex but gave no sign that he was surprised to see her, even though the bed was a mess, Baba was shirtless, and she was still buttoning her jeans. His face was hard, determined, all business.

He turned to Baba.

"Smugglers," he said. "Armed and in force."

Lex saw the color drain from Baba's face.

"Where?"

"On the path to the cave mouth."

"How many?"

"A dozen we can see."

"Weapons?" asked Lex.

"Rifles," said Ezenwa. "One may have a rocket launcher, but it's difficult to tell. It's still dark, and they are trying to be stealthy."

Baba swore under his breath. "Are the families—"

"Already moving down," Ezenwa replied.

There was a series of caves deep in the mountain that were reserved for refuge during an attack. Ezenwa hadn't shown them to Lex during her tour, but he'd mentioned them.

"And the other entrances?" asked Baba. "If they found one, they may have found others."

"None of the other guards have reported anything unusual, but I've sent reinforcements to each entrance with additional weapons and night-vision goggles for surveillance. We are low on rifles and ammunition."

"You didn't make that raid while I was gone?"

Ezenwa clucked his tongue and shook his head. "Between the rains and the resurgence in fighting afterward, it was too dangerous."

"I've got weapons," said Lex. "A few, anyway. In my room."

"Can you find your way there?" asked Baba.

Lex nodded. Thanks to Ezenwa's tour, she'd finally memorized the basic layout of the place.

"Good," said Baba as he pulled on a t-shirt. "Meet us at the armory."

Lex nodded and slipped on her shoes.

"And Lex?" said Baba.

Lex looked up. Baba pulled her in for a kiss. He looked deep into her eyes. Lex could see his concern swirling within.

"Hurry," he said.

Lex slid along the wall of the corridors, moving against the flow of women and children moving toward safety in the caves below. They all moved quickly, their eyes filled with fear, but none of them ran, none of them screamed, none of them panicked. This was a people that had already seen hardship, had lived through violence. They knew its shape and its weight all too well, and they bore it with courage and dignity.

Lex pulled her duffel bag from the armoire in her bedroom, threw it on the bed. She slid the smartphone with the satellite hookup in the back pocket of her jeans, swapped her sandals for sneakers, and checked the magazine on her Sig. She filled it, loaded it, and holstered it against the small of her back. She shoved a white smoke grenade in one pocket and a frag grenade in the other, slung a loaded rifle across her body, then threw the duffel over her shoulder.

As she pulled open her bedroom door, she heard gunfire to her right, toward the cave mouth. A dozen men with rifles ran down the corridor toward the sound, the footfalls of their boots echoing in the corridor like heavy rainfall on a wood roof. Lex hesitated, wanting to follow, to help. But she went the other way instead, toward the armory where she'd promised to meet Baba.

He stood amidst a small crowd of men and a handful of women, handing out weapons and issuing orders, an earpiece in one ear. Everyone in the crowd bore the focused looks of well-trained soldiers. Even more so because it was their home that was under attack.

When they dispersed, Lex dropped the duffel at his feet. After helping her haul it all the way across the Sudan, Baba knew its contents as well as Lex did. He motioned for someone to pick up the duffel and distribute the weapons inside.

"About time those went to some use," said Lex. "Courtesy of the U.S. government."

"You can thank them for me."

"Not much. Just a rifle and a couple handguns."

"Everything helps."

"Just wish you didn't have to use them here."

Baba nodded curtly, his lips pressed into a mirthless smile.

"Oh, here," said Lex, unslinging the rifle from across her body. Baba put one hand out to stop her.

"You keep that one," he said.

"Why? Won't it be more useful if—"

The sadness in Baba's eyes told her everything she needed to know. He looked to the side.

At Trina Huntsman and the other two journalists, talking to the soldiers, cell phones held up to record their conversations. The photojournalist, Isa, snapped picture after picture, capturing the scene.

"Them?" asked Lex. "You want me to protect *them*?"

"I want you to lead them," he said. "Away from here."

"Wouldn't they be safest in the caves? Then I could help—"

He stopped her mid-sentence with one warm hand on

her arm and eyes deep with a sadness and compassion and sacrifice Lex had never seen.

"Take them home," Baba said quietly. "They're here to hear our story. Now they need to tell it."

Lex scoffed. She frowned at Baba.

"You're talking like you're not going to make it."

Baba pressed his lips tight, those full, soft lips that Lex had been tasting less than an hour earlier. "We'll make it," he said. "Ezenwa's squad is well-trained, and we have others who know how to fight, as well." He nodded, almost as if to himself. "We'll make it." He looked at her with resignation on his face. "But it's time for you to go."

"Fuck no, Baba, I'm staying. I can help. I can fight."

"I know you can fight, little wolf," Baba smiled. "I have seen it myself. But you have a job to do."

"Fuck the job," said Lex. Anger boiled in her, boiling all the more for the truth she knew was in Baba's words. "Fuck the job," she said again, but the conviction had fallen from her words. Baba's smile faded. He nodded.

"You have a job to do," he said, "not just for yourself or your generals, but for us. For me." He stroked her cheek with the back of his hand. Lex leaned into his touch. "Those women have a story to tell. This madness in our country needs to end, and the only way that will happen is if the world decides to care about us. Get them out, little wolf. Keep them safe. Get them home. For me. For all of us."

Lex's heart dropped from her chest, leaving a gaping emptiness behind. She knew Baba was right. As much as she'd like to stay and repeat the last night over and over again, she wasn't living in that world. She wasn't living that life. That was a moment out of time. A respite.

And the real world had barged through their bedroom door.

She nodded, then pulled Baba in with her hand around his neck and kissed him, long and deep. He kissed her back.

She wouldn't ask when she'd see him again. She would leave that to hope, and to fate.

For now, she had a job to do.

47

BABA LED Lex and the three journalists through the maze of corridors, now mostly empty save for small groups of soldiers dashing from one post to another. The families were all safely tucked in the caves below, where they kept their food stores. Enough food to last for months, if necessary, Ezenwa had told Lex during their tour, with an unlimited supply of fresh running water from the underground river.

"This entrance is well-hidden," Baba said to Lex and the others. "It's tucked under an outcropping behind a stand of shrubs and trees, and it opens to the west beside a ridgeline to the south. Hike down the ridge to the northwest, then follow the river north to Birao. From there, you can take the main road up to Bangui."

Lex knew the closest U.S. military bases were the temporary bases to the south in Djema and Obo. But they would need to skirt Mont Toussoro to get there, risking travel through rough, unpatrolled country. Smugglers didn't often recognize borders on a map. If left unharrassed, they were just as likely to populate the forests just over the border as they were the forests on this side. Baba's plan was a longer route, but a safer one. Once they were over the border, Lex would make the call on her sat phone and let her contacts tell her where to go for exfil.

How she would know she was over the border was still a mystery, but Baba had said it was a few hours' hike to the Central African Republic. They would keep walking until the sun began to lower in the sky, then she'd turn on the phone and check their position.

They came around a corner to a narrowing bottleneck with a solid wall at the end. There was a small opening in the wall, low enough that Lex would have to duck to go through, and narrow enough that they would have to exit in a single file. Two guards were there, huddled around a small desk, both of them peering intently at a small TV monitor while one of the guards moved a joystick back and forth.

On the screen, Lex could see a camera panning with the joystick movements. It was a typical green phosphor night-vision view from what she assumed was the area just outside the opening. The screen was filled with the light green glow of leaves of shrubs and small trees, fading to eerie black beyond.

Night vision always gave Lex the shivers. Looked too much like a horror movie.

But the entrance seemed to be well hidden behind dense foliage. And after studying the screen for several minutes, neither Baba, Lex, nor the two guards could see any movement beyond. This entrance, it seemed, had not yet been discovered by the smugglers.

Ezenwa appeared at the end of the hallway and stalked toward Baba. They spoke briefly in Yulu, probably assuming Lex and the others wouldn't understand the language, as it was spoken by only a few thousand people in the world, the population centered in the surrounding region.

They assumed wrong. Lex understood every word they said.

But even if she didn't, the look on Baba's face would have told her everything she needed to know.

There was movement outside one of the south entrances. Since the main entrance was on the northeast side of the caves, activity to the south meant not only that there were a lot more than a dozen smugglers taking part in this raid, but that they'd discovered some of the hidden entrances.

Baba looked at the guards and nodded once. Ezenwa led them down the corridor at a jog.

"I'm coming with you," said Lex.

"Coming where?"

"To the south entrance," she said. "If the smugglers have discovered other entrances, that means there's a lot more than twelve of them."

Baba's eyes widened for a moment, then he smiled slightly and shook his head. "Is there any language you don't speak?"

"I'm coming with you," Lex repeated. "You're going to need every rifle you can find."

"No," said Baba firmly.

"Baba, don't be stupid. I can—"

"No," he said, his voice softer, but no less firm. He put his hands on Lex's shoulders. "This is the perfect opportunity for you to leave. The smugglers are distracted. They haven't discovered this entrance yet."

"Exactly. There's still time for me to help you. We can

come back here and leave once we get rid of the smugglers to the south."

Baba shook his head, staring hard at Lex. Her throat felt suddenly tight, thick, like she couldn't swallow. That emptiness in her chest yawned wider.

She knew he was right. They had no way of knowing how many smugglers were out there or what kind of weaponry they carried. They had no way of knowing what kind of intelligence they had. They had to assume the worst. They had to assume that the smugglers had done a full recon, that they knew every entrance, that they knew exactly how many fighters and how much ammunition Baba and his group had at their disposal.

The safest thing for Lex and the others to do was to leave, right then and there, while they still could.

Lex knew he was right. But everything about it was wrong.

Baba watched Lex's eyes, saw the battle happening in her mind. When he saw her come to the logical conclusion, he nodded.

He lay a rough palm against her cheek, his heat radiating through Lex's entire body.

"Go, Lex," he said. "Go." He glanced at the journalists. "Deliver our story to the world." His gaze returned to Lex, his voice falling to a hoarse whisper. "That's the only way you can save us."

One more long look, and then he glanced at the others again, nodded, and ran down the corridor after Ezenwa and the two guards.

Lex leaned one hand against the wall. The cold, hard rock robbed her of Baba's heat, of his tenderness. The emptiness in her chest threatened to swallow her whole, to drop her into a pit that she would never claw her way out of.

She took one deep, shuddering breath. She wiped the tear that had slipped across her cheek.

She had to pull her shit together. She had a job to do. For herself.

For Baba.

She turned to the three journalists. The two Brits stood wide-eyed, clearly frightened, but still functioning. Good. The last thing Lex needed was someone who would freeze when the shit hit the fan.

Trina Huntsman didn't look scared. Or, rather, her determination overpowered the fear deep in her eyes. She would do what needed doing, no matter what.

Just like Lex.

For the first time since they'd met, Lex was almost glad Trina was there.

Lex released a deep sigh. "Okay," she said to the three women, "any of you idiots know how to handle a rifle?"

48

TURNED out that none of the journalists knew how to use a rifle, but Trina had a passing familiarity with handguns. During downtime on an embed in Afghanistan, a Marine who was crushing on her had taught her how to load and fire a pistol. It wasn't much. Hell, it wasn't anything. But it was the best Lex had. She handed Trina the compact Sig from the holster at her back and flipped off the safety.

"Don't shoot anyone you know," she said. "And don't fucking lose my gun, okay?"

"Okay," Trina nodded, "and fuck you." She flicked the safety back on and tucked the pistol at her waist. "I said I wasn't experienced with guns. I didn't say I was an idiot."

There was fear in her eyes. Lex would have been worried if there wasn't. But Trina had the balls to keep moving, despite her fear. And she had enough of her wits about her to give Lex shit. That was a good sign.

Lex studied the night-vision images on the screen for a minute longer. Still seeing no movement, she waved for the others to follow her and crouched through the tiny opening in the wall at the end of the corridor.

She moved forward ten feet into the dense brush outside the entrance and stopped in a crouch, her rifle unslung and ready. The early-morning air cooled her skin. As Baba had described, a rock ledge hung above her. Behind it, she could see the sky lightening on the other side of the hill. The sun would be up soon.

Trina and the two Brits emerged and waited behind her. Fortunately, they seemed to know how to move through brush without making too much noise. The four of them waited, watching and listening, for several minutes.

The birds were chirping in the encroaching dawn. That was a good sign. Birds didn't chirp when people were moving around them. When people were nearby, birds flew away. Smart birds.

Lex waited, seeing nothing and hearing only the beat of her own heart in her ears. She focused on her breathing, listened to her heartbeat settle and slow. When she was ready, she carefully moved branches aside with the muzzle of her rifle and inched forward through the brush. The last thing she wanted was to make a ruckus and tip off any smugglers who might be nearby. They would work slowly forward until the brush thinned, then make a break for it if the coast was clear.

The sky had shifted from grey to dark blue by the time they reached the edge of their cover. Lex paused there, again waiting and watching and listening for any sign that someone might be out there ahead of them. She heard nothing, saw nothing but shadows.

She could see the ridgeline to her left, up a steep slope. The area in front of them wasn't so much a path as a clearing of less-dense foliage, but it was clear enough to walk without difficulty. If Lex kept the sun at her back and followed the downslope of the land, she'd eventually find the river.

She waved the others after her and pushed through the brush into the clearing. Just as she started toward the right, she heard gunfire behind her, on the opposite side of the ridge.

Where Baba would be.

Lex froze where she stood, waiting, listening, hoping it was nothing.

More gunfire. Automatic weapons. Lots of them.

More joined in.

It was a gunfight now, one that Baba and Ezenwa were in. And it sounded like there were a lot of guns fighting against them.

Instinctively, Lex turned and moved toward the sound.

"Lex!" said Trina. "Where are you going?"

"Stay in the trees," Lex said, pointing to her left without looking at the three women. "Get back under cover."

More gunfire ahead. Lex didn't wait for Trina to respond. She broke into a jog, headed up the slope to the ridgeline.

49

Trina Huntsman watched in shock as their guide and supposed rescuer ran toward a gunfight and left the three of them alone in a thinning stand of trees.

That bitch was going to get them all killed. Or worse.

No way. Not today. Trina had endured a firefight in Afghanistan. She'd wormed her way into Kyiv, scored an interview with Olena Zelenska six months into the war with Russia, when the entire world was in shock and her husband was still trying to figure out how to gin up money for the war effort from foreign leaders. She'd charmed Boris Johnson into inviting her to a lockdown party, then published her experience and ignited a scandal that helped to take down his administration. She was Trina fucking Huntsman. She was not about to die in the middle of nowhere in the Sudan because some asshole decided to take a bullet in the head. Trina had a gun. She had a brain. And she had a story to sell.

"Let's get out of here," she said.

"What?" said Sarah. "No, we can't."

Sarah was a good writer, but she didn't have the guts to

make it big. Gellhorn, Amanpour, Veronica Guerin. These women didn't take shit from anyone. When they found a story, they went for it. Sarah was too slow, too polite, too fucking British to make a real name for herself. She'd end up in a flat in London with two kids and a pudgy, good-natured husband, scooping the scandals of the local horse jumping championship in Cheltenham or some other lame beat. Happy, but boring.

Trina didn't need happy. And she couldn't stand boring. Or a husband.

"She abandoned us, Sarah," Trina said. "She ran straight into what's obviously a massive firefight. She's not coming back."

"You don't know that," Sarah replied, but her eyes were downcast, her voice quiet. She was already caving. She didn't even have the guts to defend her own cowardice. For the millionth time, Trina wondered again how the hell Sarah had wound up in Khartoum. Covering foreign conflict was not where she belonged.

"Yes, I do know that," Trina replied. "Come on. We'll head down the slope like Baba said."

"And then what?" said Isa.

Unlike Sarah, Isa had the killer instinct. She knew how to handle herself, wasn't afraid to get dirty, didn't get scared when the situation got scary. And she had a great eye. She was one hell of a photographer.

But she couldn't write a fucking check. Used to be that a photographer who couldn't write could still have a good career in journalism. Even a legendary one. Lynsey Addario, Isabel Ellsen, Heidi Levine. All specialized in photography.

But even if a picture is worth a thousand words, you still need words. And in the days of new media, when newspaper jobs were scarce and money thin, you needed to be able to write. Images without context don't have the same punch.

But you need pictures, too. Trina could shoot on her iPhone as well as anyone, and that was often good enough. But Trina didn't want good enough. She wanted to be the best. When all this was over, Trina might just have to steal Isa away from the Guardian. If she could only convince her to dump that stupid boyfriend of hers...

"What'll we do then, Trina?" Isa continued. "We go up the river to Birao, up the road to Bangui. Then what?"

"I don't know," Trina said. "We'll keep going into Chad. Catch a flight out of N'Djamena or something."

"That's a thousand kilometers from here."

"So? We came from Khartoum. That's fifteen hundred kilometers. What's a thousand more?"

"That woman," Isa pointed up the ridge toward where Lex had gone, "is U.S. military. She can get us out of here. Back to London. Back to our lives, our families."

Trina snorted. Maybe Isa didn't have the killer instinct after all.

"You know, families?" Isa continued. "People you love and who love you back? You remember those?"

Trina ignored the needle of pain she felt in her chest. "Look, she's not coming back. We're on our own."

"Bullshit," said Isa. "She knows what she's doing."

Trina folded her arms and stared down the hillside, searching the brush along the path she would follow, looking for signs of danger. Why did she have to hook up with these people? She should have talked Baba in to abandoning them in Khartoum. Never take a Brit into a war zone. Trina was going to put that on a goddamn t-shirt someday.

Isa sighed, changed tack.

"Since getting back to loved ones doesn't seem to interest you, how about this?" She stepped in front of Trina, forced Trina to look at her. "The sooner we get back, the sooner these stories start being read in newspapers and on websites around the world."

She had a point. Trina could make it out of here. She knew how to get around on her own. She could survive. But she had to admit, it would be easier—more importantly, *faster*—to take military transport. Then she could shop her story to the Times, BBC, Fox, AP. Even the Guardian. Trina's story would blow away whatever shit Sarah wrote for them. Maybe she could serialize on Substack or put it into a podcast and get it out that way. Or all of the above. Why not?

"Fine," Trina muttered. "But I'm not gonna sit here while she gets herself killed."

She stalked up the ridge after Lex. She'd tie that bitch's ankles and drag her back, if she had to.

"We'll wait here," called Isa. "Have fun storming the castle."

Trina snorted and shook her head. If you want something done right, you can't trust anyone else to do it. Especially not a Brit.

And definitely not Alexis Wolfe.

50

Lᴇx ʀᴇᴀᴄʜᴇᴅ the top of the ridge, half expecting to see muzzles flashing, bodies bleeding, and two lines of soldiers firing across a clearing like in Revolutionary War days.

Instead, she saw nothing. Just more stubby trees and brush scattered across a swale between two ridges, like the saddle of skin between two fingers. From this angle, a few lone rays of sunlight reached around the hilltop, searing a stark line of darkness and light across the swale halfway between the ridgelines.

Lex heard the gunfire again, saw the glint of sunlight on gunmetal as someone clambered over the far ridge and crouched through the brush nearest the cave complex. Someone trying to outflank Baba and his team.

Lex sprinted ahead, charging down the swale, squinting as she crossed from deep shadow into bright sunlight. She came up behind the soldier as he was laying beneath a branch, his rifle muzzle supported by a bipod, taking a bead through his rifle scope. She didn't hesitate, didn't even slow her pace. One quick squeeze on the trigger, a short burst from the rifle, and the man lay still, his rifle stock slumped beside his head, its muzzle staring at the sky like his own lifeless eye.

Lex crouched beside the body, unslung her own rifle, took the smuggler's, and used the scope to peer through the branches at the hillside below her. The terrain fell steeply down from the ridge and away from the hill, stippled with shrubs and trees and rocks, slashed with small embankments and sudden drop-offs where large rocks jutted from the earth.

Ezenwa was hunkered behind a boulder, his massive bulk unmistakable, issuing hand signals to his men. His team was spread among the low trees and behind the rocks on the steep terrain above. Four or five of them guarded the entrance to the caves, which were tucked behind a row of tall, jagged boulders. Lex's breath caught as she spotted Baba there. She pulled her head away from the scope. They were some distance from her, at least a few hundred yards through dense brush. She couldn't easily meet up with them to help. But she might be able to help from where she was.

She heard the report of automatic gunfire, watched Baba and the others duck down, saw a muzzle flash from the corner of her eye. She swung the scope across the hillside, steep and rocky and falling rapidly away from the cave entrance. More muzzle flashes helped her find the smugglers interspersed in a small stand of trees down the slope. Others were hiding behind rocks and natural bluffs in the hillside. Lex counted at least a fifteen smugglers, maybe twenty or more. Baba's crew was outnumbered.

She aimed at an embankment where she'd seen a muzzle flash and waited, slowing her breathing, slowing her heart rate. Someone popped their head over the top and she fired without thinking, smiled to herself at the puff of red that hung in the air for a moment where the smuggler's head had been.

She lined up another muzzle flash, beside a small tree. Her first shot found bark. Her second found its mark. The man's body crumpled at the base of the tree trunk.

She panned the scope to the left, toward where she'd seen a muzzle flash earlier. The sunlight glinted off a barrel, its round eye staring right at her in the rifle scope.

Instinct saved her. She dove for ground, then rolled backward, behind the corpse of the smuggler on the ridge. She heard the dull sound of bullets thumping into his cooling flesh.

Lex didn't wait for more. She kept rolling, then ran in a crouch back down into the swale, out of the sunlight and into the shadow, then circled around to try to get behind the smugglers and take out more of them. She worked her way, crouching, through the trees on the other side of the swale, back into the light. The sun was already hot, even this early in the morning. The back of her neck felt like she was standing under a broiler lamp. She ignored the feeling, crawled forward on her belly, and peered over the ridge to line up her rifle again.

Three smugglers were charging up the ridge toward her last location, halfway to the top of the ridge.

Without thinking, she stood. It exposed her to fire, but she could line the men up more easily without the branches and the low angle interfering. Plus, they were headed for her last location. They wouldn't be looking for her where she now stood.

She dropped one smuggler with a shot to the chest. She caught a second in the thigh, then killed him where he fell. The third smuggler dove for the trees. Lex fired after him, but couldn't be sure whether or not she'd found her mark.

As she sighted in the trees for the man, she swung her scope over the cave mouth in the distance. She glimpsed Baba, swung the scope back to focus on him. He was looking toward the ridge, confusion on his face, probably wondering where the shots were coming from. She watched him spot her and squint, watched his confusion turn to shock, watched him immediately dart toward her, away from the cave mouth.

Away from cover.

He only made it three steps. She watched through the rifle scope as his shoulder twisted awkwardly behind him, his face going slack. He took two more stumbling steps forward, then fell.

"Baba!" she screamed. She dropped the scope from her eye and raced forward, over the ridge, toward where he fell.

Dirt jumped around her feet. She heard the sizzle of bullets zipping past her, heard the splinter of wood and bark. She dove for ground, scrambled on all fours back over the ridgeline for cover, lay on her back beneath a bush.

Baba was hit. Was he dead? Lex had to know. She rolled over, pushed to her feet.

Shots all around her.

She dove for cover again. She'd seen the shooter, the third smuggler she'd fired at before. He was limping up the hill, nearly to the ridgeline.

Lex pushed through the shrubs and bushes toward a stand of taller trees. Thorns tore at her arms, her sweat stinging the wounds. She felt her heart pulsing in her neck, in her ears. Felt the raw scratch of cold air ripping her throat with each ragged breath.

More bullets whined through the air around her. She ducked away as a tree beside her burst open in an explosion of splintered wood. She spun and fired wildly, not even trying to aim, just trying to buy herself some time.

She dove behind a small boulder, tucked her legs beneath her, and tried to make herself as small as possible. She knew the smuggler would have seen her, would know where she was. She knew he'd have a bead on the boulder right now.

She'd only get one chance at this.

She wiped her palms on her jeans, gripped the rifle, and focused on her breath. Long and slow. Long and slow. Counting. Waiting. Forcing herself to count to three, slowly.

One.

The smuggler would likely expect her to peer over the top of the boulder. He would have his rifle lined up, ready to fire.

Two.

Lex would go the other way. And hope like hell that the smuggler couldn't react in time. She took one more deep breath.

Three.

She rolled low and to the side, on her back, her rifle aimed up at the man.

He was closer than she expected, practically on top of her, rifle against his shoulder, aimed straight ahead.

But she guessed right. He was looking at the wrong side of the rock.

She had him, dead in her sights.

She pulled the trigger.

Click.

She pulled it again.

Click.

Icy fear swept over Lex in an instant.

The rifle was empty.

She was a dead woman.

51

THE SMUGGLER FLINCHED at the first click of Lex's rifle. His head snapped toward the sound, fear bright in his eyes.

At the second click of her rifle, he smiled and aimed his own at her.

Lex lay on her back on the ground beside the boulder, pointing her empty rifle up at the man. He towered over her, his weight supported on one leg. Blood coated his other leg, soaking his pants, oozing in weak, pulsing blubs from a small hole at the top of his thigh.

Lex smiled grimly. He was bleeding out. She'd hit him as he dove into the trees earlier. Lucky shot.

Her luck appeared to have run out.

They were deep in the shadow of the hillside. Sunlight was just beginning to crest the summit. It lit the man's head from behind. From Lex's angle, a thin line of bright yellow-white ran across the top of his scalp. From where she lay, it looked like his hair was on fire.

Lex giggled. She couldn't help it. The thought was so comical in that moment, the man's hair catching fire from the hot sun, like he had worn too much hair gel that morning. Like he'd go racing madly around the swale, flailing flop-handed at his head, trying in vain to put the fire out.

Lex had never giggled in her life, but she giggled then, on the ground, about to die.

That giggle might have saved her life.

Instead of shooting her then and there, the man paused, frowned, then seemed to actually see Lex for the first time. His eyes scanned her body from head to toe, then back again, lingering on her chest, on her bare stomach where her slide over the dirt had pulled her shirt up. He licked his lips.

The asshole actually fucking licked his lips.

Lex knew this script all too well. Even in the middle of a firefight. Men were beasts.

She knew what was coming next. This time, she was ready.

The man stepped around the boulder to Lex's feet, keeping his rifle trained on her. Still holding her empty rifle, Lex shifted, dirt grinding against her back, moving away from the boulder to give herself room to maneuver.

"Take off your pants," the man said.

"You take them off."

He stepped closer, used the muzzle of his rifle to lift Lex's shirt, exposing one bare breast. She hadn't had time to put on her bra when Ezenwa had startled her and Baba in Baba's bedroom. Had it only been that morning, just a few hours ago? It seemed like a lifetime.

The man licked his lips again. He flicked at the button of her jeans with his rifle.

"Take off your pants," he repeated.

Lex tried to inch downward, toward the man. She needed him to take one step closer. From the way she was lying flat on her back, she needed him closer to give her enough time and leverage to act.

"No," she said.

Anger hardened the man's face. Lex tightened her grip on the rifle, ready to push away the muzzle of the man's rifle, then jab the stock of her own into his injured leg. He'd go down hard. As long as Lex could avoid being shot, she'd have the advantage. And that's all she needed.

She stared straight at the man's eyes, but she was watching in her peripheral vision for movement, for a bend in his good leg as he shifted forward, closer to her, close enough for her to act.

She watched. Waited. Saw him start to shift his weight.

She tensed her muscles, ready to act.

And then the man's head exploded.

Bone and blood and brain blew to the side, landed on the dirt with a sickening thwap, like wet paper towels dropped on a countertop.

Lex flinched away. Something sprayed over her cheek.

The man's body wobbled, then fell with a heavy thud.

Behind him to one side stood Trina Huntsman, holding Lex's pistol at arm's length like an executioner. In the pale backlight of the rising sun, Lex could see a thin tendril of smoke rising from the end of her gun.

52

Inside Trina's head, a voice was screaming.

Inside Trina's body, she felt nothing. Numb.

Her mind and her body had worked of their own accord, on auto-pilot. Trina felt like she was watching them from a distance, like a movie.

The man had been about to kill Lex. He was about to rape Lex.

Wasn't he?

Trina had to kill him. To save Lex. She had to do it.

Didn't she?

She should have reached a hand down to help Lex off the ground. Instead, she stood numb, the smoking pistol still held in her hand, her arm still extended.

Lex stood, bent to take the rifle from underneath the dead man's body.

"Thanks," she said.

Trina didn't respond.

Lex checked that the rifle was loaded, then started to run back toward the ridge, back toward the gunfire.

Even with a numb body and a screaming mind, Trina

knew that was suicide. But she didn't have to convince Lex of that fact.

The ten armed men that came over the ridgeline did it for her.

~

Trina Huntsman had just saved her life.

That was Lex's first thought.

Her second thought, once she had gotten to her feet, was of Baba. The image of his shoulder twisting backward, of his face slack with shock, replayed in her mind, over and over.

Lex had to know if he was alive. She had to help him.

When she tried to run toward the ridgeline, toward Baba, Trina grabbed her arm and yanked Lex backward. Lex spun around to tell her to fuck off, then watched Trina's eyes widen. Lex spun back and saw the men coming over the ridge. In the rising sunlight, Lex could see their faces, could see their clothes. Ten of them, armed with rifles.

They were not Baba's men. They were smugglers.

Trina and Lex had to move.

They raced up the slope and over the ridge. Isa and Sarah emerged from the brush line. Thankfully, when they saw Lex and Trina sprinting down the slope with no intention of stopping, they had the presence of mind to run with them instead of asking questions.

They had a head start on the smugglers, and if she were alone, Lex knew she could outrun them. But she couldn't assume the other three women had her speed or endurance. They would have to find somewhere to hide.

The terrain formed a row of successively higher hilltops

leading west over the border, ending with Mont Toussoro, a modest five-thousand-foot peak in eastern Central African Republic. The path in front of them curled northwest around the side of one of those hilltops, giving them some cover from their pursuers.

But Lex knew that cover would be short-lived. As she ran, she scanned the hillside above her, looking for heavy thickets of brush or, ideally, a place that looked like it might have caves they could hide in.

She saw nothing.

They ran and ran, with Lex in the lead. The path wound among the trees, following the contours of the hill's shoulder. Lex looked back at the others. Trina still had a dazed look in her eyes, but her usual determination had returned to her face. She was keeping up easily enough. Isa was a little heavier-set, and Lex had been most worried about her. But she was keeping up just fine, showing no signs of fatigue.

It was Sarah that was falling behind. Her cheeks were red and she was blowing hard, starting to look winded. Lex dropped back and took her by the elbow.

"Keep up, Sarah," she said. "Trust me. You do not want those men to catch you."

Sarah's brow furrowed for a moment, then her eyes went wide as she looked at Lex. Lex nodded. Sarah picked up the pace.

She wouldn't last much longer.

Lex spotted a place high on the hillside, a run of rocky terrain jutting between the trees. It wasn't ideal, but it would have to do.

They climbed. Lex came last, helping Sarah up the hill from behind, and wiping their tracks with a leafy branch she'd found on the ground. The higher they climbed, the better their vantage and the less likely the smugglers would be to follow.

If Lex knew anything about criminal types, unless there was money, liquor, or easy sex on the line, they wouldn't work any harder than they had to. Vengeance for the death of their compatriot was a fair motivator, especially death at the hands of a woman. But in this case, the promise of money and liquor was behind them, back at the caves. Baba's caves. The further the smugglers ran, the more fatigued they became, the more likely they were to quit and head back for the loot. Vengeance would only drive them so far.

Money, liquor, easy sex. Lex glanced up the hillside at the others, swallowed hard, and pushed the thought from her head. The money and the liquor were elsewhere. If the smugglers did catch up, Lex would make sure whatever sex they got was anything but easy.

With Isa pulling Sarah's by the hand from above, Lex pushed her the last few feet up the hillside, then did her best to quickly cover the last few yards of their tracks before she joined the others. The spot she'd found wasn't great. The boulders were barely tall enough to hide them if they crouched, barely wide enough for the four of them to fit if they pressed tight. But, through a gap in the rocks, the position did provide a clear view of the hillside below, and to her right, through a gap in the hillside and a break in the trees, Lex even had a glimpse of the curve of the path behind them.

Lex watched through that gap. After a moment, she saw the smugglers come into view. She had counted ten of them coming over the ridgeline, maybe twelve. Now, she counted only five. And they were walking, not running, their rifles held low and at their sides. It was possible the others had taken another path to try to encircle them, but Lex doubted it. If there had been other paths, she would have taken them herself to confuse their pursuers. And the heaving chests and irritated looks on the smugglers' faces told her they were losing interest in the chase.

Exactly as Lex had hoped.

As quietly as she could, she slipped the magazine from the rifle she'd taken from the dead smuggler. It was a Bulgarian AK-74, old but workable, though desperately in need of a cleaning. Guess the smugglers around here didn't put much stock in gun maintenance. The rifle scope was a recent modification, done with reasonable skill. Standard 5.45x39mm with a thirty-round mag. Lex counted only four rounds left, including the one in the chamber. Cursing softly, she snapped the mag back into place, flipped the firing mode to semi-automatic, and peered around the boulder, watching and waiting for the smugglers to reappear on the path below.

Five smugglers. Four bullets. If they spotted Lex and the others, or if Lex had to fire her weapon, things could get dicey. She looked over her shoulder at Trina. Trina was squatting low, her back flat against the boulder, staring ahead into space. The Sig she carried had fifteen-round mags. Trina had only fired once, leaving fourteen rounds left. Lex considered switching weapons with Trina, but Trina had no idea how to use the AK. And Lex didn't want to take both guns. In case she got separated from the others, she wanted to know they had some means of defense.

But the look on Trina's face told Lex she would be useless in a firefight that day. Lex had to figure something out.

Four of the smugglers walked past them, looking tired, angry, and bored.

"This is stupid," said one of the smugglers. They were speaking Dinka, spoken mostly in South Sudan. "I don't see anything."

"These women are ghosts," said another. "Let's go back to the others."

The other smugglers were nodding agreement. Lex started to breathe a little easier.

Until the fifth smuggler came into view. Unlike the others, who walked with lazy swaggers and portrayed the lassitude and attitude of a gang of high-school dropouts with their underwear showing above their low-slung jeans, this man walked slowly, studying the path and the terrain with purpose and intent.

"My brother was not killed by a ghost," he said, "and these women did not melt into the earth. Keep looking."

The other four smugglers stopped in the path just below Lex and the others, waiting for the fifth smuggler to catch up.

"Faheem was killed because he was trying to impress the captain," said one.

"He thought he was better than the rest of us," said another, smoothing a rolled cigarette he took from the breast pocket of a short-sleeved button-down shirt that might once have been white, but was now a dingy grey-brown. He licked the end of the cigarette, spat a bit of tobacco on the ground, then pulled out a plastic lighter and lit up.

The fifth smuggler walked slowly up to the man, menace in his movements. He stopped inches from the man's face. "He *was* better than the rest of us," he said.

"Better than the captain?" asked one of the other smugglers.

The fifth smuggler stared around at the others. "Better than all of us." He stared directly at the man in front of him. "Better than you."

The man stared back in silence for a long moment, a line of grey smoke rising from his cigarette, bending in the slack breeze. He opened his mouth and released a thick cloud between the two men, so thick Lex could barely see their faces.

"A woman killed him," he said. He spat on the ground once more, not taking his eyes from the fifth smuggler. "And here we are, alive. Tell me again, who is better?"

He stared at the fifth smuggler for another tense moment, then looked around at the others. "Who is better now, eh?" he said, laughing. The others laughed with him. He looked back to the fifth smuggler. "You can avenge your idiot brother, Suleyman," he said. "I'm going back to the captain."

He sauntered past the fifth smuggler, back up the path the way they had come. The others followed.

"And what will you tell the captain when you return?" called the fifth smuggler, Suleyman, over his shoulder. "That you have failed to capture the women?"

"Maybe I'll tell him you're as dumb as your brother," the man called over his shoulder, "and the woman killed you, too."

The others laughed as they continued up the path. Suleyman stood and watched them stroll around the bend. Lex waited and watched through the gap in the trees until she saw them moving further away. She returned her gaze to Suleyman.

The scent of the man's cigarette reached Lex, faint with

the distance and the breeze, but recognizable. It was not the scent of tobacco. The man was smoking a joint. With a little luck, he'd pass it around. Lex wouldn't have to worry about those four smugglers any more. Just the one, Suleyman, still standing on the path below them.

"Are they all gone?" hissed Sarah beside her.

Suleyman's head jerked toward them. Lex's heart rate spiked. She frowned at Sarah, put her finger to her lips to tell her and the others to be quiet.

Suleyman was squatting, studying the ground at the side of the path. He didn't seem to have heard them. Lex's pulse eased slightly. Suleyman touched his hand to the dirt, then trailed his eyes off the path, up the hillside.

He was tracking them. He'd found some clue, some footprint in the dirt, some broken branch, something that Lex hadn't hidden well enough.

His eyes roamed, losing their trail, then somehow finding it again, lifting higher and higher up the hillside.

Toward exactly where they were hiding.

53

Slowly, silently, Lex raised her rifle, set it in a notch between two of the boulders that hid them. She kneeled in a patch of leaves and dirt, soft in the shade of the rocks. Behind her, Lex heard Sarah peek around the boulder, suck in her breath, and duck further out of sight.

Lex peered through the rifle scope, locating the smuggler, Suleyman, then closed her other eye, shutting out the world around her, reducing her existence to one small circle, 8x magnification, a thin black crosshair in the center. She pulled in a long, deep breath through her nose, pursed her lips to a thin opening and blew her breath out slowly, letting the tension in her neck and her shoulders, in her arms and her chest, drain from her body.

She extended her senses. She could still smell a faint hint of pot in the air from the other smuggler's joint. She could smell the rotting leaves and the fecund soil beneath her, could feel the cool wet seep into the knees of her jeans. She heard Sarah's quick, panicked breaths, her soft whimpers. She heard Isa coo softly as she held Sarah, trying to calm her, trying to keep her quiet.

Lex focused her vision on the man in her crosshairs, even as she pushed her other senses even further. The soft song of birds on an adjacent hillside, the faint rush of a distant river. The smell of sex and sweat still lingering in her skin. The rent in her heart at the memory of Baba, beautiful and naked beneath her hips. The stab at the memory of his shoulder twisting backward, of the shock and worry on his face as he stumbled.

Focus. Lex pulled in another long, slow breath, pursed her lips again and blew it out slowly, bringing her world back to the one small circle, the thin black crosshair, the smuggler, Suleyman, examining the hillside.

She could take him right now, right there on the path as he stared at the trees, at the soil. One shot through his skull, and they would be free.

But would they be free? How far had the other smugglers gone? Would they hear the gunshot? Would they come back if they did?

No, the longer Lex waited, the better their odds of survival.

Suleyman stepped off the path, his rifle slung at his side, following their trail.

Lex followed his movements through her scope, keeping the crosshair in the center of his chest. He stooped to examine the branches, squatted to peer at the dirt, even picked a leaf and tossed it in the air to watch it fall, testing the wind direction.

The man was a tracker.

If he got too close, he'd be a dead tracker.

He found something, stepped up the hillside along the path Lex and the others had taken earlier, then cast about again, stooping and squatting and staring at the leaves and branches, his rifle slung by his hip. As they climbed, Lex had brushed away any disturbed leaves, had freed any branches that had been tucked or broken in an unnatural way by their passage. But had she missed something? Had there been a muddy patch that someone may have stepped in, leaving a print that wouldn't have been wiped away by her tree branch? Had they left some clue that this smuggler could follow?

Suleyman moved across the hillside, parallel to their position, then found something and stepped higher once again. So far, he was following the exact path Lex and the others had taken. Would he track them all the way up?

Lex kept him in her crosshair, hoping whoever had installed the scope had dialed it in so the rifle's aim would be true. If she had to fire the weapon, she wanted to be sure to hit her target the first time. She might not get a second chance.

He stepped up the hillside again. He was halfway between the path and the line of boulders now. Where below the soil had been softer, the terrain steeper and more shadowed, Lex recalled that here the sun had already dried the morning dew from the dirt. The ground had been harder, the leaves and dead foliage drier. Harder to leave a footprint. Harder to track.

It showed in Suleyman's face. He stooped and squatted and studied, then stood and frowned at the hillside. He looked left and right, turned around to face down at the path, no doubt retracing his steps, trying to imagine where Lex and the others might have gone.

He turned again, facing them. Lex aimed her crosshairs between his eyes. He looked up the hillside, scanned left and right, squinting into the rising sun. Then he shaded his eyes with one hand and stared directly at Lex.

He stared directly at Lex.

Fuck.

Did he see her? Could he see her behind the boulder? Lex was in shadow, but maybe she wasn't as well hidden as she thought. Maybe one of the others was careless, exposed. Lex didn't dare turn her head to check, for fear that Suleyman would see the movement.

Even if he didn't see them, he would see the boulders. Surely, he would guess that they might have gone there, might have thought to use the rocks as cover. He would come up to check, just to be sure.

And he would find them.

Lex pulled in a long, slow breath again, pushed it out through pursed lips. She would shoot him right there, but she still couldn't be sure the other smugglers wouldn't hear. How long had it been since they left? Two minutes? Five? Ten? Time in the rifle scope moved differently than time in the real world. Scope time was focused, intense. That intense focus sometimes made time stand still, sometimes made it race by. Lex had no idea how long she'd been watching the man. She had no choice but to wait as long as she could before taking the shot.

Suleyman stared directly at Lex.

And then he huffed out a frustrated breath and looked away. His head bent, his chin tucked against his chest. He put his hands on his hips and stared down at the dirt, almost as if he were saying some kind of prayer. A prayer to find his quarry, perhaps.

Then his shoulders began to shake. Subtly at first, then harder. Lex heard a noise like the squeaking of a rocking chair. It grew louder, faster. Suleyman's shoulders shook even more. He dragged in a long, ragged breath, bent at the waist as if he were nauseous, then put both hands to his face and fell to his knees.

He let his head fall back, let loose an anguished, animal cry that twisted Lex's heart. The cry of a parent cradling their child's body. The cry of a daughter losing her beloved parents.

Suleyman curled his hands into fists, pounded his thighs as he stared up at the sky, lines of wet shining on his cheeks in the sun. His face was a portrait of twisted grief, of bitter mourning.

His brother. The smugglers had been talking about his brother. It hadn't registered in Lex's mind before. That's the man Trina had killed. Suleyman's brother.

He was mourning his dead brother.

The grief on his face turned to rage. Still on his knees, he took his rifle from his side and shot into the sky, sweeping his muzzle from side to side, spraying fire at the gods. Lex heard the hiss of breath from the others, felt Sarah whimper softly and stiffen beside her, her knees drawn to her chin, her fists bunched over her ears.

Lex kept Suleyman square in her sights. He loved his brother. That much was clear from the way he'd defended him earlier, from the tears still staining his cheeks, from the truth of the sorrow behind his mask of anger.

Lex watched it all through the scope. She felt his pain. She remembered when she'd been told about her parents. Both of them, gone from her life in an instant. Four simple words. *Your parents are dead.* Meaningless apologies. *I'm sorry for your loss.* As if they had anything to be sorry about. As if they could fathom her grief, could fill the emptiness that had suddenly yawned within her.

She understood how Suleyman felt as she watched him through her scope, his rifle fire shouting down all other sounds like his primal screams would shout down his pain. She empathized with him. She knew that pain all too well.

She squeezed her trigger.

The sound of Suleyman's rifle fell dead in an instant. It echoed through the trees, then died as surely as Suleyman himself.

One shot, between the eyes.

Lex pitied him, but the shot was not an act of mercy. She never considered sparing him. He didn't deserve it. He was hunting her, her and the others.

And the brother he loved so much had been about to rape her.

Fuck Suleyman.

He and his brother deserved to die.

54

They waited only long enough for Lex to search Suleyman's body for ammunition, then ran. Lex was sure the sound of her shot would have been lost in Suleyman's rage fire, but she didn't know if the rage fire itself would have drawn the other smugglers back. She doubted it, but she didn't want to stick around to find out.

They ran down the slope along the line of hilltops, the sun behind and to their left, heading roughly northwest. Toward the Central African Republic. Toward their ride home.

With each step away from Baba, Lex felt heavier. What the hell was wrong with her? Was she in love with him? He was a good guy and a great fuck, but, shit, she'd only known him for what, two weeks? Ten days?

Baba had been shot. Lex wasn't sure if he was alive or dead, and she might never know. If life brought them together again someday, fine. So be it. But until then, she had ten million dollars on the line, if she could get out of Kafia Kingi alive, plus two and a half million a head for each of the women running behind her. Lex had a payday to worry about, not some stupid schoolgirl crush. She pushed her feelings away and refocused on the job at hand.

They hiked for hours, the air growing hotter with each step. Before long, their clothes were soaked through with sweat. If it weren't for the thorns and low branches crowding their path, Lex might have stripped off her jeans just for some relief.

Sarah was clearly flagging from the exertion, and even the others looked tired. But none of them complained, and none of them slowed from their steady walking pace. These women might not be used to gunfights, but they were used to humping. Lex had to give them credit for that.

The sun was well past its apex by the time they found the river. It was just a modest stream this close to the headwaters, but large enough that they knew it was the landmark they'd been looking for. They stopped for a rest. Sarah collapsed near the water, laying spread-eagled on the cool dirt. Isa sat on the bare ground beside her, while Trina slumped on a low rock, clearly fatigued.

In all the rush and confusion, they'd brought no food or water. Lex's tongue was swollen with thirst and her stomach was growling. Though no one said it, she knew the others would be feeling the same. The best thing for them would be to get a quick drink, wash the sweat and grime from their faces, and keep moving. Nothing keeps your mind off of your hunger like physical exertion. Once they made more distance, they could find a place to sleep for the night and Lex could hunt for food.

Baba had advised them to follow the river north to Birao, but that was not a quick walk through the woods. It had to be close to a hundred miles away, and in the wrong direction. The closest U.S. military base was in Djema to the south.

There was no point calling for an exfil until they got out of the woods. There would be nowhere for any transport to pick them up. They needed to find the road, and they didn't need to hike all the way to Birao to find it.

"Get cleaned up," Lex said. "The water will be fresh. Drink some, but not too much or you'll cramp. Try to cool off. We'll need to get moving again in a few minutes."

"Why don't we rest here?" asked Sarah, panting where she lay. "Seems like a nice spot to me."

"This nice spot is in the middle of an area notorious for ivory smugglers," said Lex. "It ain't the fucking Ritz. Still want to hang out?"

Sarah said nothing.

"How far to that place Baba mentioned," said Trina, looking up from where she sat. "Birao?"

"Birao," Isa nodded.

"How far to Birao?" Trina asked.

Lex debated whether or not to open the plan for discussion. Birao was a long hike. Without food or water, it would take them two days, maybe three. If they could find food and get some energy, they could maybe make it by tomorrow evening. Camping would be dicey. They had no tents, bags, or packs, so they'd either have to find shelter somewhere or sleep in the open, which, given the creatures slinking around at night—both human and non-human— didn't excite Lex.

The only advantage of heading south was the duration. Lex figured they would find the road sometime tomorrow morning, provided they didn't run into any trouble. But the hike itself would present the same challenges as the northern route, plus the increased danger of running into more smugglers. At least by heading north, they were heading away from that danger.

Should she give the others a vote or just force them to follow? She was tempted to just start heading south and assume they wouldn't notice the shift in direction until it was too late.

No. They were smarter than that.

And they deserved better than that. She was tired of seeing women forced to do anything against their will or their knowledge.

Lex sighed. "We have a choice to make," she said.

The ensuing debate did not go the way Lex had expected. She'd expected more emotion. Whining or hysterics or some kind of blubbering from Sarah, at least. Angry confrontation from Trina. Instead, the discussion was sober and practical. While the route south could lead to a quicker pickup, they reasoned, they would still need to spend the night in the forest, find food, water, and shelter. The added risk of discovery from smugglers, especially in the night, especially given their lack of weapons, seemed unnecessary and excessive. They all agreed that they'd rather spend an extra night in the woods and walk a longer distance than have to deal with an attack from a band of smugglers.

In fact, they convinced Lex that was the better course of action. They changed her mind. Lex could hardly believe it herself.

Once the decision had been made, they cooled their necks, faces, and feet in the icy water, sat in the sun for a while to dry and to rest, and were ready to go again within an hour. No dragging. No complaints. Just determination.

Damn if Lex wasn't starting to respect these three women. They weren't just idiot journalists who'd gotten themselves kidnapped. They were professionals who may have gotten in over their heads, but were soldiering on.

They hiked until the sun bled along the horizon. Lex got lucky and shot a small bush pig, and they roasted it over a fire, filling their bellies with meat. They ate their fill and, since they had no means to preserve the leftovers, they tossed them deep into the woods for the animals to eat.

The stream had grown to the size of a bubbling brook. There were no caves or natural shelter nearby, so they slept in a small clearing not far from the water. They slept in turns around the fire, with Trina surprising Lex by volunteering to take the first watch.

A few hours later, Lex woke, pale silver moonlight spearing through the trees. She walked toward where Trina was sitting near the river, staring at the water.

"My turn," Lex said.

"Go back to bed," Trina said without looking up. "I won't be able to sleep, anyway."

Lex sat on the ground beside her, the cold dirt seeping into her bones. She worked her shoulder joint back and forth, wishing she'd grabbed her sling before leaving Baba's caves. Her shoulder was sore as hell.

"Was that your first time?" Lex said.

Trina looked at her briefly, then stared back at the water. She didn't have to ask what Lex meant.

"How many people have you killed?" she said, sarcasm dripping from her voice.

"Until about a week ago, none," Lex said quietly. "After today," she shrugged, "maybe six? Seven. I didn't bother to keep score."

Trina didn't reply. Her face was hidden in the dark.

"He was going to rape me," Lex said quietly. "He was going to rape me, and if his buddies had shown up, they would have raped me, too."

Trina said nothing.

"And then, if they were feeling generous, they would have killed me. If not, they would have just left me in the sun to die."

Trina scooped a handful of pebbles in one hand, rolled one between the fingers of her other hand, then threw the pebble into the river. The rush of the water swallowed the sound of the impact like it had never existed.

"You saved me, Trina," said Lex. "You saved my life."

"An eye for an eye," Trina laughed without humor. "A life for a life?"

"He deserved to die."

"Is that why you killed the one on the hillside? That last one? He looked like he might have left us alone."

"Maybe he would have, maybe he wouldn't have," Lex said. "Wasn't worth the risk."

"So he deserved to die, too?" asked Trina. "Or is it all just kill or be killed in your world?"

Suleyman did deserve to die. Both for what he had almost certainly done in the past and what he would probably do in the future. It seemed clear as glass in Lex's mind. But Trina's tone suggested she wasn't as sure.

"If he had seen us," Lex said, "he would have killed us all. Or worse." Lex leaned forward so she could look Trina in the face, shrouded though it was with darkness. "Would you have taken that chance? With your life? With Isa's or Sarah's life, just to ease your conscience?" Lex shook her head. "I wasn't going to take that risk. I might have to live with the guilt, but at least I'd live."

Grey light gleamed on the water. Lex looked over her shoulder and saw the moon, a knife-edge sliver of white amid a sea of stars. The asshole moon, opening its eye once again, seeing everything and doing nothing.

"Kill or be killed," Trina murmured.

"You did the right thing, Trina. I owe you my life."

"Is your life worth more than his?"

"Worth more than a rapist ivory smuggler? I like to think so."

Trina stood, threw the pebbles in the river, brushed the dirt from her hands on the back of her pants. Her eyes were hooded in shadow, her face an eerie mask.

"Make sure it is," she said, and walked to the fire to lie by the others, leaving Lex alone under the cold eye of the moon.

VICENZA

55

THE SUN HAD JUST SET and the lights were on in the piazza outside Bar Montagna, casting a warm yellow glow that belied the crisp November air. Camerieri in white shirts and black aprons shivered as they wheeled portable heating towers into place and lit the tall flames. The navy sky was crystal clear. Soon, the piazza would be a haven of warmth, bustling with tourists and locals starting their weekend under the stars. Not nearly as many stars as Lex had seen in the Sudan, but a beautiful night sky, all the same.

"Are you telling me that, in all these years, I never knew you were Catholic?"

Lex frowned as she sat on her barstool. Inside, the bar was already more than half full. The band was just setting up for sound check on stage, and the chattering of the growing crowd echoed off the stone walls. For a moment, Lex wasn't sure she'd heard Simona right.

Simona set Lex's drink on the bar in front of her and pointed to Lex's wrist.

"Oh, that," Lex said, holding up her wrist, circled with a

string of small beads. "Just something I picked up at a market stall in this little town called Birao in the CAR. This super cool old lady was selling them."

"It's a rosary," said Simona.

"Yeah, handmade," said Lex. "From dried seeds called rosary peas. The old lady said she'd made them all herself, but she had a table full of them. I think she was full of shit."

"Those things are dangerous," said Simona as she pulled a frosted bottle of limoncello from a freezer below the bar and poured some into a tiny cordial glass.

Lex's eyebrows shot up. "You know about that?"

"Know about it? I was born Catholic. I had ten years of school with the nuns praying this rosary. *Molto pericoloso.* Very dangerous. I know this firsthand." She paused for effect, leveling Lex with a deadpan stare. "I nearly died of boredom."

Lex laughed.

"If that's what it takes to get to heaven," Simona shivered, "I'll be very happy in hell."

"Well," said Lex, "I just like the way it looks."

"You liked the old woman, you mean," said Simona. "You never could resist a little old lady selling you something. That's why you had to leave Italy, no? You'd have gone broke, otherwise."

"Italy does have a lot of little old ladies."

"It's all we have left. The internet has taken everything else from us."

"What about the weather? The coastline? The food?"

Simona blew a raspberry.

"The internet has brought the tourists to ruin those, too."

"You run a hotel, Simona," Lex laughed. "Tourism pays your bills."

"And why shouldn't I make a little money while my country goes to shit?" Simona grinned. "I'll be happy in hell, remember?"

She clinked Lex's glass with hers and threw back her limoncello, then stepped away to help a young couple. From the sound of their accent, they were American. Judging by their clothes and their entitled attitudes, Lex guessed California. Tall, skinny, geeky guy and a beautiful blonde wearing thousand-dollar sunglasses? Probably Silicon Valley.

She rolled one finger over her rosary while she waited for Simona to return. Fifty-nine beads. Lex had gone online to learn about it. She figured if she was going to desecrate a religious object beloved by over a billion adherents, she should at least know a thing or two about it. Plus, she'd had a couple hours to kill during a layover.

As far as she could tell, praying the rosary involved a couple of Our Fathers, a few Glory Be's, and a whole lot of Hail Mary's. In those proportions, it seemed to Lex like she'd found the right relic. Maybe she wasn't desecrating it after all. Maybe she had become a weapon in the hands of a righteous God.

Fat chance of that. Lex wasn't the slightest bit religious.

She'd snipped the cross off the end of the rosary, though. There was no point in pushing her luck.

"San Francisco," said Simona, jerking her thumb toward the American couple as they walked away from the bar toward their table. "Insisted on leaving me a tip. Wouldn't take no for an answer." She pulled the limoncello bottle from the freezer again and refilled her cordial glass. "When I told them we didn't tip in Italy, when I said we were paid well, we did our jobs well, and considered tipping an insult to our character and our way of life, they still got all pissy about it."

"Did you let them tip you anyway?"

"I wouldn't stoop so low as to take their money for free," said Simona, rearing back, hand to chest, feigning offense. "Besides," she said as she picked up her glass, "I'd already triple-charged them for their drinks."

She grinned, clinked her glass against Lex's, and threw back the shot.

Lex laughed and sipped her drink. She set it back on the bar and teased the beads of her rosary.

"What was his name, Simona?"

"Who? The American?"

"No."

Simona's grin faded. She looked from Lex to the rosary and back, frowning.

"That was a long time ago." She didn't ask again who Lex was talking about. She didn't need to.

"You don't remember?"

"You know I do," Simona said quietly. She refilled her limoncello and drank the shot slowly. "Why do you want to know?"

"Just... curious."

"Curious?"

"Call it research."

"Which is it, curiosity or research?"

Lex shrugged. "Curious research."

"Eduardo Cavalletti," said Simona. "May God rest his soul," she spat on the ground behind the bar, "as soon as fucking possible."

"Do you know where he is now?"

"In hell, I hope," she said. "No, if I'm going to hell, send that miserable sack of cum-soaked dog shit to heaven.

Fucking *faccia di culo*." She shook her head. "I have no idea where he is. He's not in Vicenza. That much I know."

Eduardo Cavalletti. Lex burned the name into her memory. He would be next.

She finished her drink, then slid off the barstool.

"You're not staying?" asked Simona. "Iselda is getting your room ready."

"I'll be back soon," Lex replied. "I have to see a man about a delivery."

56

THE NARROW WAITING area outside Skinner's office seemed smaller than Lex remembered. Smaller and dingier. There were no windows to let in the morning light, no breeze to dispel the dead air. The room seemed more befitting a back-alley dentist than a colonel in the U.S. Army. Which made it perfect for a douche like Skinner.

Skinner's assistant, Eunice, hulked in her usual spot behind her desk as Lex swung open the entry door. The clack of her keyboard did not slow as she burrowed her eyes into Lex. Lex stared straight back without flinching.

Nick stood from one of the chairs against the wall as Lex walked in. He stood, and he stared.

"You'd better close your mouth, Nick, or a squirrel will move in." Lex took the seat beside him.

Nick still stood, gaping.

"Sit down, Nick," said Lex.

He sat, automatically, like a little boy given an order by his mother.

"Lex," he stammered. "Your hair."

"What, you don't like it?"

The corner of Lex's mouth twisted up, a slight smile for herself. Last night, she and Simona had cut Lex's hair from the short, barely shoulder-length it had been all the way down to a buzz cut. As Lex had learned the hard way in the Sudan, even short hair could be grabbed, could be held, could be used to control her. Now, that wouldn't be possible. No one would ever control Lex's body again.

"No, I..." Nick continued to stammer. "It's... You look..."

"Don't hurt yourself, Nick. I didn't cut it for you."

He flapped his mouth soundlessly a few more times, then sat straight and stared ahead in silence. The only sound in the room was the ticking of the wall clock above their heads and the soft clacking of Eunice's keyboard.

Lex pulled in long, slow breaths, doing her best to stop the thudding of her heart. She played subconsciously with the rosary wrapped around her wrist, rolling one finger over the beads. Fifty-eight beads. There was risk in her plan. Calculated risk, but risk, nonetheless.

A mix of excitement and nervousness tightened her throat. She breathed deep. Had this room always stunk? It smelled like mold and cat piss. Maybe it was just the smell of Eunice's decaying, reanimated corpse. The woman was three hundred years old if she was a day.

"The colonel will see you now," said Eunice's corpse without looking up from its screen.

Lex was up faster than Nick, striding across the worn grey carpet to Skinner's door. She pulled it open and held it for Nick.

"Letting women open doors for you now, Lieutenant Colonel?" called Skinner from his office, where he stood behind his desk. "I guess that's what happens when women get equal rights. The whole world loses its fucking mind."

"I'm sorry, sir," said Nick.

"I'm not," Lex replied, striding in and shutting the door behind them. She didn't stand at attention, didn't wait for permission or an "at ease". She took in the room with a single sweep of her eyes—same bookcase, same flag, same folders and papers, same soulless cretin behind the desk— then flopped down on the couch in the corner of the room like she was sitting down to watch television in her own living room.

Skinner raised one eyebrow, taking in her hair, the way she was sitting, *where* she had chosen to sit. The cold leather of the couch seared the skin of Lex's palms, bringing her memories to the front of her mind. She held them there while she held Skinner's gaze with her own. If Lex's plan worked, both Skinner and Lex's memories would be put to rest today.

Skinner scanned Lex's body where she sat on the couch. His tongue slipped along his bottom lip. "Colonel Hadley," he said, "Ms. Wolfe and I have something we need to discuss." He smiled slyly. "In private."

"Oh," said Nick, glancing at Lex. "I, uh..."

"That's not necessary, Colonel Skinner," Lex replied. "I won't be staying long."

Skinner's mouth tightened. His eyes squinted for a fraction of a second.

"I'm sorry to hear that," he said.

"I'm sure you are."

Skinner stood behind the desk, tapped the desk while he considered Lex in silence, then glanced at Nick and stepped to the liquor cabinet. Lex felt her pulse flutter with anticipation at the movement. She pulled in a slow breath to calm herself.

"Time for a drink, I hope," he said. "A toast?" He pulled out three glasses and a bottle. "A new delivery came early this morning. It was starting to feel like a desert in here." He grinned over his shoulder as he broke the seal on the bottle and poured two fingers into each glass. "But I suppose you would know more about that, wouldn't you, Lex?"

"What, drinking? Or deliveries?"

"The desert." Skinner's smile as he turned was brittle and bright, his eyes steeled with hate as they scanned her figure on the couch. Lex had gotten his hopes up, and then she'd denied him. Skinner wouldn't take kindly to that. Skinner was not a man who took kindly to anything.

"Sit down, Colonel," Skinner said without taking his eyes off of Lex.

Nick hurried to take a seat beside Lex on the couch. Skinner set the drinks on the coffee table, then pulled over one of the chairs from in front of his desk. He held his glass in the air. Nick hurried to do the same.

"To a successful mission," Skinner said with that same brittle smile.

"Hear, hear," Nick replied.

Lex watched, her pulse quickening despite her breathing. She kept her face impassive, trying not to show her eagerness as Skinner brought his glass to his lips. When he stopped, Lex's breath, her heart, her whole body, froze.

Nick started to take a sip, then stopped himself hurriedly when he saw that Skinner was not drinking.

Instead, Skinner cocked one eyebrow at Lex. "You're not going to toast to our success?"

Lex forced herself to breathe again. She cleared her throat. "Our success? What did you two do, exactly?"

"Lex," muttered Nick under his breath, "don't."

Skinner smiled indulgently. "For every one operative in the field, there are five more working to support them."

"Well, let's get those five people in here then," said Lex.

She wanted—needed—Skinner to down his drink, but she wasn't about to kiss his ass to get him to do it.

The anger flared in Skinner's eyes, but he did not break his smile.

"Lieutenant Colonel Hadley and his team monitored the situation tirelessly, deterring any potential threats that might have disrupted your mission."

Lex patted Nick on the knee. "Good for you, Nick. I hope you didn't spill any coffee on your uniform while you were working so hard."

Nick stared into his glass.

"Very well," said Skinner. "If that's how you feel, then let's toast to you. You can't argue with that, can you?"

"I'm not the arguing type," Lex said.

Nick cringed and shook his head.

"To Alexis Wolfe, home safe and sound." Skinner raised his glass and stared at her. "Ready... and willing"—the predatory glint of his smile sent an involuntary shiver through Lex's entire body—"for her next adventure."

"To Lex," said Nick.

Lex leaned forward, the leather of the couch groaning beneath her. She picked up her glass and clinked it against the others, giving them a huge, fake grin.

They drank. She did not. She set her glass on the table and leaned back on the couch again, watching Skinner. She didn't know how much he would need to drink. The poison was powerful, but had she prepared the seeds correctly? Had she dosed the bottles enough? She cursed herself silently for only using one bead from the rosary. She should have used them all.

Nick took a healthy swig, then coughed like he was hacking up a lung. Nick had always been a lightweight when it came to alcohol, and he had never been a day drinker. He set the glass back on the table as Skinner scowled at him.

Skinner turned that scowl toward Lex. "You won't even toast to yourself?"

"I gave up drinking," Lex said. She held up the arm with the rosary wrapped around her wrist. "And it is Sunday, after all."

"When did you quit drinking?" asked Nick, frowning. "And when did you become Catholic?"

Skinner just chuckled. He tossed back the rest of his glass, then took Lex's.

"More for the rest of us, then," he said. He lifted the glass toward Lex, then drank. As the whiskey drained down Skinner's throat, the tension in Lex's chest drained from her body. Two glasses. That must be enough.

It had to be enough.

Skinner drained Lex's glass in two quick swallows and set it back on the table. With a stern eye on Nick, he took Nick's glass and cradled it in his lap. "This Scotch is too good to waste on you, Colonel Hadley," he said.

"Yes, sir," Nick nodded.

"And too good to waste, period," Skinner said. "If you can't drink it, I will."

"Don't waste a single drop, Colonel Skinner." A grin spread over Lex's face. "We're celebrating, after all."

The nervous tension she'd felt all morning was gone, replaced with a lightness, an elation, a feeling of justice in the world she hadn't felt since before her parents died.

As Lex watched Skinner toss back the rest of Nick's drink, Skinner's third glass, her grin grew wider.

This time, her grin was absolutely sincere.

MANILA

57

Colonel Nick Hadley tugged at the collar of his shirt as he navigated a crowded, narrow alley in the Tondo district of Manila, searching for the docks. The sky was overcast and grey, but the weather was ungodly hot and muggy.

He'd known it would be hot. Manila in May was always hot. But this was way beyond hot. This was... really, really hot. Sweat seeped through his undershirt and his short-sleeved uniform shirt within five minutes of stepping out of his taxi, expanding since to form large moons beneath his arms and a constellation of sweat-stars across his chest and his back.

He considered untucking his shirt from his pants, but that would be unbefitting his rank. He was a full colonel in the U.S. Army now, representing his country overseas. Even while traveling in an unofficial capacity, with no visible rank or insignia, he needed to honor his station and his mission.

And he needed to honor the late Colonel Skinner, whose untimely death had caused Nick to be promoted. Skinner may not have been a perfect human being, or even a good one, but he had faithfully served his country. He had died serving his country. His sacrifice was honorable, and Nick would not be the one to bring dishonor to that sacrifice.

He tugged at his collar again where it lay, soggy with sweat, against his neck. He wasn't wearing a tie. He'd allowed himself that concession, at least. He would have liked to have been wearing shorts, a t-shirt, and flip-flops like most of the men walking around him, but, again, rank and mission.

The mission was not an official one, he reminded himself. Any mission involving Alexis Wolfe would be unofficial from now on. That was the official doctrine from the top brass.

Lex had done an amazing job freeing the three journalists in the Sudan. President Burnham wasn't even pissed that the mission hadn't ended until after the election. He'd talked it up enough during the campaign, made a ton of hay and gotten a lot of votes. More, even, than if the journalists had come home before the election. And when he finally did announce the safe return of the journalists, he was able to say he was already delivering on his campaign promises. The fact that they were all still alive—alive and completely unharmed—after so many weeks missing was nothing short of a miracle, a miracle of modern American military power in the African theater.

No, it wasn't the delay that had pissed the President off. What had pissed the President off was Lex refusing to show up for the press conference in the East Room of the White House. He'd wanted to hail the American hero who had done the rescuing. Instead, he'd had to settle for hailing the brave American journalist and her British counterparts, carrying forth the bold and honorable tradition of the free press. Still a good story, but the President had taken Lex's absence as a personal affront, especially since the press generally used its freedom to report on the many scandals that followed President Burnham, his rapacious sexual appetite, and his less-than-amused wife.

Hence, Lex was to be avoided, if at all possible. And any job that did employ Lex from now on would be officially unofficial. At least until the next president took office.

But there were some jobs that only Lex could do, and they seemed to come up more and more now that she'd reminded everyone of her value. Nick had one such job for her right now. An urgent one, as always. The damn Iranians just wouldn't give up on their nuclear ambitions, no matter how many times the U.S. tried to buy them off. They needed Lex's unique combination of skills to see if they could learn what would motivate them.

Nick pressed his back against the wall of the alley as two old men rode through on their bicycles, bells ringing in the rasping sound of old-school bicycle bells. The wall behind Nick bent inward under the pressure of his body. He jerked upright, afraid the wall would collapse and he'd fall right into someone's living room, and nearly knocked one of the old men off his bike. The man wobbled the front tire and caught his balance, then moved on without even an angry backward glance.

After some searching, he'd found the food stall where he'd eaten with Lex last October. The old Filipino woman that ran the place had recognized Nick, but she didn't speak English. And, of course, Nick didn't know a word of Filipino or Tagalog. Lex was the language expert, not him. Thankfully, a young man sitting at the table eating lunch had translated and given Nick rough directions to the dock, where the old woman said her daughter Aya was working.

Nick emerged from the narrow alley onto a street that looked like a main street. It would have been four times wider than the alley if not for the clog of cars, scooters, bicycles, and pedestrians, to say nothing of the straining clotheslines, the reeking trash bags, the stray children and the stray pets that filled the space.

Traffic was at a standstill. Nick picked his way through the tangle to cross the road. Fortunately, he could see the water on the other side, so he knew he was headed in the right direction. He headed left toward the port, as instructed. The translator had said the old woman's daughter was in a converted warehouse by the docks. Nick figured it was the warehouse he'd seen when he'd recruited Lex for the journalist abductions, the decrepit, crumbling space Lex used for her self-defense classes.

Only when he came up on the building, it didn't look anything like what he'd seen in October. He recognized the location, close to the water, the strange slant of the building, one corner jutting against the roadway, the other jutting toward the water, all angles when it should have been straight and flush with the road. He recognized the row of windows along the side closest to him, where all the women had watched and waited in a crowd in the dark for their class to begin.

Aside from those few details, everything else was different. Where before the building had been made of rusted, ramshackle corrugated iron, now it had plank siding, brand new and freshly painted in a bright pinkish-red. Where before there had been no entrance aside from a small back door and the wide gates of the loading area facing the water, now there was a wide doorway facing the street beneath a huge sign declaring "Institute for Self-Defense" in tall letters in English, with what Nick assumed was a translation in Filipino above it. It even seemed like the structure itself had been strengthened, reinforced somehow to correct the swaying beams, the leaning studs, the rotting foundation.

As he walked closer, Nick could see through the side windows. They'd been clouded with grime and age before, but now they were crystal clear, and larger. Through them he saw row after row of training mats set on a polished wood floor, all filled with pairs of women working on stances and throws and moves. He counted at least a dozen other women who looked like instructors walking through the huge space, between the mats, occasionally stopping to adjust a grip or demonstrate a maneuver. Dozens more women stood or sat along the walls, watching.

The sidewalk ran across the front of the building toward the front doors, past large picture windows that gave a view to the road. Even through the glass, Nick could hear the shouts of the women, the occasional clapping of the spectators, the grunts of exertion and the squeak of rubber on wood. It reminded him of his days in basic training. He could even smell the rubber and the vinyl and the sweat, though the rubber and vinyl may have been his imagination, and the sweat he smelled may have been his own.

When he stepped through the wide front entrance, he was immediately greeted with a blast of cold, air-conditioned air. As the door swung shut behind him, Nick stood in the entryway, eyes closed, letting cold air and relief wash over him.

"May I help you, sir?"

A lovely young Filipino woman stood behind a counter. She had a trim body, jet-black hair, a round face, and beautiful honey skin that seemed to glow from within. She eyed

Nick silently. She didn't smile, but she seemed friendly enough.

"Hi, yes," said Nick, "thank you. I was just," he smiled sheepishly, "enjoying your air conditioning."

The woman's expression remained unchanged—patient, friendly, unsmiling. She said nothing.

Nick cleared his throat. "I'm, uh, I'm Colonel Nick Hadley of the U.S. Army. I'm looking for Alexis Wolfe."

"I'm sorry, sir, but Ms. Wolfe is not here today."

"Oh," said Nick. "Well, when do you expect her back?"

"We don't."

"You... what?"

"Ms. Wolfe comes and goes as she pleases, sir. She doesn't have a set schedule."

"Ah," Nick said. That did sound like Lex. "In that case, do you know someone named Aya?"

The woman paused for a fraction of a moment, then gave a curt, forbearing smile that fell upon Nick with a shameful weight that should have been beyond the ability of a woman so young.

"One moment, please," she said. "If you like," she gestured behind Nick to a seating area with cushioned wicker chairs and a table with fresh water and coffee, "you can have a seat while you... enjoy our air conditioning."

Nick did just that. While the young woman disappeared through a doorway, he poured himself a cup of coffee, marveled at the rich scent—better than Starbucks, even, and way better that the stuff they served on base—and sat down. He pulled out the back cushion to allow more air flow, shifted the chair to a spot directly under an air-conditioning vent, then closed his eyes, basking in sweet relief from the oppressive heat.

"Colonel Hadley."

Nick started, spilling coffee on his pants. A smiling Filipino woman stood in front of him. Had he fallen asleep? How long had he been out? The woman looked vaguely familiar.

"It's good to see you again, Colonel," the woman said. She pulled some napkins from the coffee station and handed them to Nick. "I'm Aya, Lex's friend."

"Right, right," said Nick, wiping at his crotch with the napkins. These were the only good pants he'd brought. He'd have to wash them by hand if the coffee stained. "Aya, of course. Good to... um... good to see you again."

He held up the coffee-stained bundle of napkins. After a long moment, Aya took them from him and threw them in the wastebasket beside the coffee station.

"Should I call you Colonel Hadley or Lieutenant Colonel Hadley?" asked Aya. "I forget the proper form of address for American officers."

"Colonel is used in informal address for both ranks, actually," said Nick as he stood, brushing down the crotch of his pants. "But you have an excellent memory. When we first met, I was a Lieutenant Colonel."

"And now?"

"Now I'm a full colonel," said Nick, standing taller, still feeling the rush of incredulous pride at the words. Full colonel, just five years after hitting major. Colonel Nick Hadley was on the rise.

"Well," said Aya, holding out her hand to shake Nick's, "congratulations on your promotion, then."

Nick's rush of pride faded, mingled as it always did with thoughts of Skinner's death, and of that horrible night Nick had spent in the bathroom, vomiting long after there was nothing left to vomit. Whatever bug he and Skinner had caught had nearly killed Nick, too. His heaves at one point were so severe, so body-clenching, that he thought he would die from lack of oxygen. His stomach still seized at the memory.

"Thank you," Nick said. "Aya, I'm looking for Lex." He wondered idly if she'd caught the bug, too. "Do you know when she'll be back?"

"I'm sorry, Colonel," Aya said, shaking her head. "Lex was here in December for about six weeks, buying this space and arranging all these improvements." She raised her hands and gestured to the building around them, a look of pride and wonder on her face. "But once everything was on track, she left. We haven't seen her or heard from her since."

"She didn't leave any contact information? A phone number or an address?"

"We have her cell phone number," said Aya, "but she doesn't answer calls or respond to texts." They probably had the same number Nick had. They were getting the same response. "Not that we contact her often," Aya continued. "She asked us not to."

"She told you not to contact her?"

"She *asked* us not to. She said we could do with the business as we wished. She left us a sizable fund and said she trusts us to manage it for her." That would be the money she got from the Sudan job. "And we know we will see her again sometime." Aya folded her hands in front of her. "When we do, we hope to make her proud."

"Hmm," said Nick. "Well, thank you, Aya. That's very helpful. Unfortunate, but helpful. If you do speak to Lex, would you please let her know I came by? We would very much like to speak with her."

Aya nodded.

Nick looked out the door at the street, at the traffic, at

the sweating drivers and bikers and pedestrians. The sweat on his back had just started to dry, and now he'd have to go out into the heat again.

"Say, do you mind if I sit in on a class here?" Nick said. "I'm curious to see what your business is all about."

"We teach self-defense to local women," said Aya with a broad smile. "We help those who are too often beaten and abused, then forgotten or ignored. We help them stand up for themselves, both physically, emotionally, and spiritually."

"That is so interesting," Nick said. "May I sit in on a class?"

Aya frowned. "I'm sorry, Colonel Hadley. The classes are for women, only."

"That's okay," Nick said. "I don't need to participate. I'm happy to just observe."

"In that case," Aya's full smile returned, "you are more than welcome to do so." She gestured toward the front door. "From the sidewalk."

MONTE CARLO

58

BEAT THUMPING HARD enough to rattle the champagne in the flutes on the tables, to rattle your skin where you stood, the sound waves washing over you, into you, through you.

Sound system clear enough, speakers spread enough that no matter where you stood, you stood in a cocoon of electronic music, synthetic trills and filter sweeps and arpeggios close and tight inside your head.

Thick funk of sweat and musk and the finest perfumes and colognes money could buy, like a wall, a solid being, another body among the throng of swaying bodies pressed close against you no matter where you moved.

The sweet tang of thousand-dollar whiskey, ten-thousand dollar champagne on the back of your tongue. Like the feel of a silk teddy the morning after, still soft, still silky, but tinged with the sober regret of the pale morning light.

But no such light here. Not yet. Dawn was still a few hours away.

Here was the spectacle of flashing lights and lasers in an otherwise dim room, of men hired to entertain in costumes that would seem elaborate at Mardi Gras or

Carnaval, of women hired to wear clothes that earn the name only as a formality. It would take longer to whisper the word than it would to remove what few scraps of clothing covered their lithe bodies as they carried the drinks or danced on the poles or swung from the ceiling. Woman as spectacle. Woman as object. Woman as thing to be used for the amusement of others. For the amusement of men.

Lex Wolfe was not amused.

She'd never liked nightclubs.

Though she'd never been in a nightclub like the Emerald Lounge, where the combined net worth of that night's guests was higher than the GDP of eighty percent of the member countries of the United Nations, Lex still didn't like it.

That night, she didn't have to like it. She wasn't there for the party. She wasn't one of the wealthy patrons, and she certainly wasn't one of their hangers-on, fresh from a day in the sun on a megayacht, watching the pretty little race cars speed by, going slowly deaf from the roar of the Formula 1 engines across the water of Port Hercules and from the incessant thump of music—always EDM, always thumping—on one high-end sound system or another.

Monte Carlo has always been and will always be a parade of decadence, where the wealthiest and most insecure go to rub money over their cocks and strut in front of their sycophants. But on race weekend, on that one weekend of each year when Formula 1 comes to town, Monte Carlo goes into overdrive.

And on the Sunday of that weekend, in the evening, when the qualifying rounds have ended and the race itself has been run and won, when the days-long party is about to end save for one last furious bacchanal, there is no hotter place to be than the Emerald Lounge.

Where Lex was.

Where Eduardo Cavelletti was supposed to be.

He was late.

Lex had been following him around for days. She'd posed as a valet to park his million-dollar Bentley. She'd boarded a septic service barge posing as a harbor worker, hoping to get onto his multi-million-dollar megayacht. She'd laid in the sun by the private pool at his high-end hotel in a string bikini and heels to catch his lecherous eye. Nothing had worked so far. He hadn't parked his own car. He hadn't appeared on the yacht. He'd already been surrounded by ten bikini-clad women at the pool, and while he nodded at Lex as his entourage walked past, his eyes slipping across her skin like rancid olive oil, he had neither stopped nor summoned her later.

And now she stood in the Emerald Lounge, clad in a sleek black skirt and top that cost more than Lex's first car and had less combined material than the napkins on the tables. And still she was modestly dressed for the crowd around her. There were women wearing outfits that consisted of strips of fabric that wound only over their crotch and their breasts, dresses in name only. Others wore little more than a G-string under sheer, body-length panty hose, leaving absolutely nothing to the imagination.

And of course, it was only the women dressed this way. Monte Carlo was a bastion of the patriarchy. While the women wore practically nothing, the men wore suits in one form or another. Expensive suits, to be sure, but suits that covered their bodies, all the same. The most skin the men would show was the occasional low-buttoned shirt, the neckline diving only as deep as their sternum.

Though, to be honest, Lex would rather not have seen most of the men with their shirts off. Most of them were old and grossly overweight, having obviously spent far too many years indulging their appetites and exercising only their bank accounts.

Eduardo Cavalletti, however, did not fit that description. He was in his late forties, but still trim and muscular. He'd kept the full head of wavy dark hair that had helped propel his father to the prime minister's post in Italy two decades earlier. He still had his chiseled jaw, the grey creeping into his dark stubble only adding to his appeal, lending a distinguished gravitas to his appearance that was catnip to the type of woman looking for a sugar daddy.

And, if the rumors were true, Eduardo was daddy to many, many sugar daughters. Lex had no idea how his wife felt about it. She probably had her own harem back in Milan and Singapore and New York and wherever else she spent her time. She and Eduardo were still seen together regularly, and in public they put forth the image of a happily married power couple. Lex could not imagine them with a harmonious household and a warm marriage bed, but stranger things had happened. To each their own. Lex was not here to judge Eduardo Cavalletti or his wife on their choice of consenting sexual partners.

She was here to judge Eduardo for the non-consenting ones.

There were no clocks anywhere on the floor. Like a casino, the last thing the owners of the Emerald Lounge wanted the patrons to think about was the time. And for Lex, the time didn't really matter, except that she needed to know when to cut her losses and look elsewhere for Cavalletti.

She'd already spent months tracking him down. His

movements weren't hidden, necessarily, but they were surprisingly difficult to pinpoint. He was a billionaire entrepreneur who, unlike many other billionaires, kept an active hand in his businesses. And he had many businesses all around the world, so he was constantly moving from city to city, country to country, for one meeting or another. And his plans could change on a dime. Lex had been about to intercept him in Paris one day only to later learn that he had ordered his plane rerouted in-flight to Prague instead, to address some sudden problem with one of his businesses there.

Monte Carlo was her best opportunity. A huge Formula 1 fan, Eduardo came to this particular race in person every single year, always staying in the same room at the same hotel, eating at the same restaurants, partying at the same clubs, following more or less the same routine every time. This was Lex's last good chance to catch him. Otherwise, he'd be in the wind again and she would have to waste more time and rely on plenty of luck to create an opportunity.

Lex didn't like to rely on luck for anything, if she could help it.

She stood in the shadows near one of the many glittering, neon-lined bars, watching the table that had been reserved for Eduardo and his party. The table had cost over forty thousand dollars to reserve for the night for Eduardo and up to ten guests. So far, it had sat completely empty for hours.

Yet another drunken asshole swaggered from the dance floor toward Lex. She fended him off with a hard stare that had him turned around before he even said a word to her. She'd lost count of the number of times she'd been hit on that night. She'd had to get physical with three men who wouldn't take no for an answer. One of them would be wearing a cast on his wrist for the next four to six weeks. All part of the job. One of the perks, actually.

She played with the rosary around her wrist, twisting it nervously while she watched and waited and tried to ignore the headache thumping in her head in time with the beat. The rosary didn't go with her outfit at all, but she knew no man would notice.

The women would, of course. They would whisper catty remarks to each other, cast cutting stares in her direction, jealous posturing in the jostle to see who could bag the richest lover. But none of that mattered to Lex. She wasn't there for sex or for money. The rosary was her totem now. Her talisman. Her good luck charm.

And her scoreboard.

Fifty-seven beads left.

One had gone into Skinner's two bottles of Scotch, with a little help from the liquor store owner in Vicenza, an old friend of Lex's with who had lost no love on Skinner over the years. Nick had caught some shrapnel on that one, but he'd survived. He certainly deserved the night he'd spent puking his guts out. Skinner had gotten all that and much more. He was burning in hell, where he belonged.

Eduardo Cavalletti would be joining him soon, if Lex could ever find him. The second bead was embedded in the pointed left toe of the heels Lex was wearing. She'd designed, built, and tested the device herself, a spring-loaded, contact-triggered needle that would inject a tiny non-toxic capsule through Cavalletti's skin. The capsule protected Lex from accidental exposure. But once inside Eduardo's body, it would dissolve in minutes, releasing the toxin from the rosary beads into his system.

It had taken Skinner nearly two days to die. Since then,

Lex had honed her dosing and delivery. Cavalletti would be dead before noon.

If he ever showed up.

A charge of activity buzzed through the room. Eduardo Cavalletti wasn't the brightest star in attendance that night. There were movie stars and rock stars and social media influencers in the club that had far more social cachet than Eduardo. But his wealth and legendary sex appeal earned him more than a few turned heads when he walked into the room. If there was a person in the building who wasn't aware of Eduardo's presence within a few minutes, that person was no one of consequence.

He strode in with an entourage of beautiful women and well-dressed men. He himself wore a tailored suit that fit every angle of his body to perfection, somehow broadcasting both his wealth and his virility. Lex could immediately see why women were drawn to him. He was a very attractive man.

Lex watched Eduardo get settled at his table. As was his custom, he sat on the edge of the half-circle booth. He was notorious almost as much for his restlessness as for his sexuality, constantly on the move, standing and sitting and pacing and walking around whatever room he happened to be in. While most fat cats liked to be in the center of their booth, arms spread across the back, women four-deep on either side, Eduardo always chose the outer-most seat.

Lex had been counting on it, and she wasn't disappointed.

She slipped past the bar and down a short hallway that led to the kitchen. The walls were blacked out so the light from the kitchen door would not disturb the dark nightclub experience for the patrons. Lex focused on a small, bright square at the end of the hallway, a window cut into the door to the kitchen.

She slipped inside the door. The kitchen staff were furiously cooking and pouring and arranging, beautiful women in gorgeous cocktail dresses coming and going, picking up trays full of drinks or desserts or even the occasional entrée, or returning with empty ones. Lex had dressed specifically to pass for either a server or a patron. She hoped she would blend in well enough. Workers tended to be more perceptive than patrons, especially after the drinks and the drugs had kicked in.

Lex quickly spotted what she was looking for, a circular tray laden with filled champagne flutes. She beelined to the counter and bent to pick up the tray.

"Hey," said a busty older woman in a white chef's coat and black pants, sweat beading on her ruddy face as she stood at a grill nearby and looked over her shoulder at Lex. "What do you think you're doing?"

Lex stared at the woman, her mouth opening and closing. "Um... I'm just—"

"Twelve flutes per tray, you idiot," said the chef. "Can't you count?"

Lex looked down at the tray, counting only eleven glasses. Who gave a shit how many glasses were on the tray?

The chef gave an exasperated huff and turned away from the grill. She wiped her hands on a towel at her waist, reached below the counter, and emerged with a chilled bottle of champagne.

"Well?" she said. When Lex stared dumbly at her, the woman pointed to a shelf of flutes behind Lex. "Get another glass."

Lex grabbed an empty glass and set it on the tray. The

chef filled it, muttering something about bimbo models who can only count dicks, dollars, and Dysport injections. Lex picked up the tray and headed back to the club floor.

She walked straight toward Eduardo's table, carrying the tray high overhead as she weaved through the crowd, smoothly dodging both the dancers and the drunks. A small army of servers had already congregated around Eduardo and his guests, lavishing him with all the attention his money had bought him, orchestrated by a tuxedoed concierge who was no doubt offering Eduardo any number of additional services that would extract even more.

Just behind the table, a woman in a sheer white one-piece twirled in a hoop suspended from the ceiling. The hoop was blacked out on one side, glowing white on the other, giving the clever appearance of a crescent moon hung above Eduardo and his crew, watching. The woman spun and twisted and writhed, her outfit hiding nothing while still affording the claim of elegance and artistry. The Emerald Club, it seemed, was basically a strip club for billionaires.

Lex timed her approach carefully. Just as the concierge attending to Eduardo stepped away, Lex brought her tray down in front of her and stepped forward. She tipped the tray as she set it down, spilling champagne across the table. The two women beside Eduardo screamed and recoiled as if Lex had set a nest of hissing vipers on the table. The concierge beside Lex sucked in a horrified breath.

Eduardo himself didn't flinch at all, either when Lex spilled the tray or when she surreptitiously kicked him in the calf with her shoe and felt the mechanism inject the capsule into Eduardo's leg. Instead, he smoothly and quickly took his napkin from his lap and set it on the table to help soak up the spilling champagne. From the corner of her eye, Lex was aware of him staring at her face, smiling slyly.

"I'm so sorry, sir," Lex stammered, scrambling to pick up the fallen flutes, struggling to contain the spill as best she could.

The concierge shouldered her aside and snapped overhead for assistance, apologizing profusely to Eduardo while offering Lex a look of fury and impending damnation. Four waiters swooped in as if they'd practiced for this very possibility, one with a bus tray to clear the table, another with a pile of towels to wipe the spill, a third with a fresh set of glasses, and a fourth with a massive champagne bottle to fill them afresh.

"Compliments of the house, of course, Mr. Cavalletti," said the concierge. "We do so apologize—"

"It's quite all right," said Eduardo smoothly and dismissively. Lex turned to leave, but Eduardo reached around the concierge and caught her by the wrist. "Do I know you?" he asked, pulling her close.

Lex looked at him, playing up the wide-eyed, embarrassed serving girl act. "I—I don't think so, sir," she said.

Her job was done, but she still needed to make her exit. The less memorable she could be while doing so, the better.

"Weren't you at the pool at my hotel?" Eduardo continued. "Yesterday afternoon?"

Lex shook her head, feigning mute confusion. "I was at work yesterday afternoon."

She was impressed. Eduardo had only looked at her for a few seconds at the pool. The man had a good memory, for women, at least.

Still holding Lex's wrist, Eduardo stood and motioned toward his table. "Won't you join me?" he said.

What an arrogant ass. "I—I have to work, sir."

The concierge gasped again and gaped at Lex as if she had committed a mortal sin by denying a VIP customer any request. Lex wondered how often the servers were taken aside by the patrons. Did they have rooms for this kind of thing? Was this place little more than a high-end brothel?

The concierge said, "Your job is to—"

"When do you get done with your work?" Eduardo interrupted, his sly smile growing. He was handsome. There was no doubt about it.

"I, um... I get off in a few hours," Lex said, ducking her head and wishing for a moment she hadn't shaved her hair.

Eduardo pulled her close. He still only touched her wrist, but his breath was warm as he whispered in her ear. "I can get you off much quicker than that."

Lex stammered and acted shy and embarrassed, playing up the routine as she shrank away from the table. Eduardo clutched her wrist for a moment longer. Lex wasn't sure if she'd have to fight to get loose, but he finally let her go, his sly smile now a salacious grin as he scanned her from head to toe, watching her as Lex backed away through the crowd.

Her meek, shy act slowly melted away as she got further from the table. Lex stood taller, took longer, smoother strides. As she stepped into the hallway toward the kitchen door, she cast one last glance from the shadows toward Eduardo's table. He still stood, watching her. Behind him, the woman in the crescent moon kicked one leg to the side and spun in a languorous circle, the light of the moon glowing beneath her, casting its dispassionate light over the table.

When she turned toward him, a knowing smile played over Eduardo's lips. Lex smiled back.

Enjoy your painful death, asshole.

She strode through the kitchen and out the back door. The Emerald Lounge sat on a hill rising from Port Hercules at the south end to overlook the Mediterranean Sea to the east. The sun was just starting to lighten the horizon beside her as Lex walked down the hill. A delivery truck rumbled in the distance far below, a dog yapping in response. She could smell the sea, could feel the salt in the breeze from her left. The breeze blew away the gnats, left the air clean and cool and fresh. It was going to be a beautiful day.

For Eduardo Cavelletti, it would be his last.

For Lex, it was a new day.

As she walked, Lex played absent-mindedly with the wolf pendant she'd attached to her rosary where the cross had once hung. She'd bought it from a street vendor in Paris, a gypsy woman who said she'd carved and sanded it with her own hands from the burnt branch of a lightning-struck acacia tree she'd found fallen at the top of a hill.

She rubbed the smooth surface between her fingers, then unwound the rosary from her wrist and ran it back and forth in her hands, felt the rough skin of the colorful beads as they knocked softly together, the unyielding twists of black cord that ran through and between them.

They reminded her, as they always did, of Baba. His deep, dark eyes. His rough hands, hot against her skin. Were those hands still warm? Were they touching another woman's skin?

Lex had started with fifty-nine beads. In the Catholic church, each was meant to be a prayer, a meditation on the mystery of the life of Jesus Christ, the joy, the glory, the luminosity, and the sorrow.

Two beads were gone from Lex's rosary. Skinner and Eduardo. Did they represent joy or sorrow?

Depends on your point of view.

Lex smiled as she walked down the sidewalk, enjoying the sudden burst of bright yellow light as the sun rose over the harbor. She gripped the rosary in a loose fist, felt the gap where the two beads were missing. As she tightened her fist, she heard her knuckles creak, felt the squeeze of her skin over them, the faint memory of an ache in her bones. The creak, the squeeze, the ache: they let Lex know she was alive. They let her know she was a fighter.

They let her know she was a savior.

Fifty-seven beads left.

Who would she save next?

ACKNOWLEDGMENTS

As always, my love and thanks to Holly. Without your support, my love, none of this would be possible.

ARTIFICIAL INTELLIGENCE USAGE DECLARATION

In the creation of this novel, I, the author, used artificial intelligence in the following ways:

- For suggestion of spelling and grammar corrections, with all final decisions made by the author
- For minor edits on cover images to remove background elements and extend backgrounds, using generative AI tools in Adobe Photoshop

ABOUT THE AUTHOR

Kevin Robert Aldrich lives in California and is the author of several mystery and romance novels:

If you love a twisting, pulse-pounding mystery, you'll love the Cameron Hauk series: Eyes in the Dark, Key Witness, Scale of Justice, Tête-a-Tête, and Burden of Proof.

If you love heart-pounding romantic suspense, you'll love Bare Trap and Flames of Freedom.

If you like vampires, witches, and forbidden love, get a copy of Spellbound now.

And if you love powerful contemporary romance, try Racing Hearts and Ollie & Alli today.

NEWSLETTER SIGN-UP

To learn more about Kevin Robert Aldrich and stay up-to-date with all of his stories and novels, please visit his website:

www.kevinrobertaldrich.com

To be automatically notified of every new release, sign up for the Kevin Robert Aldrich newsletter at the website above.